Praise for the novels of

CARLA NEGGERS

"Neggers's characteristically brisk pacing
and colorful characterizations sweep the
reader toward a dramatic and ultimately
satisfying denouement."
—*Publishers Weekly* on *The Cabin*

"Tension-filled story line that grips the
audience from start to finish."
—*Midwest Book Review* on *The Waterfall*

"Carla Neggers is one of the most distinctive,
talented writers of our genre."
—Debbie Macomber

"Neggers delivers a colorful, well-spun story
that shines with sincere emotion."
—*Publishers Weekly* on *The Carriage House*

"A well-defined, well-told story combines
with well-written characters to make this
an exciting read. Readers will enjoy
it from beginning to end."
—*Romantic Times* on *The Waterfall*

"Gathers steam as its tantalizing mysteries
explode into a thrilling climax."
—*Publishers Weekly* on *Kiss the Moon*

CARLA NEGGERS

THE HARBOR

MIRA®

ISBN 0-7783-2257-2

THE HARBOR

Copyright © 2003 by Carla Neggers.

www.MIRABooks.com

Printed in U.S.A.

ACKNOWLEDGMENTS

To Joe Fessenden of the Maine Marine Patrol,
my detective cousin Gregory Harrell,
Heidi Gould of the Jay (ME) Police Department,
Christine Wenger and probation officer and
firearms instructor Glen Stone of Syracuse,
New York—many thanks for your time,
patience and expertise…
and for the work that you do.

For my mother, M. Florine (Harrell) Neggers

Prologue

The long days of summer had come to an end, and as Olivia West sat at her kitchen table on the dark, cold October morning, she knew she wouldn't live to see another Maine summer. Tomorrow she would turn one hundred and one. But it wasn't just the odds catching up with her that led to her quiet certainty that she'd reached her sunset—she just knew. She had months, perhaps only days. Hours.

Her nephew, Patrick, wasn't deterred by autumn's shorter days. He poured himself a cup of coffee and sat across from her. He always stopped by before his walk in the nature preserve, which was just northeast of the brown-shingled 1890s house at the mouth of Goose Harbor where Olivia had lived her entire hundred years. She and Patrick both liked to be up to see the sunrise. It was one thing they had in common. Perhaps the only thing.

He was in uniform. That was unusual. Olivia licked her lips. "Patrick—"

"I can't talk about it, Olivia."

She understood. He had a job to do, but this time it hit close to home. He'd been preoccupied for some time but hadn't told her everything, not that he needed to. She knew him, and she knew Goose Harbor.

She wondered what her brother would think if he could see his only child now. Patrick West, chief of police. He'd never known his father, also a Patrick. Olivia remembered seeing her baby brother off to war, knowing he wouldn't come back, just as she knew, now, she wouldn't see another summer.

Patrick nodded at her typewriter, an IBM Selectric II. She'd given up her Olivetti manual years ago, under protest, and had no intention of switching to a computer. "What're you doing?" he asked.

"I'm revising my obituary."

"Aunt Olivia, for God's sake—"

"It's not morbid, Patrick. Not at my age. I intend to have my affairs in order. I don't want to leave that burden to you and the girls."

Patrick had two daughters, Zoe, a law enforcement officer like him but with her grandfather's zest for adventure, and Christina, who was just as rooted on Maine's southern coast as her father and great-aunt. Their mother had died when they were little girls. Patrick had done a good job raising them. Olivia hadn't bothered trying to replace their mother—she'd never married and didn't really trust her maternal instincts. She thought she was a fairly good great-aunt, though.

"You've had your affairs in order for thirty years," Patrick grumbled.

She glanced at the paper in her typewriter. *Olivia West, 101, the author of seventy-two Jennifer Periwinkle novels, died today at her home in Goose Harbor, Maine.* It was a sensible first sentence. People tended to think she was already dead. The University of Maine and Bates, Bowdoin and Colby Colleges all offered classes on her work. Her house was on the Goose Harbor walking tour. The town library had an Olivia West Room. In her mind, those were honors more suited to dead people. She knew the local paper kept an obituary of her on file. She'd asked Patrick to get her a copy of it, but he'd refused.

He got up and looked over her shoulder. She was shrunken and white-haired, her fingers gnarled, her veins prominent, her skin brown with age spots—yet she could sit here at her table, where she'd written all her books, and wonder that any time had passed at all. She glanced out at the harbor, the first of the lobster boats chugging across the quiet water in the murky predawn light. Patrick kissed the top of her head. He was paunchy and gray-haired himself, and as good a man as Olivia had ever known. "You're morbid, Aunt Olivia. I'm talking to your doctor about antidepressants to smooth out your moods."

"There's nothing wrong with my moods."

He laughed and winked at her on his way out, as if he didn't have a care in the world. Olivia knew better.

She abandoned her obituary and rolled a fresh sheet of paper into her IBM. Even slowed by arthritis and age, she managed to type quickly. *Chapter One.* She scrolled down a few lines.

And stopped.

She knew she'd go no further.

She couldn't kill off Jen Periwinkle.

Olivia had watched herself wither and wrinkle, but Jen remained forever sixteen, always ready to solve her next mystery. She was timeless. She used her wits—never violence—to solve crimes. That was Olivia's pact with her readers—Jen Periwinkle wouldn't have to resort to violence to achieve her results. She occasionally brandished a gun and once a sword, but she never drew blood.

To kill her off, Olivia meant to have her die saving someone, probably a child. Mr. Lester McGrath, Jen's evil nemesis through all seventy-two books, would have to die, too, but as a result of her intelligence and bravery, not at her hands.

"Aunt Olivia...*Aunt Olivia!*"

Zoe rushed into the kitchen from the side entrance. Olivia hadn't noticed the sun had come up, and she didn't have a good sense of how much time had passed since Patrick was here. An hour? The sun sparkled on the harbor waters and reflected the stunning fall foliage. Boats were out. Olivia tried to focus on Zoe, but realized something was terribly wrong and wanted to dive back into Jen Periwinkle's fictional world.

"Oh, Aunt Olivia." Zoe seemed to be trying to pull herself together. She was clearly shaken, her face pale, her running clothes matted with sweat and—and something else. Dark stains. Her running shoes were soaked. "I didn't want you to hear the news from someone else—I…*God*…" Her eyes, blue with gray flecks like Olivia's baby brother's, filled with tears. "Dad's dead."

Olivia saw now that the dark stains were blood. It had spattered on Zoe's gray shirt and shorts. She tried to speak, but nothing came out.

"He was shot. I found him on my run."

"But he was just here! He stopped in to see me, like he always does. Where? Where did you find him?"

"In the nature preserve. Stewart's Cove." Zoe raked a shaking hand through her short blond curls, her experience as a Maine State Police detective, accustomed to dealing with crime scenes, facts and evidence, not helping her now. But this was different. This was her father. "The marine patrol, state police and local police are there now. I—I have to go back."

"Of course. Christina—"

"She's meeting me there." The tears spilled down her pale cheeks, and when she wiped them with her fingertips, they mixed with her father's blood. "Is Betsy here? I don't want to leave you alone."

Olivia nodded. Betsy O'Keefe was her live-in caregiver, a concession Olivia had made two years ago in order to be able to continue living in her house. Betsy had learned to leave Olivia alone as much as possible in the morning.

The nature preserve was her own doing, Olivia thought. She'd bought up the land with earnings from her books and created a nonprofit organization to maintain it. And now Patrick had been killed there.

Murdered.

Olivia raised one hand, and Zoe took it, squeezed back gently and sobbed. She looked like a young woman who'd just lost her father, not the young woman Olivia had seen only yesterday, so confident and determined, preparing to head to Quantico for her sixteen weeks of training at the FBI Academy. Patrick was proud of her but worried about her zest for adventure, her need to push herself. His father was the same way and died young in the line of duty. He was afraid Zoe would, too. Instead, he had.

"I'll see you later, okay?" Zoe whispered.

"Yes, dear. Of course. I love you."

"I love you, too."

"And Patrick—oh, Zoe, I loved him so."

But Zoe was gone, and Betsy O'Keefe bustled into the kitchen, her own face smeared with tears. She was a stout woman in her late forties, a registered nurse who'd moved to Goose Harbor with her widowed mother at four. Hard workers, both of them. The mother had died a few years ago. Sometimes it seemed to Olivia everyone she knew was dead.

"You've had a terrible shock," Betsy said. "Come, let's get you to bed and have you lie down a bit."

"I don't want to lie down. Betsy…" Olivia stopped. What had she meant to say? She couldn't remember. It didn't happen often, but sometimes she'd forget things. What she'd eaten for breakfast, names—she'd lose track of what she was saying. She frowned at Betsy. "I can't—"

Olivia gasped, grabbing her chest, the jolt of adrenaline and awareness—knowledge—so sudden and forceful, it hurt. Patrick in his uniform, the job he had to do—the arrest he was making—

Betsy leaped to her side. "Miss West!"

"Betsy—I know who did it."

"What, love?"

"I know who killed Patrick."

Betsy was pale now, sobbing. "I—I bought a hundred and one candles for your birthday tomorrow. I hope we can fit them all on your cake. Zoe and Christina will come by—"

"Betsy—Betsy, why can't I remember?"

"Remember what, love?"

"The murderer's name. The bastard—"

"Maybe I should call the doctor."

"No, don't." Olivia's voice was firm. "I'll sit here a while and think. I'll remember. I know I will."

Betsy made tea and babbled about birthday cakes and the leaf-peepers and whatever pleasantries she thought would distract her elderly charge—and they did. Olivia couldn't form a coherent thought, much less call up the name of the murderer.

My God. I do know who did it.

She stared at the first line of her obituary and felt a rare tug of regret at her mortality. If only this once she could be Jen Periwinkle and forever sixteen.

One

Zoe West sat at the cluttered farmhouse kitchen table and stared out at the beautiful northwest Connecticut landscape, the hills dotted with brightly colored leaves, and she tried to piece together how she'd ended up here. It was as if one day she was headed to Quantico, and the next, she was here, canning beets and milking goats with Bea Jericho.

She knew she should be grateful. Charlie and Bea were incredible people, hardworking, determined to hang on to their land instead of chopping it up into mini-estates and making a fortune.

But Zoe didn't belong in Bluefield, Connecticut, and she knew it. She'd known it the day she'd arrived in town almost a year ago.

She needed to go home. It was just a matter of when. Goose Harbor hovered on the horizon of her life, like a fog bank she knew would engulf her in due time. Better to deal with it. Get it over with. The status quo was untenable, increasingly impossible to endure.

She'd had three calls in three days. Bruce Young, a lobsterman who'd graduated high school with her; her sister, Christina; and Greg Sampson, the one friend Zoe had left in the Maine State Police. They all wanted to tell her that an FBI agent was on the loose in Goose Harbor.

At least *they* said he was an FBI agent. Apparently he didn't want to advertise it but had slipped up with Bruce Young. His name was J. B. McGrath—Jesse Benjamin McGrath. It went right over Sampson's head but struck Bruce and Christina as suspicious, since Jen Periwinkle's evil nemesis was also named McGrath. Mr. Lester McGrath, a fictional character, but still. To them it was at best a weird coincidence.

Greg Sampson said he was at Perry's waterfront bar the night Special Agent McGrath had beaten all comers at darts. Greg had no reason to check out this McGrath character's story but thought it was legit. He reminded Zoe that a person, an FBI agent or no FBI agent, didn't make friends in Goose Harbor by beating all comers at darts.

Deep into her second month of unemployment, Zoe was determined to resist the idea that J. B. McGrath was *her* problem. He was on vacation. FBI agents deserved to take vacations. Goose Harbor was a great place for a vacation, with its strips of sand beaches, its picturesque harbor, its historic houses and quaint shops and inns. That he'd arrived almost to the day of the one-year anniversary of the chief of police's unsolved murder didn't necessarily mean a thing.

Even in her self-imposed exile in Connecticut, Zoe would have known if the Maine State Police's Criminal

Investigations Division had asked for FBI assistance in her father's murder investigation. The truth was, there were no new leads. They had his body, they had the two bullets that had struck him and they had very little else. No footprints in the sand, no DNA evidence left behind, no witnesses. For all anyone knew, Patrick West, Goose Harbor's beloved chief of police, could have stumbled onto out-of-town drug dealers who shot him and made off for parts unknown.

In the weeks after his death, although she was no longer a state police detective herself and was supposed to be on her way to Quantico, Zoe had done everything she could to find her father's killer. She'd stepped on toes of people who got in her way and toes of people who didn't—she didn't care. She just wanted answers. Why had a good man died that early October morning? Why had she been the one to find him?

And Olivia. Her great-aunt had died the next day, on the morning of her one hundred and first birthday. The doctor said she just gave out, but Zoe blamed herself, the shock of the news of her father's death. She and Betsy O'Keefe—the entire town—could have conspired to keep her great-aunt from finding out what had happened. They could have *tried.*

"I know who killed your father. Oh, Zoe, I know…"

The ramblings of a dying woman. Zoe should have realized Olivia was in trouble, but she and Betsy had coaxed her to bed for a nap. She never got up again.

After weeks of trying to find her father's killer, it was Stick Monroe who'd finally pulled Zoe aside and told her she had to ease off. Calm down. Let her colleagues in CID do their jobs. Stick was a retired federal judge and her mentor, her friend, and everyone knew he was the one person she might listen to. He reminded her that her class at the FBI Academy was set to start. All she had to do was drive to Washington, D.C., and get on with her new life.

Instead she withdrew from the academy and took off, ending up as the sole detective in Bluefield, Connecticut, a small town in the northwest part of the state. Nothing much had happened until the past summer, when the governor of Connecticut drowned in his own swimming pool in her town. It wasn't an accident. Then a Texas Ranger and a Texas lawyer showed up, the new governor and her kids were nearly killed, and basically all hell broke loose.

And when it was all over, Zoe was fired. Her chief accused her of letting the Texas Ranger "run amok," which was ridiculous—Sam Temple was a total professional. But the real reason she got the ax was that she'd stopped wearing a gun on duty in the weeks before the governor's death. It was basic U.S. law enforcement. She was supposed to carry a weapon on duty.

After she lost her job, Charlie and Bea Jericho had offered Zoe their son's room now that he'd married the new governor and moved out. She helped Bea can and freeze a ton of fruits and vegetables, and Bea was teaching her how to milk goats and knit.

But Zoe really knew she'd put law enforcement behind her last week when she got her tattoo—not because it was a tattoo, but because it was a tattoo of a beach rose. She'd designed it herself.

Cops didn't have beach roses tattooed on their hips. As far as Zoe was concerned, that was another rule, right up there with carrying a gun.

She sank back in her chair. She was losing her damn mind. At least she'd quit smoking. She'd let a pack-a-day habit creep up on her this past year but had finally kicked it.

What she needed to do now was say goodbye to Bea and Charlie, the sheep, the chickens and the goats and go home.

When her cell phone rang, Zoe assumed it was someone else from Goose Harbor calling to tell her about Special Agent J. B. McGrath.

But it was Christina, her voice shaking, her words coming out tight and fast. "Zoe—Zoe, the police just left. Someone broke into my house. Can you believe it? Who'd do something like that?"

They'd both inherited their father's house when he died, and since Christina was already living at home, she'd simply stayed there. Their great-aunt had left Zoe her 1890s house overlooking the harbor, and Christina enough money to open a breakfast-and-lunch café on the town docks. By all accounts, the café was doing well, but Zoe had yet to go there. She hadn't stepped foot in Goose Harbor since she'd fled for Connecticut.

"Are you okay?" she asked her sister.

Christina sniffled. "Yes. I wasn't here. I close up the café at three, and today I did cleanup as fast as I could—

I was done by four. Kyle and I came back here to work on his documentary on Aunt Olivia—" She took a breath, and Zoe could hear her sister's hesitation. Kyle Castellane wasn't one of Zoe's favorite people. He was young, rich, arrogant and determined to do this documentary on Olivia despite the grief Christina and Zoe both still felt at her death. To him, it was a matter of "strike while the iron's hot." Christina didn't share Zoe's frustrations—she thought Kyle was brilliant.

"Go on, Chris," Zoe said softly, reining in her own tension. No one had ever broken into their house. Not ever.

"The house—it wasn't torn up, but you can tell someone's been through here. They came in through the side door. Bruce is bringing a new one by tonight."

"Anything taken?"

"No. Not that I can see. The police think they were looking for cash, maybe because I run a café, and when they didn't find any, just ran off."

It happened all the time. Still, the timing felt odd on top of the calls about the vacationing FBI agent. Zoe sighed. "I'm sorry, Chris. What can I do?"

"Come home. Zoe, I—I don't like this. I'll admit it, I'm scared. What if this FBI agent is stirring up trouble? What if—"

Zoe stopped her—they were on the same wavelength. "I can leave here in thirty minutes and be there in about four hours."

"Really? You're sure? I don't want to wimp out. I'm not making mountains out of molehills, am I?"

"Let's hope so, Chris. I'd rather have molehills to

deal with than mountains, wouldn't you?" Zoe tried to lighten her sister's mood. "By the way, do you know how to knit?"

"Sure. Aunt Olivia taught me."

"Good. You can help me finish this scarf I'm knitting. It looks like a dead snake. Wait until you see it. I think I've dropped a million stitches—"

"Zoe!"

But Christina managed a laugh, although Zoe felt only marginally better when she hung up. She didn't have a lot of stuff. She'd never owned much. It wouldn't take her a half hour to pack—it'd take her fifteen minutes.

Two

Perry's waterfront bar was located on the southern end of Goose Harbor's Main Street. Its bank of windows overlooked the docks; its barn-board walls were decorated with wooden lobster traps, fake lobsters and framed black-and-white pictures of lighthouses and Maine days gone by. J. B. McGrath nursed a beer at a small corner table. He was thirty-six, tall, lean, black-haired, blue-eyed and had a face that would look right at home on a wanted poster. He was good at undercover work, and he'd been doing it a long time. Maybe too long. That was why he was in Goose Harbor, Maine. He was on vacation. Not his idea.

No darts tonight. He'd pissed off enough locals. He was from Montana but could handle himself in a lobster boat. He was an FBI agent but argued lobstering with people who'd done it all their lives. He was a guy on vacation who didn't have the grace to lose at darts once in awhile. None of which endeared him to the good people of Goose Harbor.

Bruce Young pulled out a chair and plopped down across from him with a frosty beer glass. "Eight o'clock and nobody's ready to kill you? Slow day, McGrath."

Bruce grinned and unzipped his Carhartt canvas jacket. He was built like a rock cliff, a big, red-faced man with scars and nicks on his hands from working his string of lobster pots day after day. His blue eyes were so like J.B.'s own, J.B. wouldn't be surprised if he and Bruce were distant cousins. But that was another thing— the locals didn't believe J.B.'s ancestors hailed from Goose Harbor. They thought he'd just made that up.

J.B. hadn't made it up. His grandmother was a Sutherland, as in Sutherland Island off the Olivia West Nature Preserve—as in Olivia's best friend, Posey Sutherland, who ran off with drifter Jesse McGrath after World War I and ended up in Montana and dead at twenty-seven.

Her father, Lester Sutherland, disowned her.

Hence, Mr. Lester McGrath, Jen Periwinkle's evil nemesis. A combination of two men Olivia West hated because of what they had done to her friend, Posey.

"I heard some of the guys talking about setting fire to your boat. They think you're obnoxious." Bruce took a long drink of his beer. "I reminded them it's my damn boat."

"Old, wooden, practically leaking."

"That's a great boat. The guys said if you don't get out of town or get an attitude adjustment, they're going to tie your hands and feet together and throw you in the drink."

J.B. shrugged. "Wouldn't do them any good."

"Uh-huh. You're a highly trained federal agent, drown-proofed and everything."

Skepticism had crept into Bruce's tone. He obviously had his doubts about J.B.'s credentials, too. J.B. didn't mind. He hadn't produced an I.D. or really confirmed one way or the other he was with the bureau. Bruce had guessed it. His truck had backfired, and J.B., still on edge from his last investigation, had gone for his weapon—not that he was carrying one. Bruce nailed him then and there. "You a cop? A *fed*?" J.B. just said he was on vacation. Period.

The talk about tossing him overboard wasn't serious—he'd invaded these men's turf, and they were *re*-marking their territory, letting him know they didn't care if he was on edge or why. He was bad company. They weren't going to give him an inch.

"Nobody believes you're here on vacation," Bruce said.

"Why not?"

"You don't look like you take vacations."

J.B. didn't disagree. He looked as if he'd spent the past year working on an undercover operation that had ended badly, leaving him with his throat half slit and the searing memory of killing a man in front of his own children. Not what J.B. had envisioned when he'd infiltrated a group of violent criminals who used their virulent antigovernment beliefs to justify robbery, murder and the possession and distribution of illegal assault weapons and explosive devices.

"I'm doing genealogical research on my Maine roots," J.B. said.

"Uh-huh. You a Mainer. I like that. You ever been to Maine?"

"This week."

"There you go."

"My ancestors helped settle Goose Harbor in the seventeenth century."

"So did mine."

"You see? We could be cousins."

Bruce wasn't amused. "Yeah, right. Listen, Mc-Grath—" Bruce sighed, staring at his nearly untouched beer. "Christina West's house was broken into today. The police think it was some idiot looking for cash, but I'm wondering—you didn't have anything to do with it, did you?"

J.B. shook his head. He hadn't heard about the break-in. "No."

"Because, you know, some people think you're here because of her father's murder last year—"

"Bruce, I'm on vacation. I know about the murder, but that's it."

Bruce rubbed a big hand across his face. "I know. It was stupid. I just—Chris is so damn young, and she's here on her own."

"What about her sister?"

But J.B. knew about the sister. Zoe West was a screwup. The rising star, the local hotshot pushed hard and fast because she made everyone else look good, too. She should have gotten her ass kicked along the way, but instead she got accepted into the FBI Academy for new-agent training. It was only natural she'd think she could solve her father's murder—only natural she'd come unglued and fallen apart when she'd had to face his death, her aunt's death, her own limitations, the kind of real-world experience she must have known was out there but hadn't had to confront herself.

Zoe West had bowed out of the academy, moved to Connecticut and got herself fired from what was likely her last job in law enforcement.

A screwup.

J.B. thought of the man he'd killed. The looks on the faces of his three children. Nine, eleven and fourteen. They were horrified, furious, filled with hate. J.B. didn't know what would become of them. Their father, a murderer and a rapist, a man who'd taught other people how to build bombs and convert legal weapons into illegal weapons, had attacked J.B. from behind, without warning, and stuck a knife in his throat, and J.B. fought back. It was self-defense. But nothing, he thought, was ever that simple.

He'd been forced on vacation by his superiors. "Take a break, McGrath. As long as you need."

Bruce drank more of his beer. J.B. could tell Zoe West wasn't Bruce's favorite subject. "Christina's just twenty-four. Zoe shouldn't have left her here on her own. I don't know what the hell she's still doing in Connecticut—she doesn't have a job. I think everyone in town's told her about you by now."

And everyone in town knew because Bruce had told them. "You talk to her?"

"Yeah. Made no difference. She went on about goat's milk when I talked to her."

"Did you tell her about the break-in at her sister's house?"

"No. I expect Chris did, though."

J.B. smiled. "You have a soft spot for Christina West, don't you?"

"Up yours, McGrath."

"She's okay?"

Bruce's expression softened. "Yeah. I'm supposed to bring her a new door. Want to go with me?"

J.B.'s instincts told him not to get in any deeper with the West sisters. He was in deep enough. He'd been interested in Goose Harbor because of his ancestors, but he'd actually come here because of Patrick West's murder. His own father had died over the winter, an old man who'd loved western Montana—and yet he never would have been born there without his tragic connection to the Wests and Goose Harbor, Maine.

J.B. knew he should cut the night short and go back to his inn, but he got to his feet and followed Bruce Young out to buy a new door for Christina West.

Bruce did most of the work. Installing a solid wood door was nothing to him. J.B. finally quit pretending to help and joined Christina and her boyfriend, Kyle Castellane, in the kitchen. The West house was built in 1827—a plaque above the door said so—on a corner lot on a side street behind the town library. Yellow clapboards, black shutters, roses. Their mother had died of lupus when the girls were two and nine. It was one of the many tidbits J.B. had learned about the West sisters since he'd decided to vacation in Goose Harbor.

Christina looked agitated. She was tall, slender and usually quick with a smile, but not tonight. Wisps of long blond hair had worked their way out of her braid and into her face, which was lightly freckled and pretty, making J.B. wonder about her older sister, the ex-detective. Christina wore the white ruffled blouse and slim black pants that were her basic uniform at her café. Kyle, the boyfriend, was sandy-haired and good-looking, dressed in his habitual gray sweatshirt and khakis. He also had on a five-thousand-dollar watch. They both stood with their backs against the kitchen counter.

J.B. had on jeans, a black chamois shirt and boat shoes he'd managed to scuff up properly during his four days on the Maine coast. His sports watch cost about a hundred bucks. He'd had to buy a new band for it after he'd bled on the old one when he got his throat slit. The scar wasn't all that visible when he wore collared shirts.

He had a feeling Christina West already knew about him, but he went ahead and introduced himself. "I'm J. B. McGrath. I'm on vacation here in Goose Harbor."

"I heard," Christina said. "I've seen you at the café a few times."

He smiled, aware of her tension. "Hard to resist wild blueberry muffins and warm apple pie. Chowder's good, too."

She couldn't muster much of a smile back at him. "Thanks."

"You're FBI, aren't you?" Kyle asked.

"I'm just a guy with some time off."

The kid didn't like his answer. "Some people are saying you're a phony."

J.B. shrugged. "It's a crime to impersonate a law enforcement officer."

Kyle Castellane liked that answer even less than the first one. "I'd like to see some I.D."

"Would you?"

"Yeah. Why the name McGrath? Don't you think that's a hell of a coincidence?"

"McGrath's not an uncommon name." It was a fact, but it left out the rest of the facts—that he knew why Olivia West had picked the name Mr. Lester McGrath for Jen Periwinkle's evil nemesis. She hadn't plucked it out of thin air. "I can't blame people for wondering."

Kyle wasn't pacified. "Why did you pick Goose Harbor for your vacation?"

"Cute name."

"I can call the local police and have them check you out."

Christina touched his arm. "Kyle…"

"It's okay," J.B. said. "He can check me out. No problem."

Her blue eyes fastened on him. "You know my father was killed last year, don't you?"

J.B. nodded. "I do. I'm sorry."

She swallowed visibly. "Thanks. It's hard not having answers." Her gaze drifted to the side door, where Bruce was almost finished with his work. "The police don't have any reason to believe the break-in's connected in any way to Dad's murder."

"Did you call Zoe about it?" Kyle asked.

"After the police left," Christina said. "You were back at your apartment."

Kyle, who'd rented the small apartment above her waterfront café, seemed put out. "Why didn't you tell me? Is she on her way?"

Christina turned to him, color rising in her cheeks. "What?"

"Zoe. Is she on her way?"

"I don't know."

She knew. J.B. could see the lie in the way she shifted her eyes away from Kyle and looked down at her hands, in the flush that spread from her cheeks to her ears, in the increased agitation. Her breathing was shallow now, coming in quick, ineffective gulps.

Why wouldn't she want to reveal whether or not her sister was on her way?

Bruce lumbered in from his door-hanging. "She drives a yellow Bug these days. She won't be hard to spot."

"She hasn't—" Christina inhaled, wrung her hands together. "She hasn't been back in almost a year. Cut her some slack, okay?"

"Right," Bruce said. "Like she'd cut us any."

"Anyway, I don't know if she's coming."

The big sister sounded like a trip to J.B. He saw Bruce give Christina a pained look, as if he was suffering to see her with Kyle Castellane, and decided it was time to make their exit. "Come on, Bruce. A game of darts?"

"Nah. It's too late. I have to be up before dawn. October's good lobstering." He pulled his gaze from Christina. "I'll drop you off at your inn."

His room at the inn had pink soap and pink-flowered wallpaper, and its four-poster bed was a first for J.B. The place was run by Lottie Martin, who had to be the sourest woman in the state of Maine. He always greeted her cheerfully just to watch her squirm. When he opened his door and saw that his room had been tossed, he knew she wouldn't be happy.

He wasn't happy.

It was a gentle toss, not a ransacking. If he hadn't worked undercover for the past five years and become accustomed to imprinting on his mind how he'd left things, he might not even have noticed.

It helped that the perpetrator had spilled his afternoon tea on the carpet.

He knew he'd done tea for a reason. The daily afternoon ritual was served on the screened porch and featured three kinds of tea and an array of tiny muffins, shortbread and scones. He'd sneaked a cup of Irish Breakfast up to his room.

He knelt down. The stain was still damp.

Interesting.

The cottage-style bureau where he'd unpacked his clothes had been gone through. His empty suitcase. The stacks of books and magazines he'd picked up to while away the hours. Nothing was quite where he'd left it.

His visitor had even pawed through his bathroom.

And locked up afterward. Which required a key to the old-fashioned door.

Also interesting.

Lottie Martin didn't strike him as the type to snoop. On the other hand, curiosity about him had risen steadily among local residents since he'd arrived in pretty Goose Harbor.

Nothing was missing. His gun was locked in his Jeep.

He left everything as it was and headed down to the front desk. Old Lottie was there in a corduroy jumper and turtleneck, her iron-gray hair pinned up in a bun that made her look like Auntie Em, except thinner. J.B. figured she'd opened the inn so she could surround herself with antiques and live in an old house. Guests were simply a necessary evil. Or at least he was.

"I heard Zoe West was back in town," he said, then made an educated guess. "I thought I saw her car pull out of here." He hadn't, but Lottie Martin didn't know that. "She's staying here? You'd think she'd stay with her sister, wouldn't you?"

Lottie took the bait. "She *is* staying with her sister. She stopped by to say hello. I've been friends with her family for years."

"Did she ever work for you?"

"Just one summer."

Long enough to help herself to a pass key. She probably had it in her old room, which meant she'd stopped at the house first and Christina had been covering for her. That explained some of her agitation. She was keeping the FBI agent occupied while her big sister searched his room to make sure his story added up. Bruce had called Christina on his cell phone from his truck to say he and J.B. were on their way with the door. The sisters could have cooked up their plan then.

He'd guess it was Zoe's idea. While she was in full screwup mode, why not break into an FBI agent's room?

"I spilled tea in my room," he told Lottie Martin.

She frowned. "On the carpet?"

"Yes, ma'am."

She seemed to think he was being sarcastic. "No harm done, I'm sure." Her teeth were half clenched as she spoke. "Mr. McGrath, I have a problem with your room. This is terribly awkward. I wanted to catch you sooner—" She paused, fixing her gray eyes on him. "I'm afraid you'll have to check out. I found a room for you in Kennebunkport. It was no mean feat since this is peak foliage weekend. I'm sure you'll be pleased with it."

"You giving me the boot because of the spilled tea?"

"No, of course not."

"Because Zoe West was here and you think I'm to blame?"

"Trouble does have a way of following her these days, but no, that's not the reason. There's a problem with the room, that's all. It happens in these old houses." She jotted down the name and number of the Kennebunkport inn and passed it to him. "I'll pick up the tab myself to make up for the inconvenience."

J.B. had to hand it to her. As socially inept and sour as she was, she'd just smoothly maneuvered him right out of her inn. He wondered if Zoe West had said anything to her, or if old Lottie had simply put the ex-detective's visit, the spilled tea and the fact that her guest was an FBI agent together and decided to toss him to avoid any trouble. She must have heard about the break-in at the West house by now.

In her place, he'd probably do the same.

He took the paper with the Kennebunkport information on it. "I'll pay my own way. Thanks. You know, my ancestors came here in the seventeenth century. Maybe we're cousins."

She didn't like that any more than Bruce Young had.

J.B. returned to his room and packed up. He had no idea where he was going, but it wasn't to Kennebunkport. Bruce'd probably put him up, but Bruce had dogs that looked as if they'd have the run of the place. Bruce was also part of whatever it was that had happened in Goose Harbor a year ago. After she'd found her father's body, Zoe West had run into the water and waved down the nearest lobster boat. Bruce Young's. He'd notified the Maine marine patrol.

It was a cold night, and dark, the clouds blocking out the moon and any stars. J.B. could taste the salt in the air, feel the dampness of an approaching storm. He dumped his stuff in the back of his Jeep and drove down to the docks, parking in the town lot. The small, protected harbor was mostly rockbound, lined with houses, with Main Street running parallel to the water above the docks. In daylight on a clear day, Olivia West's house was visible on its point on the northeast edge of the harbor. According to town gossip, she'd left it to Zoe.

Christina inherited money to buy the small clapboard building on the waterfront behind him, a run-down clam shack she'd converted into her charming café.

If he left now, J.B. figured he could be back in Washington, D.C., by morning. He had an apartment there. He didn't know what he'd be doing next with the bureau, but he expected it wouldn't involve undercover work, at least not anytime soon. There was talk of having him train new undercover agents. Yeah. He could give them pointers on how to kill a man in front of his children with your throat cut and bleeding, then how to live with yourself afterward. It didn't matter that he'd done what he had to do, that he'd had no other choice. But wasn't that the point? Leave yourself options. Always leave yourself options.

A puff of fog floated off the water and enveloped him as if it meant to, as if he was its target. He walked across the nearly empty parking lot to the intersection of Ocean Drive. If he turned left, it'd take him to Main Street and Goose Harbor village. Right, along the northeast edge of the harbor, past Olivia West's house and the nature preserve named for her.

Olivia West's house was unoccupied, sitting on its lonely point like something out of an Alfred Hitchcock movie. Bruce said Zoe kept the lights and heat on and had it cleaned once a month, but didn't know what to do with it.

J.B. did. He'd sleep there tonight.

Bruce had also said that Olivia West had never bothered to get a lock for the porch door. J.B. could walk right in. And why shouldn't he? Zoe West had gotten him tossed from his inn. He figured she owed him a night's lodging.

Three

Christina paced in the kitchen and alternated between horror and delight at what her sister had done. Zoe was just relieved Special Agent McGrath hadn't walked in while she was searching his room. She didn't know where she'd be if he had, but it wouldn't be in her sister's kitchen eating hummus and red onion on pita. Lottie Martin, fortunately, had seemed content to pretend she didn't know what was going on. She would be curious about McGrath herself, and she wouldn't want to get in Zoe's way.

Not that she'd found much of anything.

Knocking over the tea had nearly done her in. She was a better cop than a sneak, and she didn't exactly have the law on her side. More to the point, no way would J. B. McGrath not remember having spilled tea on Lottie Martin's carpet. He'd see the stain and know it wasn't his doing.

So long as he didn't realize it was *her* doing, Zoe thought she was all right. She'd slipped out, relocked the door with her pass key and managed to get out of the inn without incident.

"I can't believe you actually did it," Christina said. "*God*, Zoe, what were you thinking?"

"I was thinking he wasn't a real FBI agent."

"If he'd caught you—"

"He didn't. And I didn't steal anything out of his room. Relax, I'm in the clear. Otherwise there'd be a cruiser in the driveway right now."

"Or *him*. You haven't met him."

Zoe stretched out her legs and munched on her pita sandwich. Christina had made the hummus herself, from scratch. Over the past year, she'd added her own touches to the kitchen—baskets and brightly colored towels, gourmet gadgets, a hand-thrown pottery bowl their father would have considered extravagant. But Zoe could still feel his presence, as if he might walk in from the garden with an armload of tomatoes and chuckle at how agitated his two daughters were. He was the steadiest man Zoe had ever known. He took everything in stride. She thought she took after him, but in the days after his death, and then her great-aunt's, Zoe knew she'd been a total madwoman.

"It's weird being back," she said.

"I know it must be." Christina stopped pacing and opened a cupboard door. Kyle had taken off after Zoe returned, but promised to stop in again. "Why don't I make us drinks? What would you like?"

"Scotch on the rocks."

Christina grinned. "That's easy."

Zoe struggled to smile back. She was still thinking

about that spilled tea—and the sight of Agent McGrath's razor on the sink. She didn't know why that got to her. "The place looks good, Chris. I can't wait to see the café."

"It's great—I'm having such a good time. It's a lot of work, but I love it." She got out two glasses, filled them with ice and poured the Scotch, a brand she would have picked with the same care she took with everything related to food. She brought the two drinks to the table and sat down. "Zoe, I don't know—maybe I overreacted to the break-in."

"Why do you say that?"

"Because you're here, I guess. It makes me think—" She lifted her glass but didn't take a sip. "I don't know, I guess it makes me think the break-in must be related to Dad's death if you're here."

"I was fired in August. I should have come home sooner."

"To do what?"

Zoe drank some of her Scotch. It was her father's drink. Scotch on the rocks. Not often, and only in the evening. She didn't really like it. She knew Christina didn't, either. "I don't know what I'm going to do. First things first, okay?"

"Sure."

"I don't have any theories about the break-in, Chris. I'm not going to go off half-cocked. It's been a year—"

"I know, but you haven't been here. Zoe, I've gotten used to not having any answers. I'm not saying I like it, but I've gotten used to it."

Zoe nodded. "You're afraid I haven't."

"I *know* you haven't. It's not in your makeup."

But Zoe wasn't going there, reliving the nightmares and bad decisions, the confusion and grief of the past year. She took another sip of her Scotch and jumped to her feet. "You have to look at my knitting and see if you can figure out what I'm doing wrong."

"Zoe—"

"No, I'm serious. Knitting's a great stress reliever. I'm determined to learn. Bea Jericho took me to a yarn store in Litchfield and had me pick out a beautiful, hand-dyed yarn. Milk-gray. She insisted I'd like knitting better if I started out with yarn I loved."

Christina shook her head. "I can't believe you're learning to knit."

"Not only that," Zoe said, "but I know how to milk goats."

Teddy Shelton sat behind the wheel of his rusting-piece-of-crap pickup and tried to figure out his next move. He'd pulled into the town lot next to the FBI agent's Jeep. If he leaned forward, he could see down the docks to the yacht club and the deep-water slip where Luke Castellane had his multimillion-dollar yacht. Luke's kid had a crummy apartment above Christina West's café. He was playing the starving artist. He'd tire of Christina once he finished his documentary on Olivia West. No question in Teddy's mind. Kyle Castellane was a spoiled, self-absorbed little prick.

Teddy wondered if Kyle's documentary was just a way to stir up a bees' nest and get people focused on Patrick West's death again. The state police investigation was still active, but people'd settled down, assumed someone from out of town had killed him. Chief West could have had terrorists plotting an attack right under his nose, and he'd never notice. Not in Goose Harbor, he'd think. No way.

Yeah, well. He'd learned. Those last minutes before he'd bled to death must have been something. *Oh, shit, I should have known.*

Fat raindrops pelted Teddy's windshield. He didn't know why he couldn't afford a decent truck. At least he had all the weapons he wanted. Most of them, anyway. He'd like a couple more grenades. He had more flash-bang grenades than he needed—they were all noise and light and smoke, designed to distract and confuse, not to destroy. Maybe he could trade some for the kind of grenades that could blow a guy's legs off.

He kept his personal arsenal in an apple crate in the jump seat behind him. Sometimes it'd push up against the driver's seat. Not too comfortable on his back. But it was good to know he had an MP5 handy if some ass-hole tried to take him out on the interstate.

The lights on the Castellane yacht went out. It was ten o'clock. Jesus. He'd been in southern Maine a year, and still had no intention of ever keeping lobsterman hours. Luke Castellane was a notorious hypochondriac, always thinking something was wrong with him, probably because his father, Hollywood director Victor Castellane, had dropped dead of a heart attack at fifty-five. Luke's mother died three years later. Ovarian cancer. From what Teddy gathered, they'd been total jackasses. They used to summer in Goose Harbor, and Luke had continued the tradition after he grew up, married, had a kid, divorced and turned the modest inheritance from his parents into a bloody fortune. Now he sailed up and down the coast in his yacht all summer and spent the winter at his house in Key West.

Chubby Betsy O'Keefe was living with him. Nurse Betsy. She was plain as a bucket of oats and built like a fire hydrant, but all Luke would care about was the RN after her name. And who else would have her? Teddy figured she was in it for the goodies.

The rain picked up. It was pounding on his windshield now. He could feel the damp cold and debated turning on the engine and getting some heat in his truck. He probably should head back to that goddamn shack he rented from Bruce Young down by the lobster pound. It was barely winterized. He wanted to tell Luke that Zoe West was back in town, but he'd waited too long and now Luke had gone night-night.

If he stayed out here much longer, Teddy knew he'd fall asleep. Then some jerk cop would roust him and maybe see the guns and shit in back. Luke had never invited him to stay in a stateroom aboard the Castellane yacht. Understandable. How would he explain why he'd hired a guy like Teddy? Even that dumb-bunny Nurse Betsy would ask questions.

Teddy turned the key in the engine and switched on the windshield wipers and the headlights, which barely penetrated the thick fog that had rolled in off the water. The docks were dead on such a dark, rainy October night.

"What the hell," he said, shutting down the engine.

When he pushed open the door, he could hear the tide. He didn't know if it was coming in or going out. When he first arrived in Goose Harbor, he'd tried to keep track, but soon discovered it didn't make any damn difference. He never went on the water. Best job he could get was working at the lobster pound. He had enough claw marks from the damn lobsters to prove it. The native Mainers almost never got clawed, not like he did. His own damn fault, they told him.

He stepped onto the wet pavement and smelled the salt in the fog. The rain hit his Yankees cap. Nothing colder than a fall rain on the New England coast. He shivered, not wanting to get too wet. The kerosene stove in Bruce's shack would take forever to heat up the place, even as small as it was.

Teddy pulled a rag out of his pants pocket and wiped the rain off the driver's window on the FBI guy's Jeep. He peered inside. Not much to see. No file with "Top Secret" scrawled on it. Teddy wondered where Mr. Special Agent had gone. Talking to Luke? No way. Luke was in bed with Nurse Betsy.

"Screw it."

Teddy got back into his truck, started the engine again and drove back up to Main Street, then cruised on over to the West house. Zoe West's yellow Volkswagen Beetle was parked out front. Kyle Castellane was getting into his black BMW. Teddy could feel the sarcasm rising up in him. Starving artist. Yeah. Kyle'd be more shocked than anyone if he knew Teddy was working for his watery-eyed pop. Luke didn't like the idea of an FBI agent crawling around town. He'd thought it might bring Zoe back to Goose Harbor, and it had.

Just keep me informed. Do what you have to do.

That left a lot of wiggle room.

Teddy moved on down the road before Kyle's head-lights came on, not that he was worried about being seen. He was a nobody here. Fine with him. It gave him room to maneuver. If things went the way he thought they would, he'd need every inch he could get.

Four

The bright sunrise over the Atlantic woke J.B. early. He had no trouble remembering where he was. Upstairs front bedroom of Olivia West's house. Or why. Zoe West. Or acknowledging that he must have been out of his mind last night.

On the other hand, he liked waking up to the sound of the ocean.

He'd cracked his window and could hear the tide rolling in, the wind gusting, seagulls crying in the distance, the putter of lobster boats. The rain and fog had blown out, leaving behind a washed sky and clear, dry autumn air. His room looked straight out on the Atlantic Ocean, which sparkled in the morning sun.

He pulled on his pants and raked a hand through his hair. Probably a good idea to get moving before ex-detective Zoe decided to inspect her property. Funny she'd decided to inspect *his* first.

But instead of throwing his stuff together and clearing out, J.B. found himself wandering around the big, airy house. Three bedrooms and a bathroom upstairs. Downstairs were another bedroom, one-and-a-half bathrooms, an eat-in kitchen, a side entry and a dining room and living room that stretched across the entire front of the house, with canvas-covered furniture and tall windows that looked out onto a porch and beyond to the Atlantic. The kitchen window faced the harbor. He'd heard that Olivia West had penned all her Jen Periwinkle novels at the kitchen table.

He put an old-fashioned copper kettle on to boil and wondered if it was the same table. Probably. The house still had a pre-World War II feel to it, and from what he'd experienced of the residents of Goose Harbor so far, J.B. took them as a frugal lot. Waste not, want not.

He retrieved a tea bag from a clear class jar on the counter and duly noted the can of soy powder sitting beside it. He doubted it was the old lady's. He pulled open the Reagan-era refrigerator and noted the routine condiments, pure maple syrup, natural peanut butter and a Ziploc bag labeled "flax seed." There were cinnamon Toaster Strudels in the freezer and a bag of frozen blueberries, the little ones, which he knew meant they were wild.

When the water came to a boil, he filled a restaurant-style mug and dunked in his tea bag, then headed through the side entry and into the front room. He eased past the dining-room table, a light film of dust on its dark wood, and walked out onto the front porch. The air was brisk, the porch furniture a mix of Adirondack chairs and rockers. There was a porch swing. He pictured the West family gathering here on summer Sunday afternoons. Now only Christina and her burnt-out older sister were left.

J.B. sipped his tea, the mug warm against his hands. This place probably hadn't changed much in a hundred years. He could almost see Olivia playing on the stretch of lawn above the rock bluff as a child, having friends over—having his grandmother over.

Posey Sutherland McGrath.

He walked down the steps to the lawn and out to the edge of the rocks, where he looked northeast and saw the southern tip of Sutherland Island. It was named for one of his ancestors. He'd taken his rented hulk of a lobster boat around the island and spotted the old foundation of what the locals said had been a Sutherland house. Before he left Goose Harbor, he wanted to explore the island, walk around. Bruce said there was an old family cemetery there. He might or might not be on the level. He was capable of making something up just because he didn't believe J.B. had any ancestors from Goose Harbor.

It was unclear where Jesse McGrath was from. He'd turned up in Goose Harbor and swept Posey Sutherland off her feet. She was the wealthy, sheltered daughter of Lester Sutherland, who had no use for a drifter and forbade Posey to see Jesse. The Wests weren't as well off as the Sutherlands—without Olivia's writing, they'd have had to give up the house on the water. But she agreed with her friend's father that Jesse McGrath would bring her nothing but hardship and sorrow.

Posey ignored them both and eloped with Jesse,

moving first to eastern Montana, then west to a beautiful alpine meadow outside of Bozeman. That was where she had her son, it was where Jesse became a lawman, and it was where she died of a fever when little Benjamin was only seven years old. Jesse was killed a few years later in a shoot-out when he interrupted a bank robbery.

Benjamin—J.B.'s father—went to live with a schoolteacher in Bozeman. Olivia West paid for anything he needed. She even offered to have him move to Maine where she would see to his upbringing in his mother's hometown of Goose Harbor.

J.B. knew because he had the letter. He had all of Olivia West's letters to the friend who'd run off and left her behind. He'd found them when he'd cleaned out his father's cabin after he died over the winter. They were bundled together in a trunk that he didn't know if Benjamin McGrath, western Montana hunting and fishing guide, had ever opened.

Oh, Posey, can you believe I sold a book? You'll read it, I know. Please don't take offense at my villain, Mr. Lester McGrath. I couldn't resist.

Lester Sutherland moved to Boston not long after his daughter ran off. There were no Sutherlands left in Goose Harbor. Olivia hadn't liked Posey's father, and she hadn't liked Jesse McGrath. She'd made that clear in her letters.

J.B. noticed his tea had gone cold.

He headed back inside for more tea and a closer in-

spection of the house where Olivia West was born, lived
her entire life and died. What the hell, he was practically
family.

Zoe had apple coffee cake with her sister at the café
and then sat with a cup of coffee at a small table overlooking the harbor and tried to pretend her life was normal. It felt so normal, being back in Goose Harbor,
watching the activity on the docks. As the sun came up
and the morning wore on, there were more tourists
and pleasure yachts. The lobster boats were out in
deeper water where the catch was plentiful this time
of year.

Christina was too busy behind her glass-front counter
for chitchat. Her café was just what Zoe had expected.
White tables and blue linens, milk-glass vases with yellow mums, watercolors by local artists on the walls, a
constant flow of people. Christina and her wait staff all
wore black bottoms, white tops and blue aprons.

The food was wonderful. Zoe remembered how
Chris would get up early even as a teenager to make
wild-blueberry pancakes and set the table with their
mother's white bone china.

Finally, Zoe gave up her table and headed back outside, welcoming the cool breeze blowing in off the
water. She debated checking with the local police about
the break-in yesterday, but she knew better. They
wouldn't have anything.

She wondered where Agent McGrath was. The lobster boat he'd rented from Bruce was tied up at the dock.
Christina wanted her to talk to him and find out what

he was doing in Goose Harbor—cop to cop, she said, as if an FBI special agent would tell Zoe anything.

With any luck, he'd decided to continue his vacation elsewhere.

Then she noticed a Jeep with D.C. license plates parked in the town lot and gritted her teeth. No. Special Agent McGrath was still in Goose Harbor.

She got into her car and drove out along Ocean Drive, her stomach constricted, the apple coffee cake churning, her fingers in a death grip on the wheel as the road edged along the water. She could see it was choppy out on the ocean. She rolled down her windows and heard the waves and the wind, smelled the salt and tried not to cry.

Until she was in her late nineties, Olivia would walk from her house to the docks almost every morning. She said walking helped her think, helped a story to simmer. There was a famous picture of her leaning on her cane above the rocks on Ocean Drive. It had run in papers all over the country on her ninetieth birthday.

She hadn't died in peace. She'd died thinking she knew who'd murdered her nephew. Tortured because she couldn't produce the name.

Zoe blinked back tears and turned up her aunt's paved driveway. She hadn't expected to inherit the house. Olivia was meticulous in putting her affairs in order, but circumspect—Zoe hadn't known she would inherit the house and the rights to Jen Periwinkle, Christina a trust fund for Christina. They split the modest trust fund meant for their father. Olivia had willed the bulk of her estate to the nature preserve and her other favorite charities. She'd lived frugally and had a decent portfolio, but she'd given away money all through her life and was never enormously wealthy.

The brown-shingled 1890s house stood on the rock-bound point as it always had. All that was missing were the pots of mums Olivia put out every year. And Olivia herself. Zoe parked in the driveway and climbed out, still not used to the reality that the house was hers now. She could sell it for a fortune. It'd buy her more time before she had to get a job, but that seemed like the classic long-term solution to a short-term problem. She had to get her life in order first. Then she could decide what to do with her aunt's house.

Using the key on her key chain, she unlocked the side door and walked into the small entry between the kitchen and the front room.

Someone was here.

She stepped into the kitchen and noted the used tea bag on the counter, felt the still-warm kettle on the stove. Whoever it was could have their own key or have come in through the porch door, which didn't have a lock. Getting one had been on Zoe's to-do list for a year. But the door was seldom used, and not having a lock for it hadn't been a problem in a hundred years.

Had Christina let someone stay here and forgotten to mention it in the excitement over the break-in at her house?

"Hello? Anyone home?"

Zoe checked the front room, but there was no sign of anyone. The porch door was shut tight. Maybe Christina had let Bruce loan a room to someone. Maybe Betsy O'Keefe had moved off Luke Castellane's yacht and needed a place to stay. Zoe doubted a burglar would have fixed himself a cup of tea, but stranger things had happened.

She started up the steep stairs to the second floor. There was no sound of the shower running. No snoring. Nothing unusual.

She called again, keeping her voice cheerful. It had to be someone she knew. "Hello, anyone home? It's me, Mama Bear. Someone's been eating in my kitchen…."

At the top of the stairs, the door to the biggest bedroom across the hall was open, and she saw the unmade bed. "Someone's been sleeping in my bed, too," she muttered, not so loud, and stood in the doorway.

It wan't anyone she knew.

Heaped on the floor was the opened, soft black suitcase she recognized from her tour of Special Agent McGrath's room at the inn last night.

Just what she needed.

She wouldn't put it past Lottie Martin to toss him out for the spilled tea. Hell of a nerve, though, to help himself to a room here. Bruce could have given him the go-ahead, but still.

Zoe returned to the hall. She supposed she had no business talking about nerve since she was the one who'd spilled the tea in the first place. She'd have to find him, figure out what was going on and take it from there.

What if McGrath was the one who'd broken into Christina's house yesterday?

At this point, Zoe was willing to entertain any and all possibilities. Barely twelve hours back in Goose Harbor and things were already a mess.

She started for the stairs but noticed that the door to the attic was cracked and stopped still. A jolt of adrenaline shot through her. *Oh, no.*

It had to be the wind. McGrath *couldn't* be in the attic. Anywhere else, but not there.

She tore open the door and ran upstairs, and only when she got to the top did she think—did she really want to confront a nosy FBI agent? What if he *was* a phony?

The stairs ended in the middle of the attic, with no rail or wall around the stairwell. There was a window at each end of the huge open space. It was filled with boxes, trunks, old furniture—what anyone would expect to find in an attic. Except for the space by the south window.

Zoe snatched up an old drapery rod. She made herself breathe as she picked her way through the attic junk, unable to see if anyone was in the little nook she'd made for herself during the first weeks after her father and great-aunt had died, when she'd been overwhelmed with grief, shock, anger, insanity. She'd used two old bureaus to create false walls and added a chenille rug and a dozen pillows in varying sizes, shapes and colors, anything that didn't scream "cop," that didn't remind her of touching her father's dead body…of hearing her aunt say, *"I know who did it…."*

The only solace she'd found in those weeks was in spending time up here. She bought yellow pads and pencils, a pencil sharpener, ten different kinds of pens, and she sat on her rug amid her pillows, staring out her window at the harbor and scribbling.

She should have dismantled her secret retreat before she left for Connecticut. Set fire to everything.

Pushing back her sense of embarrassment and violation at the idea anyone had pawed through her private space, she came around the two tall bureaus that marked one of her walls.

A lean, black-haired man had his legs stretched out and one of her yellow pads on his lap, and when he looked up at her, it was all Zoe could do to hang on to her drapery rod. He might have crawled off a Winslow Homer seascape with his blue eyes and weathered appearance, more the New England seaman than a Montana FBI agent.

He smiled at her. "You must be Mama Bear."

"And you must be Special Agent McGrath."

"Zoe West?"

She nodded. She didn't know what else to say. Ex-detective West? Almost Special Agent West? She cleared her throat. "I understand you've met my sister, Christina."

"I have."

She felt ridiculous carrying a drapery rod and self-conscious seeing the yellow pad with *Chapter One* scrawled in her handwriting across the top in his lap. It was as if there was nothing left in her of the veteran Maine State Police detective or even the somewhat eccentric sole detective of Bluefield, Connecticut.

McGrath got to his feet. He was tall and obviously

very fit. Zoe used to be more fit before she took up residence with Charlie and Bea Jericho and started knitting and canning and milking goats, trying to put her life back together after her year of self-imposed exile. She didn't run, not since she'd found her father's body.

She watched McGrath take in her outfit of slim black pants, little fuchsia top, black flats and silver ankle bracelet and put that together with the image he, like the rest of Goose Harbor, must have formed of her. At least he couldn't see her rose tattoo.

He gave her a slight nod. "You want to call the police or just hit me over the head with that curtain rod?"

"It's a drapery rod. You can tell because of the hooks and the little pulley thing."

"Ah."

He tossed her pad onto a rose-flowered pillow. He moved with the kind of restrained control that reminded Zoe she was out of practice with her hand-to-hand combat skills. He wasn't wearing a weapon. He had on jeans, a thick black sweater and scuffed boat shoes.

She tried not to glance at the pad. She'd written in longhand, page after page of nothing anyone else was supposed to see. Ever. "Did you read—" She took a breath and decided she didn't want to know. "Never mind. Did Bruce give you permission to stay here? He has no right—"

"Bruce doesn't know I'm here. It was my idea to stay here."

His tone was unapologetic. He was simply stating the facts and letting her decide what she thought of them.

His voice was deep and slightly raspy, as if it'd been dragged over sharp rocks a few times.

"Why?" she asked.

"Because you got me thrown out of my inn."

"What? I did no—" She stopped herself. Why make a denial? Why lie? He hadn't asked a question or demanded an explanation. No point in painting herself into a corner. "I'll see you downstairs in the kitchen."

"As you wish."

Right. As if she had any control over the situation. She took her drapery rod with her, about-faced and headed back to the stairs, just missing falling into the stairwell and ending her return to Goose Harbor with a broken neck—which would have served her right.

Five

J.B. made his way down the attic steps thinking Zoe West must have known she wasn't dealing with a real threat or she'd never have come after him with a drapery rod. Either that or she'd gone more off the deep end as a cop than even he'd expected.

He debated packing up his stuff before heading down to the kitchen, then decided not to keep ex-detective West waiting. She had a right to be pissed at finding him in her attic, but he didn't feel bad about it. At some point in her not-too-distant past, she'd decided to resurrect Jen Periwinkle. He'd read the first chapter on her yellow pad. He knew she'd written it because she'd put her name at the top of the first page in neat block letters. It was pretty good. Her Jen Periwinkle was a little older than Olivia West's Jen Periwinkle, and she had a boyfriend. A young FBI agent. J.B. got a kick out of that. No sign of Mr. Lester McGrath in what he'd read.

He'd watched Zoe West drive up to her aunt's house in her yellow VW and could have alerted her to his presence at any time, but he hadn't. Not very nice of him, but she had searched his room. He figured she deserved to find him in the attic.

She had her kick-ass cop face on when he joined her in the kitchen. She was standing with her back to the sink and her arms crossed. He noticed she had more flecks of gray in her blue eyes than her sister did; she wasn't as tall and her blond hair was shorter. She didn't have as many freckles. With the little shirt and pants and the ankle bracelet, she didn't look as if she'd ever carried a gun. J.B. suspected that was pure prejudice on his part, but there it was.

"I'd like an explanation," she said.

"An explanation of what?"

No reaction. "Of why you're here."

"In Goose Harbor or in your house?"

"Both."

He pulled out a chair at the table and sat down, keeping an eye on her. "I'm in Goose Harbor on vacation, and I'm in your house because I figured you owed me one for pawing through my room."

"Your name's J. B. McGrath?"

"Jesse Benjamin McGrath."

"And you are with the FBI, right?"

"I was trying to keep a low profile, but yes. Do you want to see my credentials?"

She gave a tight shake of the head. "I understand your ancestors are from Goose Harbor."

"That's right."

"McGraths?"

"No."

"You know that Jen Periwinkle's evil nemesis is named McGrath?"

"He's fictional," J.B. said. "I'm not."

She muttered something that sounded like "more's the pity," then dropped her arms to her sides. "You had nothing to do with the break-in at my sister's yesterday?"

"No."

"You're not involved with the investigation into my father's murder?"

He could feel his expression softening. "No, I'm not."

"Why Goose Harbor? Why now?"

"I was due a vacation." He didn't need to tell her he'd been ordered to take some time off. "My ancestors are from here. I'd heard about your father's murder and knew it was still unsolved—I won't say I haven't tried to put the pieces together in my own mind."

"But it's not why you're here?"

He decided now wasn't the time to try to explain the relationshio between her great-aunt and his grandmother. He shook his head. "Not specifically, no. Detective West—"

"Zoe's fine. I'll never be a detective again."

He got to his feet. "I'll make my bed, pack up and clear out."

"In a minute. First you can help me get my things out of the car." She started for the side entry and glanced back at him. "Then we'll be even."

It was as much of an admission as he was going to get that she was the one who'd gone through his room last night. He walked behind her out to the side porch and down the stone walk to her VW Beetle, its back stuffed with boxes, bags and a heavy suitcase that had to be forty years old.

Zoe nodded at two knitting needles and a mass of milky-gray yarn spilling out of one of the bags. "That's my scarf. I started with a hundred stitches and now I have seventy-seven. What do you suppose happened to the other twenty-three?"

"You dropped them."

"Dropped them where?"

There was a glint of humor in her eyes—more gray in the late morning sun than blue—as she opened the driver's door. "Bruce says you're a closet eccentric," J.B. said.

"He said that about Aunt Olivia, too. Bruce is an authority on two subjects: lobstering and the Maine coast. Anything he says on any other subject is not to be trusted."

J.B. was still confident the flax seed and the soy powder were hers. "He says you refused to carry a weapon on duty and encouraged a Texas Ranger to interfere in the investigation into the Connecticut governor's death."

"I didn't encourage him—I just didn't stop him. And I didn't refuse to carry a weapon—I just didn't." She lifted out a backpack and hoisted it onto her shoulder. "Any other questions?"

"About a million, but I'll resist."

She said nothing and grabbed a plastic bag overflowing with books, the top one a primer on domestic goats.

J.B. watched her turn up the walk to the side door. He could almost see the demons swooping around her, haunting her, toying with her as she tried to tell herself she had to get used to the idea that she might never know who killed her father—that she might never know if telling her aunt about his murder had somehow contributed to her death.

She stopped on the side porch and turned back to him. "How much did you read of what I wrote?"

"None of it. You have lousy handwriting, Detective West."

"That's very decent of you," she said quietly, unexpectedly. "Thank you."

But he could see she knew he'd lied. He felt like a heel. She'd only picked through his underwear and his reading material, none of which he'd written himself.

After they got the last of her stuff out of her car, J.B. made his bed, packed, cleaned his bathroom and wiped down the kitchen counter and sink where he'd made tea. Then he offered to take Zoe West to lunch at her sister's café.

To his surprise, she accepted.

Betsy O'Keefe stretched out on a cushioned lounge chair on the afterdeck of Luke Castellane's yacht and listened to the seabirds. A lifelong resident of Goose Harbor, she still barely knew a seagull from a duck. Just wasn't interested. She closed her eyes and welcomed the ruffle of a breeze over her. It had warmed up nicely. Almost seventy degrees. Luke had on a toasty warm-up suit, but Betsy, in elastic-waist yellow jeans and an oversize white shirt, wished she'd put on shorts that morning.

Luke hissed impatiently as he read a health article at the nearby table. He was always reading health articles. After Olivia died, he'd invited Betsy over to check his blood pressure three times a day for a week. He was worried the stress of Patrick West's murder and all the publicity of Olivia's death would push him into a stroke. He was in his early fifties, sandy-haired and good-looking, if a little too whip-thin from his diet and exercise regimen. Healthy as a horse. She'd had her eye on him even before that terrible twenty-four hours last fall, but even she was surprised when he took to her.

She could do worse than Luke Castellane.

His cell phone rang. He sighed—if anything did him in, it would be his natural impatience—and answered it. "Yes, what is it?" He listened a moment. "I can't talk right now. Do *nothing* without my permission. Is that understood?"

He didn't give whoever was on the other end a chance to respond before he disconnected.

"Who was that?" Betsy asked mildly.

"What? No one. A money matter. Go back to sleep."

"I wasn't sleeping."

He didn't reply. Olivia West had always had a soft spot for Luke. She told Betsy it was because she saw what his parents did to him. His oddities, she believed, were a direct result of their psychological abuse and neglect, and that at heart, Luke was a good man who wanted to be able to connect with other people and have healthy relationships but didn't know how.

Olivia had left Betsy a generous sum that she'd immediately put away as her nest egg for the future. She didn't know how long Luke would have her but didn't delude herself into thinking it would be forever.

She swung her feet onto the deck and sat up. "I'm going for a walk. Care to join me?"

He shook his head.

"I wonder if there's any news on who broke into Christina's yesterday. I'm so glad she and Kyle weren't there. He's working like a demon on his Olivia West documentary, but I understand his materials are all at his apartment above the café, so it wasn't in any danger."

"No one's interested in his documentary."

Betsy stood up. "I suppose not. I was thinking more of vandalism or an accident."

Stick Monroe, one of Luke's few longtime friends, had stopped by that morning and mentioned Zoe was back. Luke seemed uninterested, but Betsy felt a stab of unpleasant anticipation, not because she didn't like Zoe. Because they shared a secret.

I know who killed Patrick....

Poor old Olivia. To die thinking she knew the identity of her nephew's murderer. It was ridiculous, of course, and Betsy agreed with Zoe there was no point mentioning it to anyone. Olivia had been so befuddled, and now she was dead.

Betsy told Luke goodbye and walked out onto the yacht club dock. In a week or so he'd be sailing for Florida, with various stops on the way. She thought she was invited, but she wouldn't count on it until they were actually en route—for all she knew, Luke would ask her to stay behind in Goose Harbor.

As she walked toward the town docks, she fantasized that Luke was watching her and thinking sexy thoughts about her. Instead he was probably counting his daily fat grams or fretting about his blood pressure. She tried not to delude herself into thinking she really mattered to Luke. Only Luke mattered to Luke.

She had a sudden urge for a piece of wild blueberry pie. Christina West made the best in southern Maine. How lucky her café wasn't a hundred yards off. Luke had commented not long ago that he hadn't had blueberry pie in fifteen years.

His loss, Betsy thought, deciding she wouldn't think about sugar, fat, refined flour, trans-fatty acids or calories at least for the next hour. Wild blueberries were a good source of antioxidants, but she wouldn't even think about that. She'd just eat her pie and enjoy herself.

Six

Luke Castellane was paying him to keep an eye on Special Agent McGrath and Zoe West, but Teddy thought he might have to go over to Luke's fancy yacht and beat the shit out of him. Arrogant, rude bastard. Hanging up on him. Teddy just wanted him to know that the FBI agent and Zoe West were having lunch at Christina's Café. He was reporting back like he said he would. Wasn't that why the asshole was paying him?

The FBI agent appeared out of nowhere and leaned in Teddy's open truck window. Teddy didn't rattle. He had a black tarp over his arsenal in back, an MP5 handy if he needed it. "Yeah? What do you want?"

"I thought you were having a heart attack. You're okay?"

"Yeah, fine."

"My mistake. Local?"

"Look, I'm in a hurry. I don't have time for a chat." Teddy didn't bother keeping the sarcasm out of his tone, but he decided he didn't want McGrath memorizing his license plate or lifting his prints off a coffee cup. He made himself ease off. "Thanks for checking up on me. Nice to know if I do have a heart attack, there are people around who'll do something."

"Sure. No problem."

Teddy started the engine, and the FBI agent stepped back, still with his eyes narrowed and his cop look. Teddy wondered what he'd done to attract the guy's attention. Maybe he could smell ex-cons and illegal weapons. "Heart attack, my ass."

He didn't know what he was supposed to do now. Wait for Luke to call with instructions, he guessed. He headed back through the village with its cute shops and pretty houses and took a side road down along the water just south of the harbor, veering off onto a dirt road until he came to Bruce Young's lobster pound. The place was starting to pick up with lobster boats pulling in to turn in their catches. The tide was out. Teddy couldn't stand the smell.

The driveway to the cottage he was renting from Bruce split off from the dirt road. Teddy shook his head when he saw its sagging roof and half-rotted back steps. Bruce was probably waiting for it to fall down so he could put up something new when he got the money together. He'd warned Teddy the place was a dump.

With a little luck, push would finally come to shove, and before he had to spend another hellish winter here, he'd be in good shape and moving on from Gooseshit Harbor, Maine.

"I thought you were on vacation."

J.B. heard the slight surprise in Sally Meintz's voice.

He was in his Jeep on his cell phone. Sally was at her desk at FBI headquarters. Her surprise was very slight. There was a note of sarcasm in her voice, too. Not much got to her anymore. She was one of the thousands of support staff that kept the FBI and the rest of the federal government running. She was sixty, the mother of four, the wife of a retired marine officer and a by-the-book type. She didn't like doing favors on the sly. But she would if she got talked into it, and she wasn't a tattletale.

"I am on vacation. I just want you to run a plate for me."

"State?"

"Maine."

"Right. You're there on vacation." She'd let a little more sarcasm slip into her tone. "Give me the number."

He gave her the license plate number of the rusting truck whose driver J.B. had known wasn't having a heart attack. He'd spotted the truck last night outside Christina West's house and then again this morning passing Olivia West's house, not long after Zoe had turned up the driveway. The third strike was outside Christina's Café at lunch.

"What do I get for doing you a favor?" Sally asked.

"My undying respect and affection."

"I already have that. You coming back to Washington for good after this vacation of yours?"

"I don't know yet."

"They want to keep you from going off the deep end. God knows why. I'd let you jump."

She disconnected. J.B. tossed his cell phone onto the seat next to him. Maybe it was a stretch to call Sally

Meintz a friend. He climbed back out of his Jeep and stood in the sunlight. He could see his rented lobster boat bobbing in the water. At least no one had set fire to it overnight.

Zoe was still at the small table overlooking the water in her sister's café, working on a massive piece of chocolate cream pie. J.B. had had a bowl of haddock chowder with her and watched the reactions of the people who knew her when they realized she was back in town. Alert, awkward, even nervous—or maybe it was seeing her with him. People probably wouldn't mind if they both went away.

He spotted Bruce Young on the docks and walked down to join him. He had on his Carhartt and a black turtleneck as he untied his lobster boat, a fairly new vessel with all the bells and whistles—radar, GPS, a good radio, plastic-coated wire traps, lighter in weight than the old wooden traps. The knowledge and instincts of guys like Bruce still mattered, but maybe not as much as they used to.

"Been out today?" Bruce asked, not looking up from his work.

"Not yet."

"Heard you had lunch with Zoe."

"Fish chowder. She put butter in hers."

"Best way to eat it. A pat of butter, a little pepper. People think she's here to kick your ass and teach you not to toy with the good people of Goose Harbor."

J.B. smiled. "Can she play darts?"

"Zoe? No way. She can shoot, though."

"I camped out at her aunt's house last night."

Bruce grinned at him. "She catch you?"

"In the attic."

"Good thing she doesn't go armed anymore. What'd you want with Teddy?"

J.B. frowned. "Who?"

"Teddy Shelton. The guy in the truck. You were just talking to him—"

"Oh, him. I thought he was having a heart attack. You know him?"

Bruce lifted a thick rope into his callused hand. "I'm renting him a cottage down by the lobster pound. He does odd jobs around town."

"He's not from Goose Harbor?"

"I don't know where he's from. He showed up last summer. He keeps to himself. He tried working at the pound, but he didn't like it." Bruce shook his head. "Hates the smell of the ocean."

"Why not move on?"

"Don't know. Teddy's not your big talker." Bruce tossed the rope into his boat and climbed aboard. "What'd Zoe do when she found you in the attic?"

"Came after me with a drapery rod."

"You backed down?"

"Amen."

"Yeah. You wouldn't want to lose a fight with a fired cop over a drapery rod."

Words to live by. J.B. watched Bruce's boat ease slowly out of the busy dock area and head south toward his lobster pound for another few hours' work.

When Sally Meintz rang him back, J.B. didn't tell her

he already knew Teddy Shelton's name. She said, "The plates are registered to a Teddy Shelton in Goose Harbor, Maine. Guess what else?" She paused, waiting for an answer.

J.B. sighed. "What else, Sally?"

"I did a little more checking while I was at it. He's an ex-con. Served seven years in federal prison after he was convicted on charges of transfering and possessing semiautomatic assault weapons. ATF nailed him."

"When did he get out?"

"Last July."

He must have come straight to Goose Harbor. Three months later Patrick West was murdered. "Find out what you can about his case, okay? Thanks, Sally."

"I like it when you say thank-you. It gives me hope for the rest of the world. What do I get for my trouble?"

"A cop-killer, maybe."

She sighed, serious now. "That'd be worth it."

The state and local cops had to know all about Teddy Shelton. It was a stretch to think he had anything to do with Chief West's death, but J.B. didn't like spotting an ex-con three times in less than twenty-four hours. Not at all.

Zoe dipped her fork into the last of the real whipped cream atop her pie and pretended she didn't notice J. B. McGrath down on the docks. Lunch with him had been more unsettling than she'd expected. At times he seemed to be so on edge, she thought he might jump through the window—other times, she thought it impossible to ruffle him about anything. He was intense, focused, not even close to relaxed after almost a week on vacation.

But now she had to deal with Stick Monroe. Her old friend sat across from her and eyed her over his mug of black coffee. "I thought I might find you here."

Zoe ignored his knowing tone and smiled, glancing around the crowded, charming café. "It's great, isn't it? I used to think someone ought to bulldoze this place into the harbor. I didn't see the potential Christina did. She works hard, but I think she loves it."

Stick nodded in agreement. He had on his usual outfit of corduroy shorts and rugby shirt—he wouldn't switch to long pants until it was bitter cold. He was seventy-two but looked at least ten years younger, a fit, healthy, white-haired retired federal district court judge. His family had summered in Goose Harbor for as long as Zoe could remember. He was the last of them—he'd never married, never had kids. Everyone was surprised when he gave up his lifetime appointment and retired. But he seemed content to take long walks along the water, work in his garden and read books. He'd never been much on boating. His friends included everyone from statesmen and corporate executives to lobstermen and cops. He was brilliant, but he wasn't a snob.

"You came back because of the break-in?" he asked.

"It was the catalyst. I was ready. I'm unemployed."

"So I hear."

Zoe couldn't detect any disappointment in his tone, but it had to be there. He'd been her mentor since she was a little girl, encouraging her, opening up a broader world to her. Despite her great-aunt's fame, she was content to stay in Goose Harbor. So were her father and sister. But Zoe had the feeling Stick had hoped for more from her than going into the FBI—following in his footsteps, maybe. Law school, U.S. attorney, federal judge. He'd never made it to the appeals court—maybe he thought she would.

Now she was a fired cop. A Quantico no-show. Jobless.

"I've learned to knit," she told him, then smiled. "Sort of."

"Zoe—"

She could see the concern in his warm brown eyes. "I'm not here to make trouble, Stick."

"What about the FBI agent, McGrath?"

"He's on vacation. He helped Bruce put in a new door at the house."

Stick leaned back in his chair, his coffee untouched. "I called in a few favors with contacts I still have in Washington and checked him out. He's a powder keg, Zoe. This vacation wasn't his idea."

"Something happened?"

"An ultra-right-wing, antigovernment crackpot tried to slit his throat. Almost succeeded. McGrath killed him. The guy's three kids were there."

Zoe winced. "That's awful."

"He was working undercover. I'm not supposed to tell you any of this." Stick drank some of his coffee. It must have been cold, because he took a huge gulp, swallowed it, then regarded her with obvious concern. "Those undercover types are all nuts. You know that."

It was one of the most persistent stereotypes in law enforcement, but it didn't come from nowhere. Zoe set down her fork. She wasn't hungry anymore. "What else do you know about this undercover investigation?"

"It was out west. Violent extremists constructing and trading in illegal weapons and explosive devices and plotting the assassination of local, state and federal officials. McGrath infiltrated their network over several months, posing as a buyer. It turns out a local cop was involved and tipped off the bad guys. Hence, the nearly slit throat."

"I'd need a vacation after that, too." Just as well he'd seen her out in the driveway before she'd come at him with her drapery rod and sense of violation and humiliation. She didn't want to surprise an FBI powder keg. "Well, I'll give him wide berth. What're you up to these days, Stick?"

He smiled. "Worrying about you."

"Ah." She smiled back at him. "Always good to know I've got a judge looking out for my best interests. I'm not out of control anymore, Stick. I don't know what's next for me in my life, but—"

"You want to know who killed your father."

His blunt remark caught her off-guard, and she felt herself going pale. "Of course I do."

"It's not that people around here don't want to know, it's just that they can live without it. They don't want to have to relive the grief and horror of last fall. They tell themselves it was an out-of-town drug dealer, a random act because Patrick was in the wrong place at the wrong time." He set down his mug and got to his feet, adding softly, "But not you, Zoe. You want the truth, whatever it is."

"Maybe it *was* an out-of-town drug dealer."

His gaze settled on her. He was a tall man, his skin tanned and wrinkled but not sagging. "You think the break-in at the house is connected to your father's murder."

"I have no reason to think anything, Stick—except that I've had too many milk products for lunch. Chowder, then chocolate cream pie."

He shook his head, patient, always the one who could see through her. "Keep in touch, okay?" He kissed the top of her head. "Welcome home."

After he left, Zoe said goodbye to her sister, who was obviously enjoying herself as she put together orders. The lunchtime crowd hadn't dwindled. The fall foliage was at its peak, the leaf-peepers out in droves—Zoe could hear a table of seniors as they pointed out brightly colored trees along the shoreline.

She headed outside. McGrath's lobster boat was gone. He must have left while she was talking to Stick. She walked down to the docks and squinted, picking out Bruce's old boat up toward Olivia's, making its way along the shore to the nature preserve and the cluster of offshore islands.

That was something else she had to do—go back to the nature preserve, to the spot where she'd found her father's body. Today was so much like the morning she'd found him. Cool, bright, beautiful.

Maybe it could wait until tomorrow.

She and McGrath had walked down from Olivia's. She took her time crossing the parking lot and making her way to Ocean Drive, tried to ignore the flashbacks to the countless times she'd walked this route to visit her great-aunt. She'd see her father on the way. They'd always gotten along. They'd never had any big angst-filled battles. Neither had he and Christina. Zoe didn't know if it was because they'd lost their mother so young and it'd squeezed out all of that need to rebel, or if it was just the way he was, the way they were as a family.

When she got back to the house, she decided she'd need groceries if she was going to stick around. She pushed back the wave of loneliness, the tug of grief at the emptiness of the house, and opened windows, feeling the cool, salt-tinged breeze and hearing the ocean. She started a list at the kitchen table—then stopped.

She had to know.

She ran up to the attic and made her way to her writing nook, banging her shin on a trunk. She picked up the yellow pad she'd caught McGrath holding and felt the heat rise up from her chest to her ears.

Just as she'd thought.

There was nothing wrong with her handwriting. That liar could read it just fine.

Seven

Teddy couldn't help it—to him the ocean smelled like a bucket of barf, especially at low tide. He couldn't get used to it. He stood at the water's edge of the shallow cove in front of his wreck of a cottage and watched a lobster boat pull up to the lobster-pound dock, gulls swooping around everywhere. He'd once had a gull grab a ham sandwich right out of his hand.

Luke was on the phone, bitching him out. "You moron. Betsy saw you and that FBI agent arguing."

"We weren't arguing. He thought I was having a heart attack."

Luke snorted. "And you believed him?"

"No, but so what?"

Teddy walked out onto a flat, gray rock, the water around it not two inches deep at low tide. It was more or less a puddle—a tide pool, he guessed it was called. It bled into a stretch of gray mud and small, water-smoothed rocks.

"Nothing happened," he went on. "Relax. Anybody

asks, I'm watching Zoe for you, making sure she doesn't get in over her head like last year. Because you care about her. Because Patrick West was your friend and Olivia West had a soft spot for you and you figure you owe them."

"I don't want people to know you and I have any connection—"

"Relax, will you? You should have thought this through before you asked me to spy on an FBI agent—"

"I don't have to listen to this," Luke hissed.

"Nurse Betsy say anything to you? She likes to have blueberry pie on the sly, you know. Probably figures you'll think your arteries will clog just from watching her chow down."

"Where are you now?"

"Cooling my heels. If McGrath spotted me skulking around your ex-cop sweetie, she could have, too. I'll go on back to town in a few minutes."

"Be discreet," Luke snapped, condescending, irritable.

"Why'd you agree to hire me if you're getting cold feet this fast? Jesus—"

"Don't get the wrong idea, Shelton. I'm not afraid of either one of them. I just don't want them meddling in her father's murder investigation. It'll just make matters worse and won't lead to his killer. McGrath has no right to stir up trouble." Luke breathed heavily, as if he might hyperventilate. "The West sisters have suffered enough."

Right. Like he'd hired Teddy because he was worried about Zoe and Christina West's feelings. Teddy watched the lobster boat ease on back around the point, toward the small, protected harbor. The temperature was going down, nightfall coming earlier and earlier. He could feel the bite of winter in the air. Luke'd be heading south soon. Teddy didn't have any firm plans, but he had no intention of spending another winter in Maine.

"I think your instincts about our Special Agent Mc-Grath are on target," Teddy said. "The guy's trouble. I don't care if the old cemeteries around here are full of his ancestors, he's here because there's an unsolved murder."

"It's been bad enough having the state investigators snooping—" Luke sighed. "I should have thrown you off my boat that night you showed up here."

Teddy knew he wasn't referring to the night a week ago when Luke had asked Teddy to keep an eye on Mc-Grath, and Zoe if she came back, but to a night more than a year ago. "But you didn't, did you?" Teddy walked backward off his rock. "You sold me a gun you weren't supposed to sell me."

"What's your game, Shelton?" Luke's voice was low, not so arrogant now. A touch of fear in it. "Because if you're playing me—"

"Relax. Go hump Nurse Betsy. I'll stay in touch."

Teddy clicked off. He felt almost smug—that'd teach the bastard to try to get the upper hand with him. He went back up to the cottage, a one-bedroom with cracked linoleum and cheap furnishings, and got his truck keys and headed out. He almost ran into Bruce's truck on its way out from the lobster pound. Teddy waved. The guy was amazing. His first instinct was to like people. He was totally undiscriminating. It'd never occur to him his buddy Teddy had an illegal arsenal in the jump seat. Grenades, semiautomatic assault weapons, so-called large capacity feeding devices.

Nah, not Bruce. He was oblivious.

Bruce slowed to a crawl and stuck his head out his window. "You play darts? Come by Perry's later. Maybe you can beat the FBI agent."

Teddy didn't know what to say. "Okay. Yeah, I'll see you later."

Zoe drove out to a market south of town and bought staples, like bread, juice, milk and cereal, then stopped at a farm store for local produce—Cortland apples, butternut squash, potatoes, carrots, fall spinach. She bought a jug of apple cider and a half-dozen cider doughnuts, eating one on the way back through the village.

She stopped at her childhood home, now her sister's home, and let the engine idle while she gripped the wheel with both hands and thought about the break-in. Her father had insisted on locks on the doors. He was chief of police. He wasn't going to make it easy for anyone to just walk in. He'd once stopped by Olivia's with a lock for her porch door, but she distracted him with some other project—locks made her feel like she was in prison. One was enough. The logic of having locks on both her doors defeated her.

"Oh, Christ…"

The tears came out of nowhere. Zoe breathed in through her nose, trying to get control of herself. It'd been a year, and she still missed them both, her father, her great-aunt. They'd always been there. The rocks of her life. Her anchors. Everything they'd ever wanted in life was right here. She could talk Washington, D.C., and world events and federal law enforcement with Stick Monroe—with her dad and Aunt Olivia, it had always been about Goose Harbor.

Zoe wiped her cheeks with her fingertips and ate another cider doughnut.

Maybe if she stayed in town, she could make her peace with not knowing who'd killed her father, or why, or if Olivia's death was in any way related.

I know who killed him.

"Ah, Aunt Olivia. Where's Jen Periwinkle when we need her?"

Jen used her wits to distinguish good clues from bad clues—and there were always clues. The police had Patrick West's body and the two bullets that had killed him. That was all.

Zoe pushed back her thoughts, her overwhelming sense of grief, and instead of driving back through town and fighting the leaf-peepers, she took the tangle of back streets, passing inns and summer houses, smaller homes owned by year-round locals, until she came out on Ocean Drive just above the nature preserve named for her great-aunt.

She turned onto a gravel road and drove a hundred yards to a parking area and visitors' center amid a pine grove. This time she got out of her car. The air was cooler here, a slight breeze stirring. She looked up at the pine needles etched against the cloudless blue of the sky, heard birds in the distance—it was migrating season for hawks.

The preserve's self-guided trails were open from dawn until dusk. Zoe found herself on the wide, three-mile gravel loop trail. She'd come out here to run ever since she was a teenager. After she'd resigned from the state police, she'd run the loop trail every day to train for the FBI Academy. She remembered how excited she was about her future, how her life had seemed to stretch before her. Now she didn't know what would come next. It was enough to plan dinner. She sometimes wondered if that was why she'd responded to the rhythms of the Jericho farm, milking and feeding the goats, harvesting the garden. Even with knitting, she had to stay focused on the present.

She passed interpretive signs describing the wildlife and plant life, the geology of southern Maine's curving coastline and broad stretches of beaches, the cluster of three small offshore islands with their tricky currents and narrow passages. There were benches for birdwatching and scenic views, but she didn't stop for anything.

The bright yellow leaves of a dozen thin birch trees told her she was close to Stewart's Cove. She slowed her pace, her throat tightening with tension, anticipation. It was late in the afternoon, and most of the tourists had left. She was aware that she was alone, possibly no one even within shouting distance.

Except for J. B. McGrath.

He was standing on a flat, wet rock that would be

covered soon as the tide rose. It was about three yards from where she'd found her father.

"It's a beautiful spot," he said.

She nodded tightly, fighting the images of a year ago. Her father sprawled on his stomach. His blood had seeped into the wet sand and shallow water of the rising tide.

"What are you doing here?" she asked.

"I saw your car and followed you. I came around the other way—I didn't expect to beat you here." His smile was surprisingly gentle. "No need for a sharp stick."

She edged closer to the water. The wind caught her in the face, and she wished she'd worn a jacket. She crossed her arms over her chest and tried to focus on the cresting waves out beyond the mouth of the small cove. J.B. didn't move from his rock. She let her gaze settle on him, realized he was a good-looking man, rugged, sexy, undoubtedly an independent type if he'd survived as an FBI undercover agent for any length of time.

"First time you've been back here?" he asked quietly.

She nodded. "It's a beautiful spot. So peaceful. My father was trying to lower his blood pressure and cholesterol, so he'd taken up walking before work. But he was in uniform. CID's inclined to think he was meeting someone, either here in the preserve or shortly after his walk. He stopped at Aunt Olivia's that morning. She was always up early."

"Did you have a chance to ask her what they discussed?"

"Her revised obituary. Dad thought she was morbid."

J.B. smiled and moved off his rock, his shoes sinking into the wet sand. He joined her on the packed, dry sand of the short stretch of beach. "I understand the police don't believe his body was moved. He was shot here."

"The shooter could have come in by boat or by land—it wouldn't be hard to stay concealed. At that hour, lobster boats would be out or heading out, but they're in deep water this time of year." She sighed, bile rising in her throat, and she wished she hadn't eaten so much, could feel the pie and doughnuts churning in her stomach. "It's not for me to investigate my father's death. That was made clear to me last fall."

"You run roughshod over everyone?"

"I just wanted answers. At first people understood, but when the investigation stalled—" She broke off, dropping her hands to her sides. "It wasn't an easy time. In CID's place, I'd have done the same thing. I'd resigned. I was on my way to Quantico."

"Losing your father and aunt the way you did must have pulled the rug out from under your life. I'm sorry." He shifted away from her, and for the first time she noticed the three-inch scar on his jaw, just below his left ear. He'd been a split second from becoming the subject of a murder investigation himself. But he glanced back at her and asked, "Teddy Shelton—you know him?"

His question caught her by surprise. "Not really. He worked at the lobster pound last summer—I think he's renting a cottage from Bruce. Why?"

"He popped up on my radar screen today. It's probably nothing. You must want some time here on your own. I'll see you around."

Zoe didn't stop him. She'd get his Teddy Shelton story out of him later. He walked back up to the trail, falling in with a trio of seniors, and she didn't move until they were out of sight. Then, shivering in the chilly ocean air, she sat on a three-foot boulder and watched the tide slowly roll in, the two smallest islands visible offshore, just the northern tip of the largest, Sutherland Island, visible. They were mostly rock and evergreens, but their rugged look was deceptive. Their thin soil actually made them very fragile, easily damaged by careless hikers and kayakers. Luke Castellane's father, Hollywood director Victor Castellane, had bought Sutherland Island years ago—the nature preserve wanted to add it to its onshore acreage.

Zoe stared at the short stretch of beach, not breathing, seeing herself a year ago when she realized there was no hope, her father was dead. She hadn't known if the shooter was still nearby, if she was in danger, but she hadn't been able to make herself respond like a law enforcement officer—it was her father dead before her.

She could still feel the water seeping into her running shoes as she ran out into the cove, screaming at a lobster boat down toward Sutherland Island. It turned out to be Bruce Young's.

It occurred to her then and had stuck with her for the past year that her father's murder had something to do with her. Was she supposed to find his body? It was no secret she ran in the preserve. Had she told him something in the weeks before that ultimately got him killed? Had a case she worked on when she was with the state police come back to haunt not her, but her father?

In the first weeks of the investigation, the state detectives had looked into all those possibilities. But there was nothing—no lead, no potential lead—that connected back to her.

So, what about Teddy Shelton?

She doubted it took much to pop up on McGrath's radar screen, but still.

She leaped suddenly up off the boulder, as if she'd been bitten by a spider, but it was just nervous energy, restlessness. She'd spent the last two months milking goats and knitting. Why hadn't she come back here sooner? She was convinced now, just as she was a year ago, that the answers to her father's murder didn't lie outside of Goose Harbor. They were here, in her hometown.

I know who did it....

Then again, maybe she was letting herself be misled by a dying old woman's ramblings.

"Damn."

She took a breath and walked back up to the trail. The three-hundred-acre preserve was her aunt's legacy, as much as her Jen Periwinkle novels were. Olivia had had a long, good life. It was some consolation. Her father's was cut short, in midlife. He hadn't even had a chance to fight back. For him, Zoe's only consolation was that he hadn't suffered—the coroner said he'd most likely died almost instantly.

The first murder in Goose Harbor in thirty years.

She glanced back at the cove, the afternoon light waning as the tide washed over the sand and rock. There were worse places to die.

Eight

J.B. wasn't in the mood for darts. He sat at a round table with a good view of Perry's ancient bristle dartboard and wood-shaft darts and drank his iced tea. He was staying away from alcohol. His judgment was off enough as it was. What the hell was he doing, getting involved with these people? He should leave and check into the Kennebunkport inn that Lottie Martin had recommended. Finish his vacation somewhere else.

Zoe West had gotten to him. She wasn't out of control like he was—she had such a tight rein on herself, it was a wonder she could breathe. It wasn't the picture he'd formed of her based on the stories about her from last fall. He knew about post-trauma reactions. Flashbacks, sleep problems, anger, irritability, numbness. She'd pushed herself. She'd pushed everyone.

He thought of her standing in the cove where she'd found her father's body. She still had no answers.

Bruce plopped down next to him with a beer. "I'm having a lobster roll and calling it dinner. You?"

"Sounds good."

Bruce put in their order and settled back in his captain's chair. He'd once insisted that the antique lobster pot on the wall had belonged to his great-grandfather. J.B. never knew when Bruce was pulling his leg and when he was playing it straight.

His expression darkened when Kyle Castellane entered the waterfront restaurant with two young women J.B. had never seen before. They all sat at a table behind Bruce and J.B., and Kyle snapped his fingers at a middle-aged waitress. She walked over and carded him. She had a broad Maine accent, and J.B. thought she was married to one of the lobstermen who wanted to throw him overboard and set fire to his boat.

The kid argued with her. "I come in here all the time. Nobody asks me for my I.D."

"I just did," she said.

He complied, grinned sheepishly at the two women with him. "I guess I won't mind being carded when I'm forty."

Bruce got up, plucked the darts off the dartboard and walked back to the table, sitting down heavily. "No Christina," he said under his breath. "You see that?"

"She and Zoe are having dinner together."

Without standing up, Bruce turned his chair and fired a dart at the board. It hit the wall. He fired another, hitting an outer ring. "They've had a tough year. Chris has a good thing going with her café. She's scared Zoe'll start knocking heads together, or stir up dust just because she's here—"

"She tell you that?"

"She's been saying it for months. 'What if Zoe comes back and it all starts over again?' Like that." He turned slightly to take a sip of his beer, and his eyes shifted to Kyle, just for an instant. He made a face, muttering under his breath. "I wish I knew what she sees in him."

"He's smart, rich, artistic and not from Goose Harbor."

Bruce managed a grin. "Other than that. I just want her to be happy."

"That's what I told myself when the congressional staffer I was dating last year gave me the heave-ho. It beat the truth."

"The truth was you're a jackass, McGrath."

"Possibly. I also wasn't around enough, and I didn't know the right people and get invited to the right parties."

"I'll bet you didn't get invited to any parties. Who's she seeing now?"

"No idea. I've been busy." J.B. left it at that. Bruce had exhibited very little curiosity about the details of J.B.'s work with the bureau, which was just as well since he wasn't getting any of them. "That's why I'm on vacation now."

"Where you staying tonight?"

"My boat, the rate I'm going."

Bruce liked that. "I can loan you a sleeping bag and a tarp if it rains. You could stay at my place, but I have three dogs—most people complain about the dogs."

"Do they eat off the counter?"

"I don't know. I'm not there all the time."

"Bruce, if they're good dogs, you *know* they don't eat off the counters."

"They're good dogs," he said. "They're just not prissy, overly well-behaved dogs."

Staying at Bruce's was definitely out. Their lobster rolls arrived, and Bruce examined his before pulling out a small piece of tail meat. "I think I know this guy."

J.B. laughed, feeling more relaxed. If anyone would understand how one of the West sisters could work her way under his skin, it'd be Bruce Young. J.B. started on his lobster roll, but stopped when he heard a commotion near the front door.

Christina West burst through the crowd at the bar and charged over to Kyle's table. "Caught," Bruce muttered, but he must have seen what J.B. did, because he got to his feet. "What the hell—"

J.B. stood next to him. Christina was white-faced, breathing rapidly, trying to hold back tears. "Someone broke into my café," she told Kyle. "They smashed in the door and took cash out of the register—there wasn't much—"

Kyle didn't bother to get up. "What about my apartment?"

"It's fine. They tried jimmying the door, but the police think something scared them away before they could get in. I just left there—" She inhaled sharply, brushed at her tears with the back of her wrist. She had on a black skirt and white top, black shoes that'd be easy on the feet. Despite her obvious distress, her boyfriend still hadn't gone to her. "Zoe's talking to the police."

"What for?" Kyle asked. "It's not her café."

Christina didn't seem to notice his annoyance. "We had dinner at Aunt Olivia's house, and she was driving me back. She realized the café was broken into before I did. Can you believe it? Two days in a row. I feel like I'm a target!"

Bruce stepped forward. "You okay, Chris?"

She nodded. "Yeah, I'm fine." She managed a faltering smile. "You should have seen Zoe go into her cop mode. She's still got it. The local police almost choked when they saw her, but, you know, she was so good—"

"She was the best," Bruce said softly. He touched her arm. "You want a drink?"

"That'd be great."

Using his foot, Kyle kicked a chair out from under the table for her. "Have a seat, Chris. Goose Harbor's serial thief strikes again. You'd think with the FBI crawling around town, they wouldn't dare."

Bruce rolled his eyes and stepped back, firing his last dart, but too hard. It hit the board and bounced onto the floor. He glanced at J.B. "You want to go see Zoe? You need a ride?"

"I've got my Jeep."

Bruce grinned at him. "You'd think a G-man would drive something snazzier—"

"Want to meet me there?"

He shook his head. "Nah. It's not my problem." He glanced sideways at Christina. "Kyle can help her fix her door this time."

He threw a few bills on the table and grabbed the last

of his lobster roll, finishing it on his way out. J.B. went over to Christina's table. "Your café's in a well-traveled location. Maybe someone saw something."

"That's what the police said—there could be a witness. I don't know, though. It's pretty quiet on the docks. It's so dark and cold—" She sniffled, looking a little embarrassed. "I don't know why I'm this upset. It's not as if anyone was hurt or there was any serious damage. There's no reason to think there's any connection—" she hesitated, then continued as if she wished she hadn't started "—with anything."

"I'm glad they didn't get into my apartment," Kyle said. "All my materials for my documentary are in the living room, right out in the open."

Christina angled a look at him. "The police think whoever did it was after cash, not your documentary." There was no sharpness in her tone. "Still, who knows. None of this makes sense. I suppose I could have caught the attention of some creep now that I'm running a business—oh, who knows."

J.B. knew what she meant. Speculation only brought more speculation, but it was always a temptation to run various scenarios. He thought of Teddy Shelton and wondered if the police would be talking to him. "I'd like to run down there and see what's what. Can I do anything for you?"

She shook her head, her smile stronger this time. "No, but thanks. Well, one thing—make sure my sister doesn't push too hard? She's bad enough when she has to play by the rules. Now she's just a regular person."

"I'll do what I can."

He left. He'd had only two bites of his lobster roll, but he wasn't hungry—or all that fond of lobster, which he kept to himself.

When J.B. got to the town docks, the police had gone. Zoe was sitting on the hood of her VW Beetle staring out at the dark harbor. It was a clear night, starlit, a sliver of a moon sparkling on the quiet water. J.B. could hear the endless whoosh of the tide. It'd be just past high tide now. He was becoming accustomed to its rhythms. Western Montana and the isolated alpine meadow his father had loved seemed far away, a part of a life J.B. wasn't even sure anymore had really been his. He'd left at eighteen and only went back for summers in college to work as a fishing and hiking guide. He landed in Washington, D.C., as a low-level state department worker, then decided on a career in the Federal Bureau of Investigation. He did field work out west, then ended up back in Washington.

His life wasn't anything like Zoe West's.

He parked a little way down from her and got out, but before he'd even shut his door, the old guy, the retired judge, was on him. "Agent McGrath? I'm Steven Monroe. My friends call me Stick. I'm a longtime friend of the West family." He spoke clearly and precisely despite his clenched-jaw look. "You can count me among those who don't appreciate your attitude or your presence here."

J.B. shut his door. "Okay."

Monroe didn't react. "The break-in yesterday at

Christina's house and today at her café—I think they happened because of you. I checked you out. You should be in a treatment center, not in a town where good people are trying to put a terrible experience behind them."

"I'm not getting into it with you, Judge."

"Don't hold Christina and Zoe West hostage to your personal agenda. Don't stir up trouble here so you don't have to think about what happened to you this summer."

J.B. shrugged. "Okay. Anything else?"

Monroe inhaled through his nose and tilted his head back. He had to be aware of Zoe on her VW hood, but he gave no indication of it. "You're a smart-mouthed prick, aren't you?"

"Isn't retirement fun? You can say stuff like that. It's cold out." J.B. glanced at the guy's corduroy shorts. "Your knees have goose bumps."

"Just because you're fucking FBI—"

"There it is again. What do you think? Should it be 'you're FBI'? Or 'you're *the* FBI'?" J.B. ignored the guy's hiss of irritation. "I know it's not 'you're fucking FBI.' That's disrespectful." His voice softened. "Even from a retired judge who's just looking out for his friends."

"They've had a difficult year."

"I can see that. Need a ride anywhere?"

Monroe gave a tight shake of his head. He was white-haired, with age spots on his face and hands, but in good shape. "I like to walk."

He left without another word.

J.B. walked over to Zoe, who glanced sideways at

him and smiled without any humor or obvious pleasure. "You sure know how to make friends around here, don't you, McGrath?" The temperature had dropped precipitously with nightfall, but she didn't seem to be cold. "You missed all the excitement."

"I saw Christina at Perry's."

"She's okay?"

He nodded. "Just upset. Kyle Castellane's with her."

Only a faint lift of her eyebrows suggested Zoe wasn't reassured. "Bruce?"

"He didn't offer to fix her door this time. Went home to his dogs."

"Don't feel sorry for him. Half the women in Goose Harbor are in love with him."

"All over fifty," J.B. said.

She almost managed a laugh. "The café'll be fine overnight. There's nothing to take. You get to Kyle's apartment through the café, but he has a locked door."

"Witnesses?"

"I'd hoped so, but it's not looking good." She slid down off the hood, her shirt riding up and exposing a few inches of pale midriff. "Do you have any idea what's going on? What about this Teddy Shelton character?"

"You tell the police about him?"

"No. I wasn't sure—"

"I'm on vacation, Zoe. I'm not on a case."

"Right, your ancestors and all that."

He decided this still wasn't the time to bring up his grandmother. Zoe stabbed a toe at a loose pebble on the pavement, her shoulders hunched against the cold. J.B.

thought she looked alone, a woman with the world on her shoulders. He wondered if she'd left behind a boyfriend in Connecticut.

"Shelton spent seven years in federal prison on a weapons conviction. He got out last summer. Who knows, he could have picked Goose Harbor because he wanted to smell the ocean air after sitting in a cell." J.B. sat on the hood, placing his hands next to him on the cool metal. "I thought he might be following you." He related the three times he'd spotted Shelton.

"Is that why you were at the nature preserve?"

He nodded. "I don't know, maybe I'm just bored. The guy could just be getting his act together. I'm sure the locals know about him."

"If Bruce is renting him that damn shack of his, you bet they do. My father wanted the town to condemn it. Bruce says he wants to renovate it—with a match, maybe. Burn it down, collect the insurance." She smiled, a little more genuinely this time. "Not that I'm encouraging arson or that it'd even enter Bruce's mind."

"I'm getting a cold butt." J.B. stood up from the hood. "You heading back?"

"I guess I should. I'm just getting cold out here. I suppose you don't have a bed for the night?"

"My boat. No food, either. I didn't finish my lobster roll. I like it better with a little tarragon."

"Tarragon? That's disgusting. Must be a Montana thing."

"Actually, I got the idea from a restaurant in Kennebunkport."

"One that caters to Montanans." But her humor was only fleeting, and she glanced back at her sister's café, crossed her arms tightly over her chest and shivered. "Bad guys everywhere, even here in Goose Harbor. My father tried to pretend he had it easy—no murders during his tenure as chief. Until his own."

"Zoe—"

She turned to him, the moonlight shining in her eyes. "I'm staying at Aunt Olivia's house tonight. I have to sometime or another, and my sister and Kyle—I'm not going to think about it. She said if she needs to, she'll camp out with me." She sighed, and J.B. saw how pretty she was, despite her obvious stress. "You can have your room from last night. I have a bad enough reputation with the FBI without letting one of its finest sleep on a decrepit lobster boat."

He didn't know why, but he tucked one finger under her chin. "I can tackle any bad guys that come your way."

"I'm not that out of practice, McGrath." She eased around to the driver's side of her car and opened the door, looking over it at him. "I can still tackle my own bad guys."

Nine

Somewhere—a magazine, probably—Betsy had read that sparkling wine went to the head faster than regular wine. She could believe it. She was on her third glass of an expensive champagne that Luke had chosen himself, although he seldom indulged in more than a sip or two. She was feeling the effects of the alcohol, finding it difficult to concentrate on what Luke and Stick Monroe were saying. She kept having to stifle an inappropriate giggle or yawn.

The police had been by to ask about the break-in at Christina's café. Of course, she and Luke hadn't seen anything.

Luke was concerned about Kyle, since he had an apartment above the café, but the police said neither he nor Christina had been there and nothing of Kyle's was stolen or vandalized. The café was fine, too. Just some money missing from the cash register.

Stick had dropped by a few minutes ago. It was getting late for Luke to be up, but they were all in the yacht's main salon, which was decorated in rich, buttery colors, with modern artwork and mirrors opposite the bank of windows that overlooked the harbor. The effect was an atmosphere of intimacy, elegance and style, but cost was important, too. Luke would want people to know that everything he owned was of the highest quality, the best taste, and that he could afford it. He didn't make movies like his father or catch lobsters like Bruce Young—Luke made money.

Betsy sank onto a curving sectional under the windows and had to squint to keep the room steady. It wasn't because of the ocean undulating under them. It was the champagne. She looked out at the harbor, where lobster boats bobbed gently under the starlit sky. The water was nearly still. She was struck by the contrast of Luke's multimillion-dollar luxury yacht and the rugged working boats. Each boat had its own buoys, with unique colors that identified its traps. By law they were required to display their buoy colors on their boats for others to see.

Betsy had never fit in in her hometown. Growing up in Goose Harbor, living here as an adult. She wasn't an old Yankee, a summer person, a fisherman, a part of the tourist industry. She was a nurse. Her mother had been a nurse, too. Her father had died in the very early days of Vietnam. That was the one thing she'd had in common with Olivia West—a close relative killed in war.

Luke pretended he didn't give a damn about fitting in, but Betsy thought his contempt for such trivialities was a defense mechanism. She thought he was a man who desperately wanted to fit in somewhere, anywhere. He romanticized small-town life.

She watched him pour a glass of champagne and hand it to Stick Monroe. Betsy felt the room spin a little more. Stick was definitely a man who didn't worry about fitting in. If people liked him, fine. If they didn't, fine. But it wasn't something he had to pay attention to—people generally liked him. He was handsome, successful, confident, imposing yet well-mannered, authentic. People tended not to like people who always fretted about whether or not they were liked.

Stick was saying something about Zoe West and that FBI agent. Betsy leaned forward in the soft cushions and forced herself to concentrate, placed her fingertips at her temples as if that could still the spinning in her head. Stick had on shorts and a sweatshirt in spite of the chilly evening. Betsy was almost thirty years younger than he was, but she expected he had more energy now than she did at her best, when she wasn't feeling the effects of three glasses of champagne.

"You have no idea what's going on with these break-ins?" Stick asked.

Betsy sat back abruptly at the obvious insinuation and expected Luke to throw Stick off the boat. But Luke, in khakis and a pale blue cashmere sweater, remained on his feet and didn't react heatedly. "Of course not. Why would I?"

"Kyle—"

"Kyle's not involved."

"He's Christina's boyfriend. He lives at the café."

Luke narrowed his eyes. "Are you suggesting my son could be the target of the break-ins?"

Stick shook his head. "I'm not suggesting anything."

Luke came around from the bar, his skin color a bit off. Betsy suspected the conversation was more unsettling to him than he wanted Stick to know. They'd been friends for years—both had adored Olivia West and considered Patrick their friend.

Stick let the stem of his glass slide between two fingers. "What do you know about this FBI agent?"

"Nothing," Luke said. "His name's J. B. McGrath. He rented a boat from Bruce Young. He's on vacation. He's been beating everyone at darts. He annoys people, I think."

"Kyle?"

Luke didn't answer at once. Betsy knew he wouldn't want to involve his son in a discussion about a mysterious FBI agent in town. For all his oddities, Luke did love his only child. "I don't think Kyle's had anything to do with him, frankly."

Stick drank more of his champagne. "McGrath seems very interested in Zoe."

"Do you think he hasn't been straight with everyone about his reasons for being here? Isn't that illegal, or at least unethical for an FBI agent?"

"I don't know. I just worry about Zoe." Stick smiled, almost embarrassed. "I guess I can't help it."

Betsy tried to make eye contact with Luke, but he wouldn't look at her, or simply had forgotten she was there. She had no idea where Stick was going with this conversation. He'd always treated Zoe like some kind of protégée, ever since she was a little kid and he was the well-connected, respected judge. He'd believed Zoe could do anything. When she'd been accepted to the FBI Academy, Stick said she could be the first female FBI director if she wanted to.

Betsy wondered if Zoe was a disappointment to him now that her father's murder and her aunt's death had thrown her into a tailspin. Not only did she not go to the academy, she'd run off to a small town in Connecticut and got herself fired from her police job there.

But Stick would never say a bad word about Zoe West, and if she wanted him to, he'd help her pick up the pieces of her career and figure out what to do next. Betsy was convinced of that.

Olivia had always been suspicious of Zoe's commitment to law enforcement and often wondered aloud to Betsy about whether her niece would stick with it or burn out before she was thirty-five. Olivia would sigh and say, then what? Then what would Zoe do? Now it seemed almost like a premonition.

"I have nothing to hide," Luke said. "If that's what you're implying."

Stick sank onto the far end of the couch, at least two yards from Betsy. He was another one who'd watched Luke grow up, summer to summer, in Goose Harbor, who'd known what wretches his parents were. Stick cupped his champagne glass in his palm, the stem between his fingers. "What about Teddy Shelton?" he asked.

Clearly caught off guard, Luke staggered back toward the bar. He placed one hand on the polished wood and steadied himself. Betsy could see he was rattled. No wonder. Teddy Shelton was a creep. She frowned at Stick, but he ignored her. He wasn't the old friend anymore but the truth-seeking judge, the arbiter of justice. He was neither kind nor unkind. That wasn't his role, not at this moment. He wanted the truth and thought he'd get it by intimidating and blindsiding Luke.

"Luke's got nothing to do with that dirtbag Shelton." Betsy jumped to her feet, prompting a wave of dizziness so profound she thought she might vomit. Heat surged up through her, fierce enough that it seemed to make even her hair feel hot, but she didn't back off. "Stick, what's the matter with you, coming in here like this and insinuating Luke's done something wrong?"

He didn't spare her so much as a glance, his incisive judge-eyes staying on Luke, as if he could see right through him and read his mind. "Luke?"

"You're talking through your hat." Luke's voice was calm, but Betsy could see he was shaken, if only from the insult. If Stick Monroe thought he was mixed up with the likes of Teddy Shelton, who else did? "You don't know anything."

"Call him off, Luke." Stick spoke in a quiet, measured voice, but there was no mistaking his seriousness. "You can't control a man like Teddy Shelton. I don't care how innocent your arrangement with him sounds to you, trust me that it won't sound that way to anyone else."

Her head spinning, her hands sweaty, Betsy staggered toward the two men. "What arrangement?"

Neither answered. She might have been invisible.

Luke's nostrils flared. His lips thinned and took on a purplish tint, but Betsy hoped it was just a combination of the lighting and his emotions, usually so repressed, rising to the surface. He was such a hypochondriac that if he were in real medical trouble, he'd throw Stick out and have Betsy call an ambulance.

"Do yourself a favor and head south," Stick went on. His tone was gentle now, the calm, wise older friend giving Luke sound advice. "You're normally gone by now, anyway. No one will think twice about it. There's no point staying here any longer. Call Teddy Shelton off and leave. Then you won't have to worry about people jumping to the wrong conclusions."

"Zoe and that FBI agent, you mean," Luke said.

Stick nodded. "Precisely."

"I had nothing to do with Patrick's death." Luke's voice was raspy, as if he were being strangled. "Neither did Shelton."

"I didn't say I or anyone else suspect you of any wrongdoing. I just don't think you want the likes of Zoe West and J. B. McGrath asking questions about why you hired Teddy Shelton." Unruffled, Stick polished off the last of his champagne and got slowly to his feet. He set the glass on the bar. "They're going to want to know who *you* suspect of wrongdoing. How far will you go—"

"Go to hell!"

Luke reared back to punch Stick, but the old judge shook his head, as if his disapproval alone would be enough to ward off the attack. It was. Luke backed away, breathing in rapid, shallow gulps, spit oozing out at the corners of his mouth. Betsy had never seen him so angry.

"Get off my boat," he spat. "Now."

Stick still didn't react. "Luke, I'm not accusing you of anything except hiring Teddy Shelton. I don't question your motives. Others might, but I don't. I know you wanted him to check out this FBI agent and keep an eye on Zoe—because you're afraid for her, afraid for Christina, afraid for your son."

Betsy was stunned, and she lost her footing, stumbling on the flat carpeting. "Luke? What's going on?"

"Your loyalty to Olivia is no secret," Stick continued. "Given Zoe's behavior this past year, we all want to make sure she doesn't self-destruct. I imagine we all have things we'd rather hide from the prying eyes of the police. A murder investigation spares no one. But to spy on Zoe here in Goose Harbor requires a subtlety and expertise Teddy Shelton doesn't have. People might draw the wrong conclusion if they find out."

"I don't care what people think. I've done nothing wrong!"

"Luke," Betsy said, "that FBI agent was talking to Teddy earlier today—"

He swung around at her. "Stay out of this, Betsy."

Stick waited. Betsy, breathless, could feel her pulse thumping in her temple and thought—watch, I'll drop dead of a stroke and Luke'll be fine.

"Patrick was my friend as much as yours," Luke continued, calmer but obviously only because he was forcing himself. "Just because I'm wealthy doesn't mean I'm arrogant and accustomed to having my own way. Don't make assumptions about me, Stick."

"Oh, for God's sake, Luke." Stick seemed almost amused. His tone was matter-of-fact, as if he were stating the obvious. "You *are* arrogant and accustomed to having your own way. So is your son. I'm here because I'm your friend. I'm not implying you know anything about Patrick's death or have anything to hide. I'm merely asking you to cut your ties with Shelton and head south. If this liaison with Teddy Shelton goes sour and someone gets hurt, what do you think will happen to you? Who do you think will stand up for you? You don't have a lot of friends in Goose Harbor as it is."

"When Olivia was alive—"

"She was a great lady and may be the only person in your life who ever loved you unconditionally, but she's gone, Luke. I know Zoe as if she were my own daughter, and I just had an encounter of my own with J. B. McGrath. Don't be fooled by his easygoing manner, playing darts with the guys, letting them tease him, teasing them back. He's tough as nails. Suspicious, well-trained." Stick stood back from the bar. "I'd listen to me if I were you."

Luke was silent, breathing hard. Betsy stumbled forward a few steps and touched Stick on the elbow. "It's time to leave, Stick. Luke's done. You won't get any more out of him tonight."

His expression softening, Stick didn't jerk his arm

from Betsy's grasp but instead reached across with his free arm and patted her hand. "You're the salt of the earth, Betsy. I'm just trying to get him to see this situation for what it is. If I had any information, any inkling, Luke was trying to protect a murderer, I'd take what I knew to the authorities."

"Don't interfere, Betsy," Luke said. "Do yourself a favor for once and mind your own business."

"Luke," Stick chided him. "You're lucky to have a woman like Betsy in your life."

Luke said nothing.

Betsy tried to hide her embarrassment with a polite smile. She'd always been intimidated by Stick—it wasn't his fault. His reputation, his intellect, his manners, the fact that he'd lived in and seen more of the world than she ever would—everything about him made her feel frumpy and inadequate. At seventy-two, he could walk farther than she could. He grew prettier roses.

"Here," she said quietly, "I'll walk you out."

"It's all right, Betsy, I know the way." Stick kissed her warmly on the cheek. "I'm sorry about all this. Think of it as a form of tough love. I had to get through to him."

He nodded at Luke, who said nothing, his lips bloodless, and left.

When she was sure Stick was gone and out of earshot, Betsy grabbed up his empty champagne glass. "I hope the old fart trips and falls headfirst into the harbor. A dose of cold Maine water might give his system just the shock it needs." She noticed Luke was sweating, trembling. "I suppose he means well."

"Betsy…"

She didn't move to his side. She'd learned not to go near him unless he wanted her there. "What do you want me to do, Luke?"

"Help me…" He gasped for air. "Help me to bed."

"Are you sure? It's still early—"

His eyes shot through her, and she realized that even as upset as he was, anger and humiliation seethed just beneath the surface. She knew he hated the idea of someone like Stick Monroe thinking he'd done something stupid. "Help me."

"Do you want me to check your blood pressure?"

He shook his head. "I know it's high. I can feel it."

He motioned for her to come close, and when she put her arm around his lower back and took his hand, she could feel that his skin was clammy. But there wasn't a thing wrong with him. He'd live to be a hundred, unless it turned out all the supplements he was taking were no good for him, after all.

She guided him back to his stateroom. She had her own. He kept a little bell by his table in case he needed her in the night, not just for medical care. For sex, too. It was just a little arrangement they had. It made him feel more secure, and she didn't mind. Her stateroom was beautiful, and she appreciated the quiet nights when she could just sit in bed and read. But she'd die if anyone knew she responded to a bell.

She helped Luke out of his clothes. There was nothing romantic or loving in her actions, nothing remotely sexual. This was work. She was the nurse now, the professional.

"I don't think Kyle's relationship with Christina is anything that'll last, but if he—" Betsy found herself unable to get a proper breath. "Luke, I know you can't think your son had anything to do with Patrick's death."

"I *asked* you to mind your own business. None of this is your concern. Betsy—" He shivered as if suddenly he was cold, and she pulled back the covers of his bed and helped him slip beneath them. He took her hand, his eyes brimming with tears. "I'm sorry. Betsy, I don't know how I'd manage without you."

Pure drama. He'd be fine without her. He knew it. Betsy wasn't fooled. He just didn't want her to tell Kyle about Stick's visit. Let the plain, single nurse feel wanted and loved, and she'd do anything. Betsy had no illusions about Luke or their relationship.

"Let me know if you decide you want to get up," she said, keeping her tone clinical, professional. "Ring the bell. I'll be up for a few more hours."

He nodded. "I can't believe Stick came in here like that. Who does he think he is?"

"I don't know, Luke. I think he just wants to look out for you."

"Later." He raised his hand higher and pressed two fingers against one of her nipples, through the fabric of her top, an example, she thought, of the sort of abrupt, inappropriate gesture that had kept most women out of his life. "I might want you later."

Betsy thought of several sarcastic remarks about heart attacks and strokes, but she withdrew to the main salon without comment and checked the bottle of champagne. Another glass left. She poured it for herself and sank back onto the sectional.

She stared out at the dark harbor, wondering how long she had before she heard the tinkle of Luke's little bell—and what was wrong with her for staying to find out.

Ten

Despite the cold night, Zoe slept with the window open and awoke to the sounds of the ocean and the sea-birds, and for a moment, she felt as if her life was normal again. Then she remembered she was in the twin room because McGrath had the big bedroom, and she could hear him in the shower down the hall. Picturing him naked was enough to propel her out of bed. She pulled corduroy pants and a fisherman's sweater out of her backpack and jumped into them, bolting downstairs before she could bump into her houseguest coming out of the shower.

It had been a long-enough night as it was, just knowing he was in the next room.

She ended up telling J.B. about her year in Connecticut while they carried her belongings upstairs. How she'd asked questions about the governor's drowning death that the state detectives were slow in asking or not asking at all. In Maine, she'd have been one of them, so she'd tried not to step on toes—but she was persistent.

Then it had all, literally, blown up. Bombs, shootings, national *Breaking News* happening right in the tiny Connecticut town where she was the sole detective.

J.B. had surprised her. He'd stood in the hallway and said, "I'm sorry about your father, Zoe. It must still be very hard for you and your family."

Then he went into his bedroom, shut the door and left her alone.

She'd failed her father. He'd have expected more of her. At the very least he'd have expected her to stand and fight until his killer was brought to justice.

Except that wasn't true.

He'd have wanted her to mourn him and then go on with her life. Leave the investigation to CID. Go to Quantico. She could almost hear his soothing voice... *It's okay, Zoe, it's okay, you don't have to worry about me.*

It had been one long damn night, she thought, pulling open the freezer. Only one Toaster Strudel left in the box.

"Ah-ha," J.B. said from the doorway, "so the Toaster Strudels *are* yours. I thought you were the flax-seed type."

"I am. I sprinkle ground flax seed on the Toaster Strudels. You can't even taste it."

"That, ex-Detective West, is disgusting."

He smiled, and that just made everything worse. She'd noticed how good-looking he was again last night while he was carrying boxes and trying not to bug her about the break-in at the café and Stick Monroe being such a jerk and Christina and Kyle and all of it. It wasn't the first time she'd noticed, but it was the first time she'd admitted to herself she was attracted to him. Physically, in a kind of elemental, rock-you-to-the-core way that generally only led to trouble.

She didn't trust her reactions. Responding to his blue eyes, his irreverent smile and his long, lean legs and scarred hands, his shoulders and flat stomach, could just be an unconscious ploy to keep her from confronting why she was even in Goose Harbor. Maybe even why he was.

He came up next to her and shut the freezer door. He had on a navy pinwale corduroy shirt and jeans. If he was physically aware of her, he gave no sign of it. Probably just didn't want to split the Toaster Strudel with her.

"Wait," she said. "I almost forgot. I have cider doughnuts—"

"Save them. Why don't we have some of your sister's wild blueberry muffins? We can see how things are at the café this morning."

She nodded. "Make sure the police didn't miss anything."

"I'm not second-guessing them."

"Right. Of course not." She smiled, and for an instant, she wondered where she'd be now if she'd followed through and gone to Quantico. "We can walk. On the way I'll tell you how I've come to my senses and decided you shouldn't stay here, after all."

"Why not?" His voice was low and amused, and he stood very close to her, making her think he might actually be physically aware of her. He said softly, "I behaved."

Oh, God.

She darted past him to the side entry and pushed

open the door, welcoming the gust of brisk autumn air, the sparkle of the sun on the water and the gleam of brightly colored leaves. But J.B. was right behind her, and she had to fight an image of him in the shower. The ends of his hair were still damp.

This was not good.

Dew had collected on the mums and the grass and glistened in the morning sun, and she could hear the wash of the waves down on the rocks. It was cool enough for a jacket, even over her sweater, but she didn't want to take the time to go back for one—she wanted to get to the café and join other people as soon as possible. She didn't need to be alone with J. B. McGrath for one minute longer than was absolutely necessary.

She was feeling awkward and out of control this morning, but it wasn't just him. It was last night, too. She'd talked with Donna Jacobs, the acting chief of police, a former captain with the Portland Police Department—very good, but wary of having Zoe back in town, especially with two break-ins within twenty-four hours of her return.

The water was choppy in the harbor as they walked along Ocean Drive, no sign of fog or mist or rain in the clear air. The bright reds and oranges of the huge, stately maple trees in yards above the harbor were breathtaking against the blue sky. Soon the leaves would start to fall, the reds first, the rusts and burgundies last.

Zoe had to choke back a tug of emotion. Autumn was her favorite season in Maine. She used to associate it with cooler weather, beautiful scenery, plentiful lobsters, hikes and Olivia's birthday—for years, they'd all wondered if she would make it to her next birthday, never re-alizing that she'd die *on* her birthday. Her one-hundred-first.

"I think you should probably find a different place to stay," she said.

J.B. shrugged. "Let me get more information on Teddy Shelton first. Then you can decide what to do with me. You don't go armed anymore, ex-detective. I might come in handy."

"I'm going to let you think you're funny."

"Who's trying to be funny?"

"McGrath, you're not armed. You're on vacation—"

"I can be armed. Just watch me."

From her own experience in law enforcement, Zoe knew that FBI agents could carry a weapon in any state, without a local permit, on duty or off. "How long are you on this vacation of yours?"

"It's open-ended."

"Meaning they don't necessarily want you back?"

"Of course they want me back. They just aren't sure what to do with me."

"No more undercover work?"

"I never said I worked undercover."

"Stick—"

"Judge Monroe can say what he wants." He glanced over at her, his very blue eyes unreadable. The more ag-itated she got, the calmer he seemed to get. "I can't talk about it."

"He says you were almost killed. Your throat—"

"Your friend Stick must have good connections."

"Excellent connections." Zoe narrowed her eyes on him, aware not only of her quickening heartbeat but of just how damn sexy he was. It was nuts. She had to be going out of her mind. "I've got enough going on in my life right now without hanging around with a loose cannon of an FBI agent."

"You'll have to draw your own conclusions about me," he said quietly. "Yes, I'm just off a rough investigation. Yes, I'm on vacation to help put it behind me. I did my job. It wasn't easy. End of story."

"Bruce thinks you're just obnoxious. Christina says the guys all want to throw you overboard and set fire to your boat."

"That's because I know more and can do more ocean stuff than they think an FBI agent born and raised in Montana should."

Zoe smiled. "Like Bruce said. Obnoxious."

The docks were quiet at this hour. The working boats were already out, the pleasure boats—fewer of them in October than during the summer months—were still in. A handful of walkers and runners cruised the waterfront streets, but most of the tourists were still tucked in bed or having scones and muffins at their inns.

Pulling her hands up into her sleeves, Zoe looked across the harbor and saw two lobster boats churning out to sea.

J.B. hunched his shoulders against a sudden gusting breeze. "You can almost see Jen Periwinkle crawling around on those rocks, can't you? I've only read a few of your aunt's mysteries, but her fictional Maine is a lot like the real one."

"All Jen Periwinkle's mysteries get solved," Zoe said.

"No DNA labs, either. She does it with her wits and clues scattered through the book. It's fun, a puzzle to be solved. Real life—"

"Real life's different. Aunt Olivia knew that."

J.B. nodded, as if he'd known her himself. "I'm sure she did."

"She never took anything here for granted. That's why she created the nature preserve and left most of her money for its protection and continuing work." Zoe glanced out toward the head of the harbor and her aunt's famous house, a Maine landmark. Hers now. An honor and a burden, but a problem for later. "She was born and raised in Goose Harbor and lived here her whole life, but she didn't assume that everything she loved would automatically be here for future generations."

J.B. moved on toward the café. "Did people mind when she bought up that much prime coastal acreage and set it aside as a nature preserve?"

"At first it was controversial, but you can't develop every single inch of coastline. People know that. And it turns out the preserve attracts tourists and ultimately makes money for the town."

"Even with two break-ins in two days, there was a lot more crime in Jen Periwinkle's Goose Harbor."

Zoe looked out past the mouth of the harbor at the endless blue horizon, where sky and water seemed to meet. "At least the crimes Jen had to deal with only affected fictional characters, not real people."

Eleven

Christina's Café was between crowds. The lobstermen had grabbed their coffees and muffins and gone, and the tourists hadn't arrived yet. On his first few days in Goose Harbor, J.B. wandered in with the lobstermen, then went out on his rented boat and stayed out of their way—at least his definition of out of their way. The lobstermen wanted him back in Washington.

He didn't know about his next few days in Goose Harbor.

He sat with Zoe at a small table overlooking the water. The busted lock on the door was the only evidence of last night's break-in. Christina was in a cranky mood, slamming around behind the counter and barking orders at her waitresses. She completely ignored her older sister.

Finally, she put her hands on her hips, exhaled loudly and apologized. "I didn't get enough sleep last night." She smiled over the glass-front counter at Zoe, who'd gotten up to inspect the muffin offerings. "Hey, breakfast's on me. What'll it be?"

Zoe grinned. "Since it's on you instead of your unemployed sister, I'll have blueberry pancakes with sausage and coffee."

"Orange juice?"

"Sure."

Christina leaned over the counter and called down to J.B. "What about you, Agent McGrath?"

"Same thing, except I'll pay my way. And you can call me J.B."

She held up a hand. "J.B. I can do, but you should seize the moment about me paying. I'm usually not this generous." Her crankiness had disappeared so fast and so completely, he wondered if he'd imagined it. "Give me a sec and I'll bring over two coffees."

Zoe returned to her seat, and when she gazed out at the sunrise, J.B. saw the pain in her eyes, fleeting, not meant, he thought, for him or anyone else. It couldn't be easy for her to be back here, with the onslaught of memories and unanswered questions, her uncertainty about her own future.

Christina swooped out from behind her counter and set two mugs of coffee on their table, pulling up a chair and sinking into it as if she'd been on her feet all night instead of just a couple of hours. "Kyle didn't want to come back here last night," she said. "He insists he wasn't spooked, but we ended up having a couple of drinks and talking for *hours* about his documentary. He's really into it. Obsessed, I'd say."

Zoe poured milk into her coffee from a pottery

pitcher painted with a sprig of wild blueberries. "I hope it works out for him."

Christina sighed, and J.B. could tell some unspoken sisterly communication had just occurred between them. "Come on, Zoe, it can't hurt to talk to him," Christina said.

"It doesn't matter, I'm not going to." Zoe seemed to be struggling to keep her tone neutral. "Don't take it as anything against him, Chris. I just don't want to do it."

"Fine. I won't pressure you."

Zoe ignored her sister's irritable tone and smiled at her instead. "Thanks."

Christina slid to her feet. She had on her informal uniform of blue apron, white ruffled shirt and black pants. Her hair was up, her eyes a darker blue-gray this morning, sunken from lack of sleep. She looked exhausted and troubled. And annoyed, but trying to pretend she wasn't. "I'll get your breakfast," she said, probably wishing she hadn't insisted on paying.

She swung behind the counter, and a waitress, who obviously knew Zoe, rolled her eyes behind the boss's back, as if to say to steer clear. Must have already been a long morning with the younger Ms. West, J.B. thought.

He pushed back his chair to give himself more room to stretch out his legs. "She thinks Kyle is handsome and brilliant."

Zoe shrugged. "Maybe he is. I don't care." There was no harshness in her tone, just determination. "He can do his documentary without my help."

"What does he want from you?"

"I have no idea. We've never gotten that far."

The waitress, not Christina, brought out their pancakes, thin and buttery, dotted with blue-and-deep-purple wild blueberries. J.B. dribbled just a little real maple syrup on his—he was buzzed enough from coffee and too much late-night thinking without overdoing on sugar. Zoe had no such compunctions. Her pancakes were swimming in syrup. She even dunked her sausage.

"What're you doing today?" he asked.

"I wouldn't mind going kayaking, but I'll have to see what the conditions are like. It's been awhile—I don't want to roll. Too cold." She stabbed more pancakes, and he could see they were an indulgence for her, something she mustn't have had in Connecticut. "I haven't known what to do with myself for two months. I'm sort of used to it."

"Not a bad life if you can afford it."

"I can't," she said. "Not forever, anyway."

"Sorry you got yourself fired?"

She shook her head. "Not really. I had it coming. I don't regret the Texas Ranger, but I should have carried my weapon."

"Where was it?"

"Locked in my car."

"Then it wasn't an oversight," he said. "It was deliberate. You knew what you were doing."

"Yes. I did."

She swept a triangle of pancakes through her river of syrup, and J.B. knew the subject of her and guns was closed. "How did people around here react when you quit the state police to go into the bureau?" he asked.

"Fine."

She was into these short answers. J.B. knew he was moving onto shaky ground. "They thought you could cut it at the academy?"

She raised her eyes. "Of course."

He sipped more of his coffee. "People liked the idea of you leaving Maine?"

"No."

"You're only answering the question asked, Zoe."

She set down her fork. "My father wasn't killed because I was on my way to Quantico."

"Did he like you following in his footsteps into law enforcement, going beyond what he did?"

"I don't think of it that way. I was on my own path. I didn't think of myself as going 'beyond' him because I was on my way to becoming an FBI agent and he was a small-town police chief."

J.B. nodded. "I know. It's not how I think, either."

She managed a self-deprecating smile. "I fell for your interrogation tactics, didn't I?"

"We're just having a conversation—"

"Right." She didn't bother to hide her skepticism.

J.B. smiled back at her, setting down his mug. "Your father wanted you to stay in Goose Harbor and run a bed-and-breakfast, didn't he?"

She ignored him. "I could look into this Teddy Shelton character. Talk to a few people, see what they know about him. How much trouble can he be if you spotted him just like that?" She paused, giving him a long look. "Or are you that good, Special Agent McGrath?"

He laughed. "I'm that good."

"Excellent. I wouldn't want to hang out with a lousy FBI agent. What're you planning for the day?"

"Don't know yet."

"Meaning you're waiting to see what I do. Well, I am not going to be responsible for you not having a proper vacation. Go on and enjoy yourself. Don't fret about me."

The waitress refilled their coffee mugs, and J.B. found himself noticing Zoe West's slender fingers and neatly polished fingernails. There was something off-center about her, as if she'd just started getting in touch with a part of herself she'd stamped down during her years in law enforcement. She might have belonged there for a while, but she didn't anymore. He could see that now, wondered if she did, too. He thought about Bruce's comment that his childhood friend was a closet eccentric. Then he thought of her writing secretly in the attic.

"What about you?" she asked. "Did you always want to be an FBI agent?"

"Nope. I wanted to be a fishing guide like my father and grandfather."

"That didn't work out?"

"It got me through high school and college. Then I went to Washington, D.C., and knew I wasn't going back home except for vacations."

"Not this vacation," Zoe pointed out.

"True." He didn't expand.

"Now you're an FBI agent. You hate it Stick found out about you, don't you? You undercover types. Pains in the butt."

"No comment."

He finished his coffee and got to his feet. Zoe followed, and he turned to her abruptly, catching her off guard. He stood so close to her that her sweater sleeve brushed against him and he could see the gray flecks in her blue eyes. "You don't trust me, do you, Zoe?" he asked softly.

She didn't back up even an inch. "Tell me who you trust."

"That's not what I asked—"

"Of course not. I know you won't answer, so I'll tell you. No one. You trust no one. That's why you can do the work you do." A steely hurt worked its way into her eyes, a kind of pain he thought he understood. "When I found my father, I stopped trusting. It happened just like that. The blink of an eye."

"It's a tough way to live."

He didn't know if she could see in him the lingering effects of what he'd done. Escaping his own death, causing another. Putting an image into three kids' eyes that they would have to live with forever, just as Zoe did the one of her murdered father. J.B. didn't think he didn't trust people but he was the only son of a solitary and self-reliant man, and undercover work had come naturally to him.

If Patrick West's murder had been solved, J.B. doubted he'd have come to Goose Harbor. Maybe for a three-day weekend, to see where his grandmother was born, maybe deliver Olivia West's letters to the West family. But he wouldn't have picked it now for this particular vacation.

Zoe spun off, telling her sister what a great breakfast they'd had—in a better mood, Christina thanked her, said she'd talked Bruce into fixing her café door. Zoe greeted an older couple who'd come in, people from Goose Harbor she'd apparently known forever. Then she disappeared outside, the screen door banging shut behind her.

J.B. stopped at the counter, and Christina smiled feebly at him. "It's harder for her than for me. I know that." She spoke as if he'd understand what she meant, without her having to provide context, and he thought he did. She brushed her forehead with the back of her wrist and shifted her gaze to her broken door, then back to him. "You're one of the good guys, right?"

He nodded. "Yes."

"Then do what you can before it's too late and she starts again, running roughshod over everybody, not eating, not sleeping. Please. Most of the time Zoe knows when enough's enough, but with Dad's death…" Christina trailed off, her own skin a little paler.

J.B. smiled, trying to ease some of Christina's obvious tension. Zoe's return to Goose Harbor wasn't easy for her little sister, either. "Did you know Zoe eats Toaster Strudels sprinkled with flax seed?"

"Oh, God. Is that the *worst?*"

But Christina had smiled, even laughed, and J.B. headed outside, the sun so sharply bright as it rose up over the harbor that it gave him an instant headache. He had no deep sense of belonging here. None at all, no matter how many of his ancestors were buried in Goose

Harbor cemeteries. To him, at that moment, it was a strange and beautiful place, and he understood why his grandparents had cleared out and headed west.

Twelve

Zoe was aware of J.B. easing in behind her, then beside her, as she made her way along Ocean Drive. He'd prodded and poked at her for information and reactions, and maybe he'd needed to because of Teddy Shelton and the break-ins—and maybe she'd let him because she wanted his fresh take on what had happened here last year. But it'd been difficult for her, even just that much questioning.

Because all along, deep down, she was convinced she'd said something, done something, that had caused her father to be shot dead early on a beautiful autumn morning.

"You okay?" J.B. asked.

She nodded. "It's different when it's your father lying there."

He said nothing, for which she was grateful.

"Zoe! Hey, wait up!"

It was Kyle Castellane, running to catch up with them. He jumped off the sidewalk onto the street and came up on her left. He was out of breath, his longish hair pulled back in a ponytail. "Wild night last night, huh? Looks like we have a serial thief on the loose in Goose Harbor."

"Let's hope that's all."

"Ooh," he said, grinning, "always the doom-and-gloom cop."

She wanted to hit him. "What's up, Kyle?"

"Nothing—just wanted to say hi. Chris tell you we stayed up until all hours brainstorming on my documentary?"

"Sounds like you're making progress."

He shrugged, still out of breath from his run up from the docks. "I run into the occasional stone wall."

Like Chris's big sister, he seemed to imply. Zoe didn't bite. "That's the way it goes, I guess."

"Chris tells me you don't want to get involved. That's okay, but maybe you can point me in the right direction on something." He paused, walking a few steps, but Zoe didn't take the bait and say yes before she knew what he wanted. "Did Olivia ever tell you about her best friend when she was growing up? Posey Sutherland. She lived across Ocean Drive, about a half mile from Olivia."

J.B. stiffened noticeably next to her and Zoe assumed Kyle's intense, self-absorbed manner got on his nerves. It was a beautiful morning, she was just back in Goose Harbor since her father and her aunt's deaths, and Kyle Castellane wanted to pick her brain for his documentary.

Zoe shook her head. "I know the Sutherland name, of

course, but I don't recall Aunt Olivia ever mentioning, -at least to me, a Posey Sutherland, friend or otherwise."

Kyle nodded, frowning as he considered her answer. "Posey was the youngest daughter of John Lester Sutherland. All kinds of bells and whistles went off when I saw his name. That has to be where Olivia got the Lester for Mr. Lester McGrath, Jen Periwinkle's evil nemesis."

As if he had to tell her who Mr. McGrath was. Zoe slowed her pace, dropping just slightly behind J.B., but enough for her to get the full brunt of a gust of wind blowing up off the water. But she could feel the temperature rising now that it was midmorning. "It could just be an innocent coincidence."

"I don't think so. The more I learn about her, the more I think Olivia was deliberate about everything she did. It's my guess she didn't think much of her friend's father and this was her private revenge."

"But if you have no proof—"

"I can raise the question without answering it. But I want to know what she thought of Posey's father—I want to know what happened to Olivia West's best friend from childhood. What happened to Posey Sutherland? I can't find a thing. Not yet, anyway. I'll keep looking."

"I can't help you," Zoe told him.

"I checked town records. Posey was a year younger than Olivia. They grew up together. I'm checking with the local school district to see if they have pictures of them in their archives. I imagine they already gave everything they had on Olivia to the town library."

J.B. picked up his pace, and Zoe imagined he'd had his fill of Kyle. She tried to smile at him. "You *are* into this documentary, aren't you?"

Kyle hardly paused. "Zoe, this is all so fascinating. You find the answer to one question, and it leads to another. This Sutherland connection to Lester McGrath— no one else has that. It's new material. She named one of the most famous villains of the twentieth century after someone she knew."

"For whatever reason," Zoe added.

He hunched his skinny shoulders against another cold, hard gust of wind, which tangled the ends of his longish tawny ponytail and made Zoe think twice about kayaking today. But Kyle was into his topic now. "I talked to Bruce Young's grandmother. She's in her nineties—she remembers hearing something about a scandal involving Posey Sutherland, but no one would discuss the details. That's provocative, don't you think?"

Zoe wondered how bored J.B. was, but, to his credit, he didn't try to change the subject. She angled Kyle a look. "Is this why my sister was out of sorts this morning, because you kept her up talking about the mystery of Posey Sutherland?"

Color rose to his cheeks, whether from the wind or self-consciousness Zoe couldn't be sure. "Yeah," he said. "She's a good sport when I get going. You know, this would all have been easier if I could have started when she was still alive—"

Zoe inhaled sharply.

To his credit, Kyle realized what he'd said. "I'm

sorry—I didn't mean to imply it was inconvenient of her to die when she did. I—" He stopped, peering across Zoe and looking sideways at J.B. "There must be a reason Olivia named her evil nemesis McGrath, too."

"McGrath's not an uncommon name," J.B. said.

"Yeah, but I'm thinking if Lester's from a real person, so is—"

"Stop!" Zoe groaned but tried to keep any sting out of her voice. "Kyle, I just had a huge breakfast that I need to walk off. I have no idea where Aunt Olivia came up with the name for Mr. Lester McGrath. I can see you're serious about this documentary, but I loved Olivia—I still miss her and think about her every day. This is all fun and interesting for you, but for me—"

"I understand," Kyle said quickly, almost sheepishly, and dropped back and shoved his hands into his pants pockets, his nose red now. But he was sullen, too, insulted. "I don't pretend I had the connection to her that you do, but she knew my family for decades—"

J.B. cut him off. "You've got a famous grandfather. Why don't you do a documentary about him?"

Kyle shook his head, taking J.B.'s question seriously. "That'd be taking on too much too soon. I'm not ready to touch my grandfather." He seemed to have no idea that anyone might consider his comment offensive and moved along. "There's something else. Christina said I'd have to ask you—she's unbending on the subject and won't give me permission herself. She says it's your house now. If you'll let me, I'd like to take a look in Olivia's attic."

"There's nothing up there," Zoe said, refusing even to glance in J.B.'s direction.

"Maybe as far as you're concerned, but she died only last year." Kyle's tone was formal, as if he were in a real negotiation and not just asking a favor of a friend. "Given the circumstances, I'm guessing you haven't had a chance to go through all her belongings yet. The house has been sitting empty for the better part of a year. If I can just go through—"

"Kyle, I know it must be so tempting for you, but you have to realize that Aunt Olivia took great care to make arrangements for when she was no longer around. She left nothing to chance. If there's anything in her attic, it'll only be what she wanted her family and any ghouls to find—"

He stopped dead in his tracks. "Is that what you think I am? A ghoul? This is a serious documentary."

"Of course it is," Zoe said. He looked so hurt. "I didn't mean to imply you were a ghoul. Look, let me think about it, okay?"

"Fair enough." He grinned suddenly, cuffed her on the shoulder. "Hey, it's good to have you back. I'll see you around, okay?"

He turned and trotted back down toward the docks, apparently delighted with her response. Zoe had the feeling agreeing even to consider his request was more than he'd expected. Feeling the cold, she knotted her hands into fists and slipped them up inside her sleeves again, picking up her pace as another cold breeze gusted off the water. She hadn't counted on the wind.

"That kid isn't doing a scholarly documentary," J.B. said. His tone was matter-of-fact, not critical. "He's looking for drama, titillation, scandal."

Zoe nodded. "You're probably right, but I hope not. Christina isn't worried—she knows him better than I do."

"Blinded by her feelings for him."

"That's cynical."

"Just stating the obvious." He wasn't argumentative, and he looked at her without expression. "Your father's death will be in it."

"It has to be, doesn't it?" She didn't mean for him to answer, and he didn't. "Aunt Olivia died the next morning."

"You blame yourself?"

"I shouldn't have told her." She pictured her great-aunt that afternoon, her thin white hair sticking out in soft white waves, like angels' wings, as she tried to remember the name of whoever it was she believed had killed her only nephew. Zoe pulled her lips between her teeth, fighting for self-control. "I thought she'd find out and it'd be better to come from me, but I should have had her doctor with me—"

"Everyone says her doctor told you it wouldn't have made any difference. That wasn't what killed her."

I know who killed Patrick. Oh, Zoe, why can't I remember anything anymore?

"Damn."

She shot ahead of McGrath, then started to jog, her legs aching almost immediately, the wind whipping tears out of her eyes. She'd been on a run on a morning just like this a year ago, an incredible future ahead of her, everything she wanted, everything she'd worked so hard for, at her fingertips. All of it had evaporated the moment she'd spotted her father's body in the wet, cold sand.

J.B. fell in beside her. He wasn't running, hadn't made a sound. He was just suddenly there, inches away from her as she slowed to a walk. "I thought I could handle being back here." She was breathing hard, not just from running but also from the tension and swirl of emotions—grief, fear, anger, frustration. An FBI agent in Goose Harbor, the break-ins, Teddy Shelton. Did they have any connection to her father's murder? Crazy to think so. Yet she couldn't stop herself. "I've been away a year and haven't resolved anything—I know that. But I thought—I thought at least I could get up this morning and have a nice breakfast, go out kayaking—"

"You had a nice breakfast. You can still kayak." A hint of humor came into his tone. "Might want to wait for the wind to die down."

She stared down at the gray, jagged rocks, a short stretch of pebble-and-gravel beach. The tide was out. Two seagulls picked at an exposed clump of dark green, slimy seaweed.

She'd gotten to her father before the gulls had. She remembered that.

J.B.'s calm was a counter to her sense of frenzy, her uneasiness. "How many people knew you liked to run in the nature preserve?" he asked abruptly, quietly.

She didn't hesitate. She'd answered this question before, at least a dozen times. "I don't know. Everyone. No one. I never thought about it."

"No way someone would mistake your father for you."

She shook her head as if he were asking a question. "No. I can't believe that. There's no evidence—nothing to suggest whoever killed him was gunning for me. Technically—" She broke off, shaking her head. "Technically it's possible, but it doesn't seem likely."

"Any leftover cases from your state police days?"

"CID looked into it, and I've racked my mind for months. No, there's nothing." She breathed out, smelling the low tide now, wondering how she'd stayed away for as long as she had. "You'd think there'd be a record if my dad was investigating Teddy Shelton. You sure that guy was keeping tabs on me?"

"No. Could be a coincidence."

"But you don't think so."

"I'm keeping an open mind."

Her own smile took her by surprise. "You're on vacation—you don't need to keep an open mind."

He glanced at her. "Like being a civilian, don't you?"

"It has its advantages."

He acknowledged her words with a small nod. His nose, she noted, was red, too, but she still had that sensation that he belonged out here, on the Atlantic, Montana or no Montana. He had the hard-bitten look of a man who'd spent his life at sea.

"Teddy Shelton could have an innocuous reason for being here, you know," she said.

"He's not your problem, Zoe. I got into it with him. I'll play it out."

She tilted her head back and eyed Special Agent J. B. McGrath, decided he was very serious for someone on vacation. "You're supposed to be relaxing and having fun."

He smiled. "I am relaxing and having fun."

His smile eased the tension between them and seemed to go straight through her, penetrating her natural reserve when it came to men. The way it brought a sexy gleam to his blue eyes, the way it tilted up one corner of his mouth and not the other—she found herself licking dry lips.

Without thinking, without even knowing she was doing it, she put one hand on his hard shoulder and kissed him lightly on the mouth.

He could have stopped her. He was a trained FBI agent.

She could have stopped herself, except she hadn't stopped herself from doing anything insane in a year.

He tasted like salt, and she wanted more.

Then she realized what she'd done and jumped back, swearing under her breath. "Oh, damn. I *must* be going nuts."

"I don't know." His voice was that studied calm, laced with amusement. "Nuts can be good."

She bolted. She called on all her mental and physical training, her ten years of experience in law enforcement, and got the hell out of there, pushing herself hard and not even feeling the wind now.

When she reached the house, she was gasping for air

and had a sharp stitch in her side. She staggered up the driveway, thinking she might throw up her blueberry pancakes.

That'd be just great. Kiss an FBI agent, then throw up.

Everyone in Goose Harbor would know by noon. She'd never hear the end of it. She'd have to move back to Connecticut and stay there for good.

She could feel the exertion in her calf muscles and had to slow down when she hit the stairs to the second floor. Not in as good a shape as a year ago. Definitely. She'd tried to keep her body fat below twenty-two percent.

When she reached her bedroom, she shut the door and thought about barricading herself in, but that seemed a little over the top. She'd reacted to the moment. She was entitled. No one would blame her for being just a tad out of control her first days home.

Except maybe the man she'd kissed out of the blue.

His footsteps sounded on the stairs. "I'm going for a boat ride," he said calmly, as if nothing had happened. By his standards, maybe nothing had. "Wind's dying down. Need help getting out your kayak?"

"No. Thanks." She sounded relatively calm and normal herself.

"Water's fifty-eight degrees in the harbor."

"Chilly."

"Yeah. You might think about rolling on purpose. Cool you right off."

The bastard. The *bastard.* Zoe almost burst through the door and told him what an unfeeling, obnoxious man he was, making fun of her at a moment of peak embarrassment.

But she was smiling, too, although she doubted that was a good sign.

"Don't worry," he said. "Next time you won't catch me off guard."

Next time?

He trotted down the stairs. Even through her door, she could hear the kick in his step. He might think she was completely insane, but he hadn't minded being kissed.

"Well," she muttered, digging in her still-unpacked boxes and bags for suitable kayaking attire, "doesn't that just make my day?"

Thirteen

Zoe waited until it was a rising tide before she got out on the water in her lime-green sit-on-top kayak. She dragged it down the bluff from the garage and launched from a small, protected area among the rocks. She had her life vest and safety whistle, but didn't bother with a dry bag of emergency supplies, since she didn't plan to go far and would stay within yelling distance of shore. She didn't know what had happened to her wet suit and instead had put on exercise tights, an exercise shirt and a fleece vest.

At first the paddle felt awkward and even the slightest wave or breeze put her on edge, but within a few minutes, she had her kayaking rhythm back.

Kyle and his documentary and Teddy Shelton and whatever he was up to—J.B. and his questions, even his steady calm—had all zapped her energy and frazzled her nerves. Kayaking should help.

She should have stayed with her sister after breakfast and fixed her door.

Not kissed McGrath.

Maybe her blueberry-pancake sugar high had crashed, explaining her impulsiveness.

She breathed out and dipped one end of her paddle into the water. It was just her and the gulls. The lobster boats were in deep water. Most of the pleasure boats were south or north of the harbor or docked. She noticed the Castellane yacht hadn't moved.

The wind was in her face, but it'd be at her back on her return trip, when she'd really be feeling the effects of her first time in a kayak in a year. As she crossed the harbor, she avoided the shipping channels so she wouldn't run into the path of a bigger boat, which wouldn't easily see a small kayak, even a lime-green one. Bruce liked to threaten to run her over with his lobster boat. He thought most kayakers were irresponsible and out of their minds.

She kept her weight centered in her boat and used her shoulders to dip the paddle, first on one side, then the other. Her kayak was stable and easy to maneuver, but not meant for long treks.

The sounds of the gulls and the ocean soothed her raw nerves. Normally she'd have headed northeast to the quiet waters among the small islands along the shore of the nature preserve. There were spots with tricky currents, strong tides, shallow, narrow passages and underwater ledges that could be treacherous for both kayakers and power boaters, but Zoe knew where they were. She loved the islands, but the reminders of a year ago would be everywhere and she didn't want that, not today.

She rested a moment, letting her kayak bob in the

water, her shoulders aching but not unpleasantly so. Her father and Olivia used to sit on her aunt's front porch and watch Zoe and Christina kayak along the shore as teenagers. Christina didn't go out as often once she started college, but Zoe stayed with it, kayaking a great way for her to relieve stress. She wondered if her sister would take it up again—Kyle Castellane had an expensive kayak capable of handling long treks and virtually any condition. He'd never taken a lesson.

Too busy trying to get into Olivia's attic, Zoe thought, suddenly put out with him for bringing up his request when she was still getting her feet under her now that she was back in Goose Harbor, when she was trying to figure out what was going on with the two break-ins.

Then again, she supposed she should give Kyle credit for not walking in through the front door the way McGrath had.

She stiffened, going very still in her boat. Christina had locks on her café doors and her house doors—forced entry wasn't necessary at Olivia's house. Just go through the damn porch door.

Could whoever had broken in to her sister's house and café have gone through Olivia's as well? Were she and Christina the targets, or just Christina, or were the break-ins random and had nothing to do with either of them?

Zoe shook her head, nearly throwing herself off balance and turning over her boat. But she quickly centered herself and continued paddling, moving closer to shore now that she'd passed the town docks.

No one had broken into her aunt's house. The only uninvited guest she'd had was her FBI agent.

Staying close to shore, she paddled past a rock-bound point and out of the harbor, the water less choppy now, no wind. Bruce's lobster pound was up ahead, quiet at midday. She headed toward the protected salt marsh and figured she'd turn around in the cove there.

As she passed Bruce's wreck of a cottage, just thirty feet from her, she noticed a heap of a truck parked out back, then saw Teddy Shelton walk out onto the rotting deck. He waved to her. "How's the kayaking?"

"Invigorating."

"Zoe, right? Zoe West? I heard you were back in town."

She nodded. "It was time. You renting this place from Bruce?"

"Yeah. Fancy, huh?"

"Nice location."

"Stinks at low tide."

She smiled. "You get used to it."

"Not me."

He walked down the two half-rotted porch steps and followed a sandy path through the tall beach grass and wild beach roses and stood at the water's edge, the tide nearly in now, lapping at his feet.

Zoe could feel her boat scraping the sandy bottom of the shallow cove. It was high tide, but the water wasn't much more than two feet at its deepest here. At low tide, the cove would be a wide stretch of mud. She skimmed her paddle over the still, clear water and tried to keep her boat from pushing in toward land with the tide. She was at a disadvantage and should say goodbye.

But she didn't. "I understand you got off on the wrong foot with my houseguest."

"That FBI asshole? Yeah, I did."

Zoe noticed Shelton hadn't hesitated when she referred to J.B. as her houseguest. But given Bruce's big mouth, she wouldn't be surprised if it was all over town by now.

"He should clear out," Shelton said, pushing a toe into the wet, soft sand. "He's pissing people off."

Zoe gave a neutral nod and said nothing.

Shelton lit a cigarette. He was a big man, probably in his early forties, and wore faded jeans, a denim jacket over a white T-shirt and a belt with a huge silver buckle. He shook his head, blowing out smoke. "You cops. Always suspicious. They teach you that in cop school, pester people who're sitting in their truck minding their own business?"

"I'm not a cop anymore."

"That's right. I heard that. You back for good?"

"I don't know yet."

A sudden swell lifted her kayak and pushed it toward shore, the bottom scraping hard in the sand. If she ran aground, she'd have to get out and shove off again, and she didn't want to do that, not with Teddy Shelton standing there smoking his cigarette and lying to her.

"I have to go." But she added, "Did you hear about the break-in at my sister's café last night?"

Shelton nodded thoughtfully, holding his cigarette between two fingers. "Any leads?"

"I don't know. I haven't talked to the police since last night. I doubt there are."

He grinned at her, exhaled more smoke. "Still got your cop instincts, don't you?"

She smiled without any meaning, any pleasantness behind it. No wonder this guy had popped up on J.B.'s radar screen, as he'd put it. "I have training and experience—I'm not sure I ever had any instincts. If you see Bruce, tell him I said hi, okay?"

"Sure. No problem."

Zoe felt his eyes on her as she turned, her back to him as she and her lime-green kayak scooted over the calm water. Her strokes were even, rhythmic, with more energy than before she'd talked to him. She paddled past the lobster pound and started to move in closer to the rockbound point, but an ancient, battered lobster boat was in her way, motionless in the water about twenty feet from shore. Approaching it on its non-working side was a good way to get run over—the pilot could easily swing his boat around before he realized she was there.

She paused in the water, debating her options.

Then she squinted at the faded buoy atop the pilot-house and recognized Bruce's colors.

It was the old boat he'd rented to McGrath.

"Ah, hell."

He must have seen her talking to Teddy Shelton. He'd positioned his boat so that she'd have to paddle in a wide arc out into choppier water or cut between him and the shoreline, where she'd be within just a few feet of him. Working or nonworking side didn't matter, because J.B. wasn't on the water to catch lobsters.

Zoe was too tired and sore even to try sneaking around him the long way. Straightening her spine, she took powerful strokes and maneuvered her kayak toward shore, debating whether she should just land here on the rocks, hoist her kayak on her shoulder and walk the rest of the way. But then she'd be acting as if she'd done something stupid, and she hadn't.

The stern of J.B.'s boat was pointed at her. She could see him in the pilothouse and decided just to paddle along the shore as if she didn't have a care in the world.

J.B. sauntered out and leaned over the gouged working side of his boat, where Bruce and before him his father had checked and rebaited their traps, day after day, in every manner of weather. "Want a ride?" he asked as if he just happened to be there.

"I'm fine. Thanks."

"Long way back across the harbor."

She kept paddling. "Wind's at my back."

"I saw you have a little chat with Shelton." His tone was unreadable. "Thought I'd have to jump in the water and come to your rescue."

Zoe narrowed her eyes up at him, and all she could think was—damn, he really did look like he'd jumped off a Winslow Homer seascape. He was tight-lipped, stoic-looking, sexy, so at ease in his boat he might have grown up on the water.

But he also wasn't happy with her at all. Not that she

let it bother her. "What if Teddy is what he says he is and you're just on his case because he thinks you're a jerk?"

"Did he tell you I was a jerk?"

"Actually, he referred to you as 'that FBI asshole.'"

"That's what you two talked about? Me?"

"We didn't talk about anything." She was beginning to feel restless, exposed. "I have to get going. If I stop paddling, my shoulders are going to seize up on me, and then you *will* have to rescue me."

He stood up straight and smiled at her. "Could be fun."

She ignored him and the unsettling picture in her mind of the two of them in the cold Atlantic. "I'll see you later?"

"Most definitely."

He'd been kissed and called an asshole. J.B. figured that provided a certain balance to his day. He puttered on back to the town docks and tied up his boat, then walked over to Christina West's café for her incomparable Maine crab cakes and coffee. It was cold out on the water. He could see Zoe still making her way across the harbor. Her cheeks were red from the wind and cold when he'd cornered her.

Just as well she didn't trust him. Who knew what would have happened if she'd climbed into his boat with him.

The café was packed with tourists. He had to wait, then settle for a table by the door. But the crab cakes and coffee were hot, and that was fine with him.

Christina slipped out from behind her counter to join

him for "thirty seconds." She looked calmer than she had at breakfast. "Did you see my lunatic sister on her kayak?"

J.B. dipped a chunk of crab cake into a red-pepper coulis. "Looks like she's having a good time."

"That's Zoe. If she's sweating, she's having a good time."

For no reason at all, at least none that he wanted to contemplate, J.B. thought of slim, blond-haired, blue-eyed, very female ex-cop Zoe sweating in bed with him. He said nothing to her little sister, and, mercifully, Christina slipped back behind the counter.

It was going to be that kind of day, and he couldn't blame the little nothing of a kiss, never mind that it had been a lit match to a fuse. He'd been thinking about Zoe in bed with him even before she gave in to impulse.

Almost as if on cue, the café crowd gave out a collective gasp.

At one of the window tables, an older woman said, "Oh, my! That kayak turned right over, didn't it?"

The woman across from her nodded. "She got caught in the wake of that speedboat."

J.B. rose, and Christina shot back around the counter and joined him. "Is she okay?"

Zoe had almost made it to her aunt's house on its rocky point before she went ass over teakettle into the water.

Her kayak was still upright, and she was trying to climb back in.

Christina touched his arm. "Don't go after her. You won't get there in time to do any good. If she needs help, she'll blow her whistle." She gestured at the offending speedboat. "Most of the boaters look out for kayakers, but that guy's a menace."

J.B. spotted Bruce Young's lobster boat coming back into the harbor from the northeast. "Bruce can get to her if she's in trouble."

Christina rolled her eyes. "He's probably laughing his ass off."

"Is anyone besides you happy your sister's back?"

She smiled. "You are. You were looking kind of bored before Zoe showed up."

He said nothing and watched Zoe flop into her kayak. She reached back into the water and grabbed her paddle, and in another few seconds was paddling again, making good time.

A cheer erupted from the café.

"I've got to get back to work," Christina said. "Why don't you and Zoe come over for dinner tonight? *I'll* cook. Zoe tends to throw things into dishes that don't belong there. Like her flax seed and Toaster Strudels."

She retreated, and J.B., resisting the image of Zoe in cold, wet, tight-fitting clothes, returned to his coffee and crab cakes before they could get cold.

Fourteen

At high tide, like it was now, Bruce's cabin wasn't too bad. At low tide, it smelled like dead fish. The wet, gray sand developed pinprick holes that made tiny sucking sounds, like something was alive down there. Probably was. Teddy didn't want to know what. He'd worked at the lobster pound, but he just did what he was told. He was out of his element on the ocean. If he had any sense, he'd quit this job and head back to New York.

He'd never have come to Goose Harbor in the first place if he had half a brain.

He flipped a card onto the red-and-white-checked oilcloth that was duct-taped to the table. He was playing solitaire with a limp, grimy deck of cards with a picture of a lobster on the back, hoping some kind of plan of action would materialize in his head.

There was nothing for him in New York. An ex-wife who'd dumped him over the guns, long before he'd ended up in prison. No kids. His parents were dead. He had a brother somewhere.

He'd decided in prison that his family had something wrong with them. They had bad luck. In his early days behind bars, he read a bunch of Stephen King novels and concluded his family was cursed. Made sense to him. His father had been angry and abusive. His mother had been a mouse when he was around and a tiger when he wasn't. They had no other family—there were vague references to other Sheltons upstate, but who knew? His parents were also liars. Teddy hated liars.

He joined the army at eighteen thinking he'd at least get away from these people, maybe make something of himself. But he'd never worked at it harder than some asshole officer made him work, and after his stint, he was done. Without the army, he had no structure. He had no purpose, even if it was only one defined for him. He'd seen other guys do fine in the military, fine when they went back to civilian life. They got jobs, they had families, they made a contribution.

They gave up weapons they weren't supposed to have.

At least this nitwit job with Luke Castellane paid well. Luke had made allusions to a big bonus at the end of it. The guy was just dying at the idea of Zoe West and the FBI agent crawling up his ass. He didn't understand that Teddy had his own reasons for taking the job—for being in Goose Harbor at all.

He had the front door open and could hear the wind whooshing in the trees and the tide lapping all the way up to the grass. The place was such a hole. Saying he was renting it was too strong—he was just keeping up the taxes and utilities. Bruce wasn't making a profit.

The front room had a couch and a musty chair, the table with the oilcloth and three rickety chairs. Teddy had nearly blown himself up lighting the pint-size gas stove in the galley kitchen. No coffeemaker, just a pitted percolator.

He didn't know what Luke wanted him to do about Zoe West and the FBI agent. Why'd she come sneaking around? Was she on to him and checking him out? Had she found out about his prison time? His job with Luke? Maybe she and the G-man had found out about Luke's bullshit story that he wanted to protect Zoe and didn't believe it, either.

Teddy got up from his solitaire game. He was losing, anyway. Except for his arsenal, he hadn't broken the law. If and when he did, he'd make sure he had his escape route planned out ahead of time.

He should get on that.

He glanced at his array of cards on the crooked table. Clock. It was a moronic game. He used to play it as a kid, up in a closet when he was hiding from his crazy mother.

He went through the kitchen and out the back and got in his truck. He checked his apple crate of weapons in the jump seat. All nice and tidy. If the cops got wind of his arsenal, he'd be toast, but so far, so good. He'd come close to getting discovered not long after he arrived in Goose Harbor, when he ran into Patrick West on the docks. West was off duty, not in uniform. A friendly guy. He asked Teddy if he knew boats. Teddy didn't know why, but he didn't like people just walking up to him and starting talking. He'd asked West what business it was of his.

Patrick West hadn't gotten ruffled. He wasn't a big man, and he was steady, self-confident. He explained that he knew Goose Harbor, he knew its people. He understood the kind of guys who came through looking for work as opposed to the kind who came for their ocean fix, their lobster and clam dinners and walks on the beaches, their treks through cute shops. He figured Teddy for the former. It wasn't technically the case, but Teddy didn't argue with him.

"Lobster pound's hiring if you're interested," West told him. "Tell Bruce Young I sent you."

It was god-awful work. Teddy had lasted only a few weeks.

Then Patrick West was dead.

"And here I am," Teddy grumbled, starting his truck. "Lucky me."

He was out to the main road when his cell phone rang.

"I want you to maintain the status quo," Luke Castellane said, without so much as a how-was-your-morning.

Teddy frowned. "What's that mean?"

"It means I like things as they are. It's better for all concerned if Patrick West's murder remains unsolved."

"Yeah? So far so good. It's been a year—"

Luke cut him off. "I don't like having Zoe here. I don't like having this FBI agent snooping around."

"What about the break-ins?"

"I just don't want any more trouble."

"Yeah, and I'm supposed to do what to stop it?"

But the line had gone dead. Teddy figured it must mean he was supposed to fill in the blanks for himself.

He tossed his phone onto the seat next to him. The boss had just upped the ante. Had to be. Keeping an eye on Zoe West didn't require any action or decision-making on Teddy's part. He just watched and reported back to Luke Castellane. But maintaining the status quo? Stopping her and Agent McGrath from kicking up dust? That could take work. Action. Crossing the line.

How he went about it, apparently, was his call.

Teddy turned toward the village and kept his truck under the speed limit. He didn't want to be stopped now, have one of Maine's finest get suspicious about his apple crate.

After a year in Gooseshit Harbor, he didn't know if he liked the idea that he might have to go as far as killing Zoe West to keep that weird bastard Luke happy.

But, nah. Teddy shook his head. He wouldn't have to kill her, maybe just beat her up a little.

The FBI agent he might have to kill.

Fifteen

Zoe sat on the porch with a pot of hot peppermint-licorice tea and wrapped herself in a red wool blanket that still smelled faintly of the rosemary-scented powder her aunt preferred. She listened to the ocean and the shorebirds and tried to stop shivering after her dunking in the harbor. It had been a good half hour, and she was still frozen.

The sun was behind the house now, off the water, the porch cool and shadowy, hinting at the short, dark winter days that were just around the corner.

"You Mainers." J.B. came around from the side porch, the floorboards creaking under his weight. He looked dark and warm, not as if he'd had to climb out of the freezing ocean. "Most people would sit by the fire after they took a spill in cold water."

"*Frigid* water. I'm out of practice." She held her mug with both hands, absorbing its heat. "You saw me?"

"All of Goose Harbor saw you."

"I'll never live it down. I was preoccupied, and the

pilot of the speedboat was an idiot—" She sighed, vividly recalling the exact moment when she realized she was broadside to an enormous swell and going over. She glanced up at J.B. "Were you ready to come to my rescue?"

"Me and a couple of old ladies on a bus tour."

"I'd have blown my whistle if I were in real trouble."

"No, you wouldn't." He dropped onto a wooden rocker painted a dark green. "You'd have drowned or died of hypothermia before you admitted you needed help."

"Are you implying I'm stubborn?"

"Self-reliant to a fault, maybe. Proud, stubborn. Possibly overconfident." He rocked back, shrugging. "But that's only a guess. I'd have to be around you for an hour or two more before I could say for sure."

He looked windburned and rugged, as if he'd been going out to sea for years, as if he were born to it. But Zoe pushed back her attraction to him, her curiosity about him, as if they were something she could control.

"Still mad at me for talking to Teddy Shelton without your say-so?" She smiled. "I don't know if I'm insulted or amused."

"I ran into Bruce on the docks. He said he was hoping he'd get a chance to fish you out of the water, just to have something to hold over you for the rest of your lives. He blamed the speedboat. That was decent of him."

"It was *accurate*."

J.B. obviously had no intention of letting her off the hook. "Your mind wasn't on what you were doing. You know it wasn't."

There was no point arguing with him. He was already convinced he was right. Zoe drank more of her tea and finally felt a bit warmer. She wondered if her lips were still purple. She was shivering uncontrollably and still cursing her inattention when she got to the rocks below her aunt's house, then dragged herself and her kayak up the steep trail. She'd left her boat in the yard and made it upstairs to her room without collapsing from hypothermia, then peeled off her wet clothes and found an old bathrobe in her bedroom closet to put on.

J.B. couldn't see her bathrobe under her blanket. It was one of Olivia's, or perhaps had been left by a former guest. It looked like something Lucy Ricardo might have worn.

She decided to change the subject. "Kyle called while I was making tea. He wanted to know if I'd thought about his request."

"Have you?"

"No. I went kayaking to avoid thinking about anything."

"Didn't work, did it?"

She ignored him. "Periodically for about three years before she died, Aunt Olivia would have me burn stuff she didn't want to leave behind after she was gone. I protested, but she was adamant. She'd have done it herself if I'd refused."

"Sounds like a character."

"She didn't want anyone—family, scholars, gossip hounds—pawing through her private thoughts and possessions after she was dead. She knew she was famous. Kyle knows all this, you realize."

"So no big surprises in the attic."

"I doubt it."

"Did she know you wanted to write?"

Zoe was so startled by his question, she ended up spilling her tea over her hand. She yelled out, but he was there, taking the cup from her, setting it back on its saucer.

"Did you burn yourself?" he asked.

She nodded, feeling flushed and exposed, as if he could see not just through her, but into her, which she knew was all in her head—a result of being off balance. She sucked on her burned knuckle. "I didn't want to write. I *don't* want to write. I was just…scribbling. I don't know. It wasn't anything."

J.B. stood back and sat on the porch railing, the lawn and beach roses, the bluff and the ocean behind him. "You resurrected Jen Periwinkle."

She lifted her gaze to him. "I thought you couldn't read my handwriting."

He shrugged. "I could read that much. Did you start writing before your father was killed and your aunt died?"

Zoe slipped both hands under her blanket and tightened it around her, her fingers stiff from the cold and nerves. "No, after. I stayed here by myself. I made the nook up in the attic, but if it was warm enough, I'd write out here on the porch sometimes. It was a way to get my mind off everything."

"Funny that your aunt left you the rights to Jen Periwinkle." J.B. placed his hands on the porch railing on either side of him, and she noticed several scars, not that old. "If most of the books are out of print, maybe she wanted you to keep her going, reinvent her for the next century."

"I don't even know if there'd be an audience. And in her will, Olivia made it clear that I was under no pressure from her from the grave—she'd tried to kill off Jen herself but couldn't."

J.B. laughed. "And here I've been thinking your aunt was a practical old Mainer—sounds like she could be loosey-goosey."

For a moment, Zoe felt as if Olivia was out here with them, her wisps of white hair in her face as she enjoyed the fresh air and the incomparable view. Her throat caught. "She was something, J.B."

"Tell me about that last day," he said. "When you told her about your father."

"There's nothing to say. I barreled into the kitchen like a crazy woman and blurted that Dad had been murdered."

"Was anyone else here?"

"Betsy O'Keefe."

"The woman living with Luke Castellane?"

"Not then. She was my aunt's caregiver. She's an R.N., but she also served as a companion and personal assistant. They worked out the arrangements. Olivia was prickly at first, but Betsy was so patient with her, always willing to compromise. She had just the right mix of spine and kindness for the job."

"Ever imagine her with Luke?"

Zoe shook her head. "Betsy never seemed interested in romantic relationships, or even friendships. She's always struck me as a solitary sort. Nice, not someone who needs a lot of people in her life. I suppose that makes her good for the kind of work she does."

J.B. said nothing for a moment, and Zoe thought about how little she knew about him—a powder keg according to Stick, yet he hadn't done anything out of control or nuts as far as she could see. Unless she counted helping himself to a room in her house.

"How'd she end up with Luke?" he asked.

"I don't really know. Aunt Olivia always liked him. She said he was an abused and neglected little boy and that made him a self-absorbed and often not very pleasant man, but she held out hope for him. He was devastated when she died."

J.B. eased off the rail. "I've seen Luke Castellane around town a few times. He strikes me as an arrogant son of a bitch." He smiled. "But maybe your aunt was more tolerant than I am."

"I'd call her observant more than tolerant." Zoe fought off a sudden wave of nostalgia, regret, sense of loss. "She always expected the good in people to triumph."

"That's not a bad way to live."

"You think so? I'd have expected you to say it's naive."

"One kiss and she thinks she knows me." He moved toward her, deliberately, dominating her view, and smiled. "That brought some heat to your cold cheeks, didn't it, Detective Zoe? Still shivering?"

Not anymore, she thought. "It was staying in my wet clothes that did me in. If I could have gotten out of them sooner—" She stopped, aware of a darkening of his eyes. She warned herself not to read anything into it, but she could feel how scantily clad she was under her wool blanket. She'd at least pulled on dry, warm socks. Hiking socks and a silky bathrobe. Very sexy. "I'm much warmer now."

J.B. stood directly in front of her, his toes almost touching hers, and seemed to hesitate a moment, as if he thought she might jump up and run back into the house—or giving her the chance to.

Then he skimmed a crooked finger over her cheek and caught the damp ends of her hair. "You got soaked, didn't you?"

"Head to toe," she managed to say.

He let his finger slide under her jaw and tilted her face up toward him, then slowly lowered his mouth to hers. He gave her another chance to scoot inside, to back him off, if she'd wanted to. But she didn't, and instead she parted her lips slightly, taking in a small breath as his mouth touched hers. He pulled back a little, and she thought that'd be the end of it, but she was wrong. He cupped his hand at the back of her head and kissed her for a long time, letting his mouth play against hers.

Her blanket slipped off her shoulders, and her flimsy bathrobe fell open, exposing the swell of her breasts but, mercifully, not her nipples. Her skin was overheated now; the contrast to the chilly air seemed erotic.

He trailed one hand down her throat, let his fingertip skim over the curve of one breast before he took in a sharp breath and whispered into her mouth, "I need to stop now or I won't." He stood up straight, but his gaze shot straight to her breasts, his jaw tightening as he raked one hand through his hair. "Hell, Zoe."

"I don't know." Her voice was hoarse, and she quickly tugged her blanket back over her shoulders. "At least my kiss this morning wasn't a toe-curler."

"Oh, you don't think so?"

"It was spur-of-the-moment."

"Ah-ha."

"It *was*."

"So you think I walked out here with the specific intention of kissing you?"

She swallowed. "I didn't say that."

"Where'd you get the robe?"

Her throat was tight, dry, and she could feel her skin tingling under her blanket, wondered what she'd have done if he hadn't pulled back. Made love to him out here on the porch? Let him carry her inside? She shook off the images. "Bedroom closet. It reminds me of Lucy Ricardo, except I don't have red hair."

He went to the porch door and pulled it open with more force than was necessary, and she realized he was on edge, fighting for self-control. His muscles seemed tensed, his back rigid. He glanced back at her. "Your sister's invited us to dinner tonight."

His clenched teeth undermined the normality of his words. Zoe took a quick breath, remembered Stick's warning about him. An undercover agent who'd killed a man in front of his children. Who'd almost been killed himself. A potentially dangerous man who was supposed to be in Maine cooling his heels, not getting mixed up in a year-old murder investigation.

She took a breath and followed his lead, keeping her words mundane. "Both of us?"

"Yes, ma'am." His eyes sparkled, his humor back as abruptly as it had vanished. "Probably the whole town saw you kiss me this morning. We're an item."

"McGrath!" Zoe almost jumped out of her chair but saw his quirk of a smile and stopped herself. "You're kidding, right?"

"You need to be kidded more, Detective. Life's been damn serious for you for too long."

"For you, too, don't you think?"

"Absolutely. That's why I picked Goose Harbor for my vacation."

She leaned back, wiggling her toes inside her heavy socks. "Is it? I don't know, Special Agent McGrath. I don't think Teddy Shelton's told me the whole story about why he's here. But neither have you."

"I haven't known you two whole days," he said. "I haven't told you the whole story about anything."

And he smiled, winked and headed back inside.

Zoe flopped back against her chair, sighed at the porch ceiling, then made herself pour another cup of tea. An erotic, toe-curling kiss, a dunk in the harbor and a million questions had her reeling. Her peppermint-licorice tea would calm her down. She didn't need warming up, not anymore.

What could J. B. McGrath possibly be hiding?

She shook her head at the simplicity of her question,

because she had a feeling there was nothing simple about her houseguest.

And she knew how insidious the aftereffects of a traumatic experience could be. Her former colleagues in the state police and her father's small, shattered police force in town had all been more than patient with her in the first weeks after his murder. They understood she'd just wanted to find out who'd shot him on an isolated stretch of Goose Harbor coast and why.

It wasn't the wanting that got her into trouble—it was pushing herself, and them, beyond all reason. She'd made a pain of herself, complained about the lack of progress in the investigation, demanded answers to questions she knew they weren't going to answer. She meddled. She didn't believe she was somehow magically better than her former colleagues because her father was the victim, or because the FBI had accepted her as a new trainee—she simply couldn't stop herself.

The last straw was when her criticism of the slow progress of the investigation ended up in the *Goose Harbor News*. The Boston media picked up the story.

Finally, Stick Monroe had called her over for a visit.

They'd stood in his garden as he'd stirred his compost and read her the riot act. If the FBI found out she was handling this crisis this badly, they'd boot her. She could forget the academy. Kiss her career goodbye. "We all understand," he said. "Zoe, I know it's hard, but it's not your case. If you keep this up, you're going to end up on the wrong side of a jail cell, never mind get disinvited to the academy and lose friends."

She hadn't cared, not then. It wasn't that she didn't want to—she couldn't step back from the brink of her own need to keep acting, doing, not thinking. She remembered thrusting her chin out at her old friend. "I found him, Stick. I saw his blood mixing with the sand and saltwater. I felt for his pulse. His skin was cool, mottled—you know, that bluish-purple marbled effect bodies get—"

"Stop it, Zoe."

"I can't!"

"That's why you need to let CID do their job."

She'd fought tears, felt so out of control, more than she'd ever experienced in her life, even when her mother died—because both her father and her aunt had been there then, anchoring her, absorbing some of her trauma. "Aunt Olivia—if I hadn't told her—"

"She still would have died, Zoe." Stick was patient, firm. "You know that. *She* knew it. She'd been working on revising her obituary that morning before you arrived."

"I feel so terrible. I've made such an ass of myself."

"No, you haven't. Patrick was a good man. We all miss him. We all hate what happened to him. But it's time to back off."

All the rage and fight had gone out of her as she watched Stick use his pitchfork to turn over rich, black dirt made from scraps from his yard and kitchen, his special worms, his care and time—most of all, time. She didn't say a word. She just stared at that new soil and listened to the birds overhead, felt the warm autumn sun on her back contrasting with the cool breeze coming up from the water. No wonder he'd retired to Goose Harbor. No wonder her father and her great-aunt and her sister had stayed.

Then, still saying nothing, she'd turned on her heel and left. She packed up her car that afternoon and headed south. She stayed in Boston for a few days and bowed out of the FBI Academy. Forget it. She wasn't coming. She contacted people she knew who didn't live in Maine, and within two weeks, she was offered the job as the sole detective in Bluefield, Connecticut.

And now here she was, back again. Her problems hadn't changed. Her father was still dead, her aunt was still dead, and a murderer was still on the loose.

Sixteen

Betsy ate a double-chocolate brownie from Christina's Café as she walked up Ocean Drive to the house where she'd spent two years of her life. If Zoe was there and let her in, it would be the first time Betsy had been into Olivia West's house since her former charge's funeral.

Those awful days last October weren't easy to think about.

Olivia had been a forceful but engaging personality, and her fame had given Betsy's work a certain cachet. She wasn't the caregiver for just any old woman, but the creator of Jen Periwinkle.

Few people were aware, because Betsy kept it to herself, of the generous nest egg Olivia had left her.

Her legs ached. She needed more regular exercise, but Luke's compulsive "physical training" turned her off. As a little private rebellion, she didn't exercise at all. She could feel the effects now as she puffed and coughed after just half a mile. As a girl, she used to see Olivia walking around town at all hours of the day.

Betsy had always imagined she was plotting fictional murders. When she started working for her years later, she discovered that Olivia in fact liked to walk when she was plotting a book or was stuck.

No wonder she'd lived to be a hundred.

Betsy turned up the driveway and surprised herself at the overwhelming sense of sadness she felt being here. Olivia was gone. Her nephew, such a good man, was gone. Really, all of Goose Harbor was still dealing with their loss. But how much more awful for the West sisters to endure two deaths in one twenty-four-hour period. Betsy had watched them scatter the ashes, in separate urns, of their great-aunt and their father into the ocean and thought—I'm not going to put off living anymore. I'm going to have fun. Enjoy my life.

Every day she'd known Olivia West, every day she'd worked for her, Betsy had watched Olivia try to make the best of what she had. She didn't pine for lost opportunities or days past but lived in the moment, the present. Betsy saw that as the key, the answer. She'd promised herself never to forget it. She had to be practical—she didn't have the financial resources of someone like an Olivia West. But that wasn't the point. The point was no more feeling sorry for herself, no more living in the past or the future.

She'd marched herself down to Luke's yacht and made sure he knew she was interested in him. She'd be his nurse. Romance could come later.

And it had. Sort of, anyway.

A leaf-peeping tour bus crawled down Ocean Drive,

a string of bumper-to-bumper cars behind it. Betsy noticed J. B. McGrath's Jeep in the driveway next to Zoe's VW and almost turned back. This couldn't be a good development. Zoe needed to move on with her life, not look for reminders of what she'd given up by letting herself get involved with an FBI agent.

Would the two of them guess what she'd witnessed between Luke and Stick Monroe last night? Was it even relevant?

Zoe would have an opinion about Betsy's relationship with Luke. Zoe had an opinion about everything. Would she think Betsy had settled somehow? That one or the other of them wasn't worthy of the other? Betsy, because she was the salt-of-the-earth nurse who deserved better than a self-absorbed, mercurial man. Luke, because he was rich and could get more.

But Betsy resisted making assumptions. She knew she had a bit of a chip on her shoulder, and she didn't like it.

Before she could change her mind, she ran up the walk to the side entry.

Zoe already had the door open. "Betsy! I spotted you coming up the driveway." She seemed genuinely pleased. "It's great to see you. Come on in."

Mumbling something about being glad to see Zoe, too, Betsy followed her into the kitchen. Although she had no idea why, Betsy had always been self-conscious around Zoe, who looked so trim and pretty with her blond curls and blue-gray eyes. She had on slim side-zip pants and a close-fitting dark pink sweater with a

V neck that was downright sexy. But she was probably unaware—she'd always seemed oblivious to how attractive she was.

Betsy felt frumpy in her old L.L. Bean barn coat and elastic-waist chinos.

She stood in the middle of the kitchen, noticing that Olivia's typewriter was gone. Otherwise it seemed the same as a year ago.

"Would you like a cup of tea?" Zoe asked.

"Oh, no, I can't stay long, but thank you." Betsy wondered if Zoe, with all her experience as a police officer, could see through her white lie. What did she have to get back to? Luke was off on his seven-mile run. In truth, she had nothing to do. "I just wanted to stop by and say hello."

"I appreciate that."

"I noticed you have company."

Something came into Zoe's eyes, then was gone again before Betsy could identify it. "Right. It's a long story, but he's upstairs."

"It's the FBI agent everyone's been talking about? J.B.—"

"McGrath."

Betsy smiled. She supposed she was being silly pretending not to have the FBI agent's name on the tip of her tongue. "Now I remember. Like Mr. Lester McGrath. I didn't mean to pry."

Zoe gave her a reassuring smile. "You're not prying."

"It's hard to believe she's been dead a year, isn't it?" Betsy stared at the empty table and unexpectedly found herself on the verge of tears. She cleared her throat. "Those two years with her were good ones for me. I did what I could for her at the end."

"I know, Betsy." Zoe's voice was soft, steady. "No one could have asked more of you. We were all so grateful."

"It was just her time." Betsy hesitated, uncertain of what to do with herself. Sit? Walk around? Go into the front room? When she'd worked for Olivia, she'd had a sense of authority, a place. "You're staying here at the house?"

Zoe nodded. "I lost my job in Connecticut. Time to figure out what comes next."

"The break-ins are worrying, don't you think?"

"No one's been hurt, nothing taken. Good signs, I hope. It could just be someone scrounging for cash."

But she didn't think so. Betsy could see that. "I hope so." She ran her fingertips over the oak table. Even if she didn't mean to, Zoe always made her feel inadequate, as if she came up short to her and Christina. Betsy knew better, but she couldn't help it. She managed a quick, awkward smile. "I don't know if you've heard, but I'm living with Luke Castellane on his boat. He and I—we hit it off."

"I'd heard. You seem happy, Betsy. That's great."

There was no condescension in Zoe's tone, but Betsy bristled, angry with herself for reading anything into Zoe's words, for wanting this woman's approval, as if Zoe West was somehow an extension of Olivia. That was how Luke saw her. That was why he was protecting her. Betsy doubted Zoe would understand that Luke had hired Teddy Shelton to spy on her and Agent Mc-Grath out of a noble desire to do right by Olivia, a woman who'd done right by him. He'd been devastated by her death. He wasn't over it even now.

"Betsy," Zoe said, "is something bothering you?"

She stared out at the water and suddenly wished she hadn't come. "Just being back here, I guess. I'm sorry—"

"It's okay, but if something's on your mind…"

"I'm afraid for you, Zoe. I'm afraid for all of us, maybe." Betsy couldn't believe she'd blurted that out, but she couldn't stop herself now. She flew around at Zoe, knowing she must look wild with her wind-tangled hair, the intensity she felt surging through her. "I remember what you were like in the weeks after your father and Olivia's deaths. We all do. It's understandable. No one blames you, Zoe. You wanted answers, and you weren't willing to stop at much to get them."

Zoe sank into a chair at the kitchen table and nodded with remarkable calm. "That's not much of an exaggeration. I can understand you'd be worried that now that I'm back, especially with these two break-ins, that it'll all start over again and I'll make people's lives miserable."

"And still end up with no answers." Betsy surprised herself at her own boldness. She eased gingerly onto the chair opposite Zoe and reached across to take her hand, squeezing it gently. "Let sleeping dogs lie, Zoe. The police haven't found anything in a year. You know they've worked hard at it—your father was one of their own. There's no rock, no stone they haven't turned over and looked under. The media aren't letting them off the hook, either. They'll all keep at it."

"I know. I'm not here to make a mess of things, Betsy. I'm just trying to get on with my life."

Betsy pulled her hand away and could feel her heart beating like a scared bird's inside her chest. She felt cold, on edge. Nothing she was doing made any sense— she had no plan. And Luke—Luke would be furious with her.

"Olivia was out of her head that last day," she said, her voice almost inaudible. "You know that, don't you?"

A flicker of pain came into Zoe's eyes. "Betsy—"

"She was always making up stories. She didn't write them down anymore, and I think they filled up her head. She could have had one of her stories in mind when she said that about knowing who your father's killer was. She wasn't making sense."

"Do you think that's why I'm here?"

Betsy felt her jaw jut out. "You suspect the break-ins are connected to your father's death, don't you?"

"It doesn't matter what I suspect, and anyway, I'm trying not to jump to conclusions. Betsy, I went over all of what Aunt Olivia said in my own mind last year. Even if she had a hunch—even if she *knew*—who killed my father, the police couldn't arrest on that basis. They'd need evidence. And there was none. There *is* none."

"It was a stranger," Betsy said firmly, as if saying it could make it so. "It was a drug dealer or a bird poacher from someplace else, an escaped convict, an escaped lunatic. It wasn't anyone from Goose Harbor. Olivia only knew people from here—that's all she saw during her last weeks on this earth, were people from Goose Harbor." Betsy got to her feet and glared at Zoe, as if somehow she was being an obstructionist. "You *know* that."

The more agitated she got, the calmer Zoe seemed to get. She stayed in her chair at the table and looked up at Betsy. "And what? You think I believe someone from Goose Harbor killed my father? You think I'll start digging into people's lives here? Betsy—why would I do that without any reason, without any suspicion—" She stopped, narrowing her eyes. "Do *you* suspect—"

"Everyone has something to hide," Betsy blurted. She wished she hadn't eaten the brownie, sitting like lead in her stomach now, perhaps the chocolate and the sugar pushing her past the threshold of common sense, common decency. She continued to glare at Zoe. "I'll bet even you have something to hide. Even Olivia. Even your father."

Zoe went very still, her face draining slightly of its color. She looked pale even against the pretty pink of her sweater. "Betsy, I take your point. Is there anything else you want to tell me?"

Stricken by her own behavior, Betsy covered her mouth and gasped against her hand, then blinked back tears. "I'm sorry. I had no right. You and your family have gone through so much this year. I should be more understanding, at least more diplomatic."

"Forget it." Zoe gave her a weak smile and got to her feet. "What happened last year was difficult for you, too. And your larger point's well taken—I don't want to go off half-cocked, either."

"It's just that you haven't been here every day, with the police, the questions, the little invasions of privacy. It all adds up. Maybe your coming back like this, the break-ins, the time of year, have made some of us—me—realize that we're ready to move on, as difficult as that is to say when your father's murderer is still on the loose."

"I understand."

But her words were choked, clipped. Betsy moved toward the door, anxious to be out of there now, feeling embarrassed. What made her think she had a right to tell Zoe anything? She and Zoe weren't friends. They were just people from the same hometown, people who'd both loved an old woman now dead for a year.

"It's a beautiful afternoon for a walk," she said lamely.

"I'm glad you came." Zoe had to clear her throat to get the words out, but she sounded sincere despite her ashen look. "Tell Luke I said hello. I've seen Kyle already. He's awfully excited about the documentary he's doing on Aunt Olivia, isn't he?"

Betsy nodded, relieved that Zoe apparently wasn't going to hold what she'd said against her. "*Obsessed* is the word, I think. Luke will want to see you. Why don't you come out to the boat tomorrow night and have dinner with us? We'll be heading south soon. I'll get together some friends. It can be your welcome-home party."

"Thanks, Betsy, but you just warned me off."

"I know. I put it all so badly. Forgive me. I got carried away." She glanced into the front room past the dining table to the big window that looked across the porch to the Atlantic, quiet, shimmering in the afternoon light.

"I haven't been in here since the memorial service. It's brought back all my own fears. When Olivia said she knew—" Betsy swallowed, shifting her gaze back to Zoe. "It was bone-chilling."

"You handled the situation well, Betsy. She was a very old woman and didn't have long to live." Zoe folded her arms on her chest, and Betsy could see she was shaking, just a little. "Dinner would be lovely."

Betsy sagged in relief, as if her muscles couldn't hold the tension any longer. "Wonderful. Luke's into wines. I'll see to it he opens a good bottle for you. Bring—bring your FBI agent, if you want."

Zoe managed a small smile. "He's not my FBI agent, but I'll invite him. Thank you."

Betsy nodded and fled, nearly stumbling in the driveway, which would have been just perfect. She'd have to explain skinned knees to Luke. But she *didn't* fall, she reminded herself, and when she made it down to Ocean Drive, she slowed her pace and felt almost calm. Should she find Teddy Shelton next, tell *him* not to stir up trouble? To disappear and forget that Luke had hired him?

What were they up to, the two of them?

She shook her head, as if she were arguing with herself. Teddy was Luke's problem. She had an excuse to see Zoe, none at all to track down a creep like Teddy Shelton. She'd met him last summer and had heard rumors that he'd served time in prison. Luke was so naive about people—he'd have no idea. And Betsy knew she could do only so much to protect him.

Seventeen

J.B. walked into the kitchen after Betsy O'Keefe left and helped himself to a cider doughnut. He felt much better now that he'd done the kissing and then had a chance to kick himself and get over it.

Zoe didn't move from her position in the entry doorway.

"Thinking about going after her and saying no to dinner, after all?"

"You eavesdropped?"

He sat at the table. "Overheard." He bit into his doughnut. "I see you changed out of your robe."

"Don't go there."

He smiled without remorse. "I don't have to, do I? You're already there. And will be for a while, I suspect."

"You know, McGrath, as houseguests go—"

"You could do worse." He finished his doughnut in two more bites and dusted the cinnamon sugar off his fingers. "There's something I should tell you before the Castellane kid figures it out. My ancestors settled here in the 1600s. I think George Sutherland was the first one. Sutherland Island's named after him."

He could see he had her attention. She eased out of the doorway but still was stiff, preoccupied. "How distant are these Sutherland ancestors?"

"Not very. My grandmother was a Sutherland."

She kept her reaction under control, but he could see her shock in her eyes. "Posey Sutherland? The woman Kyle just happened to mention this morning?"

"She was my grandmother. John Lester was my great-grandfather. An SOB as far as I can tell."

Zoe shot into the kitchen and grabbed the last doughnut, but didn't take a bite as she leaned back against the counter and shook her head. "Forget it. I don't believe a word you're saying. You made that up after you heard Kyle mention her name. You're just trying to distract me because Betsy read me the riot act. You're incorrigible." She bit into her doughnut. "I'm talking to Bruce. He and the guys really should toss you overboard."

J.B. ignored her. "Posey eloped with my grandfather, Jesse Benjamin McGrath, and moved west with him. Her father—"

"John Lester," Zoe supplied, dubious but apparently willing to let him keep digging this hole for himself.

"Right. John Lester disowned her. She died when my father was seven. Jesse became a lawman in western Montana and was gunned down chasing bank robbers during the Depression."

"I see. What about your father?"

"He became a guide in western Montana. He died in

February. He didn't marry until he was in his forties, and my mother died when I was a baby. So, it was just the two of us. Me and my old pop. He loved Montana. It was where he belonged. Do you ever wonder about that, Zoe? Where you belong?"

Zoe's expression softened, and she set her half-eaten doughnut on the counter and took a small breath. "You're telling the truth, aren't you?"

"Yes, ma'am."

"Did you know your grandmother and Olivia were friends?"

He nodded.

"How, if she and your grandfather both died when your father was just a little boy—"

"I have letters," he said. "From your great-aunt to my grandmother."

She stared at him. "Letters? Letters Aunt Olivia wrote?"

"Letters a very young woman wrote to a friend who'd run off with a stranger and never came home. Olivia and Posey." His voice caught with unexpected emotion. "They were both just kids."

"My God. I had no idea."

"I didn't bring the letters with me. They're still in Montana." He leaned back in his chair, his eyes on Zoe as she steadied herself, one hand on the edge of the counter. "Olivia had no use for Posey's father or her husband."

"Hence, Mr. Lester McGrath."

"It was hers and Posey's secret."

Zoe shook her head in amazement. "I had no idea. Olivia was almost seventy when I was born—she'd already lived a big chunk of her life. And your grandmother had been dead for years. How did she die? What happened to her?"

"Some kind of fever. It wasn't an easy life for her in Montana."

"Do you think she was happy?"

"I only have Olivia's view of things. She had her doubts, but I gather my grandmother kept insisting she was happy. But I think she was also aware of what she'd given up to be with my grandfather, to follow his dreams."

"Do you have a sense of what kind of man he was?"

"Not an easy one. My father was just ten when he was killed. He wasn't a big talker. Sometimes when we were out hiking, he would tell me stories—he said his father was a hard man but basically good, and he never got over Posey's death."

"How sad," Zoe murmured. "Your grandfather wasn't from Goose Harbor?"

"Nova Scotia, as far as I know."

"It was such a long time ago. Yet just last year, Aunt Olivia was sitting right here at this table—" But Zoe stopped abruptly, some of her surprise wearing off, and frowned at J.B. "You could have told me this sooner, you know."

"Why?"

She had no good reason to give him. "It would have been polite."

"You broke into my room at mean old Lottie Martin's inn and came at me with a drapery rod."

"I did *not* break into your room."

He raised an eyebrow.

She smiled. "I had a pass key."

Her smile pleased him more than it should have. It meant she was feeling better—and his reaction meant he was sliding in deeper with her. Any deeper and he might not be able to climb out again. And he'd have to. He knew it. Something was wrong in Goose Harbor, Maine, and she'd run from it a year ago. But she wouldn't again.

He was supposed to be on vacation. His superiors back in Washington would skin him alive if they knew he was dipping a toe into the unsolved murder of a small-town Maine police chief.

Zoe's father.

He had his life away from here. He needed to go back to it.

"As for the drapery rod," she said, "you're lucky I didn't beat you over the head with it. That nook isn't for public consumption."

He pushed back his dark thoughts and stretched out his long legs, sexy, deliberately provocative. "Meaning it's blackmail material? I wonder what I could get in return for my silence."

The warmth spread through her—he could see it. It unsettled her, got her moving. But she didn't back down. She stood over him, leaned in toward him. "Eavesdropping on private conversations, trespassing, not hiking and boating and relaxing like you're supposed to—I wonder what I could get in return for *my* silence."

"Lots." He folded his hands on his stomach, just above his belt, unabashed by the stirring in his groin. She had to know by now what they were moving toward. "Just depends on what you want."

But that, apparently, was all Zoe could stand. She bolted for the front room. "I can see why Aunt Olivia named her evil nemesis McGrath. If your grandfather provoked people the way you do—"

"She never killed him off," J.B. said. "I think she kind of liked him."

"I should sic Kyle on you. Do you know what he'd do for original letters from my aunt to her best friend? Letters no one else has ever seen?"

"Maybe she never intended for anyone else to see them. Maybe my grandmother didn't, either, and she only saved them because they reminded her of Goose Harbor."

Zoe turned suddenly, tears shining in her eyes. "It's a sad story, isn't it? Your grandmother must have been in her twenties when she died. That's so young. I feel almost selfish, missing Aunt Olivia as much as I do."

"She was a presence in your life for a long time."

"The letters—did you read them all?"

"One by one," he said. "I went back to Montana to bury my father. It was cathartic to go through his cabin. I found the letters in an old trunk—I don't know if he'd ever read them. He wasn't an introspective man."

"I'm sorry. You must miss him."

J.B. nodded. "I do. There's a line in one of the letters—your aunt's clearly responding to something my grandmother had written to her about her little boy."

"Your father," Zoe said.

"Your aunt wrote, 'Perhaps your son was meant to be in Montana.'"

"Meaning it was all worth it?" She sounded skeptical.

"I don't know. I think it helped your aunt understand why her friend left."

"Posey hadn't just been swept off her feet by a rogue—she'd played out some cosmic destiny."

J.B. rose but felt weighted, as if the forces of gravity had suddenly decided to grab him by the feet and drag him to the center of the earth. He had to make himself take another step. "My father *was* meant to be in Montana, Zoe. Somehow a Maine writer who never moved out of the house she was born in, who never met him, knew it." He shrugged, and he even had trouble moving his arms. "That's all I can say."

"J.B., are you okay?"

He didn't answer. He pictured himself in the cabin on a snowy winter night as he dug into the trunk and found his father's old christening gown that Olivia West had sent from Maine, three first-edition copies of her first books, signed by her, a black-paper photo album of fading pictures—and the letters. He'd come to know his grandmother through the eyes of another woman.

Zoe smiled gently, and he noticed the slenderness of her fingers as she placed one hand on the doorjamb. "I wonder if Aunt Olivia knew, on some level, that Posey

Sutherland and Jesse McGrath's lawman grandson would end up here, back in Goose Harbor. If that was meant to be, too."

Luke was still on his run when Betsy got back to the yacht after seeing Zoe West. She fixed herself a margarita and sat out on the afterdeck, only to experience a jolt of restlessness mixed with fear, the kind of powerful emotion she knew propelled people into acting on impulse, doing things they shouldn't.

She'd already set down her drink and was slipping through the plush, luxurious yacht, stealthily, her very manner giving her away. She knew she was taking a stupid risk, knew she was about to do something she had no business doing.

Prying, meddling, spying.

She was Luke's lover and his nurse, but he didn't share much about his finances with her. They weren't intimate in that way.

She came to his stateroom. It was his sanctuary. Determinedly masculine, richly appointed. She was not allowed in here unless it was with him, at his behest. He'd made that clear. He was odd, she thought, but not cruel.

The brass bell occupied its usual spot on his nightstand. She felt a rush of embarrassment and shame. How could she explain the bell to anyone? Who would understand? The bell was beyond odd. The bell veered toward cruelty.

Now that she'd come this far, she went ahead and knelt in front of a two-drawer filing cabinet, its deep, polished dark wood making it fit into the stateroom's decor. He kept it locked.

Betsy knew where to find the key. She'd learned to recognize what she might need to know if something happened to her patient, including things they might never think to tell her or want to contemplate—or hide. She considered knowing a part of what was expected of her as a caregiver.

Reaching up to the nightstand, surprised that she wasn't more nervous, she lifted the bell and tucked two fingers up inside it, where the key was taped. She'd noticed it because sometimes it affected the ring of the bell. She hoped she'd have enough time to retape it when she was finished. If not, she'd do it later, even if she had to empty a sleeping pill into Luke's herbal tea and knock him out.

But she couldn't think about that now, let it panic her.

She unlocked the cabinet and slid open the top drawer. Given his obsessive-compulsive tendencies, Luke maintained the files himself and had every one of them neatly labeled. Betsy flipped through them, expecting she'd know which one she wanted when she saw it.

She did. It was a slender folder stuck between two fatter folders, labeled *Miscellaneous.*

There were two sheets of green ledger paper inside the manila folder. Luke didn't trust computers. The writing on the pages, in black ink, was clearly his. At the top of the first page, he'd written in capitals, *T.S.*, as if that would fool anyone, and recorded three payments. The earliest was last fall, *before* Patrick West's death.

That almost stopped Betsy's heart. But the payment wasn't for that much, surely not enough for a man to commit murder.

The second two payments were made in the past week, for considerably more.

The second sheet surprised her. At the top, again in all caps, Luke had written, *S.S.M.*

Who?

Her heart jumped, and she almost yelled out in surprise. *Steven Stickney Monroe.*

"What on earth?" she whispered, shocked. Her vision blurred for a few seconds as she stared at the list of numbers, unable to make them out.

They were payments *to* Stick, not from him.

Why would Luke need to pay Stick Monroe? They both liked a poker game now and then, but Luke was too much of a control freak to get in over his head. She didn't know about Stick.

Well, they both were honest men. It was a lot of money by her standards—she added up thirty thousand dollars—but undoubtedly not by Luke's or even Stick's, although he wasn't nearly as wealthy.

A small loan between friends. It was in the same folder as the record of payments to Teddy Shelton because they both were informal, if not illegal.

Teddy worried her. She couldn't help it. He worried Judge Monroe, too.

Instead of resolving her questions, the file only added new ones. Warning herself not to jump to conclusions, Betsy quickly returned the folder to the filing cabinet, shut the drawer, locked up and returned the key to its spot inside the bell. The tape still stuck. She didn't have to replace it.

The ice had melted in her margarita when she returned to the afterdeck. She added two more cubes from the ice bucket, took a huge gulp and sat down.

Luke was out on the dock doing his post-run stretches. He was drenched in sweat, and she thought he looked nasty, hated the idea that he had secrets from her. Possibly explosive secrets. What had he paid Teddy Shelton for last *September?*

But Betsy had secrets of her own—she'd never breathed a word to him about Olivia's certainty that she knew the identity of her nephew's killer.

When he climbed onto the afterdeck and kissed her lightly, a drop of his sweat landing on her shirt, she didn't mind. Whatever he and Shelton and maybe even Stick were up to, Luke meant well, and he was very rich.

Eighteen

When Zoe decided to walk to dinner alone, J.B. didn't argue with her, not because he liked the idea but because he might kiss her again, and she could get spooked and throw him out. Then he'd have to camp out on the rocks, in the cold to keep an eye on her. He could anchor his boat off the bluff, but that made a quick reaction to any goings-on impossible.

And he'd probably have to get wet.

Either way he'd be cold.

The larger point was he didn't like what was going on in Goose Harbor. He had a bad feeling about Teddy Shelton. Betsy O'Keefe's visit. Kyle Castellane's documentary on Olivia West. None of it felt right, so not right that he'd dug out his 9 mm pistol from its locked compartment in his Jeep and clipped on his belt holster. Time to go around Goose Harbor armed.

Since he was driving, he gave Zoe a head start before finding his way along the maze of narrow streets behind the library to the yellow clapboard house she'd grown up in.

The two sisters were out back talking gardening with Stick Monroe. Christina, in jeans and a sweatshirt as a change from her café clothes, offered J.B. a glass of Chianti from a colorful pitcher on the patio table. He declined. He'd put on a jacket to cover his pistol, but if Zoe or her sister or her friend the retired judge noticed he was carrying a firearm, they didn't say anything. Which meant Zoe, at least, hadn't noticed.

He'd called Sally Meintz before he left for dinner and given her all the names. Betsy O'Keefe. Luke and Kyle Castellane. Bruce Young. Steven Stickney Monroe. And the Wests. All of them. Patrick, Zoe, Christina. Not because he didn't trust the state and local police to do the job but because he was thorough and he'd been blindsided enough this year. In February, by his father's death. Over the summer, by a violent criminal willing to kill a man in front of his own children.

Sally had typed the names into her computer in silence, then asked if he wanted her to make reservations for him somewhere else, like Costa Rica, because it sounded like he needed something new to keep him busy.

Monroe was in a better mood than last night and tipped his glass to J.B. "We were just discussing the glories of good compost. Are you a gardener, Agent McGrath?"

"Afraid not."

"Do you have any hobbies?"

"I used to fly-fish," he said. "My father was a guide in Montana."

"Is that right? That's a gentleman's sport, isn't it?"

He didn't seem to mean it as a dig, but J.B. didn't answer. Out of the corner of his eye, he could see Zoe settling into her seat, tucking her feet up under her. He wondered if she realized how close he'd come to carting her up to bed after their kiss on the porch.

All in all, Sally Meintz was probably right. He should head for Costa Rica for the rest of his vacation.

"You'd hate fly-fishing, Stick," Zoe said. "It involves water."

He grinned at her. "Ah, you're right. I like to look at the water, but I don't care for getting in it. Fresh or salt. A wonder I retired to a seaside village. You'd think I'd have picked the mountains." He gestured broadly with his Chianti glass, obviously not his first of the evening. "Agent McGrath—J.B. You don't mind if I call you J.B.?"

"Not at all."

"J.B. it is, then." Monroe was in shorts and a Princeton sweatshirt despite the dropping temperature, but he didn't seem chilled. "You can see how Goose Harbor grows on a man, can't you? But the locals—I've been coming here since I was a boy and I know better than to think I'll ever be one of them. They're a tightknit lot. One local finds out you're with the bureau, the entire town finds out. You beat one local at darts, you've beaten them all." He grinned broadly. "Especially if it's Bruce Young."

Christina sighed. "I don't know why Bruce is so popular."

"Because he's a nice guy," Zoe said. "Stick, you exaggerate the clannishness of those of us who were born and raised here."

"Be careful, Zoe. You left. You might have to reapply to admission as a native."

She laughed. "Oh, give it up, will you?"

His dark eyes twinkled. "There's a rumor J.B.'s staying with you at Olivia's."

J.B. wondered how long it would be before anyone would refer to the house Zoe now owned as hers instead of her aunt's. If it even mattered. She leaned forward and poured herself some Chianti. "If you want to know the truth, J.B. got kicked out of his inn. He spilled tea on his carpet."

"Actually," J.B. said, "Lottie Martin said there was a problem with the room."

"A rare display of diplomacy on her part," Stick said. "I heard she just got spooked having an FBI agent under her roof."

Zoe sampled her Chianti. She seemed relaxed here with Stick and her sister, maybe more than she realized. She smiled at the judge. "I decided I've burned enough bridges with local, state and federal law enforcement in the past year that the least I could do was offer the guy a room."

After he'd already helped himself to one, she could have added. But she didn't, and Stick slung a skinny arm over her shoulders, fatherlike. "I should be more careful what secrets I tell you—I seem only to have encouraged you to dive deeper into the vipers' nest, not jump out of it." He spoke lightly, a little drunkenly. "But since our

Agent McGrath unraveled a network of violent, gun-toting lunatics, he's the hero of the moment. Ah, retirement." He polished off the last of his Chianti, then smiled, letting his arm drop from Zoe's shoulders. "I don't have to worry about being neutral or politically correct. I can call a lunatic a lunatic. Operation Copperhead, I believe it was called. J.B. here was lucky to survive."

Christina blanched. "What happened?"

J.B. said nothing. Too much Chianti or not, Stick Monroe knew he was out of line.

"He had his throat slit. Not all the way, obviously, but here—" He pointed at J.B. with his glass. "You can see the scar."

"Stick," Zoe said. "For God's sake—"

He kept his attention on Christina. "I told your sister yesterday. I told her to take a look—I should be more careful of the advice I give her, shouldn't I? I'm talking out of school, of course, but so be it." He shifted his gaze to J.B., any warmth gone from the older man's eyes. "That's why you're on vacation, isn't it? Because you needed a break. You killed your attacker. Ferocious, hand-to-hand combat. It must have been terrible."

He waited, but J.B. wasn't playing this game. The man needed to go home and sleep it off.

"Unfortunately, the attacker's young children witnessed the whole thing." Stick paused, letting the stem of his glass slide between his fingers. His voice was deceptively sincere, filled with the horror of what he must have supposed J.B. had seen and done. "No wonder you were compelled to take some time off."

Zoe reached over and plucked Stick's glass from him. "No more Chianti for you. Next you'll be giving away state secrets."

The old judge shrugged without apology. "My point is—"

"I know what your point is, Stick. You want me to be careful. Thank you. I get it."

"You always were a quick study." He didn't seem bothered by Zoe's tart reaction to what he had to say—bluntness was obviously a part of their long friendship. "I meant no offense, J.B., but can you honestly say you trust your own judgment right now?"

J.B. broke his silence. "About what? Whether to order haddock chowder or crab cakes for lunch?" He refused to let Monroe provoke him. "I chose crab cakes today. Christina makes good crab cakes, don't you think, Judge?"

He didn't tell J.B. to go to hell but rose, rocking slightly on his feet, and smiled coolly. "Yes. Absolutely. Christina makes the best crab cakes in Maine. Pay no attention to me, J.B. I've had too much Chianti, and all I'm good for these days is gardening advice. Fortunately, I love it." Then he added, smiling, gentleman-like, "Gardening, that is, not giving advice."

He thanked Christina for the Chianti and kissed her and Zoe on the cheek, then gave J.B. a polite nod and headed out. He'd walked. No surprise, since he walked everywhere.

Once he was gone, Christina groaned loudly. "Well, J.B., I'll bet you're just thrilled we found out you're an

FBI agent. Too bad you're not working an undercover operation. Then none of us would know. You'd have us convinced you were a lobsterman from up north."

Zoe bit back a smile. "Never. We'd have exposed him in a heartbeat."

"Christina thinks I could pass for a Maine lobsterman," J.B. said.

"It'd be easier for you to pass as—what did Stick call them?" Christina paused a moment, obviously pretending she had to think to remember. "Violent, gun-toting lunatics. How'd you blend into that crowd?"

"Your friend Stick knows I can't go into operational details," J.B. said. "He shouldn't have said anything."

Christina, who seemed to have a slightly off-center but cheerful view of life, made a face. "Does that mean we're going to be handcuffed and gagged and carted out of here in the dead of night?"

Zoe groaned. "My sister has strange ideas about law enforcement, never mind that our father was the police chief for thirty years and I was a state detective. Makes no difference. She gets her facts from movies."

"*Serpico*," Christina said. "It's one of Kyle's favorites."

It was getting dark and the temperature was falling, but the West sisters were intent on eating outside provided it didn't snow. They went about bringing out supper and turned down J.B.'s offer to help. Christina brought him a glass of iced tea, and he thought about their encounter with Judge Monroe. J.B. saw it differently than the two women did. To them, Stick was speaking out of school because he trusted them and had gotten too far into the Chianti. To J.B., the judge had acted deliberately—it was why he'd shown up. He thought J.B. was a disaster waiting to happen. He wanted J.B. to understand that Steven Stickney Monroe, retired U.S. district court judge, would be looking out for Christina and Zoe West.

Not that they'd asked him to or needed him to but it wasn't a bad thing to have a powerful friend.

"You didn't happen to see Kyle on your way here, did you?" Christina asked as she set a salad bowl on the table.

J.B. shook his head. "No, was he planning to join you?"

"I invited him. I just called his cell phone, but no answer." She seemed put out, not worried, and let the screened back door bang hard behind her when she returned to the kitchen.

Zoe stared at the shut door and sighed. "That bastard's going to break her heart."

"Relax, big sister. If he does, Christina will handle it."

"I know." But she sighed again, more deeply. "At least I hope so. She still seems so young to me. I wasn't there for her when she needed me after Dad and Aunt Olivia died. Then I took off for Connecticut."

"Sometimes you have to save yourself."

She didn't answer. J.B. was aware of her mood slipping, noted that the pink color of her sweater seemed out of place amid the burgundy and orange leaves, but maybe she wanted it that way—maybe she didn't want to quite fit in around here. Keep her distance. Avoid getting sucked back into the vortex that had gripped her last fall.

"Anyone ever break your heart, Detective West?" he asked.

She glanced at him, a glint of humor sparking in her pretty eyes. "There was this organic farmer in Connecticut—"

He didn't let her finish, didn't let her use humor to deflect him. "You keep that heart of yours where no one can touch it, don't you? At least you try. You had it ripped out of you last year. You must have felt very exposed."

"I still do." Her voice cracked, and she had to clear her throat. "I don't trust myself, never mind anyone else."

"Some people say that's where it starts, you know. With learning to trust ourselves again."

"Do you? Do you trust yourself? After what you went through this summer?"

"I trust myself with some things. Not all."

"With me?"

He hadn't expected that. He wondered if she could see that she'd caught him off guard, but probably she did—probably she'd planned it that way. She was an experienced detective. She knew how to interview people.

Christina banged out of the house again, and Zoe shot off to help her finish getting dinner on the table, as if she regretted her question and didn't trust herself one little bit around him.

Dinner was grilled chicken, salad, rolls from the café and warm apple crisp. J.B., feeling lazy, insisted at least on refilling the two sisters' wineglasses.

Christina was still obsessing on Kyle's absence. "He must have got caught up in working on his documentary. He was filming background scenes today. The harbor, the library, the lobster pound, other places around town. Just getting a feel for what it all looks like on tape."

"Maybe he lost track of time," Zoe said.

"He wants to do a good job. He knows he can't get by on the Castellane name. In fact, the critics will probably be tougher on him because of it. Of course, he says he's not thinking about that sort of thing now—he's just thinking about the work itself." She smiled, but J.B. could see she was hurt her boyfriend hadn't shown up or called. "I'm sure you're right, Zoe. He hyperfocuses. That must be what it is."

Zoe sat back in her chair, the early evening shadows flickering on her face. "He's serious about this documentary, isn't he?"

"That's what I've been telling you. He says he wouldn't dare touch Aunt Olivia's life if he wasn't serious—she'd haunt him."

Zoe laughed. "She would, wouldn't she?"

"I wish you could have known her, J.B.," Christina said. "She was a lot like Zoe, except Zoe never wanted to stay in Goose Harbor and Aunt Olivia couldn't imagine moving. That's where she and I were alike. When I was at the New England Culinary Institute, all I wanted to do was come home and get on with my life."

"It's true," Zoe said. "It's not that I didn't like Goose Harbor, but I couldn't be a police officer in my hometown, not with my father as the chief of police. But Chris—it's like that café was meant for you."

"It's been fun. That's how I decide I'm doing what I should be doing—when it's fun. But I guess that's probably not the case with law enforcement. I mean, it can't be fun in the way making a good haddock chowder is fun."

Zoe smiled. "*Satisfying* would be a better word."

J.B. just listened. As different as they were, the two sisters seemed to get along. He'd had no siblings. Forever, it'd just been him and his father. They'd got along fine. His father had never said a word when J.B. took off, never asked him to stay. When he came back for visits, they enjoyed each other's company. J.B. had never felt the lure of going back to stay—he loved Montana but it wasn't where he belonged. He knew that.

Through dinner, whenever something reminded her that Kyle Castellane had stood her up, Christina either sank into her seat, looking hurt and defeated, or slammed something on the table as if she'd chop his balls off when she caught up with him.

J.B. took a stab at teasing her. "What about Bruce Young? I think he likes you."

Zoe and Christina both almost choked on their Chianti.

"Hey, he's a decent guy," J.B. said.

Zoe nodded. "He's a great guy, but—J.B., the reason you've been able to beat Bruce at darts as many times as you have is because if he's not on the water or at the lobster pound, he's at Perry's."

"That's because he doesn't have a good woman in his life."

Both sisters groaned. "Bruce likes lobstering and boating," Christina said. "Women for him are an afterthought. He's one of those guys who'll suddenly fall for someone and get married within a month."

J.B. got up and started clearing the table. "If Bruce couldn't make it for dinner, he'd call."

He'd pushed his luck. Christina snatched a plate out of his hand. "I'll clean up. You and Zoe run along. It's a nice night. Enjoy it. Go play darts."

"Christina, I apologize." Never good at apologies, J.B. sounded stiff and awkward even to himself. "That was supposed to be funny, but it was out of line."

Zoe snorted. "It was way the hell out of line."

"Just *go,* both of you," Christina said, and fled inside.

"Real nice, McGrath," Zoe muttered under her breath. She started after her sister, but J.B. grabbed her by the elbow. She glared at him. "What?"

"Let's do as she asked and get out of here."

"We can't leave her with this mess—"

"Zoe."

"Okay." She pulled her arm free. "Maybe you did Chris a favor in ticking her off. She was looking for an excuse to let off some steam. She'll bang around in the kitchen, and Kyle'll show up—" She broke off with a shudder. "Yeah, let's get out of here." She called to her sister, "Dinner was great, Chris! I'll see you tomorrow."

There was no answer from the house. Zoe, still clearly reluctant to abandon her sister in this mood, led the way back to the driveway. The sun had gone down, darkness coming fast. She slid into the passenger seat of J.B.'s Jeep. "Lesson learned? No teasing about the boyfriend."

J.B. climbed in next to her. "You had it right, Zoe. That guy's going to break your sister's heart."

But she was staring at him. "Damn. That's a 9 mm you're packing, McGrath. What for?"

"Zoe, I can carry a firearm on or off duty."

"I *know.* But you're on vacation."

He didn't answer and instead checked his cell phone. Luckily, he had a message. A reprieve from explaining to Zoe West, who'd been fired for not carrying her firearm on duty, why he'd decided to carry his off duty.

In a brief message, Sally instructed him to call her back. He did so, and wasn't surprised to have her pick up. "Working late?" he said.

"I have my cot set up in case I had to wait all night for you to call."

He smiled. "Sarcasm doesn't suit you, Sal."

"Did you know that Zoe West was accepted into the academy and dropped out before her first day?"

"I did know that."

"I thought you might. And Patrick West was the chief of police in Goose Harbor until last year, when he was shot and killed? You knew that?"

"I did."

"Am I aiding and abetting your insubordination?"

"No, ma'am."

"Luke Castellane's father committed suicide. He tells people it was a heart attack."

"Interesting. Anything else?"

"Steven Stickney Monroe sentenced Teddy Shelton to seven years in federal prison."

Christ. The local cops either knew and hadn't said or didn't know because they hadn't gotten the break J.B. had. Or they'd checked out the connection and it was nothing. "Anything else?"

"I love Victor Castellane's films," she said, and hung up.

"What was that all about?" Zoe asked.

J.B.'s undercover training and experience kept him from registering any reaction to Sally Meintz's information. Or maybe it didn't.

"J.B.?"

"Nothing. I don't scare anybody anymore."

"Sure." She sat back, dubious. "I believe that. If it's any consolation, you scared the hell out of me."

She wasn't serious. He appreciated that. "Was it the kiss or showing up armed?"

"Take your pick."

Nineteen

❧❧❧❧

Zoe couldn't remember the last time she'd actually been inside Perry's. She wasn't much of a drinker or dart-player, and its fare of fried fish and thick slabs of meat, although popular, wasn't what her diet needed. An evening on Olivia's porch suited her more. One reason, as J.B. would no doubt inform her, that she'd never really had her heart broken.

Bruce Young was tossing darts and nursing an ale the color of mud. He waved a hand at J.B. "You want a game?" Then he saw her and grinned, her personal nemesis since high school. "Hey, Zoe. Nice dive this morning. Water cold?"

"About the same as the air temperature," she said.

"That's not saying much in October. Come on, you can play a game, too." He walked over to the dartboard and, holding his beer, used his free hand to pull out the darts. "Beer?"

"No, thanks. We just had dinner at Christina's."

"How's her new door?"

Zoe had to smile at his infectious good humor. "Her new door's just fine. She had the one at the café fixed— it didn't need to be replaced."

"Have you seen Kyle Castellane around?" J.B. asked.

Bruce handed J.B. one set of darts, thrust another set at Zoe. "Nope."

Zoe winced at J.B.'s diplomatic skills. Since Bruce had a crush on Christina, why not ask him out of the blue about her current boyfriend? She singled out one of the darts, its tip slightly bent. "He didn't show up for dinner."

"He's been filming around town. He was out at the lobster pound." Bruce set down his beer and fired a dart, hitting an outside score. "I heard you had a chat with Teddy Shelton while you were kayaking."

"I didn't know you were renting him your cottage," Zoe said. "Hell, Bruce, I hope you're not charging him much. As handy as you are, you'd think you'd at least fix the steps so the guy doesn't break his neck."

"Teddy? He doesn't care. No point putting time and money into the place. I'll just wait and tear it down when I have the money together to build something new."

J.B. suddenly threw a dart and hit the bull's-eye. Zoe tried not to look impressed. Without looking at Bruce, he asked, "How well do you know Shelton?"

"Not well. I don't keep tabs on him. Jesus, loosen up, you two. You look like a couple of kick-ass cops."

J.B.'s intensity was palpable. Zoe expected it had something to do with his phone call. She knew what he was doing—checking names with a cooperative source in Washington.

Bruce took a big gulp of his beer. "That bull's-eye doesn't count, McGrath. It's not your turn. So, what's the deal? You spending another night at Olivia's?"

Zoe gritted her teeth. The two of them, she thought. "If anyone asks, tell them he's my houseguest."

"People are starting to think you two knew each other from before—"

"Don't start with me, Bruce."

He grinned at her. "Touchy, touchy. I guess it's just as well McGrath didn't end up camping out on your boat, in case someone forgot it's my boat and tossed in a Molotov cocktail."

"Bruce!" Zoe was lining up her darts on a nearby table but thought she might take one and throw it at him. "That's no way to talk."

He was unrepentant. "J.B. knows I'm kidding, right, J.B.? An alert, trained federal agent—someone tries to torch your boat with you in it, you'd go overboard and catch the bad guys before dawn."

J.B. had his remaining darts neatly folded into his palm. "I'd keep that in mind should the pyromaniac in you decide to come out."

"No pyro in me. I don't even like lighting the grill."

Although technically it still wasn't his turn, J.B. threw another dart in a move that was smooth and destined not to make him any friends. It didn't hit the bull's-eye but struck close to it. Zoe didn't know much about dart scoring, but he seemed satisfied. He stood back, fingering another dart, which, despite her best efforts, struck her as sexual.

"I should check in with Chris and see if Kyle turned up."

"It's dark," Bruce said. "He should have finished his filming by now."

"When did you see him last?" Zoe asked.

"Couple hours ago. I guess he must want film of an old-time Maine lobster pound for background. I don't have a lot of faith in this documentary."

J.B. laid his two remaining darts on the table next to Zoe's. "Rain check, Bruce. Or you can win by default."

"I'll take the rain check. I want to beat your ass fair and square, McGrath."

But Zoe knew Bruce's heart wasn't in it—he liked playing darts. He didn't give a damn about winning. He'd never been particularly competitive. She sometimes thought that if he'd been more assertive, Christina might have realized he was serious about her, not just joking around.

As they left, J.B. took such long strides across the bar that Zoe practically had to run to keep up with him. She was sore from kayaking, tired from getting dunked and on edge from everything that had gone on since Christina had first called her about someone breaking into her house.

And taking nothing, Zoe thought. Hurting no one.

It was something to keep in mind. She could be on edge more because she was back home for the first time in a year, not because of any real dangers—or perhaps because of J.B., his intensity, her reaction to him.

The temperature had dropped precipitously, a taste of winter in the cold, clear night air. It was fully dark now, the stars and sliver of a moon sparkling over the harbor.

A beautiful day, now a beautiful, freezing night. With a shiver, Zoe climbed into McGrath's Jeep. She was aware of how close he was. What if Stick was right and he was more out of control than she thought? What if she was letting herself get caught up in his need to find a new adrenaline rush to give himself an excuse not to have to confront his demons? She knew what that was like.

But she didn't think that was what was going on, at least not entirely.

"I assume we're going to check on Kyle," she said. "Do you know the way?"

He gave a curt nod.

He drove faster than seemed necessary to her. She borrowed his cell phone to check with Christina—no Kyle. Her sister had tried his apartment and his father's yacht, but no sign of him. She wanted to call the police. Zoe reported what Bruce had said about seeing Kyle at the lobster pound.

"You're going out there? It's dark, Zoe. He can't be there, unless—" She stopped herself. "I know I'm thinking the worst because of the break-ins. It's all just so creepy."

"Chris, if you don't want to be alone, call Stick or Bruce or someone."

"I'll be fine. Let me know, okay?"

Even with the windows closed, Zoe could smell the low tide as J.B. pulled into the small dirt lobster-pound lot. Bruce's cottage was next to it, through a tangle of small brush and trees on the south side, then, bordering the cottage, a hundred acres of sprawling, state-protected salt marsh and sand beach. Zoe hoped Kyle hadn't gone wandering and gotten himself lost out there. It'd be morning for sure before they found him.

J.B. shut off his headlights. The area was dark and quiet, no sign of Kyle or his black BMW. Zoe rolled down her window and listened, hearing only the gentle lapping of the water as the tide started to come up again. The air was downright frigid, and she half wished she'd brought her parka.

She rolled up her window. "We should check with Shelton. Maybe he's seen Kyle."

J.B. sighed. "He could be at Perry's by now, trying to figure out how to tell Christina he got carried away with his documentary and stood her up."

"And she'll forgive him, you know." Zoe looked out at the stars sparkling on the expanse of dark water. "Well, maybe she should. I admit I've never been fond of the Castellanes. You've only seen Luke around town? You havn't met him?"

"That's right."

"My aunt was more tolerant of his quirks than I ever have been, not that I've had that much to do with him."

J.B. still didn't move his Jeep. "What about your father?"

"He stayed neutral. 'Luke is what he is,' he'd say." Zoe pointed to a stand of trees, a blackish-purple silhouette against the ambient light of the stars and moon. "There's a shortcut to the cottage over by those trees. It's not much of a road, but your Jeep can handle it."

J.B. started up the Jeep's engine again. The shortcut

was, in fact, just a rutted strip of sand, marsh grass and gravel, but the Jeep bounced over it without a problem and came to a stop behind the cottage. Its back-door light was on, but Teddy Shelton's truck was gone—and, again, there was no sign of Kyle or his BMW.

Zoe pushed open her door and stood out on the dirt driveway, the cold air impossible to ignore. She shivered. "Maybe Shelton decided to take off after he had both of us sneaking up on him."

J.B. got out. "I thought you just saw him by accident."

She smiled over the Jeep roof at him. "I did. I'll go knock on the door—"

"Hang on."

But she didn't wait for him. She trotted up the back steps and peered through the back door's cracked window. She tried the knob. "It's not locked. Bruce knows we're out here. He'd expect me to make sure nothing's wrong and the place is secure." Bruce wouldn't give a damn if the place spontaneously combusted, but Zoe wanted an excuse to go inside.

J.B. mounted the steps behind her. He nodded. "Go."

His mood was so serious and grim, Zoe wouldn't have been surprised if he drew his weapon. But he didn't, and she pushed on the door. It stuck, and she had to put her shoulder to it to get it to budge.

She reached along the paneled wall to her right and flipped the switch for the overhead fluorescent in the galley kitchen. It slowly flickered on. "Looks like no one's home," she said.

Dirty dishes were stacked in the sink, and a half-played game of clock solitaire was laid out on the table. Without a word, J.B. checked the back bedroom and the bathroom and returned in less than a minute, still grim-faced. "Nothing. Bed's unmade, used towels on the bathroom floor. No personal items or a suitcase or backpack."

"Maybe Shelton did clear out. That's not a good development."

Zoe walked over to the picture window. She couldn't see the view, just her reflection and that of the flickering kitchen light. She thought she looked shaken and ragged, a ghost of the law enforcement officer she'd been even just a few months ago.

"Forget it," she muttered. "You look around. I'll wait in the Jeep."

"What's wrong?"

"Nothing."

She turned abruptly, running into the solid wall that was J. B. McGrath. She was so preoccupied, she hadn't noticed him move toward her. That wasn't good. What if he'd been Shelton? Someone else? She was out of practice. Her head wasn't in the right place. She glanced away, trying to quash her agitation and uneasiness. "I don't think I can handle being back here."

"You are handling it. It's just not as easy as you'd like it to be."

"If I cause anyone to get hurt—"

"Zoe."

She held up a hand. "It's okay. I'll snap out of it. It's been a long day." Being that close to him got to her, and she shot across the ancient linoleum floor to the door out to the deck. "I'll take a look outside and meet you back at the Jeep."

She walked out onto the deck, its floorboards soft and sagging, but the below-freezing temperature quickly penetrated her cotton sweater. Crossing her arms for added warmth, she ventured down the steps to the narrow footpath cut through the tall grass. The shallow cove was straight ahead, the water was so far away now, just past low tide, that she could barely hear it. She could smell the salt-drenched mud and sand, the seaweed. The stars and moon were breathtaking sprinkled across the night sky.

J.B. had followed her, his tall figure casting a long shadow across a stretch of moonlit path. The kitchen and porch lights in back didn't do much out here. Zoe paused, letting her eyes adjust to the unrelenting darkness.

"I don't suppose you undercover FBI agents have built-in night vision equipment?"

"I've got some goggles in my Jeep."

She glanced back at him. "You know, I have no idea if you're serious or not. I'm going to guess not. Why would an undercover agent need night vision?"

"We like our toys."

"What about a simple flashlight?"

She saw his smile. "I have that, too."

But he reached out suddenly and touched her arm, his other hand on the grip of his pistol, his eyes focused on the stretch of light woods between the cottage and the lobster pound.

"Did you hear something?" Zoe whispered.

Then she heard it herself, a rustling sound. And a moan.

J.B. drew his pistol, touched her shoulder in unspoken communication she recognized—he'd investigate, she'd stay put. Basic. He was the armed law enforcement officer. She wasn't.

Then came a pained, male voice. "Ah, hell. Zoe? Zoe, is that you? It's me, Kyle. I could use a hand before I freaking freeze to death."

Zoe lunged forward, but J.B.'s grip tightened on her elbow. He shook his head, and she understood. She'd responded like a friend, not a cop. "Are you alone?" he called to Kyle.

"Yeah. I think so."

"Can you walk?"

"I just got the crap beat out of me—ah, shit. I'm covered in mud." But they could hear him moving in the brush, making his way toward them. "What a cesspool."

J.B. didn't budge. "Just keep walking."

Zoe could see Kyle now, a solitary figure emerging from behind a nearby spruce. He stumbled onto the path, and she caught him around his thin waist, taking most of his weight. He wasn't wearing a jacket and was cold to the touch. When he looked up, a ray of moonlight struck his face. It was battered, bruised and bleeding. A mess.

"Good God, Kyle," Zoe said, "what happened?"

His lower lip was split, his nose was bloody, his left eye was swollen. His right cheek looked bruised and raw. J.B. kept his hand on the grip of his 9 mm. Kyle managed to hold up a shaking hand. "Relax, okay? Both of you. He's gone. That guy, Shelton. He punched me out and took off."

"How long ago?" J.B. asked.

"Awhile. I don't know." He brushed at his bloody nose with the back of his hand. He'd started to shiver uncontrollably. "I've been pretty out of it."

"Come on," Zoe said. "Let's get you inside and get some ice for these cuts, although you'd think you wouldn't need any as frozen as you are. J.B. has a cell phone. He can call an ambulance and the police—"

"I'm okay. I don't want to make a stink. Shelton overreacted, but I had it coming. He caught me sneaking around his truck—he wasn't in the mood to ask questions. I don't blame him. For all he knew, I was going to shoot him and steal the damn thing."

Not likely, Zoe thought, but she let it go. This wasn't the time to push him for answers. He was in pain and cold, his teeth chattering. She helped him onto the porch, aware of J.B. behind her, on high alert.

Once she got him inside, Kyle sank onto Bruce's duct-taped couch and moaned again, drool oozing over his cut lip as he continued to shiver. His khakis were soaked and muddy at the knees, his sweatshirt smeared with blood from his lip and nose.

J.B. took a musty blanket off the back of a chair and laid it on Kyle's lap. "Looks like Shelton hit you more than once."

"Twice that I remember. I don't know, maybe three times."

His speech was slightly slurred, but Zoe attributed it

to his swollen lip and shivering. She found an ancient ice tray in the freezer, whacked it on the counter and dumped the ice in the sink, then scooped a half-dozen cubes into a dish rag and handed it to him.

"You should have that lip and eye looked at," J.B. said. "Your nose might be broken, but I doubt it. What about your teeth?"

"I didn't lose any." Kyle placed the ice pack on his lip. "I'll be fine. It was stupid, the whole thing. I mean, the guy saw me and went apeshit."

"Did he say anything?" Zoe asked.

"Yeah. He said, 'Get the fuck away from my truck.'"

J.B. didn't smile. "Then what happened?"

"I told him, 'Yeah, man, cool, I'm moving,' but he had me by the arm. Jerked me around and pounded my face. I mean, shit. I'm no fighter. But I told you, I'm not messing with him—I'm not pressing charges."

Zoe sat next to Kyle on the couch. He seemed nonplussed more than angry or scared, as if he still didn't quite understand, couldn't absorb, what had happened to him. "Christina missed you at dinner, and Bruce saw you out at the lobster pound shortly before dinner. Was that when you ran into Shelton? Around dinnertime?"

"I guess. I don't know. I think I was knocked out." He yawned, more a reaction to stress and exposure, Zoe thought, than tiredness, but she could see the simple motion caused him pain. He winced and moaned in pain, licking along the edge of his lip where it was cut, the blood mostly dried. "You know, one minute Shelton's beating the shit out of me, next thing, I'm facedown in the mud."

Zoe frowned. "Kyle, if you lost consciousness or were incoherent for even a few minutes, you need to see a doctor."

"I don't know, maybe I was just in shock or something." He moved the ice up to his eye. "How bad do I look?"

"Pretty bad," Zoe said.

She could feel J.B. taking in every word, every nuance as he stood motionless in the middle of the room. He'd returned his pistol to its holster. "Did you hear Shelton leave?" he asked.

Obviously losing energy, Kyle sank back against the couch. "I don't think so, no."

"Where was his truck when he saw you?"

"In the driveway."

"The cottage driveway?"

"Yeah."

J.B. didn't relent, but his tone was steady, nonthreatening if not gentle. "What were you doing here?"

"I was filming—" Kyle paused, bolting up straight as if he had a fresh surge of energy. "That's right! I dropped my camera. The fucker came at me, and I dropped it—I didn't even think of hitting him with it. It must still be out there. I was filming at the lobster pound, then I walked over here, because I—I don't remember. I saw a hawk or something."

"Where's your car?" J.B. asked.

"My car? Oh, yeah. It's down by the boat launch. I didn't want it to get in the way. You know these lobster guys. They'd bulldoze a BMW right over if it got in their way."

That explained why they hadn't seen it, Zoe thought. She eased to her feet, every inch of her body telling her she'd already overexerted today. Her shoulders ached from kayaking, her legs were tired, and she was sleepy, ready to collapse into a warm bed and get unconscious. But she had to feel better than Kyle did. She held out her hand for him. "We can take you to the emergency room—"

"I'm *fine*."

She didn't argue. "And if you don't want to press charges against Teddy Shelton, that's your prerogative, but you need to tell the police what happened."

"Why?"

He took her hand reluctantly, and she helped him back to his feet. "Because if you don't, Special Agent McGrath here will. Or I will. Either way, the police need to have a chat with our Mr. Shelton."

Twenty

The Castellane kid didn't let his injuries stop him from arguing with Zoe all the way back to the village. She wanted him to talk to the police. He didn't want to do it. J.B. was in favor of hauling him straight to the police station and letting Goose Harbor's finest sort out what went on tonight. Zoe was more willing to compromise.

"It was just a fight," Kyle said. He was warmer now, his speech less slurred. His lip had started to bleed again, probably because he wouldn't shut up. "Can't a couple of guys get into a fight anymore? Why involve the police?"

"They need to be aware of how Teddy Shelton reacted to you," Zoe said.

J.B. debated leaving them both out of the decision-making and pulling up to the police station. It was next to the town library with its Olivia West Reading Room. What was the kid going to do, jump out of a moving car?

He threatened to. "If you try to take me to the police, I swear I'll jump out of here. A few more bruises aren't going to matter."

Good, J.B. thought. I'll provide them. He was ready to call Kyle's bluff, but he reined in his irritation and passed the call off to Zoe. Her town, her sister's boyfriend.

She caved. "Fine. We'll drop you off at your father's yacht."

"What for? He'll have a heart attack or blame me for bleeding on his rug. Come on, Zoe. Give me a break. I just want to clean up and crawl into bed. Drop me off at my apartment or Christina's. My father goes to bed at ten, anyway."

Zoe shook her head. "I'm not leaving you alone or with my sister. What if Teddy comes back to have another crack at you? Have you thought of that?"

When he drove into the parking lot at the docks, J.B. saw that Christina's café was lit up. She must have spotted his Jeep, because she ran out and waved them down.

Zoe glanced back at Kyle, her expression neutral— her ten years in law enforcement finally showed. "She's worried sick about you."

J.B. braked, but before he could come to a full stop, Zoe had the door open. "Chris, it's okay. Kyle's with us. He got in a fight—"

She saw him and cried out. "*Kyle!* Oh, my God, look at you! Who did this?" Ignoring Zoe, Christina reached for him in the back. "What happened? God, Kyle, you're *bleeding*. Zoe, why aren't you at the hospital?"

"He won't go."

She went through the bare bones of the story while Christina clucked and sobbed over her beaten-up boyfriend. He seized his moment and slipped out of the

Jeep. J.B. could have stopped him, but what was the point? The kid wasn't cooperating. He was enjoying the drama and attention and presuming he could get away with his rendition of events.

It wouldn't work. J.B. would see to it.

"Let me get you some fresh ice—I've got a freezer full." Christina looked at her sister. "It's okay if we go?"

Zoe thought a moment, then nodded. "The police are going to want to talk to Kyle, but—sure, go on. Your door's fixed, right? Lock it. And call me if you need anything."

J.B. considered his options, decided not one of them was appealing and kept his mouth shut. For the time being. He stood out in the parking lot, noting how quiet it was now that it was dark and below freezing. No tourists, no night walkers, no yacht parties. Goose Harbor must be a different place in late fall and winter.

Christina hung on to Kyle's waist, steadying him, as they walked to the café. "I can't believe you got in a fight with Teddy Shelton. He's twice your size!"

Kyle remarked that he'd held his own.

Another version of what'd happened tonight. Another lie.

J.B. could see Zoe gritting her teeth, but she said nothing. They both got back into the Jeep, and he started it up, glancing over at her. "Think your sister'll ask you to be maid of honor at the wedding?"

"Go to hell, McGrath."

He grinned. "And I was worried you were afraid of me now that I'm armed."

That brought a grudging smile. "Not a chance. You know where the police station is?"

"I do."

He had no trouble finding a parking space on Main Street in front of the station. The village was deserted at night. He leaned back in his seat. "Tell them they can get in touch with me if they want to." He gave her his cell phone number. "They can call anytime."

"You're not going in with me?"

He shook his head. "No."

"Why not? You had the run-in with Shelton yesterday. You're the armed FBI agent."

"It wasn't a run-in. I told him I thought he was having a heart attack. He blew me off." He glanced over at her, aware he'd aroused her suspicions. "Suggest they look into Teddy Shelton's prison record. Who the judge was at his trial."

Even in the darkness, he could see how pale she was. "J.B.—"

"Let them figure it out, Zoe. We need to pull back."

"Stick—was he the judge? Is he in danger?"

"I'll wait here."

She waited another two seconds, but he didn't budge. Without a word, she pushed open her door and climbed out. He saw her hesitate. Never mind the story she had to tell about tonight, that she'd offended the people she had to tell it to—the building itself was where her father had worked her entire life. It had to hold countless memories.

J.B. didn't envy her.

It took her ten minutes to get the job done and get out of there. She tore open the Jeep door, flopped into her seat and burst into tears, lowering her head so he couldn't see her as she sobbed, quietly, miserably.

"Even rougher than you thought it'd be, wasn't it?"

She didn't answer, and he didn't expect her to.

With her bent over like that, her sweater rode up a few inches, revealing the top edge of what looked like a tattoo of a pink beach rose just above her left hip.

J.B. inhaled a deep breath, started the engine and drove slowly back to Olivia West's house on the bluff.

Zoe jumped out before he'd come to a full stop. By the time he followed her into the house, she was running up the stairs as if the hounds of hell were on her.

It hadn't been so easy, these first days back home.

J.B. found a heavy crystal decanter of Scotch on the sideboard in the dining room. He got a glass from the cupboard and splashed in about half an inch and smelled it. Seemed fine. Olivia West died on her one hundred and first birthday. It was safe to assume the Scotch hadn't been around for more than a century.

He stood at the window and drank, and he thought of a woman out here on this bluff alone for the better part of a hundred years. If his grandmother had stayed, would she have lived longer? Would she and Olivia West have remained friends and gone to church suppers and played bridge together?

J.B.'s father might have become a lobsterman.

More likely he'd never have been born.

Yet nothing in her letters to her friend in Montana

suggested Olivia was lonely out here. She never married, but from everything J.B. had learned about her in his days in Goose Harbor, she hadn't lived a solitary life.

He thought of Zoe's writings and wondered if that was what she'd run from as much as anything—not her father's murder, but her aunt's death, inheriting the rights to Jen Periwinkle, as if Olivia was daring her to write, daring her to embrace a different kind of life than Zoe had imagined for herself.

Must have been scary, picturing herself sitting out here on this rock bluff all alone for the next seventy years.

J.B. finished the last of his Scotch.

Well, what did he know? At least it gave him something to think about besides what the rest of Zoe's rose tattoo looked like.

"You beat up my son? What the fuck's the matter with you?"

Teddy yawned at Luke's hissing. The guy was frothing at the damn mouth, but who was on a toasty-warm yacht and who was freezing his ass off in a rusting truck? Teddy was cold and uncomfortable, stuck in the boonies for the night. He'd parked out in the salt marsh, probably right on top of a rare bird's nest or something, but before he showed his face again, he wanted to make sure the kid didn't go to the police.

"It was a misunderstanding." Teddy figured it was the best spin he could put on it. Misunderstanding, hell. The shitbird was snooping in his truck. Two minutes later, and he'd have been into the apple crate. He got what was coming to him. Any jury'd see it Teddy's way. "He's okay?"

"He's in pain. Betsy took a look at him. He didn't want to wake us, but Christina West insisted. They were supposed to have dinner together, and she became concerned when he didn't show up. Zoe and that FBI agent heard his car was spotted at the lobster pound and investigated. A lucky thing."

Do-gooders. Bored cops. Pains in his ass. "Your kid wasn't hurt that bad. He could have driven out."

"Apparently he was so incoherent from the beating you gave him that he couldn't find his way back to his car."

"Nah, he just got lost in the dark. He pressing charges?"

"No."

"I didn't realize it was your kid until it was too late."

"Kyle has a natural, unrestrained curiosity."

Kyle was a spoiled brat, but Teddy said nothing. An owl hooted nearby. At least he thought it was an owl. Somebody had once told him moose were out here, too. Just what he needed. A goddamn moose sticking its nose in his window. The moose he might shoot.

"Teddy, hiring you wasn't illegal, but people won't understand if it comes out. If it does, they'll learn about the mistake we made last fall."

The gun, Teddy thought. The Smith & Wesson .38 revolver that Luke had sold him last September. For such a finicky guy, Luke was lax in keeping up with Maine gun laws. Like he wasn't really there for months at a time on his yacht and didn't have to do the required paperwork. But his mistake was worse than not having the right permits—he'd sold a gun to a convicted felon.

His voice was calmer now, but still with that snotty undertone. "That's why confidentiality is such an important part of our agreement. It's why I'd like to offer you a bonus when we're finished with this job. And another bonus if you'll agree to leave town and never contact me again."

"How much?"

"Thirty and fifty."

Not bad. "Fifty and fifty."

"Done."

There wasn't even a hint of relief in Castellane's voice. Teddy held his knuckles up to his mouth and in the moonlight saw they were swollen and cut from where he'd slugged Kyle Castellane. He licked on one cut. "What's next?"

"The same mission. Maintain the status quo."

Luke clicked off.

Teddy tried to get comfortable in the front of his truck, but there was just no way. He pulled one of the tarps off his guns and ammo and used it as a blanket. It smelled like oil and dead fish, and it wasn't very warm.

The owl wasn't going to quit.

He'd examine his options in the morning. Even if he ended up having to clear out of Gooseshit Harbor, it wouldn't be until he'd had some sleep—and it wouldn't be until he got his hundred grand bonuses.

* * *

Zoe sat cross-legged in the middle of her bed and worked on her milk-gray scarf until she thought she'd go blind.

She didn't drop any stitches. She kept checking.

It was after midnight, and she'd heard J.B.'s door close down the hall. She hadn't meant to be rude, but she looked like hell when she cried, and what could he do but feel awkward and helpless, which she hated? But now she had a headache, and her sinuses were clogged. She didn't know when she'd feel like sleeping.

Donna Jacobs, the acting chief of police and forty-five-year-old mother of three, was in her office when Zoe arrived. That was a surprise, but Jacobs said she was going through paperwork and listened to Zoe without interruption.

Then Jacobs thanked her for the heads-up and showed her the door.

If the local police had any information on Teddy Shelton, Donna Jacobs wasn't saying. If she had misgivings about having an FBI agent and ex-detective on the loose in her town, she kept them to herself, too. She was professional and serious, and she treated Zoe as she would any other private citizen, never mind that she had her job because Zoe's father was dead.

It was exactly what Donna Jacobs should have done.

And it had nothing to do with why Zoe had dissolved into tears once she got back to the car. The emotion of walking into the police station where her father had worked for so many years, had overwhelmed her. That simple, that awful.

She was both surprised and pleased that J.B. had summoned the patience and grace to leave her alone and let her pull herself together, because she knew he had about a million and one questions about what had occurred with Kyle and Teddy Shelton out at Bruce's cottage.

She'd have to tell Bruce that J. B. McGrath, grandson of a Maine native, wasn't as obnoxious as people thought.

She remembered his startling, toe-curling, spine-melting kiss on the porch and smiled to herself, the tension easing out of her body. He'd come to Goose Harbor to recuperate after a grueling undercover operation, one that had ended with him having to kill or be killed in front of children.

He really *had* picked Goose Harbor because of his Maine roots.

More or less. Her father's unsolved murder and her aunt's death on its heels must have helped settle it.

The scar on his throat told her how close he'd come to being another name on the FBI Honor Roll.

She counted her stitches one last time.

Ninety-nine. It was supposed to be a hundred. She'd unraveled back to where she'd screwed up and started from there—and she'd dropped a stitch.

"No!"

She held up her scarf-in-the-making and saw immediately where she'd gone wrong, about four rows back.

That was the good thing about knitting. She could pinpoint what she'd done wrong and go back and get it right this time. If only life were like that.

Twenty-One

Gold-tinted marsh grass moved gracefully with the morning breeze in the protected area south of the lobster pound and the cottage Teddy Shelton had rented. The fingers of saltwater were a dark blue under a sky dotted with puffs of fair-weather clouds. A migrating hawk flew high overhead. It was all a pretty sight, but J.B. was focused on Teddy Shelton's truck. Yellow birch leaves had fallen onto its windshield.

Once he found out about last night, Bruce Young had gone on the hunt for Shelton so he could throw him out of the cottage, never mind that it appeared he'd already left voluntarily. J.B. ran into him at the lobster pound and suggested he do the driving. Nobody, even Bruce, liked the idea of Shelton beating up an unarmed twenty-two-year-old without more provocation—as much as they didn't mind the idea of Kyle Castellane with a fat lip.

Bruce was the one who'd spotted the tire tracks in the protected marsh's delicate, picturesque landscape, most of it without trails. The tracks led them straight to the truck. It was locked. Bruce was willing to crowbar it, but J.B. dissuaded him.

"It's a long walk to town," Bruce said. "Maybe he stole a boat at the lobster pound or hitched a ride with one of the guys. I'll check."

J.B. nodded. "I'll drop you off. Let me know what you find out."

When they arrived back at the lobster pound, Bruce jumped out of the Jeep, then hesitated. His coat was open, a cold breeze lifting the ends of his hair. "You sure Kyle's okay?"

"I saw him at breakfast," J.B. said. "He's colorful, but he'll be fine."

"Hate to see anyone go through something like that. Think he's not pressing charges because he's scared Shelton'll find him and finish the job?"

J.B. had thought this one over on his own. "I think it's because he didn't tell us the whole story."

Bruce nodded. "Maybe he wasn't just standing next to Teddy's truck."

"Could be."

"Teddy could have freaked once he realized he'd knocked the shit out of a Castellane. He could be long gone, you know." Bruce exhaled, obviously not relishing this development. "Christina? She okay? I didn't stop by the café this morning."

J.B. had breakfast there with Zoe, who was distant, not cool, just not that approachable. Since he had things on his mind, too, J.B. didn't mind eating his eggs and home fries in silence. She'd had a goat-cheese-and-chive omelet. One of the lobstermen teased her that year she'd spent in Connecticut was showing. Christina had seemed very pale and drawn, even more tired, just going through the motions of her café routine.

"She's hanging in there," J.B. said.

"Yeah. Well, I'll see what I can find out about that jackass Teddy."

"Don't go up against him, Bruce."

He grinned. "What, you think if he can beat the crap out of Kyle, I'm a goner for sure?"

"No, I think he's probably armed to the teeth. He likes guns, Bruce. That's what put him in prison."

Bruce shook his head in mock amazement. Not much got to the guy. "You think the FBI's got a file on me?"

"If not, I'm making one. Keep me posted."

"I'd ask you to do the same, but I know you won't."

Fifteen minutes later, J.B. was back at Olivia West's house, standing on the bluff as Zoe dragged her lime-green kayak through the rose bushes, which made him think of her rose tattoo, which in turn brought up his long, tortured night. Not good. He was in deep with this woman. It was like having someone grab him by the ankle and jerk him over a cliff. He was plunging head-first, no bottom in sight, anything possible, from a smooth dive into the water at the bottom to smashing himself to death on the rocks.

He stood at the edge of the waist-high roses. "Glutton for punishment, aren't you?"

"You know how it is." Her kayak was at her feet, half pushing her down the steep path. She had on leggings, a turtleneck and fleece vest, her orange life vest hanging open. She squinted up at him, the sun high and bright above her. "You've got to get right back up on the horse again. If I get dumped out today, I might consider a new hobby."

"Do you have another kayak?"

That took her by surprise. "What?"

He smiled. "Another kayak. I can go with you."

"Have you ever been kayaking?"

"Nope. Looks easy enough."

"This cockiness of yours is why people around here want to set fire to your boat. I guess compared to what you do for a living, probably kayaking does look easy." She sighed, gestured toward the house. "There's one in the garage. It's shocking pink."

"Not going to let me use the green one?"

She grinned at him. "Your reputation might benefit from a pink kayak."

He found it in the back of the garage and dragged it, a paddle and a life vest out to the path. Zoe was lifting her lightweight kayak over a stretch of jagged rocks. She wasn't doing this because she got dunked yesterday— she was doing it to make sure she minded her own business and stayed out of the police's way. Let them find Teddy Shelton and talk to him.

J.B. knew he should follow her lead, but that wasn't why he'd offered to join her. He didn't want her out on the water alone. It wasn't a protective impulse so much as a common-sense one. Zoe could take care of herself, but she wouldn't naturally or easily regard anyone or anything in Goose Harbor as dangerous. J.B. didn't have that problem.

He made his way down the steep rock path and slid his kayak over the gravel beach. The air was clear and ice-cold down by the water. If he didn't take to kayaking, it could be a rough few hours.

Zoe zipped up her life vest. "Quick lesson. Wear your vest. Put it on properly. If you get into trouble, blow the whistle."

"Got it."

Next she demonstrated how to hold her paddle. "You want to stay centered in your boat. Don't lean with your shoulders or your torso or you'll go over. Just find that center line and hold it."

J.B. noticed the dark circles under her eyes. He doubted she'd slept well. "I don't want to capsize."

"Then don't lean."

Next she showed him how to paddle. Stay centered. Use his shoulders. Develop a rhythm. To turn, paddle on the opposite side he wanted the boat to go. She showed him how to do a power turn to reverse direction, but he didn't know if he'd remember that maneuver. She said it was easy. Natural.

"We'll stay in calm waters, close to shore," she said. "The hard part is when you run into winds, currents, big swells, rapids, swirls, unexpected rocks. You should have a proper lesson, but at least I'll be with you if something happens." She grinned at him. "Then I can blow my whistle."

"Okay, Captain, let's launch."

"Another thing. You'll get wet. It's unavoidable. You'd do better in a wet suit, especially on a day like today. But so would I."

He had on khakis, a canvas shirt and his boat shoes. If he got wet, he'd stay wet. He noticed her outfit emphasized the shape of her slim body. "That'd be something. You in a wet suit."

"Don't even go there."

But he already had, and would again before his first-ever kayaking expedition. It'd be something to do out on the water. Think about Zoe in a wet suit.

He had to be out of his mind. He'd need another vacation to get over this one.

She pushed her tights up to mid-calf. She was wearing beat-up water sneakers with no socks and just plunged into the rising tide, dropping seat-first into her kayak and shoving off with her paddle. Her moves were competent and effective if not smooth. She used her paddle to keep from getting pulled back to shore with the tide. "I forgot to tell you how to get in the boat. Did you see me? Butt first. Legs next. Don't drop your paddle. And zip up your life vest. It won't do you any good if it falls off."

Or if he froze to death before he could get back in his boat. J.B. complied with her instructions, but he wasn't smooth or competent in launching—and he got wetter than she did. But he ended up in his boat, and after some remedial instruction from his guide, he was paddling along fairly well. As promised, he did get wet.

They meandered northeast along the rocky coast,

past Sutherland Island and amidst the small islands off the Olivia West Nature Preserve. Because of the narrow passages and shallow waters, J.B. had stayed away from the smaller islands in his lobster boat. He'd never live down getting hung up on an underwater ledge or running aground in the mud.

Zoe finally led him to a pocket beach on the northwest shore of Sutherland Island. She hadn't shown him how to land, either, but there was nothing to it. She explained that it was important to pick out a sandy beach, some place where they'd have a minimal impact on the environment—he wasn't to be fooled by the rugged appearance of the landscape.

J.B. thought she looked relaxed and in her element.

They peeled off their life vests and sat together on a rounded, sun-warmed boulder above the water and several low-lying wild blueberry bushes. Zoe had a dry bag and offered to share her water bottle and Christina-made ginger cookies. Her rear end was just as soaked as his, but her tights would dry faster than his khakis.

"So, this island's named after one of your ancestors," she said. "George Sutherland. Did you know he fought in the Revolutionary War? He's buried here."

"On the island?"

"Mm. There's an old cemetery. Do you want to see it? It's not very far."

She was already on her feet, ginger cookie in hand. He followed her across an open expanse of sloping gray rock, the tide crashing below—much rougher here than where they'd landed. They curved inland, taking a visible but overgrown path under pines and spruces, until they arrived at a tiny, shaded cemetery enclosed in a crumbling three-foot wrought-iron fence. Maybe a dozen slender stone rectangles marked graves.

Zoe climbed over the fence and examined the largest of the stones, leaning slightly with time. "George Sutherland. There he is."

J.B. joined her at his ancestor's stone. 1742 to 1797. Just fifty-five when he died. J.B. knelt in the weeds and touched the smooth, cool stone, and tried to imagine what life must have been like on this small island over two hundred years ago.

"When did the Wests get here?" he asked Zoe.

"Not that early. Olivia and her brother were the first Wests actually born in Goose Harbor. Before that they were in Portsmouth, I think. My mother's family came down from Castine—it's just below Mt. Desert Island."

J.B. checked the other gravestones. Many also bore the name Sutherland. There were two babies, a teenaged girl. "No one lives on the island these days," he said.

"Not since the late nineteenth century."

A bramble stuck on Zoe's upper thigh, and she picked it off unconsciously. Gravestones or no gravestones, J.B. noticed the shape of her legs, the curve of her hip, thought again of that rose tattoo. She seemed oblivious.

They climbed back over the fence. He could feel his kayaking in his arms and shoulders. Zoe seemed unaffected, but he had no doubt she'd fake it just to lord her greater experience over him. He tended to bring out the

competitiveness in people, make them feel as if they had
something to prove to him. It wasn't always a bad thing.
Wanting to stick it to him could bring out the best in people, too.

On their way back to their kayaks, he noticed a par-
tial stone foundation amidst the birches and pines, the
dry undergrowth. Zoe explained it was the foundation of
the original Sutherland house, which, according to local
legend, had burned down the same night Abraham Lin-
coln was shot. The entire island nearly went up in flames.
Island fires and boat fires. Both were treacherous.

"There's an old boathouse at the tip of the island,"
J.B. said. "I noticed it when I was out on my boat last
week. New door, new lock."

"Really? I wonder if Luke worked out a deal with the
preserve. He owns the island, but Olivia left the preserve
enough money to buy it from them—of course, I think
he should just donate it." She smiled as if she knew she
was expecting a lot. "I know the preserve wants the island for public access. They think it'll help discourage
people—especially kayakers—from stopping on the
smaller islands and disturbing the seabird nests. They
can picnic and prowl around here instead."

J.B. nodded, looking out through the brightly colored
leaves and the dark green of the spruces and pines.
"Gravestones, cellar holes, history, wildlife and scenery.
Not a bad combination."

They returned to their kayaks, and after more water
and cookies, set off back down the coast, the wind holding back until they reached Olivia's point. J.B. had no

illusions he could handle white water and tough currents or one of Maine's notorious fog banks floating in, but he decided he did all right his first time in a kayak.

When they pulled their boats out of the water, he thought he noticed Zoe might be examining his wet butt. He smiled to himself. Yesterday's kisses hadn't been a fluke, a response to the stress of her first full day home. The woman had something going for him. He didn't mind at all.

They left their kayaks in the front yard and headed up to change into dry clothes, but they didn't make it to their respective bedrooms. They got as far as the upstairs hall before J.B. scooped her up and found her mouth, lifted her onto him as she wrapped her arms around him.

"Damn," she whispered, "it must be the kayaking— I can't seem to resist you."

"Good."

She kissed him back deeply, hungrily, her arms over his shoulders, her fingers clasped behind his neck. When he lifted her higher, pressing her against him, his hands slid over her wet tights, the curve of her hips, between her legs. The wetness there wasn't cold at all.

But his intimate touch startled her, seemed to bring her back to reality. She slid down off him, back to the floor, and caught her breath, pushing both palms through her short blond curls. "I should get changed," she mumbled, and disappeared into her room.

J.B. didn't push it.

Retreating to his room, he put on dry pants and checked his voice mail. He had a message from Bruce

Young. No boats missing at the lobster pound. No one saying they'd seen Teddy Shelton or given him a ride. "The guy's gone, McGrath," Bruce had said. "Maybe it's just as well."

Teddy Shelton had hit the road. Kyle Castellane wasn't pressing charges. J.B. clipped his belt holster back on and decided it wasn't necessary. He didn't need a gun. He needed a dose of common sense. He should go back to D.C. and let these people get on with their lives. If he hadn't tapped on Shelton's window, probably nothing would have happened. He wouldn't have beaten up Kyle last night and spent the night in the marsh. J.B. wouldn't have found out Stick Monroe had sentenced him to seven years.

Maybe he wouldn't have kissed Zoe the way he had.

She met him downstairs in the kitchen, and J.B. filled her in. She shook her head at Bruce's suggestion that Teddy Shelton was gone. "We're not going to be that lucky. He's still here. Lunch at Christina's? I haven't had my annual fried fish sandwich."

J.B. smiled. "No fish for me. I want meat."

She muttered something about Montanans, but at least she was smiling and the circles under her eyes didn't seem so ominous. He thought it might be that near-lovemaking in the upstairs hall, but she'd probably say it was the kayaking.

Twenty-Two

Betsy O'Keefe poked at a slice of warm apple pie. She was at a table in the far corner of the café, the only one without any window at all. She didn't want Luke to see her. Luke would disapprove of her apple pie. He seldom ate out. He worried about food poisoning. Normally she didn't have to worry about him seeing her, but he and Stick Monroe had gone for a walk together.

The café was crowded, but Betsy thought she looked like all the other tourists in her stretchy pants, windbreaker and walking shoes. Except she was alone. None of the tourists were alone.

"Hey, Betsy."

"Kyle." She was so relieved at seeing him she almost made a fool of herself. "Please, sit down. How are you feeling today?"

"Like shit." But he smiled, wincing in pain as he did. His swelling was down, but his bruises had blossomed, blues and purples oozing out across his face. Teddy Shelton had done a job on him. Betsy noticed last night that Luke hadn't mentioned to Kyle that he even knew Teddy, never mind that Teddy was on his payroll. "Sneaking out for pie, huh? Good for you, Betsy."

"Can I order anything for you? Pie, a milk shake—anything?"

"No, I'm fine." Despite his ordeal, he was in reasonably good spirits. "Chris used local apples. She has this thing about picking just the right apples for her pies. She likes Cortland, Baldwin, Northern Spy—I forget what else. Not Macs. She says they're best for eating. Me, I used to think an apple's just an apple."

"She's a wonderful cook," Betsy said. "And I noticed she was there for you last night."

"Yeah, after she thought I stood her up for dinner."

"I know from your perspective this doesn't matter right now, but truly, Kyle, you're very fortunate you weren't hurt worse."

"I know." He reached over and grabbed a bit of crust from her plate, eating it on the less-injured side of his mouth. "Betsy, do you think if she were alive, Olivia would object to my documentary?"

"I don't know. Probably."

"Why?"

"She was a private person, and she was very careful with what she let people know about her. She realized she couldn't control what they *said*, but she could try to keep them from learning all her secrets. Her books were her way of communicating with the world. For her, that was enough."

"Think she had any secrets?"

"We all have secrets, Kyle."

He tried smiling again. "Not you, Betsy."

She thought of herself breaking into Luke's files. "Everyone, Kyle. It's just that my secrets don't matter."

"You're the good nurse," he said. "You'd never divulge a patient's secrets, even if you knew them. Right?"

"That's right. I admire your tenacity, Kyle, but I can't let you interview me about my relationship with Olivia. That would be unethical. I was her caretaker for two years. She was a wonderful employer. That's all you need to know."

"Think you can get me up to her attic? Talk Zoe into letting me up there to take a look?"

Betsy didn't know whether to laugh or slap him. "What could you possibly think is in that attic?"

"That's just it. I don't know. I bet no one knows."

His ordeal last night hadn't lessened his zeal for his topic one iota, as far as Betsy could see. "I guarantee Olivia knew."

"But she had trouble getting around the last few years. Come on, Betsy, when's the last time she was up there? Two flights of stairs, hauling boxes. Damn, she was a hundred, you know?"

Betsy didn't remember Olivia ever going up to the attic, ever sending anyone up there with instructions as to what she wanted thrown out, not in the two years Betsy had worked for her. But she resisted catching Kyle's enthusiasm. "Zoe inherited the house—"

"Olivia's been gone for a year. Before Zoe left she didn't have the time or the inclination to clean out the attic. Look, who knows what I'll find. Maybe nothing, maybe just an old picture I can use that no one else will have. The smallest things can make a huge difference, lift a documentary like this from the mundane to something—I don't know, something at least Maine public television might want."

Zoe and J. B. McGrath entered the café, both looking young and fit and almost smug to Betsy. But she didn't know if that was fair. She still regretted her encounter with Zoe yesterday, but the attack on Kyle— even if he refused to call it an attack—had put it out of her mind.

Kyle fingered a sugar packet, deliberately avoiding their eyes. "Just my luck those two found me last night. An ex-detective and an FBI agent." He spoke in a low voice, as if he thought they might hear him all the way from the front of the café. "You should have heard them grilling me while I'm bleeding and out of my head."

As far as Betsy was concerned, Luke's only child was smart and well-intentioned, but also a spoiled young man. "You told them the truth, didn't you?"

His dark eyes, Luke's eyes, settled on her, reminding her of his father's arrogance, his sometimes casual cruelty. But Kyle wasn't abused as a boy, and had no excuse. Not that anyone did, Betsy thought. She stared at her pie and wished she'd stayed in her stateroom and read a book.

But Kyle laughed suddenly, softly. "Easy, Betsy. I'm not going to bite your head off. I'm just doing a documentary on a famous local writer. I don't know anything about Teddy Shelton, and I don't want to know anything."

She nodded, relieved. "Fair enough."

"And I'm not that interested in who killed Patrick West. Not to sound heartless, but we all know it was a drug dealer or some dumb-ass Mainer out shooting birds. Oops, missed."

"Kyle!"

McGrath and Zoe took a table vacated by two tourists, and Kyle glanced at them, waved slightly and calmed down. He gave Betsy an apologetic look. "I'm sorry. That was uncalled for."

But she was appalled, unwilling to let him off the hook that easily. "Patrick West didn't deserve to die the way he did. Look how young Christina is. Neither sister will have their father at their wedding, at the birth of their first child."

"I should be more diplomatic—"

"You should be *nicer.*"

He got up and leaned across the table, coming very close to her face. "With the father I have, I have to work at nice, Betsy. You know that. You sleep with the bastard."

She gasped, shocked, but he walked away, greeting J.B. and Zoe pleasantly, thanking them for their help last night. Betsy couldn't listen. She stared at the remains of her pie and fought back tears. Why didn't she just leave Goose Harbor? She had enough money, not nearly as much as Luke did, but enough for a fresh start somewhere else. She could get a nursing job in Portland, or another caregiving job almost anywhere.

But I want a life.

She didn't know what that meant anymore. It was always something she'd put on hold for the future. When she worked for Olivia, she promised herself she'd have a life after Olivia passed on. It'd be her last full-time caregiving job. She'd enjoyed Olivia's company and didn't mind the work, but it left her no time for anything else. Or no energy, at least. Now she had Luke, and even if he had his quirks, for the most part he was quite good to her. And he had so much money. She'd struggled to make ends meet all her life. Was it wrong of her not to want to struggle anymore?

She had no one to talk to, no one to ask but herself. She'd lived with her mum until she died and had never made very many friends, not close ones. Damn it, she was lucky to have a man like Luke Castellane. Count your blessings, her mum would tell her.

What would Olivia say? She'd had her soft spot for Luke but was hardly blind to his faults.

Suddenly feeling bloated and old, Betsy pushed her plate aside and left money for the pie and the tip on the table. *Her* money. Not Luke's.

When she reached the parking lot, she realized J. B. McGrath was behind her. He was eating the last of a little bag of oyster crackers. "Zoe had me out kayaking. I'm starving." He was good-looking in a rugged sort of way and had such an easy manner, but Betsy wasn't misled. This was not an easy man. He walked next to her as she headed toward the water. "Kyle's looking better."

She nodded. "I think that cut on his eye could have

used a stitch, but it might have been too late by the time you found him, I don't know. I encouraged him to see a doctor."

"A lot of stubborn people around here."

She gave a small laugh, her melancholy lifting. The cool air helped, the smell of the ocean. She'd lived in Goose Harbor her whole life, and the thought of taking the yacht south with Luke, flying to Utah for part of the winter, both thrilled and terrified her. He'd have no patience if she got homesick, if she ended up needing any emotional support at all from him. She was on her own, but she'd always been on her own.

She zipped up her windbreaker. "I invited you and Zoe to dinner tonight. Did she tell you?"

He smiled, and Betsy relaxed even more. But she thought that was why he'd smiled, to get her to relax. Everything he did was probably calculated, deliberate. "I'm doing all right with my meals," he said. "How to stretch a federal employee's vacation dollar. Mind if I stop by your boat after lunch? I'd like to talk to you and Luke."

Her heart jumped. She hadn't expected this. "Well, I don't know, I—"

"Just have to eat my burger, and that apple pie you were having looked pretty good." He turned, starting back to the café, unhurried, but not a man Betsy wanted to counter. "I'll pop over in about forty-five minutes."

She didn't know what to say. She'd never argued with an FBI agent before, and she didn't know if it mattered that he was on vacation. Could she tell him he couldn't come over? Was that forbidden? Would she get her and Luke into trouble?

She was having chest pains, knew it was stress, fear at what she'd done, how easily she'd let J. B. McGrath manipulate her. Did he know about Luke and Teddy? But that was ridiculous. Only she and Stick knew anything at all, and she doubted that was everything. Luke just wouldn't tell them. Talk about someone who kept secrets. She guessed his biggest secret was that his parents had abused him as a child—yet it was one everyone knew. And he'd benefit from talking about it.

Betsy walked slowly back to the yacht. She could hear the tourists up on the street. If she were on vacation, would she pick Goose Harbor? On her last vacation—three days off—she'd taken the bus to Boston for a Red Sox game.

The pie sat heavily in her stomach. Maybe Luke was right and she should eat lighter foods. More fruits and vegetable, more fiber.

"Oh, Lord."

She sank onto a chair on the afterdeck and felt the water undulating beneath the boat. Usually she didn't notice.

How long before J. B. McGrath arrived?

She prayed Luke and Stick would stay on their walk long enough for her to get rid of him.

Twenty-Three

Teddy sat in his truck in front of the Goose Harbor Public Library and decided he'd dodged enough bullets for one day. The police had talked to him. He told them he'd thought Kyle was stealing his truck and regretted hitting him. It was a misunderstanding, just like Kyle'd said. No hard feelings.

They pointed out if Kyle had died of exposure out there in the mud, Teddy'd be up shit creek. He agreed. No idea Kyle got lost in the dark. Poor kid.

Then they asked him about Stick Monroe.

Coincidence, Teddy said. He was shocked to his toes when he found out Monroe lived in Goose Harbor.

Bullshit, of course, but nothing they could do about it. He could live where he wanted to live. It was a free country.

He went back for his truck after the FBI agent and Bruce Young had checked it out. He'd hidden in the woods like a sniper, saw them and knew he'd been right to hop-to and stash his weapons and ammo. He'd tucked them in the marsh grasses while he figured out what to do.

How was he supposed to keep an eye on McGrath and Zoe West now that they were on *his* case? How was he supposed to make sure they didn't get everyone stirred up about Patrick West's murder? *Maintain the status quo.* Hell of a vague assignment.

He'd picked up food for lunch and drove out to the Olivia West Nature Preserve for a picnic. He walked down to Stewart's Cove and watched the tide roll in where Patrick West was murdered.

As he ate a couple of ham sandwiches and chips, Teddy collected his wits and came up with a plan, step one of which was to reclaim his arsenal before the ducks crapped on it. He drove back to the marsh and loaded his apple crate back into the jump seat. By the time he finished, he was sweating. He needed a shower, a decent night's sleep. He should just show up on Luke's multimillion-dollar yacht.

Luke'd have a stroke on the spot.

He needed a place to stay. He figured he was as good as evicted from Bruce's cottage. The motels and inns were packed with leaf-peepers. They were clogging the streets, on foot, on bicycles and Rollerblades, in cars and buses.

He started up his truck and waited a hundred years before he could pull out onto Main Street. Then he got behind a carload of rubber-necking old people. If they'd turned onto Ocean Drive, he'd have run them off the road. They didn't, and he scooted right on up to Olivia West's house.

He turned left, away from the water, and parked on a side street under a diseased elm tree. He walked down to Ocean Drive and as he crossed in front of Olivia West's house, he was damn near blown over by a cold gust off the water.

Zoe's yellow car was parked in her aunt's driveway. He knew she wasn't there—he'd seen her down on the docks with the G-man. If she had doubled back in the meantime, Teddy would tell her he'd heard she'd found Kyle Castellane last night and ask how the kid was doing. Friendly.

Otherwise he'd take a look around the place. He didn't know what he was looking for or what he'd find, but he wanted more information on what she and Agent McGrath were up to. What if the two of them had been working together all along? What if they knew each other from her state police work or her year in Connecticut?

Lots of questions. Now it was time for answers.

Teddy strolled up the driveway as if he had nothing more nefarious on his mind than a knock on the door. He could hear the wind howling down on the water, but once he was up on the bluff, it didn't reach him. The air was cold, colder than it had been yet that fall.

The side door was locked. He'd hoped old Olivia wasn't the door-locking type. Probably the cop nephew and grand-niece's influence.

He really didn't want to break in. He walked around to the front porch and looked out at the Atlantic Ocean, a straight shot to Spain. He saw a couple of lobster boats and some birds but didn't get that excited about the view. The ocean didn't do much for him.

He tried the front door on the porch. Bingo. Opened right up.

"Hello? Anybody home?"

The front room was cool and quiet, a big old sofa covered in blue canvas, a dining room table with eight chairs. It had an old-fashioned feel to it but was homey, not as fussy and claustrophobic as what he'd expect of a spinster born at the turn of the twentieth century.

He didn't waste time and headed back to the kitchen. He grabbed a cider doughnut off the counter and ate it while he checked out the rest of the first floor. He called a few more times, just in case Zoe was taking a nap. Mc-Grath wasn't around. Teddy figured he'd have a gun at his ear by now. He wondered what Special Agent Mc-Grath carried. A Glock? Teddy wasn't worried about Zoe coming after him with a gun—she was out of practice. People said she'd mellowed since she'd taken up knitting and goat-herding.

Licking cinnamon sugar off his fingers, Teddy trotted up the steep stairs to the second floor. If he got caught, he'd think of some excuse for being here.

FBI had one room. Ex-cop had another room. That was interesting. No bed-sharing yet.

Teddy thought he heard something and paused in the hall, deciding against slipping his .380 out of his ankle holster. He'd strapped it on before he'd slipped into the marsh at the crack of dawn. He had no permit—being a recently released felon, he couldn't legally own a firearm. Anyway, a gun would automatically complicate his just-here-to-check-on-Kyle story.

Maybe the wind had kicked up or it was just the old house creaking.

He listened another few seconds, heard nothing and retraced his steps back to McGrath's room. There was a backpack to go through. It'd only take a minute or two.

But there it was again, and this time Teddy realized it was coming from behind a door in the hall.

The goddamn attic.

Someone was up there? Hiding, sneaking around, doing nothing?

As far as he could see, there was no good reason for anyone to be up there. They'd have heard him call. So what was the deal?

Moving quickly, he snatched open the door.

The kid, Kyle Castellane, fell out on the floor, rolled onto his back and gulped in a breath as he stared in shock up at Teddy. "You!"

Teddy was no less surprised. "What the fuck are you doing here?"

He jerked Kyle to his feet, his face bruised and swollen from last night's thrashing. He was scared. "Look, I don't want any trouble. Just let me go."

"Anyone else up there?"

"No."

"Side door's locked. You sneak in through the front?"

"I don't have to explain myself to you."

Even after last night, even as scared as he was, the kid had to be sullen and combative. Teddy bent the kid's arm around his back, taking it just to the point where

Kyle would know another half inch and he'd be in a cast. "We're going downstairs," Teddy said.

"Okay, yeah, just don't break my arm."

Teddy shoved the kid down the stairs, but they didn't get far. Detective Zoe was on the scene. Teddy hadn't heard her come in. She'd come almost two-thirds of the way up the stairs.

"What's going on?" Her voice was firm and calm, without a hint of fear. "Stop right there and explain."

Kyle sputtered. "Zoe, Jesus, thank God, this crazy son of a bitch—"

Teddy put pressure on the kid's arm, prompting a loud yell of pain. Zoe started to react, but Teddy shoved Kyle face-first down the stairs, forcing her to choose between helping to break the kid's fall or getting out of the way.

She chose to help. It was a long way for Kyle to go, and he was out of control—he could break his neck. He careened into her, and Zoe managed to pull him toward the wall and down onto the steps with her, instead of letting his momentum carry them both down the near-full flight of stairs.

Teddy had a split second's chance before she'd be able to untangle herself and go cop on him. He scrambled down the stairs, leaping over her and Kyle.

But Zoe was quick. She disengaged herself and charged downstairs after him. He glanced over his shoulder, saw she wasn't armed and decided it wasn't in his interest to stop and try out a story on her. She'd be calling the police. She wouldn't be listening.

In a maneuver he'd practiced on his own a hundred times, Teddy, still running, whipped the Llama out of his ankle holster, turned and fired over her head. She was a cop. She'd know he didn't mean to kill her, once she had time to think. Right now she dove, pulling a hardwood chair in front of her for cover—it was the best she could do with him right there, shooting.

The bullet shattered the glass front of the china cupboard.

Teddy kept running, making his way into the side entry. He wouldn't get down the driveway on foot. Zoe West was a runner—she had him in the fitness department.

But at least now she knew he had a gun, and that'd slow her down.

He spotted her keys on the kitchen table and didn't hesitate. He detoured into the kitchen, snatched the keys and ran back into the entry. Zoe was on her feet. He didn't take the time to wave his gun or shoot her—he charged outside and jumped into her little car, sticking the key in the ignition. His stupid hand was shaking. Jesus! He'd trained for this sort of moment. It was as near to combat as he'd ever gotten. Last night, beating up Kyle, didn't count. No guns. And when he was arrested—what a letdown. They'd put cuffs on him, read him his rights and walked him out the door.

He made it down the driveway, out onto Ocean Drive. He barreled up the side street and pulled in behind his truck.

He stared at his gun, his fingers stiff on its grip.

What had he just done?

"You shot at an ex-cop and stole her car, you stupid fuck."

The cops would be after him for sure now. Status quo, right. He'd upped the ante all by himself.

Teddy pushed that one out of his mind. He'd deal with Luke later. Right now he had to figure out transportation. Going any farther in Zoe's car would just invite more trouble.

He left the keys on the VW's dashboard as a way-late gesture of good will, returned the Llama to his ankle holster and climbed into his truck. He had a few minutes, anyway, before the whole goddamn state was after him. He needed to ditch his truck.

His heart was pounding. Damn, he was supposed to be keeping an eye on Zoe West, not shooting at her. She was hanging around with the freaking FBI. Great. Just great, Teddy thought. He was supposed to be keeping an eye on McGrath, too, not provoking him.

Hell. Talk about biting the hand that feeds. This wasn't maintaining the status quo. Luke'd be furious. Teddy figured he'd just totally screwed himself out of any chance at a bonus. Then again, who knew? He wasn't caught yet, and he still had guns, ammo and grenades.

Twenty-Four

Teddy Shelton had run off. Kyle had run off. A bullet had shattered the old glass in Olivia's china cupboard. Zoe, absorbing what had just happened, set the dining-room chair back on four legs. Her right shoulder ached from saving Kyle from a broken neck. Nice of him to stay and help her.

"Sorry, Zoe," he'd said as he'd run past her.

She could have thrown her chair at him, but there was glass all over the floor and she basically didn't trust herself not to kill the little bastard.

Only now did she notice the blood on her hand. She grimaced, realizing a shard of glass must have grazed her left wrist. The cut stung and was oozing blood, but it didn't look deep.

She cursed and gave the chair a kick.

When she'd entered the house through the side door and tossed her keys on the kitchen table, she immediately realized she had company. At first she assumed J.B. had made it back before her. He'd gone down to the docks after lunch, and she'd stayed at the café to chat with her sister and some old friends after the lunch crowd had thinned out.

But she heard Kyle yell and charged upstairs—not the smartest choice she'd ever made. After that, she'd called upon her training as best she could to protect herself and her sister's idiot boyfriend.

In a hundred years, her great-aunt had never had a break-in.

Her hand throbbing now, Zoe stumbled into the kitchen and grabbed the phone, dialing 911 as she probably should have when she realized it wasn't J.B. in the house with her. She wasn't a cop anymore.

Kyle must have been terrified. He'd taken a thrashing from Teddy Shelton last night, too. Zoe couldn't blame Kyle for bolting. Fight or flight. He'd fled.

The dispatcher came on and asked her the nature of the emergency. As Zoe described the situation, she wrapped her hand in a dishcloth, blood soaking into it.

J.B.'s Jeep pulled into the driveway. She felt a rush of relief at having someone with her and, at the same time, renewed annoyance with herself for not having done a better job of handling the situation. Kyle was gone. The bad guy was gone. She was bleeding.

On the other hand, Kyle wasn't dead, kidnapped, or beaten to a pulp. And neither was she.

She saw both doors of the Jeep opened. Kyle got out of the passenger side, looking sheepish. J.B. met him and moved in close, all but marching him to the house. They burst into the side entry.

J.B. dumped Kyle onto a chair at the kitchen table. "Shelton stole your car?"

Zoe nodded. "The police are on the way."

"The police?" Kyle looked stricken—and bloody. The cuts on both his eye and lip had opened up. "What for?"

She stared at him, incredulous, her earlier moment of compassion deserting her. "Now, why do you think? Thanks a lot for staying to make sure I was okay, you weasel. I should have let you fall down the damn stairs."

"I was scared." He coughed, looking more irritated and insulted than scared. "I didn't know what the hell was going on—"

Zoe cut him off. "You didn't want to explain to me what you were doing here."

"That's not true! I was looking for you. I heard someone and thought it was you, but it turned out it was Shelton."

"You're lucky I gave up violence, Castellane. I don't believe a word you're saying."

J.B. walked over to her and silently lifted her hand, her dishcloth bandage not particularly effective. "You okay?"

"Glass cut. The bullet didn't hit me. He shot over my head."

"What kind of gun?"

"He had it on his ankle. A .380, I think. I didn't get a good look. I was busy hitting the deck. You grabbed Kyle making his getaway?"

"He told me he panicked."

"Yeah, right."

"Come on, Zoe," Kyle said. "Cut me some slack. I

was scared shitless. This bastard pushed me down the stairs, right into you—you were there. You saw him. He could have killed me."

"He could have killed *both* of us." But she knew some of her anger was at herself, not just him. As far as she was concerned, she'd acted like she'd never spent a day in law enforcement, never mind a decade. "Forget it. It's over."

"I know you could have stepped aside and let me fall all the way down the stairs, but you didn't, and you know why? Because you're good, Zoe. You're not an asshole like Shelton." Kyle tried smiling, but it obviously hurt. He touched two fingertips to his bleeding lip. "We're okay. That's what counts."

Zoe sighed. "Either you have very bad luck or something's going on with you and Shelton that you haven't admitted yet. Well, now you can tell it to the police. How do you like that? Do you need some ice for that lip?"

Kyle shook his head.

J.B. peeled a couple of paper towels off a roll and handed them to Zoe. "I'll take a look around. Don't beat him up while I'm not looking."

"It wouldn't make me feel any better."

He nodded. "I know."

He drew his pistol, a 9 mm SIG Sauer. She was aware of how serious he was, the professional at work. She wasn't. Not here, not now. Not ever again. The realization hit her suddenly, hard. She saw now that she'd spent much of the past year disengaging from law enforcement, leaving behind that part of her life. She'd done her duty as best she could in Connecticut, but when she was finally fired, she was ready for it.

She just didn't know what came next.

Whatever had happened to him over the summer—whatever he'd had to do—J.B. still had the focus and the drive to do his job. As he moved into the front room, she could see that every fiber of him was tensed, committed to what he was doing. It didn't matter he was on vacation, or that he'd kissed her. Not at that moment.

"That guy," Kyle said, motioning toward J.B., managing a weak grin. "He's something, isn't he? The FBI stud. Bet the local cops are going to love finding a fed here."

"Kyle—"

"I didn't mean to leave you, Zoe. Honestly. I don't know, I thought Shelton was still sneaking around, and I figured if I ran and got help—"

"He was here when you arrived?"

Kyle stared down at the table.

"Damn. You slipped in here, didn't you? What were you doing, pawing around in the attic?"

"I didn't get that far." He still didn't look at her. He sounded almost contrite. "I was going up the attic stairs when I heard him. I didn't know who it was—I figured it was you or McGrath. I felt—" He broke off, and Zoe thought he might have sobbed. "I felt like such a lowlife. A weasel, like you said. I'm sorry."

"Did Shelton hear you?"

"Yeah. He must have. He yanked open the door and

jerked me out like I was some kind of peeping Tom. Scared the hell out of me."

Zoe smiled and patted him on the shoulder with her uninjured hand. "Good."

He managed a smile. "You're a hard-ass, you know that? I thought getting fired might mellow you out, but no way."

"Oh, but you're wrong. If I'd been in top-cop form, kiddo, I'd have managed to break your fall, nail Teddy Shelton on the stairs and tie you both out on the rocks for the gulls to pick your bones clean."

"Come on. We're bigger than you."

"Size isn't everything."

He grinned at her, and she saw that he did, indeed, have a tear or two on his dark eyelashes. "Bet Special Agent J. B. McGrath would've kicked some ass. Man, I almost peed in my pants when he pulled over and hauled me into his goddamn Jeep."

Zoe laughed, although it wasn't easy to let go of her irritation with him. "How did he know something was wrong?"

"I don't know. Fed radar or something. I think he saw Shelton screaming out of here in your car. He asked if you were okay."

"You told him Teddy shot at me?"

"Yeah. He got all grim-looking. You cops." But he glanced nervously out the window when the Goose Harbor Police, the department Zoe's father had built, arrived. "Going to rat me out for trespassing?"

"No, of course not. That's a private matter."

"If Chris finds out—"

"I'm not keeping secrets from my sister, Kyle."

J.B. returned from his cursory search of the house. He had his shield out, his gun holstered for when he greeted the locals. He glanced at Kyle. "Tell the police everything. No bullshit. Teddy Shelton shot at Zoe and stole her car. He's not a good guy."

Kyle licked his cut lip. "He could have killed her, but—"

"You shoot off a gun that way, anything can happen. I'm not arguing with you. I'm telling you what you need to do."

Kyle made a face but sank lower in his seat, and Zoe could see he was finally intimidated. It wasn't because J.B. was armed—it was his directness, his clarity of purpose.

She let the police in, including the acting chief, Donna Jacobs. "Nice homecoming," Donna said as she entered the kitchen. "Three break-ins in a row."

"I don't know if this one's related," Zoe said, then stopped herself. "I guess you'll figure that out."

"How's your hand? Does it need medical attention?"

"A Band-Aid, but they're here somewhere. I'll be fine. Thanks."

Zoe noticed that J.B. had backed off, letting Jacobs and her guys do their jobs. A deputy sat at the kitchen table and took Zoe's statement.

When the police finished, Acting Chief Jacobs gave Zoe a bit of simple advice. "Buy a lock for the porch door, get that wrist looked at and try to stay out of the line of fire. We'll let you know when we find your car."

"Thanks."

"And I'll be in touch with CID," Jacobs added. "They need to know what's going on."

When she left, Kyle seized the moment and slipped out with her. He'd given the police his corrected version of events. Zoe supposed now he wanted to get to Christina before her big sister did. Or maybe just get out of her house before he had to be alone with her and J.B. again.

She sank onto a chair at the kitchen table. Her cut was throbbing now. She glanced at J.B., who'd given his own statement. Brief, unemotional, to the point. The professional. "I noticed Chief Jacobs didn't give you any advice," Zoe said.

"That's because I don't need any."

"If you're implying I went off half cocked—"

"I'm not implying anything." He got to his feet, his mood difficult to read. "Let's have a look at that cut. There's a first-aid kit here?"

"On top of the fridge."

He retrieved it, a shoebox that Betsy had stuffed with first-aid basics. He set it on the table and dug out a roll of gauze, tape, a gauze pad, scissors and antibiotic ointment. "I'm assuming you're not going to a doctor."

"I want to look for my car."

"Yeah. Your car. You'd love to find it with Teddy Shelton inside." He lifted her hand onto the table and unwrapped her makeshift bandage of paper towels and a dishcloth. "If I think you need stitches, you're going to the emergency room."

"You can handle it, Dr. McGrath."

He eyed her with just the barest hint of a smile. "Don't mind me touching you, do you?"

She felt herself flush at the sudden memory of his hands on her hips, her body pressed into him. "Awfully cocky, aren't you?"

He shrugged. "Some things are obvious."

He dumped the bloody cloth in the sink and dampened a fresh one, which he used to dab at her cut. She didn't pull back. He was gentle but unrelenting.

"See," she said, "it's not that bad."

"Ever been shot at?"

She shook her head. "First time. There were a lot of bombs and guns this summer in Connecticut, but none directed at me. You?"

"Yep. Shot at, knifed, kicked, bit. Well, one guy tried to kick me. He did not succeed."

"I've been drawn on," she said. "Lots of people have screamed at me. Maine's a low-crime state. Bluefield's a small town. Like I said, there were the bombs this summer—ouch."

"Sorry."

He set down the wet cloth and squirted on a dab of antibiotic ointment, using his finger to spread it over the cut. It stung, but more from the pressure than anything in the ointment itself.

He snipped off a length of gauze. "Did you tell yourself not to fall for anyone in law enforcement?"

"Never thought about it."

His look was disbelieving. "Right."

"My last date was with an organic farmer in Connecticut. Great guy. We went to a goat show together."

J.B. tore open the gauze pad, lifted her hand and placed the pad on the wound, then wrapped it with the length of gauze he'd cut. He tied and taped his bandage. "There you go. Does it hurt?"

"It's throbbing, but it's okay."

He winked. "You tough Mainers."

"What about you?" she asked. "No law enforcement types in your romantic life?"

"I haven't had much time for romance in the last year."

His tone was neutral, but she knew better. "Losing your father and barely surviving a dangerous undercover operation—that's a lot."

"Yep."

She could see he wasn't going to talk about it. "I'm not a cop anymore."

"I can see that. Otherwise you'd have had a gun."

"Not necessarily. If I was off duty, I wouldn't have had a gun. If I was still working in Connecticut, I couldn't just waltz into Maine—"

"All right. You win that point. Even if you'd been armed, Shelton still could have shot you."

"He shot *at* me," Zoe corrected. "It's the glass that hit me."

But J.B.'s teasing mood had ended, and with one finger he tilted her chin up, his eyes locking with hers. "I heard the shot. I saw Shelton scream off in your car, and I grabbed Kyle. He told me you weren't dead."

His intensity—his fear—unsettled her, and she tried to

cut it with humor. "You knew I wasn't dead? Then why'd you come here? You should have followed my car!"

It didn't work. His intensity didn't ease. "Kyle had seen the blood from your cut." J.B. traced her lower lip with his thumb. "I'm glad you're okay."

Before she could even get her breath, he was back on his feet, collecting up the first-aid materials. He returned the box to its spot on top of the refrigerator, and Zoe, watching him, realized the kisses and touches, the awareness, weren't fleeting, meaningless, of the moment. She didn't know where they'd lead, or if they stemmed from their mutual need for distraction—J.B. because he was running from his bad memories, her because she was running from herself.

Coming home hadn't settled anything. If anything, it had triggered more questions, more problems, more danger.

She didn't like it. Something had to give.

"Do you think Teddy Shelton's responsible for the other break-ins?" she asked. "I'd suspect Kyle, too, but he doesn't need to break into the café or Chris's house."

J.B. leaned against the sink and smiled. "I suspect everyone." He nodded at the window by the table. "Your pal Stick is here."

Zoe hadn't noticed him walking up the driveway. He knocked on the side door, but didn't wait for her to respond before he came in. "I heard what happened," Stick said. "Good Lord, Zoe. What can I do to help?" He glanced into the front room, shattered glass still all over the floor and dining room table. He paled visibly when he turned back to Zoe. "Christ in heaven. This is getting out of hand."

"Kyle and I are both okay, Stick."

Behind her in the kitchen, J.B. dropped onto his chair and said nothing. Stick was her friend. This was her house. She supposed it was possible J.B. was acknowledging her role, but decided he was just playing the observer and keeping his own theories to himself.

Stick was clearly worried and shaken. She invited him to sit, but he shook his head. "Zoe, I don't know—I don't like how close you came to getting killed today."

"He wasn't trying to kill me."

"But he could have. You know that. Maybe you should consider asking for police protection until he's caught."

"I'll be fine. Don't worry, okay?"

She might not have spoken. Her old friend raked a hand through his thinning white hair. "Christina should have round-the-clock protection, too. Zoe, I'm serious. It's been quiet all year. Then these break-ins, and you show up—" He broke off. "I'm not blaming you, of course."

Zoe sank back against her chair. "I know that."

J.B. poured himself a glass of water at the sink. "Have you had anything to do with Teddy Shelton since he got to Goose Harbor?" he asked Stick.

"I've seen him around town. That's it. Why?"

"You'd think you'd want to keep an eye on a man you sentenced to seven years." J.B. leaned back against the sink again and drank his water. "At least you'd be curious about why he decided to come here."

Stick sighed. "I should have known you'd check. Yes, I sentenced Shelton. I was the judge at his trial. For a long time, I didn't make the connection—I just wasn't paying attention, I suppose. Then we ran into each other on the waterfront, and he seemed as surprised as I was."

"After Patrick West's death—"

"There's no connection between Teddy and Patrick. Don't try to make one."

J.B. set his water glass in the sink, his reaction difficult to read. "You didn't mention your connection to Teddy to the police?"

"No, why should I? He served his time. I'm retired. We're living in the same town. There's nothing more to make of it. If Shelton wanted revenge, he's had plenty of time—he's been here over a year." He shifted his gaze to Zoe and smiled, but she could see he hadn't liked J.B.'s questions. "I just wanted to check on you."

"Thanks. I don't know, Stick, maybe we're all on edge for no real reason. Kyle's so obsessed with his documentary—he's managed to annoy me about it. He could have gotten under Teddy Shelton's skin and that's all this is."

"You mean he could have put Shelton on the defensive," Stick said, but shook his head. "You don't believe that."

It was true. She didn't. She glanced at J.B., but he'd thrown his stick of dynamite into the conversation and backed off.

Stick kissed her on the forehead, squeezing her uninjured hand. "This was too close, Zoe. Please be more careful." He shot J.B. an unfriendly look. "Where were you?"

"Obviously not here," J.B. said.

"Obviously."

Zoe watched Stick walk back down the driveway and hated the idea that she worried her friends, that her old mentor had to hear that someone had shot at her.

But she smiled at J.B. "Stick's hard on you because he's worried about me. You know that, don't you?"

"I know that's what you believe." He moved toward the door. "I had a talk with Betsy O'Keefe. That's where I was. She says Luke is concerned about your well-being and safety now that you're back in town. Another one. Something about his sense of loyalty to your great-aunt."

"Luke? Worrying about me? That's news."

"Betsy says he doesn't want you to know."

"Why not?"

"He realizes you don't like him, but he doesn't care because Olivia was so good to him and he feels he owes her."

Zoe frowned. "Has he acted on this concern for me?"

"Betsy wouldn't say."

"But you have a guess, don't you?"

"It's just a guess. Betsy isn't very good at deception, but I think she's afraid Luke's in over his head and wants to keep him from getting in any deeper." He stood in the doorway to the entry, but Zoe knew not to misread his calm. "It's a fair bet Luke hired Teddy Shelton to keep an eye on you. Maybe me, too."

"Then what, Teddy sneaks into my house and shoots at me?"

A quirk of a smile. "I didn't say it was a smart move on Luke's part."

Zoe noticed a fresh drop of blood had seeped through her bandage. "Betsy won't want to mess things up with Luke. She's a good woman, J.B. She thinks less of herself than she should, and if she's found happiness with him—" She broke off, sighing, her hand throbbing. "That's a good thing. Olivia would be pleased."

"Betsy clearly loved her."

Zoe nodded, feeling her adrenaline rush wearing off. Her shoulder was throbbing now, too. "She invited us to dinner tonight— I can try to talk to her."

"Meanwhile," J.B. said, "do you want to stay here and sweep up glass, or do you want to go with me and look for your car?"

Twenty-Five

Luke and Kyle paced in the main salon like two angry bulls. Betsy had never seen them so furious with each other. She didn't think they were even aware of her. She sat as far down on the sectional sofa as she could but thought about slipping out to the afterdeck, except that might draw attention to herself.

"You should learn to mind your own goddamn business! I never asked for your help." Luke was clenching his fists, yelling, which he never did. "I've done *nothing* wrong. Do you hear me? *Nothing.*"

"Oh, yeah. Sure." Kyle all but sneered at his father. "Get with the program, Pop. Teddy Shelton will turn you in before he goes down himself."

Luke went very still in that superior, intimidating way he had. "Turn me in for what?"

"Oh, fuck you," Kyle said, flouncing off.

Luke started to charge after him, but Betsy jumped up and interceded, grabbing his hand. "Give him a chance to cool off," she said. "He's not making any sense. He's had a terrible scare and he's looking for someone to lash out at."

"Why me? I'm his father—"

"That's why you." She smiled gently. "Once he's pulled himself together, he'll realize he was way off base and apologize. He'll understand that you hired Teddy because you were worried about Zoe."

"Zoe?" Luke sniffed, his skin clammy and gray as he extricated his hand from hers. "I don't give a damn about Zoe West. She can take care of herself. I'd hoped she wouldn't come back here."

Betsy was stricken. "Luke."

"Why so surprised? You don't like her."

"It's not that simple. I sometimes feel inadequate around her, but I don't know—no, I do know that's not her fault."

"Women," Luke muttered, dismissive. "I wanted to know if Zoe would try to link the break-ins at the café and her father's house—her sister's house now, I suppose—to his murder and start back on that again."

Betsy swallowed. "Oh."

He smirked, stepping back from her. "Betsy, you're so naive. You always want to think the best of people."

"You say that like it's contemptible."

"It can be, if it makes you willing to overlook the truth, if it blinds you to what's right in front of you." His voice was cold, his condescension palpable, but Betsy tried to tell herself it was a cover for his fears, his deeper emotions. "Do you think Zoe West cares about any of us?"

"Yes. Yes, I do."

"If we came between her and her father's killer? You, me. Kyle."

Betsy's knees went out from under her, but Luke didn't help her when she stumbled. She sank onto the sofa. "Luke!" Her voice was strangled, her heart skipping beats. "You can't think Kyle had anything to do with Patrick West's death?"

"Why not? He thinks I did."

Like it was a contest. Tit for tat. A game. You think the worst of me, I'll think the worst of you. Betsy tried to absorb what Luke was saying. "*My God.* You two have to talk. You have to get this straightened out."

Luke spun around and hissed at her. "Be quiet!"

But he was too late.

A white-faced Christina West was standing at the entrance to the salon. She was still wearing her apron from the café. She seemed unable to speak.

Betsy got shakily to her feet. What had she done? "Chris—"

Luke didn't move, didn't look at either woman. Christina whispered something unintelligible, flew around and ran out.

"Go after her!" Spit flew out of Luke's mouth, and he pressed his palm into the middle of Betsy's back and shoved her, propelling her across the carpeted floor. "Undo the damage you've done. Then pack up and get off my boat."

"Luke—Luke, I know you're tired—"

He pushed her again. "Go!"

Sobbing, Betsy staggered for the afterdeck, tripping

over chairs as she stumbled onto the slip. Christina was faster, younger, upset but not as shattered, not as terrified as Betsy was. Betsy was shaking. She couldn't walk properly. The finger slip undulated under her with the wake of a passing sightseeing boat. She thought about flinging herself into the water. Maybe she'd drown. Maybe she'd die of hypothermia. Maybe Luke would rescue her.

But she wasn't going to kill herself.

And nobody would ever rescue her.

A damp southwest breeze brought with it gray clouds and the smell of impending rain. J.B. noted that Zoe's color was better than when he'd first charged into her house with Kyle Castellane. She was perched on an old wooden lobster pot in his rented boat, staring out at the harbor and thinking. Or maybe not thinking. She wasn't talking.

They'd found her VW on a side street about a half mile from her house, the keys on the dashboard. Shelton must have parked his truck there and walked down to Ocean Drive, crossed over to the water and gone about his business. J.B. called the police to let them know.

Since Shelton had shot at Zoe, the police wanted to go over the car thoroughly. After she and J.B. gave statements, he drove her down to the town docks and Bruce's disreputable boat.

Zoe had jumped right in, a reminder she'd grown up on the coast and had been jumping in and out of boats all her life.

Bruce was out in deep water. J.B. radioed him, but Bruce had heard about Shelton. "I haven't seen that asshole," Bruce said, referring to his former tenant. "Zoe okay? She got shot?"

"Shelton missed. She cut her hand on a piece of flying glass."

"Christina?"

"Wasn't involved."

"I'm coming in. See you soon."

Zoe breathed in deeply, as if she wanted to suck in as much of the ocean air as she could, as if it had secret healing powers or maybe just would crowd out the demons. "Bruce's father took me out on this very boat when I was a little kid. I figured out pretty quick I didn't want to be a lobsterman. It's almost a calling in a lot of ways."

"When did you know you wanted to be a cop?"

"Then." She blinked up at the sky, her eyes the same gray as the clouds, the blue flecks seeming to have disappeared. "I knew I wanted to catch bad guys like my father. I didn't want to catch lobsters. It was one of those rare moments in life of absolute clarity, where you just know what you're meant to do."

Those were rare moments, J.B. thought.

She turned from the water, the late-afternoon light making her short curls seem a tone darker, the wind blowing wisps off her face. "It seems I was wrong."

"Not for the past ten years. Maybe for the next ten."

She shifted back to the water. Her back seemed stiff, and blood had oozed through her bandage. She'd declined again to go to the E.R. "It must have been a mo-

ment of a different kind of clarity this summer with the
man you killed."

The man you killed.

That was what he'd done. Forget the euphemisms,
forget the reasons. He'd killed a man.

"Maybe it would have been worse," Zoe said quietly,
"if his children had to watch their father kill you."

"Maybe it would have been better if I'd seen it coming and prevented it."

"Hindsight."

J.B. nodded. "I know. I did what I had to do. I don't
have regrets so much as—" He looked out at the gray
water, still, mirrorlike as the breeze died down. "Demons, I guess."

"They're not why Teddy Shelton shot at me today,"
Zoe said. "My demons are."

He was silent. There didn't seem to be anything to say.

She rose stiffly, wincing, and glanced around. "This
is a very scary boat. Only Bruce and a risk-taking undercover FBI type would think it's seaworthy."

"You don't want to go for a ride?"

She smiled. "I don't think so. I'd like to have a chat
with Luke. You?"

"Next item on my agenda."

They walked along the dock, mingling with sight-
seers and a stray dog Zoe recognized and had to pet.
Luke was drinking a bottle of spring water on his afterdeck but didn't invite them on board. "If you're looking
for Betsy, she's gone for a walk. Kyle? Here earlier, but
gone, he didn't say where. If it's Christina you want, she

was here a moment but ran off, apparently having misunderstood a discussion Betsy and I were having." He glanced up at Zoe. "Does that answer all your questions?"

She didn't wait to be invited and climbed on board, and J.B. followed her lead. He'd had a look around the Castellane yacht earlier when he'd talked to Betsy O'Keefe. It was a hell of a nice boat, but he thought he liked his better.

"I haven't seen you since I've been back, Luke." Zoe pulled out a chair at the round table and sat down. "How's it going? Kyle tell you about his second encounter with Teddy Shelton?"

Luke's lips thinned, and he took a swallow from his water bottle without answering.

"You know Teddy," Zoe went on. "Drifter type. He showed up in town last summer."

"Yes. I know Teddy Shelton." Luke's tone was stiff, borderline unfriendly. "I've noticed an increase in tensions around here since you came back. Connecticut didn't work out?"

"For a while. Then, no, it didn't."

"Betsy saw you on *Breaking News* this summer."

"That was a wild few days," Zoe said.

His resentment of her was plain. "You got your killer."

She said nothing.

Luke sighed audibly and set his bottle on the table. "I considered your father a friend. I adored Olivia. I don't know you and Christina as well, but I've tried to do right by you since their deaths. When Special Agent

McGrath turned up in town, I was concerned his very presence, whether or not he was on vacation researching his genealogy, would put people on edge."

"So you hired Teddy Shelton?"

"After I got worried about McGrath. Just to keep me informed. Then you came back, and I asked him to let me know if you started to unravel again." He raised his watery eyes to her. "You know what I mean. I don't have to spell it out."

"You didn't want me to hit the self-destruct button again," Zoe said.

J.B. noted her tone was objective, but she'd started to rub one finger along the edge of her bloody bandage, staring at it. Luke made a small gesture with one hand, as if he wasn't agreeing or disagreeing with her. "I had no idea Teddy would beat up my son or take a shot at you."

"Have you seen him or talked to him since it happened?" J.B. asked.

"I left a message on his cell phone, firing him."

Another breeze stirred, and J.B. thought he felt a drop of rain. "Did you tell the police?"

"Of course. I gave them his cell phone number, not that they can't get it on their own. I have nothing to hide, if that's what you're implying."

J.B. shrugged and didn't respond.

"I don't know what Teddy's game is. He could be working for someone else. He could be running his own angle. Kyle could simply have caught him at the wrong time, in the wrong place, and we're all overreacting."

"Could Teddy have followed Kyle to Olivia's?" Zoe asked.

Luke replaced the cap on his bottle of water. "I have no idea."

"Have you seen what he's collected for his documentary? I'm wondering if Teddy thinks there's money to be made there." She pushed back her chair, rising. "Even blackmail money."

"You're reaching, Zoe. Now, if you don't mind—"

"Kyle's not trying to find my father's murderer, is he?"

Luke was on his feet but stiffened visibly at her question. "I don't have to answer your questions, do I? This isn't an official visit, is it?"

Zoe didn't back down. "Who else knows you hired Shelton?"

"You might not approve, Zoe, but my arrangement with Teddy wasn't illegal. What he's done on his own isn't my fault. I won't allow you or anyone else to tarnish me because of it." He yawned, covering his mouth. "If you two will excuse me, I have work to do. I'm leaving Goose Harbor in the morning. I don't usually stay this late in the season as it is."

"What about Betsy?" Zoe asked.

"She won't be coming with me."

J.B. thought that was the first bit of good news he'd heard. Betsy O'Keefe deserved better than this snot. He looked at Zoe. "I guess this means dinner on the yacht tonight's canceled."

Luke ignored him.

Zoe spun on her toes and got off his boat. J.B. could

sense her anger. She shot ahead of him and was out to the main dock before he caught up with her. She marched along at a brisk pace. "I can't believe Aunt Olivia didn't see what a coldhearted bastard he is. I know people who've come out of abusive childhoods. They don't treat people like cockroaches. They—" She stopped herself. "It was the tone he used when he mentioned Betsy that got to me. Like she wasn't worthy of going south with him. The summer stuff you leave behind in Maine."

"He's a condescending prick."

She gave him a sideways glance. "Your professional opinion?"

"They teach us to recognize condescending pricks in the academy. You should have gone."

For the first time in hours, she laughed. It was good to see. J.B. slipped his hand into hers, and she didn't pull away. "You need a new bandage."

"Christina has a first-aid kit at the café."

He nodded. "I thought you might want to talk to her."

Twenty-Six

Christina wouldn't let them in. She'd locked the café door and was down on her hands and knees, scrubbing the floor with a bristle brush. Zoe pounded on the door. "Chris! Come on. I know you're upset about something Luke said."

She didn't respond at once. Zoe, more worried than annoyed, gave her a chance to collect herself. Christina didn't like to be pushed. Finally, she got up and unlocked the door, then turned away quickly, dropping her brush into her bucket so hard, water and suds splashed out.

Zoe had seen her tears but wasn't sure J.B. had. The café smelled of cleaning detergent and looked as if it'd been scrubbed from corner to corner. Christina was on a tear.

"Chris?" Zoe's voice was gentle, and she approached her sister slowly, reaching out one hand tentatively, as if Chris might bite it. "What's wrong? What happened with you and Luke?"

"Oh, that's not important." Her back was rigid as she stared into her cleaning bucket, fat locks of hair hanging in front of her face. "I heard you were shot at. That's much more important than anything I've been through."

Zoe heard the hurt in her voice, the fear, recognized that Christina wasn't being bitter or sarcastic but trying to put into perspective whatever had happened to her. Zoe didn't move, didn't touch her. "Shelton wasn't shooting at me, Chris. I'm fine. He shot over my head to drop me in my tracks and give himself a chance to escape. He'd stumbled on Kyle—"

"That's right. My sneak of a no-good boyfriend."

Christina whirled around, her apron dripping, her ruffled blouse soaked up to the elbows. Her face was raw and red from crying. But she didn't seem to notice. She was focused only on Zoe. "Why did you come back? Maybe the first break-in was nothing—just someone looking for silver."

"Chris, we don't know that Teddy Shelton has anything—"

She refused to listen. "Kyle—Kyle never would have sneaked into Aunt Olivia's attic if you'd shown any interest at all in what he's doing. Now—" She spun back around and gave her bucket a kick, more water splashing out on the floor. "Now his own father thinks he was involved somehow in Dad's death. That *bastard*."

"Is that what you believe?" Zoe asked quietly. "That Kyle was involved?"

"No! How could you suggest such a thing?"

"I'm not suggesting anything. I'm asking. Because if you don't believe it—"

Christina faced her sister again, her gray eyes dark with emotion. "I don't believe it."

"What about Kyle? Does he know his father thinks—"

"Of course. He must."

"Have you asked him?"

She shook her head. "The two of them are hard to figure out. I've quit trying." Her voice was hoarse but calmer, some of the fight gone out of her. "I wouldn't be surprised if he's afraid Luke had something to do with Dad's death, if the two of them aren't trying to protect—" But she didn't finish, squeezed back tears. "I can't—Zoe, can you understand? Can you understand that I just don't want to think about it anymore? I don't want it to be a part of me anymore. Dad's murder. Aunt Olivia. The whole mess."

Zoe nodded. "I can understand."

"I'm sorry." She spat it out, then softened. "I know it's not your fault."

"Where's Kyle now?"

"I don't know. I haven't seen him. I'm sure he's feeling stupid and inadequate over what happened with you and Teddy Shelton. I'll finish up here and go look for him." She cleared her throat, quickly stepped out of a puddle she'd made, apparently not realizing she'd been standing in it all along. "What about your car?"

"We found it," Zoe said without explanation.

"Well, that's good, isn't it? One thing, anyway."

Christina attempted a smile, but it faded quickly. "Maybe we're letting Shelton spin us around until we're all nuts, and none of this has anything to do with who killed Dad."

"That's possible. We'll just have to see."

J.B. stepped forward, steering clear of the wet spots on the floor. "Let us help you finish up here," he said quietly.

Christina looked at the mess she'd made and peeled off her dripping apron, dropping it in a puddle on the floor and swirling it around with her toe like a makeshift mop. She smiled at them through her tears. "Sure. Mops and sponges are out back."

Bruce Young materialized in the doorway. "This'll be fun. I want to see an FBI agent mop a floor." His natural good humor seemed to infuse the place with positive vibes, and he walked right in and tugged on Christina's long, messy braid. "You okay, kiddo? You look like shit."

"Now I feel great, Bruce. Thanks." She rolled her eyes at him, but smiled.

He turned to Zoe. "Crappy day?"

"You could say that."

Bruce acknowledged her words with a rare display of seriousness. "Teddy didn't kill your dad. I'd bet both my boats on that, Zoe. He's just your basic meat."

J.B. retreated to the back room, got a sponge mop and a bunch of rags, returned and shoved the rags at Bruce. "Swab up some of this water. You ought to be good at that."

"Aye-aye, Captain. Hell, you armed? Were you wear-

ing that thing last night at Perry's? No way am I playing darts with you if you've got a goddamn gun. It's
loaded?"

J.B. ignored him and started mopping the floor.
Christina shivered in her wet blouse but seemed more
cheerful. Bruce pulled off his Carhartt and slipped it
over her shoulders, and she murmured her thanks.

Zoe noticed Betsy O'Keefe down on the docks by
herself and decided to try to talk to her without the FBI
standing next to her. Not that Luke's rudeness was J.B.'s
fault—Luke was going to be difficult with or without
J.B. there.

She started backing toward the door, but J.B. pointed
his mop at her. "Uh-uh. You're staying put."

Bruce grinned. "Whoa, the FBI has spoken. Zoe?
Were you intending to give Agent McGrath the slip?"

"Bruce, I swear I don't know why your father didn't
throw you overboard when you were six."

"Because he knew you at six and figured you'd need
someone to give you a hard time when you were thirty."

Zoe could have taken that answer and run with it, but
she directed her attention at J.B. "Betsy's down on the
docks. I want to talk to her. Two minutes."

He nodded. "Stay in sight."

It wasn't so much an order as a reminder to use common sense. She'd been shot at once today, Teddy Shelton was still on the loose and J.B. was armed. And Zoe
had a lot on her mind. J.B. would see that.

Christina stepped back onto a dry section of floor.
"She's just trying to get out of helping." But she sniffled

at her sister, and the earlier tension between them might never have existed. "You want me to go with you?"

"If you think it'd help," Zoe said.

"It could."

Bruce dropped the rags into the puddle of water. "I meant what I said. Teddy's a meat. He's impulsive. He doesn't think things through. But he's not bright enough to get away with murder." Bruce sighed heavily, working at the rags with his toes. "Don't you wish you knew whose side he's on?"

J.B. squeezed out his mop. "I'm not sure it matters."

"Yeah. A friend kills you, you're just as dead."

Zoe touched Christina's shoulder. "Let's go."

"Tell that little fuck son of yours to stay out of my way." Teddy, parked in an out-of-the-way corner of the salt marsh south of the lobster pound, spoke in as low and deadly a voice as he could manage. He wanted to scare the hell out of Luke Castellane. Enough was enough. "He sneaks up on me again, he'll be lucky to live."

Luke was remarkably calm. "My son is an artist. He doesn't think the way you do."

"No shit."

"I didn't call to ask you to defend your actions. Our work together is done. I've already told Zoe, the FBI agent and the Goose Harbor police that I've fired you."

"That right?"

"That's right." There was that cool, snot-nosed tone again.

Teddy didn't know how long he had before the cops

picked up his trail, but he wasn't letting Luke get the
upper hand, take control. "I suppose now you want me
to get out of town."

Luke sniffed. "It makes no difference to me, but I
imagine it would be the prudent thing for you to do."

"Gooseshit Harbor. Yeah, I'd love to clear out. Last
night, I smack the hell out of your jackass kid. Today,
I smack the hell out of your jackass kid. What's his
problem? Why's he always in the wrong place at the
wrong time?"

"You also shot at a former police officer."

"'Former' is a key word, don't you think?" Teddy
stared out at the marsh, pretty even with the gray light
and clouds. "What about maintaining the status quo? I
thought that was worth a bonus—"

"Goodbye, Mr. Shelton. I'm sorry our association
had to end this way. There will be no bonus."

Click.

Done. The ax had fallen.

Teddy had the Goose Harbor police, the Maine
State Police, the Maine Marine Patrol, an FBI agent,
an ex-cop and who knew else all out looking for him.
And Luke, that rich puke, was in the clear. But he
must have figured out another way to exercise control
over events and make sure Patrick West's murder
stayed unsolved.

Or maybe he wasn't worried about that anymore.

It was nothing to Teddy. He'd never given a damn
about the Castellanes. Didn't now. The bonuses would
have been nice, but he had to remember he was in Goose

Harbor for one reason and one reason only—that regal bastard, Judge Steven Stickney Monroe.

Betsy extricated herself from her conversation with the West sisters as quickly as she could, too upset and on edge to trust herself not to lash out at them because of her own volatile emotions. They didn't seem to notice. They merely asked if she'd seen Kyle since he'd left Olivia's house after he'd talked with the police.

Betsy assured them she hadn't. She'd noticed the crude bandage on Zoe's wrist and shuddered at the thought of Teddy Shelton shooting at her—the thought of him possibly almost killing Kyle, of Luke being mixed up with a thug like that. Why didn't the two Castellane men understand how much she cared about them?

Zoe said she and J. B. McGrath had been to see Luke. Betsy didn't mention their argument. She didn't know if he'd forgiven her, but she'd forgiven him. He was upset because of his ridiculous, irrational fear that his son was somehow involved in Patrick West's death.

She promised Zoe and Christina if she saw Kyle, she'd tell him they were looking for him.

As she walked back to the yacht, Betsy found herself feeling sympathy for Luke, wanting to reassure him. No one should have to endure such groundless fears and suspicions. Given his unyielding hypochondria, the anxiety behind it, she guessed that he must have seized on any inkling he had about Kyle and blew it all out of proportion, the way he did a sniffle or a spot that anyone else would dismiss.

She was almost to the boat when Kyle approached her. She grimaced at his bruises and pale, grayish skin. He'd had enough shocks to last him for a long, long time. "I saw my dad. He says he's leaving tomorrow. Alone. Just him and his crew."

"We had an argument," Betsy said.

"Betsy—" Kyle shook his head, looking pained. "Never mind."

She bit down on her lower lip. "You don't think he ever meant to take me with him, do you?"

"He's an odd duck. You knew that going in."

She smiled sadly. "And aren't you relieved you're not like him? Christina West adores you because of it. The romantic, creative artist misunderstood by his difficult, philistine father—"

"All that's true, but he'd do anything for me." Kyle's voice was quiet, surprisingly mature, self-aware. "I know that."

"Do you really?" Betsy continued toward Luke's yacht, feeling steadier on her feet now. "I suppose having your father out of Goose Harbor will make it easier for you to continue your work on your documentary. He won't hinder your access to the Wests." She paused, realized the air didn't feel as cold anymore as she looked at this young man she'd known since he was a baby. "That's why you're seeing Christina, isn't it? Because she's Olivia's niece?"

"No, of course not."

"She's a good girl, Kyle. She's got simple desires. Don't use her to fulfill your own ambitions. Think about her and what she wants."

"I am. Don't worry, Betsy." He flashed her a smile, handsome and rakish even with his split lip and black eye. "You're a good soul, aren't you? Worrying I'm the rich bastard who's swept the naive small-town girl off her feet."

Betsy couldn't help herself and smiled at him. "You're awfully full of yourself, Kyle Castellane, and you always have been. You used to stand out on the dock and pee in the harbor when your mum was trying to potty-train you. We all should have known then."

He grinned at her. "That's where I have to give my old man credit. He didn't beat me for anything, not even peeing in the harbor."

Everyone in Goose Harbor knew Luke'd had terrible parents, and yet he acted as if he'd had a loving and privileged childhood, pretended the abuse he'd endured wasn't just his private hell but something that had never happened at all.

However good his intentions, Betsy doubted Kyle's relationship with Christina would last after he finished his documentary. She was part of that obsession now. In time he'd move on to a new one and forget what it was that had attracted him to her in the first place. It wasn't that he wasn't sincere—Betsy didn't doubt he loved Christina. But after his documentary, he'd move on to a new obsession, a new love, as impossible as that would seem to him now if she mentioned it.

He didn't join her on his father's boat but retreated back toward the café and his apartment.

Luke was out on the afterdeck, a surprise given the damp weather. "Mind if I come aboard?" Betsy asked softly.

"You still have to get your things."

She pushed back the hurt and joined him. He got up suddenly. "Come with me."

He took her below to the smallest of the staterooms, where he had his gun cabinet. He unlocked it silently, punching in the code to the alarm. He'd shown Betsy his modest but very expensive firearms collection once before, but she didn't care anything about guns. Luke could have guns or not have guns. It didn't matter to her. She'd never owned one, had never touched one. Since he was so meticulous about everything else, she assumed he had the proper permits. She'd never known him to shoot any of his weapons, on a firing range or in self-defense.

"The police haven't released any information they have—or don't have—on the weapon that killed Patrick West." He spoke calmly, swinging the glass-and-wood door open. "I don't know what ballistics evidence they have. The bullet could have hit bone and shattered, or it could have been dug out of him relatively intact, in which case it could tell them a great deal."

Betsy could feel her pulse throbbing in her temple. "The police would want to keep that kind of information under close wraps, wouldn't they? They wouldn't want the killer to know what they had on him. That's the way it's done, isn't it?"

Luke nodded. "To be honest, I don't know that much about ballistics or investigative procedures." He spoke calmly, clinically, but she had no idea why he was telling her these things, why he'd taken her down here. "I assume if they can get hold of the actual murder weapon, they can match it to the bullet. If they have one, of course. Short of that—well, I don't know."

"Luke. What's going on?"

He gestured at his collection. "I own two hunting rifles and six handguns, including two antiques. I sold a handgun to Teddy Shelton last September, not one of my six."

"That's legal, isn't it?"

"In this case, no. Teddy's a convicted felon. I didn't know at the time. Stick Monroe mentioned it. He doesn't know about the sale. There were other problems—paperwork—"

"Is Teddy—" Betsy's lips were so dry. "Is Teddy blackmailing you?"

"No. He's a true gun nut, the kind who gives responsible gun owners—well, I don't know if I can say I'm responsible anymore. Look at what I've done. But Teddy's only interested in the weapons themselves." Luke sighed, his color off. "That's not why I brought you here. Count the handguns, Betsy."

"Luke—"

His eyes leveled on her. "Count them. Please. I want you to understand."

She did as he asked. "Five, Luke." She could hear her

own breathlessness. "There are only five handguns here. You said you had six."

"I'm a health nut. I exercise and watch what I eat. I'm a control freak in a thousand different ways. I know that about myself." His tone was quiet and intense, but still unruffled, as if he were discussing a weather report. "What I am not is paranoid about other people, especially my friends and family. I don't know why—I probably should be, given my upbringing. But I have faith in them. I believe in them."

He'd never once, in their months together, referred to his childhood negatively, or to other people so positively. Betsy found she couldn't speak. Who was this man? She knew now she didn't have a clue.

Luke swallowed, looking vulnerable, ashen. "After Patrick's death last year, I discovered the missing gun. It's a Colt Python .357 revolver. It's a fine weapon."

"How long after Chief West was killed?"

"The next day. After I heard Olivia had died. I don't even remember why I checked."

"Did you report it?"

He shook his head. "No."

Betsy was silent. Her stomach ached.

"Now it's too late," he said.

She nodded. "I—I understand."

"No, you don't. You think I'm covering up for my son. I'm not. Betsy, I don't believe Kyle killed Patrick West. I never believed it."

"But you were worried the police would."

"I was worried Zoe would find out and kill him."

"Luke!"

He closed up the cabinet and locked it. "She wouldn't have. I see that now, but at the time, I was as caught up in the drama as everyone else."

She thought of the payments to Stick Monroe. "What about Stick?"

"He knows about the stolen gun. He knows I didn't report the theft to police. I should have, especially when I knew it could have been the weapon used in Patrick's murder. I paid Stick for his silence. Cash. He wouldn't take it—he says he's retired and has no intention of ratting out a friend. But I insisted. I don't know what he does with it. Tosses it in the ocean for all I know."

"He's not—you don't consider that blackmail, do you?"

Luke shook his head sadly, his disappointment palpable, as if he'd hoped she'd have figured it out by now, understood him after all. "No, Betsy. I consider it an act of friendship."

To pay a man for his silence? Betsy didn't get that. But she supposed that was Luke's whole point. That she didn't get it, didn't get him.

"Once I realized the Python was gone," Luke went on, "I couldn't sleep, I couldn't eat. I was terrified that a gun I owned, legally, for the most innocuous of reasons, would end up being the murder weapon, not only in Patrick's death—"

"But someone else's," Betsy said. "You hired Teddy

because you were afraid the murderer was getting ready to strike again."

Luke shut the gun cabinet and reset the alarm. "I still am."

Twenty-Seven

~~~~~~~~~⟳⟳⟳~~~~~~~~~

Zoe slipped up to the attic and sat on her thick chenille rug among her pillows and scribblings. She picked up one of her yellow pads and sighed at how awful her writing was. She didn't have Olivia's zest for adventure, her accessible style, her insight into Jen Periwinkle.

At least it didn't seem so at that moment.

Last year, sitting up here with her feet propped up on pillows and the window cracked so that she could feel the breeze and smell the ocean, she'd thought she was brilliant. The words flowed, the scenes developed one after another in her head, and she couldn't stop writing.

She hadn't written a word since she'd left Goose Harbor, not even after she was fired and living with Charlie and Bea Jericho, canning vegetables and milking goats and learning to knit. She'd meant to pretend that she'd never written at all.

Probably still a good idea. She could burn this mess and go find a job.

"Zoe?"

It was J.B. She'd left him in the kitchen to scrounge up dinner now that their evening on the Castellane yacht was off. She figured he'd drag her to Perry's for fried shrimp, beer and a game of darts.

"I'm here," she said. "Come on up. You've read this garbage, so it's not like it's a secret."

He seemed even taller as he made his way toward her under the slanted ceilings. "I told you—"

"Yeah, right, you can't read my handwriting. I don't need to polygraph you on that one—I know it's not true."

He smiled. "I take it I'm not disturbing you?"

She shook her head. "No, it's not like I'm writing." She sighed at a curling yellow page. She'd thought about writing with a fountain pen, the way her aunt had started in her early twenties, but decided on pencil. "This was just a catharsis or something."

J.B. stepped over her discarded drapery rod from what seemed like a thousand years ago. "Do you believe Kyle's story that he didn't get all the way up here?"

"That part. He wouldn't have been able to resist if he knew I'd played around with Jen Periwinkle. It seems like an invasion into Aunt Olivia's imagination, don't you think? Jen and Mr. Lester McGrath were her creations, not mine."

"Then make them yours. She left you the rights to her Periwinkle novels for a reason. Maybe that was it. So they could live through you—"

"Trust me, I was a better cop than I ever will be a writer."

He stood in front of the bureau at her feet. "Except for that little incident with the gun and the Texas Ranger."

"Did the governor's murder get solved or did it not? And without too much damage to the good guys." She leaned back against a fat pillow, eyeing him. "You'd have fired me, too, wouldn't you?"

"I'd have fired you the first time I caught you without a weapon while you were on duty." His presence made her writing space seem even smaller, more intimate. "You disengaged from the work, didn't you?"

"Over time. It didn't happen all at once."

He sat on the chenille rug and stretched his legs out straight, crossing his ankles an inch from her hip. "I can understand how Stick Monroe and Luke Castellane could see themselves as your protector—Luke because of his loyalty to Olivia, Stick because of his loyalty to you."

"Luke's protecting himself. Anyway, I can take care of myself."

"That's not the question. It's not about you. It's about them and their relationship to you, to your father, to your aunt. It's a tough position to be in. For all of you." He watched her a moment, then the corners of his mouth quirked. "Especially for them. You're noncompliant."

"Not me." She smiled. "I'm good at taking orders."

But he'd gone serious on her. "You're more out of control than I am."

Her throat caught at the quiet truth of his words, and she looked away, staring out at the harbor. It was dusk, the water still, glasslike, reflecting the moored boats and the bright leaves of trees on the shoreline.

"If Teddy Shelton knows anything about who killed my father, why—"

"Let the state and local police figure it out. If they choose to, they can bring in the bureau. Zoe, you have to stand down. You have to let people do their jobs, let them help you. You ran last year because you knew you couldn't keep it up, you had to back off."

She shook her head. "I ran because I knew the answers to my father's murder are here in town, not outside. That's what people want to believe. That's why they're all so nervous around me." She shut her eyes and inhaled, then exhaled slowly. "I just want to know why he was killed, J.B. Who did it."

"I know."

"And then I want a normal life." She tried to concentrate on her breathing and not to relive the image of Kyle Castellane flying toward her, Teddy Shelton shooting at her. She'd had no idea he was armed, hadn't even considered it. Law Enforcement 101. "All this past year I told myself coming home was a normal thing to do and nothing would happen. I could make my peace with Dad's death and figure out what comes next in my life. I could live here. I could eat blueberry pancakes every morning."

"Everything you've just said makes sense."

She managed a halfhearted smile. "Not the blueberry pancakes."

"Zoe—"

"I knew it wasn't true. I knew I couldn't just come back here and it'd all be normal again."

She looked down at her bandaged wrist. He'd helped her put on a fresh bandage, but since she wasn't hurting as much when he did it, she'd responded to even his slightest touch. Another reason she'd bolted up to the attic. That was what it was, she thought. A place to hide. Her writing, too, was a place to hide.

"Well," she said, "I guess I anticipated dodging bullets and having my car stolen, but I sure as hell never expected to go kayaking with an undercover FBI agent."

J.B. moved his legs closer to her. "It's not the kayaking that's got you off balance."

"You're not going to give me an inch?"

"Honey, I'm not giving you a millimeter. And no more undercover work for me. They won't put me back in. I've done my bit. Nearly didn't make it back this last time."

"Won't you go stir-crazy at a desk?"

"I'll learn yoga. Get exercise." He smiled. "Have a proper sex life."

Zoe tried not to let him get to her. Stick was right. J. B. McGrath was a powder keg. "What about emotional commitment to others?" she asked lightly. "That was something you could avoid undercover. If you're just a regular FBI agent—"

"I'll never be that."

"Do you talk to your superiors that way?"

"I've got a place in Washington, and there's talk of having me put together a UCA training course."

"UCA means undercover agent. The FBI and its acronyms."

"You'd have been an NT. New Trainee."

"I'd have made it through the academy, you know. I didn't drop out because I was afraid of failure. I dropped out because—"

"Because you had Jen Periwinkle in your head."

Maybe he had a point. Maybe she'd gone into a tailspin not just because of her father and Aunt Olivia, but because she wasn't meant to stay on the course she was on.

He stared out the attic window, and she wondered what he saw when he looked at the harbor, the docks, the boats. He wouldn't see her father lumbering along the waterfront, her aunt with her cane as she set out on a bright morning to borrow books from the library. It'd be like if she were in Montana. She'd see an unfamiliar landscape, beautiful, but one that didn't conjure up images and memories. He'd never known his grandmother. Posey Sutherland wasn't real to him the way the best friend she'd left behind in Goose Harbor was real to Zoe.

"You know when it's time to stand down," he went on quietly. "You don't think you'll know when you're so into the work that's all you can think about, but when the time comes, you know." He leaned his crossed ankles closer to her, touching her thighs with his toes. "As for emotional commitment to others—right now I'm committed to keeping you from doing something stupid."

"That's not emotional."

"Oh, but it is."

She scowled at him, but couldn't sustain it and smiled. "You have no sense of romance."

"Look who's talking, the hard-bitten Mainer."

"I'm not hard-bitten. I know how to knit."

"And you have a tattoo of a rose on your left hip."

She gasped in spite of herself. She could see he knew he'd get to her with that remark. He smiled, cocky, pleased with himself, and pushed aside a half-dozen pillows and crawled over the rug to her.

"Right about here," he said, slipping the waistband of her pants down over her hip. "A beach rose. Pink."

"It's my own design." Her voice seemed disembodied, her mouth suddenly gone parched. "I had it done a couple weeks ago. It hurt like hell. One hot little needle prick at a time."

"Did it take long to heal?"

"It's healed now. It itched, and I had to beat it with a rolled-up newspaper—"

"Zoe."

He skimmed his fingers over her tattoo. She inhaled. "What?"

"You don't have to say anything. Just relax." He kissed the edges of the rose, flicked his tongue over her skin, whispered, "Trust me," and eased her shirt up, trailing his mouth up her hot skin.

He reached her bra, and she fell back into the pillows, not protesting when he undid the front clasp and exposed her breasts, took first one nipple, then the other, between his lips. Finally, he found her mouth, kissing her deeply, saying more words of comfort, desire, assurance, words she absorbed but couldn't quite make out, aware only of her own overwhelming desire and urgency. He eased her shirt up over her head, her bra off her arms, and held her close as he drew her pants over her hips.

"Tell me if you want me to stop," he said.

But the feel of his hands against her bare skin had her head spinning, her body aching. She held him, his sweater soft, his chest warm and hard against her breasts. "Don't stop."

He dispensed with her pants, laid her back against the pillows and gazed down at her with a frankness that made her self-conscious. But she didn't pull away, didn't grab a pillow and cover herself. He positioned himself alongside her, stroking her gently, boldly, until she was unaware of anything else, just his touch, her response.

"I want…"

But she didn't finish, instead rolling onto her side so she could slip her hands under his sweater. She felt his hot skin, then probed lower, immediately seeing, feeling, that he wasn't immune to what was happening between them.

He pulled off his sweater first, then his pants, and he came to her, taking her hand and placing it on him, letting her stroke him, touch him. He was thick, hard, sleek, and when she lay back onto the soft rug, he came with her, onto her.

"I'm not asking for anything," she whispered. "Just this."

"It's enough." He entered her slowly, as if he knew she hadn't made love in a long time, like this, never. "It's more than enough for right now."

But his gentleness didn't last, his need matching hers, then overtaking it, forcing her to stop thinking, to lose herself in the feel of his thrusts, of one moment after another that she wanted to etch forever in her mind.

He came in a series of hard, fast, deep thrusts that completely undid her, had her crying out with her own release.

They held each other for a long time, and he laughed softly, stroking her left hip. "I only meant to check out your tattoo."

"Ha."

"Zoe…" He kissed her hair. "Ah, Zoe."

She touched two fingers to his lips. "Don't talk. We can talk another time."

And they made love again, just as wildly this time, without words, and when they finished, the harbor was dark except for the glitter of lights from some of the boats and the gleam of the moon on the water.

J.B. pulled a blanket over her, then managed to crawl into his pants. "Come downstairs whenever you're ready. I'll find something for dinner. It just won't involve flax seed."

Zoe smiled at him. "I have a feeling this sort of thing never happened when Aunt Olivia lived here."

"I don't know, Zoe. I've read dozens of your auntie's letters to my granny. She knew the score."

"She didn't—she didn't mention a lover, did she?"

He laughed. "That revived you, the idea of old Olivia having a lover in her youth. No, she didn't say she did or she didn't, but she comes to life in those letters. She knew what went on between my grandparents. She understood the physical attraction."

"Jesse Benjamin swept Posey off her feet, didn't he?"

"He did."

"You're a chip off the old block, then. A bad-boy lawman, and you swept me right off my feet."

"You were already lying among your pillows. The rest was easy." He smiled down at her. "And I'm not your evil nemesis."

He left, and Zoe rolled onto her back and stared at the slanted ceiling, but without J.B.'s warm body there next to her, she soon realized it was cold up in the attic. She scrambled into her clothes, her body aching. She'd kayaked, she'd been shot at, she'd been cut and she'd been made love to not once but twice, all in one day.

She glanced around at her tousled pillows and her scrunched-up chenille rug, and she had her doubts if she'd ever be able to write up here again.

Twenty-Eight

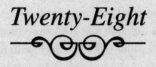

Teddy knew he wouldn't make it two inches out of the salt marsh with his truck. Some cop'd spot him. He waited until three in the morning to make his move. He was frozen and uncomfortable and badly in need of a shower, and hungry—damn, he was hungry. But he summoned the energy to haul his weapons and ammo out of the back of his truck and set it all in the wet grass. Then he started carting it back to Bruce's cottage. That was work. Took three trips, although the third one was because he counted his grenades and two were missing. He went back and found them under the front seat.

He was pissed at everybody now. Luke, Zoe West, her prissy little sister, the FBI agent. That Kyle prick. Bruce was okay. He wasn't pissed at Bruce. He was sorry that if his plan didn't work out, Bruce would end up with the local cops, the state cops, the ATF and the FBI crawling over his property. Couldn't be helped. But the plan would work.

Not that Teddy had ever been much at planning. Usually he implemented other people's plans. Last time he planned, he ended up in federal prison. He'd had a much bigger arsenal in mind then. He'd had it all planned out. Then he got caught buying illegal weapons from illegal sellers, and next thing he knew, he was staring up at Judge Monroe in a fancy courtroom.

Teddy saw through Stick Monroe immediately. He was the kind of guy who was born with a silver spoon in his mouth and tried to pretend he didn't look down his nose at other people but did. As far as Teddy was concerned, Monroe had rigged the damn trial. He denied Teddy's lawyer every motion and made him look like an idiot in front of the jury. Teddy just wanted a fair shake. That was all.

Stick hadn't wanted him in his courtroom. He wasn't a big-enough case. He wanted terrorists and mobsters and serial killers. Teddy wasn't even a good-enough criminal.

When he finished hauling his stuff, he was so hungry and tired he thought he'd pass out. He went into the cottage and found a box of crackers he'd left. He gobbled them up while he made his way over to the lobster pound. It had rained earlier, but now it was just drizzling. His fingers were numb from the cold.

An old rowboat was turned over in the grass and muck alongside the launch. He'd seen it the other night with Kyle. He kicked it over and decided it'd do—it wouldn't sink before he was finished. He dragged it to the water and floated the bow out, keeping the stern on the cement launch. There was only one oar. He'd have to manage.

He didn't think the boat could handle all his weapons and ammo, so he'd left a bunch of it hidden in the brush and scrub pines by the cottage. None of it could be traced back to him, and nobody'd ever believe Bruce Young would be playing around with illegal weapons. Not that Teddy was worried. No way would anyone stumble on his stash before he could get back for it.

It was a good plan. He knew it was. He'd thought through his options. Of course, he always believed he thought through his options. He did okay when he had structure, routines, orders to follow. Mostly, anyway. Unless the orders were stupid. His mother used to say, "Teddy, you have to learn to make good decisions." His father would just slap him up the side of the head and say, "You stupid son of a bitch, what did you expect?"

A prison shrink had told him those were mixed messages.

He'd kept a half-dozen flash-bang grenades, a couple of fragmentation grenades, his 9 mm, his semiautomatic and enough ammo to make him feel secure. He dumped it all into the back of the rowboat, shoved off and climbed in.

He paddled with the one oar as if he was in a canoe.

He made almost no noise and stayed within a few yards of shore, half rowing, half paddling. He went right past Luke Castellane's yacht. It'd be alarmed and locked up tight. Teddy considered lobbing a flash-bang over the bow. That'd serve the bastard right for firing him. Scare the hell out of him.

But that'd happen soon enough.

His boat leaked. The cold water oozed over his shoes, but he was sitting up on the seat. His ass wouldn't get wet. He kept rowing.

It was cold and dark, just the hint of dawn, a paler gray light far out on the horizon. A Maine sunrise was something to see, but with the rain, it wouldn't be much this morning. He'd be out of here by then, anyway.

The FBI agent's boat, the one Bruce'd rented him, was tied up down by Christina West's café. Teddy managed to steer his boat up to its bow, right at the end of the slip.

The leak was worse. Water was pouring into his rowboat.

He was glad he had his weapons and ammo wrapped in a waterproof tarp. He pulled them onto the seat next to him, then heaved them onto the dock without making a sound.

Kyle Castellane's BMW was parked next to the café. Teddy had a key. He'd swiped the spare when he'd gone over to the yacht last week to discuss keeping an eye on Agent McGrath with Luke. He'd had a feeling he might need a BMW before this job was over.

Christina West was up already, getting the coffee on and making muffins. That could be a complication. The lobstermen would be rolling in soon, too.

He carried his stuff up to the parking lot and set it down, fairly certain Christina couldn't see him at this angle. He put on earplugs and goggles and got out one of his flash-bang stun hand grenades. He was excited, nervous. This had to work.

He walked back down to the docks as calm as anything. His rowboat was sinking fast. At least it hadn't
sunk with him in it.

Holding his breath, he pulled the pin in the grenade
and lobbed it perfectly into the stern of the G-man's lobster boat.

Then he turned and ran like hell.

One second, and *boom.* A 175-decibel explosion and
searing, blinding light. It was doing just what it was supposed to do. Make a lot of noise, disorient, distract,
confuse and basically scare the hell out of people.

That'd wake up Gooseshit Harbor.

Teddy didn't linger to admire his handiwork. He
climbed into the BMW, started it up and pulled out his
earplugs as he backed out.

Twenty-Nine

"Get down here." Bruce Young's voice was intense but under control on the other end of the phone. "Someone just torched your boat. *My* boat."

J.B. had heard the explosion and was halfway out of bed. "Anyone hurt?"

"No. The marine patrol and local cops are already here. They think it was a flash-bang stun grenade. A lot of noise and light."

Zoe, wide awake, held the blanket up to her chin as she sat up, whether because she was cold or had just come to her senses and realized where she'd spent the night, J.B. didn't know. "Is that Bruce? What's he saying? What was that explosion?"

"McGrath? You there?"

"I'm here. Flash-bangs are intended to cause confusion and disorientation, not damage—"

"Yeah, so maybe that was the point."

J.B. rolled out of bed. He was stark naked and cold and had meant to spend a gray, drizzly morning in bed with a troubled hothead of a woman he didn't know if he'd ever get enough of.

He saw that her bandage hadn't come off her wrist during the night. There was no sign of fresh bleeding. She was watching him impatiently, as if she should be the one talking to Bruce. J.B. thought of last night. Lovemaking in the attic. Dinner. More lovemaking.

Life could be good. Definitely.

"McGrath—"

"I'm on my way."

He hung up, and Zoe frowned at him. "Someone tossed a flash-bang into your boat?"

He nodded. "I'm meeting Bruce on the docks."

"I'm coming with you."

Still holding the covers in place, she kicked her legs off the side of the bed and reached onto the floor for her clothes. After their lovemaking in the attic, she'd showered and put on fresh clothes. They hadn't lasted, J.B. remembered. He'd carried her up here and removed them piece by piece.

She found her bra and shirt. Her curls were tousled, her skin luminous, the blue flecks in her eyes standing out against the gray early dawn light.

J.B. had on his pants and boat shoes and headed for the door, his shirt in one hand, his gun and holster in the other. "I'm not waiting. Meet me down at the docks."

He saw the flash of her rose tattoo as she threw back the covers and reached for her pants. His chest muscles seemed to clamp down on his lungs and heart, constricting his breathing, and it was as if every moment of last night came at him as a whole.

It had been good, but insane.

He slipped out into the hall. Just as well he had a grenade explosion to deal with.

No one could ever say Olivia West was haunting the place. If she were, she'd have flung him onto the cliffs or struck him with a bolt of lightning before the night was over.

Maybe that was what the boat was. Maybe her aim was just off.

By the time he reached his Jeep, he was normal again. Making love to Zoe had been natural, perfect, what they both wanted. No need to feel guilty or worry about ghosts or any of it. His mind was focused, and he concentrated on the task at hand. Get to the docks. Talk to Bruce. Talk to law enforcement. Most likely he'd be explaining himself to the Boston FBI field office before the day was out. They covered Maine. They wouldn't like grenade explosions of any kind.

The dampness penetrated his shirt and jacket. He could taste salt on the drizzle. It was cold out, the air still and very quiet.

A marine patrol boat was down by the docks. Police and fire truck lights penetrated the gloom. It was a low ceiling, not that foggy—which wouldn't last. There was more fog and rain coming.

As he climbed into his Jeep, Zoe ran out of the house barefoot, carrying her shoes, and jumped in next to him. "Luckily all my clothes were right where you threw them."

"So were mine."

As he drove, she pulled on socks over her painted toes, then tucked her feet into her sneakers and tied them. Just over a week ago, he'd had to refer to a map to get here, and when he'd driven down Main Street, he'd thought…how quaint. He'd found the perfect place to do nothing for a couple of weeks. Boat, walk, look at gravestones, eat lobster and blueberry pie and let his demons depart out of sheer boredom, out of disgust with the cloying charm and beauty of Goose Harbor, Maine.

One murder in thirty years. J.B. couldn't pretend it wasn't part of what had drawn him here.

"A grenade explosion will bring on the feds," Zoe said. "Bruce must have told the police by now that you rented the boat. They'll love that. I worked with marine patrol on a boat explosion once. A guy tried to off his wife by blowing up his boat with her in it. Wanted to make it look like an accident."

"She survived?"

"Yes. *Not* a happy woman."

J.B. parked next to Christina's café. State and local police cars and a couple of fire engines had pulled in as close to the docks and his boat as they could get without going into the water themselves. If it'd been a destructive grenade of any kind, the entire area could have caught fire—the boats, the docks, the buildings. Bruce Young was standing by himself a few yards from a group of cops, his big arms crossed on his chest as he grimly surveyed the scene.

Zoe got out slowly, her Maine cop eyes taking in who

all was down at the waterfront. She'd know people, names. J.B. didn't. He met her in front of his Jeep. Bruce spotted them and waved, and they walked down to the dock. He was still in the parking lot—the police weren't letting anyone on the docks.

"How do you like this?" he asked. "I was in my truck on my way here when—*boom!* Jesus, it scared the hell out of me."

Zoe shoved her hands into the pockets of her fleece vest. "You called it in?"

He shook his head. "Your sister did."

"Christina? She's here?"

"Making muffins for us rise-at-dawn types." But Bruce obviously didn't like it, either. "The cops are in with her now."

Zoe absorbed his words with a small, tense nod. "She's okay? Did she see anything?"

"She's fine, Zoe. I don't know what she saw. I haven't talked to her." He glanced at the cluster of law enforcement officers, the stretch of yellow police tape, and sighed heavily. "You don't think these guys are telling me anything, do you?"

J.B. noticed Donna Jacobs and what he guessed was a state detective exiting the café. "What about Kyle Castellane?" he asked Bruce. "Was he in his apartment?"

Bruce shook his head. "No idea."

Jacobs joined them, quickly explaining that she had no information on who'd tossed the flasher in the boat or why. "We're still looking for Teddy Shelton. Maybe he can help us." She glanced at J.B. "FBI and ATF are on their way. I told them I've got a fed here."

"I'm on vacation."

"Yeah. That's what I told them." She turned to Zoe, and J.B. thought her expression softened slightly—but not much. "Talk to your sister. She can fill you in on some things. I just don't have the time."

She didn't wait for an answer.

Zoe glanced at J.B., then Bruce. "You two want to come with me?"

Bruce rubbed a big palm over the top of his head and heaved another sigh. "Nah. I want to see about my boat. Geez, it was an eyesore on a good day." He turned and gazed out at the harbor, the horizon all gray now, sky and sea indistinguishable. "Weather sucks. Hey, if I learn anything, I'll let you know, okay?"

J.B. nodded. "I'm sorry about the boat."

"So long as it wasn't some scumbag who followed you to town. If that's the case, we won't be letting any more vacationing cops in town, fed or otherwise." But his stab at humor didn't last. "I bet it's that dumbass Teddy Shelton. I gave the guy a break, and this is what I get. A torched boat. What if a spark'd touched off a fire? The boats in close like this, you'd get a chain re-action, they'd all go up in flames. It'd be my boat that started it, a guy I helped. I'd have to leave town."

Zoe put out a hand toward him. "Bruce—"

He gave a curt wave. "Forget it. Go talk to Christina."

They found her behind her counter. A half-dozen lobstermen had gathered at the tables by the harbor-front windows to drink coffee and watch the show. There was no teasing this morning.

Without a word, Christina filled three mugs with coffee, set them on a tray and carried them to a table away from the lobstermen. She pulled out a chair and sat down, then J.B. and Zoe did likewise.

Christina looked drawn and tired, but her hands were steady as she held her mug and stared at her steaming coffee. "Do you ever feel like bad things start happening and they just keep happening, and there's nothing you can do to stop them? You don't want to be along for the ride, but there you are. And there's just nothing you can do."

Zoe nodded. "I've felt that way a lot this past year."

Her sister bit off an angry sigh. "I hate being a whiner."

"What happened this morning?" J.B. asked.

"I was in here working. I heard Kyle go out, and then I looked up and there was this awful explosion and the harbor was on fire. That's what it looked like. It was still dark, that gray light you get just before dawn. I didn't even know it was your boat." She paused, but neither J.B. nor Zoe interrupted her. "I ran out—I don't know why. I wasn't thinking." She stopped again, blinking back tears, and she had to set her mug down. "Kyle's BMW careered right at me. I thought it was going to run me over."

Zoe said nothing, but J.B. was becoming more aware of her reactions, her defenses. She was shaken by what her sister had said. He added sugar into his coffee. Normally he drank it black, but having a stun grenade explode in front of her must have made Christina heavy-handed with the coffee measure. It was almost too strong to drink.

When she didn't go on, J.B. prodded her. "Did you see the driver?"

She shook her head. She was still very pale, her stark expression a contrast to her pretty, ruffly clothes. "I think I was a little blinded by the explosion. I—I couldn't see much of anything except that car coming at me."

"What about Kyle?" Zoe asked quietly.

"I don't—" She turned away, still fighting her tears. "I didn't see him. It must have been him behind the wheel, but I can't say for sure. I don't know what happened to him. The police—the police want to talk to him." She sucked in an audible breath, let it out in a whoosh, as if she were trying to stave off a panic attack, keep fear and hysteria from overwhelming her. "We had a fight last night. Otherwise he'd have been down here helping me out. Most mornings he helps early on, so I don't have to hire a waitress or run myself ragged."

Zoe touched her sister's shoulder. "Chris, it's not your fault—"

She sniffled, nodded. Her hand was shaking now as she picked up her mug. She took the smallest of sips.

J.B. could feel the strong coffee, even with the sugar, burning in his stomach. He thought about Kyle Castellane and Teddy Shelton. Luke. Stick Monroe. These women's dead father. A police officer killed in the line of duty. "You and Kyle argued about him sneaking into your great-aunt's attic?"

"And other things. We covered a lot of ground." She seemed embarrassed, her emotional reserve as natural and intractable as her sister's. "He was such a *jerk*. He said he never asked for Zoe to rescue him."

Zoe hadn't touched her own coffee, and J.B. thought she looked ragged, cold, so different from last night. But she'd buttoned down her emotions. She was in control. "Did you two talk about Luke's fear that Kyle was involved in Dad's murder?"

"He thinks we're out to blame it on an outsider. Why not his family? Why not *him?*" Chris took in a sharp breath, her lingering distress over their argument evident. "They're not from Goose Harbor, so we locals will turn anything we can on its head and use it against them. He says that's why his father said what he did. He's worried we'll all somehow find a way to pin everything on Kyle. And Kyle says if not him, his father."

Zoe took a sip of coffee, set it down and dumped in both sugar and milk. "Chris, you know the police will follow the facts and the evidence. No one's out to pin the blame on anyone. I'm sorry Kyle and Luke feel—"

Her sister snorted. "They're both so selfish. This isn't about them! They're just worried about their own skins. They don't care that Dad's *dead*. They don't care that his murderer is still out there—he could kill again, he could get away with what he did!" She was furious now, shocked and frightened, but J.B. could feel her determination. "I know—oh, Zoe, now I know what you felt like last fall. I was in such a state of denial. I just wanted all this to go away. It won't."

"Chris, we don't know that any of this is connected to Dad."

"It is."

Zoe didn't argue with her. "Luke made his deal with the devil when he hired Teddy Shelton. The police will talk to him and get to the bottom of it. He could be covering up nothing, or he could have real information."

"I know. We have to be patient." Christina smiled, self-conscious. "I seem to recall people telling you that a lot last year."

"We'll get through it, Chris," Zoe said.

"Yep. We will."

"It's possible Kyle saw something," J.B. said. "That could be why he ran out."

Christina looked at him, her eyes as gray now as the horizon. "Then where is he now?"

Good question. J.B. didn't have an answer for her, so he left it hanging.

"Bruce got here before anyone else—I was already calling the police, although I think they heard the explosion." She breathed out, a hint of color high in her cheeks. "Bruce is a rock, I'll say that for him." She looked around suddenly, as if she were just now tuning into her surroundings. "Do you two want anything to eat? I didn't have a chance to make muffins, but I can whip up some eggs."

"Coffee's fine, Chris, thanks," Zoe said.

"Damn, Zoe, I'm sorry for going off on you yesterday. Don't think I don't want the truth to come out about what happened to Dad, because I do."

"I know that."

"Whatever it is, I can take it. It's one thing to live with not knowing who shot him because his killer's in Colombia or New Jersey or someplace and there's just no realistic chance we'll ever know. But if he's here in Goose Harbor, if we can find him, or her, or them—" She trailed off, leaving it at that. "I need to get back to work."

She took her coffee with her and swung off, more energetic and focused if not calmer.

"Hey, Agent McGrath," one of the lobstermen, a wiry guy somewhere between fifty and a million, called to him. "You going to find the bastard who tossed a grenade into your boat? We can't have some asshole running around town torching boats."

It was one thing to tease him—they knew they'd never act on their threats, that they were all in good fun. It was another to have someone come damn close to destroying all their livelihoods.

"The police are on it." He got to his feet and glanced down at Zoe. "I should go back down there. You?"

She rose, handing him his coffee. "Take it with you. I have an in with the owner. We can bring our mugs back when we're done. I don't know about you, but this stuff's burning a hole in my stomach, although I could use about a gallon of coffee this morning."

"Not much sleep last night?"

"As much as you got, Agent McGrath."

The drizzle had picked up, now a fine, bone-chilling,

misting rain, but the cops didn't seem to notice. The fire-fighters were heading out, which meant they were satisfied there were no other explosive devices in the vicinity and the fire danger was over. Although he had an urge to hold Zoe close, keep her warm, J.B. just walked beside her down to the water.

Stick Monroe was hovering on the edge of the taped-off crime scene in his corduroy shorts and sweatshirt. "I heard what happened," he told Zoe. "What an asinine thing to do. What the hell was the point? It must have been Teddy Shelton. He's an idiot. I warned Luke."

Zoe stared at him. "You knew Luke'd hired him?"

"Not immediately. I thought about telling you but decided it would only upset you unnecessarily." He glared down at the lobster boat. "It was a judgment call."

"Not a very good one! Stick, what were you thinking?"

He settled his dark eyes on her. "I was thinking about you. So was Luke. He was concerned, not irrationally, I might add, that McGrath here would stir up trouble and you and Christina would get caught in the crossfire."

"Luke wasn't trying to protect me."

"You underestimate your importance to people, Zoe. You always have. You help them, you're there for them, but when they try to do the same, you question their motives."

Zoe didn't push. "Luke says he fired Shelton."

"Let's hope." Stick sighed, shifting his gaze back down to the ruined boat. "He had nothing to do with this little show. Shelton's playing his own game now. Don't for one second think he's gone away. He knows Luke's rich. He'll find a way to try to blackmail him, extort money from him."

"What about you?" J.B. asked. "Do you think Shelton will come after you?"

The old judge snorted. "I hope he does. He'll land up in prison for an even longer stretch this time."

Zoe hunched her shoulders against the rain and the cold, and J.B. could feel her focus, her determination as she beat back her concern for her friends and family. "Kyle's BMW pulled out of here a minute or two after the explosion. It almost ran Chris over. She didn't see the driver. They both could have been blinded by the explosion, but who knows."

Stick frowned. "It wasn't Kyle?"

"She doesn't know."

"If it wasn't—"

"Stick, you've dealt with Teddy Shelton. Is it possible he snatched Kyle as a way of putting pressure on Luke and extorting money from him?"

"It's possible, but money isn't what motivates Teddy. At least it's not his central motivation. He likes guns. You'd think seven years in the custody of the federal government would have had an effect, but I remember thinking when I sentenced him that he'd be back—he'd never give up illegal weapons."

J.B. could feel the drizzle collecting on his hair. "The police—"

The judge cut him off. "They have Teddy's record. They know everything I know, and then some, no doubt." He turned back to Zoe and touched a finger to the glistening drizzle on her hair just above her ear. "You'll be okay? How's your hand?"

"It's fine." She smiled at him, her lips a little purple. "You're retired. Go dig in your garden."

"It's compost day." But he seemed distracted, an old man unsettled by the goings-on in the quiet, pretty village where he'd retired. "I heard the explosion. I wonder if this is what Teddy wanted—all of us up and focused on grenades and blowing up boats while he—" He broke off, shaking his head. "Well, I don't know. That's why we have law enforcement."

After he left, Bruce rejoined Zoe and J.B. "You're the talk of the town, J.B. Look—" He pulled J.B. aside, out of Zoe's earshot. "There's a rowboat sinking in the harbor. Marine patrol's all over it. I'm guessing it was Teddy's transportation."

"From?"

"The lobster pound. If I'm right, it's the rowboat that was turned over off to the side. I was going to salvage what I could from it and get rid of it, but I never got around to it. It probably made it here and gave up the ghost."

J.B. considered the logic of taking a rowboat from the lobster pound to the harbor and the docks. It would be slow but quiet. Unexpected. Risky—Shelton had to know the police were looking for him and he'd be in big trouble if they caught him with his flash-bang.

"I'm thinking about driving down to the lobster pound and taking a look around," Bruce said.

"Bruce—"

"I know. You're the freaking FBI. You've got procedures." He seemed oblivious to the weather and grinned at J.B. "You coming?"

Zoe thrust herself back in between them, apparently having been left out of the conversation for as long as she was going to stand. "What're you two plotting?"

J.B. handed her his coffee mug. "Bruce and I are going down to the lobster pound. You'll stay here with your sister?"

"I like the way you make that a question instead of an order. Maybe I should go instead of you. I've already been fired."

"What?" Bruce winked at her. "We're just going to talk lobstering. McGrath thinks he knows everything about it."

Zoe rolled her eyes. "You're both full of it. Go. Just keep me posted."

Something about her struck J.B. as vulnerable, a lightning rod for too many people's sense of personal inadequacy, a woman who had her world shattered and was still trying to fight back. An image of her last night came at him, and he decided—screw it. He leaned toward her. "Want me to kiss you goodbye, warm you up a little? You can prove to all of Goose Harbor you're not a repressed Yankee."

"You know, McGrath—" But she stopped, and without warning, kissed him lightly, boldly. She smiled cheekily. "Now who's embarrassed? I don't know if your pals in the FBI have rolled in yet."

"One thing about me, Detective Zoe—I don't embarrass."

Bruce grinned at him. "You work fast, don't you, McGrath? Leave it to Zoe. She gets fired, she learns to knit. Now she falls for a bad-boy FBI agent."

The repressed Yankee in her was back. "I haven't fallen for anyone."

"Yeah, right." Bruce wasn't buying it. "Come on, Agent McGrath. We'll take my truck."

Thirty

Zoe slipped behind the counter and fixed eggs and home fries with a little onion and green pepper while her sister, humming a sad tune, popped a pan of apple-cinnamon muffins into the oven. The lobstermen had all gone out to pry information out of the police, then hit their boats, late, with plenty to think about as they worked their strings of traps.

Christina hadn't put out a Closed sign, but between the lousy weather and a grenade going off on the docks, customers were few. But Betsy O'Keefe was one of them. She took a table overlooking the harbor. Zoe set the eggs and home fries in front of her and sat down. "You look like you could use a good breakfast, Betsy. Did the festivities this morning wake you up?"

"Oh, I never went to sleep." She smiled weakly, and Zoe could see the strain in her face. "Home fries? Zoe, I haven't had home fries in months and months."

"One of life's great indulgences. Look, they're not those deep-fried things, either. They're proper home

fries. I even burned the edges of a few of the potatoes."

"Okay, I give in!" She tried to laugh, but it was a hol-
low sound and only made her look more drawn.
"Where's Agent McGrath?"

"Off with Bruce Young."

Betsy stared out at the harbor. "How long will the police stay?"

"As long as necessary. A while, I would think. It'll
take time to gather evidence."

"Two state detectives talked to us a little while ago.
Luke and me. We didn't see anything—we were in bed."
She stabbed at a few potatoes but seemed to have trouble holding on to her fork. "I can hear the innkeepers and
shopkeepers screaming now. A grenade going off can't
be good for business. It was a blow to have our first murder in thirty years, and the chief of police no less." Betsy
gasped in horror at her own words and dropped her fork.
"I'm so sorry, Zoe. I didn't mean to sound cavalier."

"Forget it. I know what you're saying. Goose Harbor's a fishing village and a tourist town. When either
gets threatened, people worry." Zoe slipped a triangle
of toast from Betsy's plate. "I'm going to guess you
didn't tell the police everything you know."

"Zoe—"

She bit into her toast and looked at Betsy, realized how
frightened and uncertain she was. "Tell me. I can help."

"Can you? I don't think so. It's gone too far now."

"How far, Betsy?"

"Luke—he's heading south today without me. We

had a dreadful argument yesterday. I thought I'd regained his trust, but—" She picked up her fork again and poked at her potatoes, her eyes lowered. "I was wrong."

"I'm sorry," Zoe said.

"Oh, it's probably for the best. I had a feeling it wasn't a forever kind of relationship." She smiled, dismissing her own feelings, her sense of hurt. "Luke's terrified."

"Because of Kyle?"

She nodded tentatively, as if she shouldn't. "But I can't—I can't tell you—"

Zoe finished her toast, hoping Betsy would want to fill in the silence. She didn't, and finally Zoe said, "Do you believe Kyle killed my father?"

"No!"

"Do you believe Luke did?"

She shook her head. "God, no. Zoe, I'd never have stayed with him if I believed that."

"Then what are you afraid of?"

She didn't answer right away. She grabbed the salt and pepper and shook them on her eggs and home fries, and Zoe could see she was, if possible, even paler. But she wasn't crying. She seemed to be past crying. "Last year," she said, her voice almost inaudible, "not long after your father was killed, Luke discovered that one of his handguns was missing. A .357 Colt Python, I believe. It was in a locked, alarmed cabinet."

"Kyle has the key and the codes?"

"Access to them, at least."

"Anyone else?"

Betsy put a forkful of potatoes in her mouth, but she didn't start chewing. She looked as if she'd spit them out, but finally she chewed, swallowed and wiped her mouth with her napkin. "I don't know. I wasn't involved with Luke then. He has a boat crew. Anyone who knows his habits would be able to calculate when he wasn't going to be around. He has his locks and alarms, but he's not meticulous about security. The lure of Goose Harbor, you know. Safe, pretty, no need to watch your back."

"Teddy Shelton was around then."

She nodded, picking at her eggs. She seemed exhausted, physically and emotionally wrung out. She lowered her voice, as if someone might hear. "Luke sold him a gun."

Zoe tried not to react. "When?"

"In September. I don't know what kind, but I know— it wasn't a legal sale."

"Has Teddy been blackmailing him?"

"I don't know. I don't think so. At least not in as many words."

"But Luke's afraid of him," Zoe said.

Betsy lifted her shoulders. "I don't know that, either. I overheard them talking—Luke didn't sound afraid. He was totally in charge."

"Teddy probably realizes he doesn't have enough leverage on Luke. It'd be a first offense for Luke, but not for Teddy. If Teddy goes to the police, he's cooked, too." She sank against the back of her chair and looked out at the harbor, picturesque even on such a gray day. "But Luke suspects Kyle of stealing the Colt Python, not Teddy? Why?"

"Zoe—Zoe, Luke would just die if it turns out a gun he owned was the weapon in your father's murder. I don't know why Luke collects guns. He's difficult, impossible at times, but he's not violent."

Zoe nodded. "A gun collector isn't necessarily violent, but Luke behaved irresponsibly, even criminally. He sold a firearm to a convicted felon and didn't bother to report the theft of another firearm that he had reason to suspect was used to commit murder."

Betsy took a shallow breath. "It's like collecting guns is his secret passion or something. I don't understand it."

Zoe sat forward, Christina's strong coffee churning in her stomach, and she had to fight the effects of caffeine, lack of sleep and adrenaline. "Luke didn't tell the state detective this morning any of this?"

"He says it can't possibly make any difference."

"Then I'll tell them."

"He'll know it was me! Zoe!"

"Betsy, you knew when you started this story that I'd have to tell the police."

She set down her fork. "You'd never look the other way, would you, Zoe? No matter who it was who'd done wrong. Your father was like that."

"If you mean professionally, you're right. He wouldn't look the other way, and neither would I. That would be unethical, corrupt. On a personal level—" She sighed. "I try to be a forgiving person. I know life isn't black and white."

"Olivia would look the other way. She would see the whole picture, how complicated people are, what their motives are, and decide—" Betsy swallowed visibly. "I wonder if that's why she couldn't come up with the name of the murderer. She knew who it was, or at least guessed, but she'd looked the other way. Maybe she thought it cost your father his life."

"How much of all this does Kyle know?" Zoe asked abruptly. She had no intention of discussing Olivia's last hours with Betsy—not now.

"I have no idea."

"His documentary—what if it's a ruse for him to get more information about my father's death, his father's involvement?"

Betsy considered the question. She seemed calmer, more in control of herself now that she'd told someone her story, or at least most of it. Zoe suspected there was more.

"It's possible," Betsy said. "Sometimes I had the feeling Kyle was trying to satisfy himself that his father wasn't Chief West's killer."

"Did you tell him what Olivia said?"

She shook her head.

"Betsy, are you afraid? If you are, I can make sure you're protected."

"I'm afraid, Zoe, but not in the way you think." She blinked rapidly, but there were still no tears in her eyes. "I want him back. Luke. I can't help it. I've spent my whole life in Goose Harbor. I've worked hard. Two years with your aunt alone. I've never had much of a life."

"I hope you didn't feel unappreciated for what you did for Aunt Olivia. She adored you, relied on you, and we all—Betsy, I've always respected you and what you do."

"Thank you." She picked up her fork again, tried the eggs, chewed as if they had no taste. "I'm being selfish."

"That wasn't what I was thinking."

Betsy stared out at the harbor, the yellow police tape, the police cars. Zoe recognized the lead detective on her father's case. The fire trucks had left. "Luke threatened to charge me with harassment and trespassing if I tried to see him again," Betsy said quietly.

"I'm sorry."

"Me, too." She turned back to her food, a tear sliding down her cheek. "Tell the police, Zoe. You're right. I told you my sad story so you'd tell them."

"They'll want to talk to you."

She nodded. "I'll be here."

Teddy didn't like the looks of the kid. A scared shitless golden boy. "Are you going to puke? Do it out the window. I don't want you stinking up the car."

Kyle Castellane's big brown eyes widened. "Don't shoot me."

"Jesus Christ, relax, will you? The gun's to keep you in line. I won't shoot you unless you do something stupid. If you're smart, you'll be fine. Okay? Just do what I say."

"You have grenades."

"Mostly flash-bangs. They're mainly for show. The frag grenades are the ones that do the real damage."

The kid was close to hyperventilating. "I should have stayed in my apartment and called the police. I never should have run after you—"

"Water over the dam, pal. Stop thinking about it. You thought your old man was a killer."

"I *didn't!*"

"I wouldn't want to admit it, either."

When Kyle came flying out of the café and tried to stop a moving BMW, Teddy had considered running the kid over. The show on the docks was intended to put the fear of God into Luke Castellane and make him reconsider the bonus. Now he had Luke's kid. Funny how things worked out.

You have the plan. Things happen. You revise the plan.

Luke had already called. Teddy was worried about the police tracing his cell phone signal, but decided they hadn't gotten that far yet—the phone was in Luke's name. Luke had loaned it to him when he hired him last week. He wanted Teddy to drive to the Olivia West Nature Preserve and await further instructions—like he was still the one in charge, never mind Teddy had his kid. At least Luke's voice had sounded more strangled than usual.

The lousy weather was keeping the leaf-peepers away, and it was still very early. A month ago, Teddy would have been burrowed in his lumpy bed at Bruce's cottage.

He pulled into the gravel lot. No one, not even any staff, was around yet. But he didn't like it—there was only that one dirt road in and out of the place.

"If the cops bother us, you're going to tell them we're cool, right?" Teddy fingered the grip of his Llama. A damn fine gun, except it was unregistered and as a convicted felon, he wasn't supposed to have guns. "I picked you up on the docks this morning. You wanted to interview me for your documentary. We heard the flash-bang go off and decided the harbor was under attack and got the hell out of there. Didn't see anything."

Kyle stopped hyperventilating long enough to give Teddy a sour look. The kid's face looked like hell, the bruises all blue and yellow and purple now, very ugly. "Why would I want to interview you? So you could tell me how you killed Patrick West and Olivia West?"

"Nobody killed Olivia West. She died of old age. She was a hundred and one, for Christ's sake. You tell that shit to the cops, you'll find out how fast a bullet travels two feet right into your stupid head. Actually," he added, as a point of interest, "I should aim for center mass. Bigger target. Still deadly."

"I've got my own money," Kyle said. "I can pay you."

"Not as much as your daddy can."

And as if on cue, Teddy's cell phone rang.

"I'll bring your bonus in cash," Luke said, still in that weird, strangled voice. "Meet me on the beach where Patrick West was killed."

"What're you doing, bringing the Zodiac?" It was a small, fast, maneuverable boat that Luke had aboard his yacht for short excursions—Luke had never used it that Teddy knew. "In this weather?"

"I'll be there."

Teddy looked around. He still didn't like the location. "Let me pick out the place—"

"No. You'll get caught. Do as I say."

"All right. Deal. And just in case you want to play games, say hi to your boy."

Teddy shoved the phone at the kid, who didn't cooperate. "Dad—Dad, he's a *fuck*. Don't do it. He's got guns."

"Asshole," Teddy said, and put the phone back to his ear. "Nice to know the kid cares, isn't it, Luke? The FBI loves kidnapping cases, but I'd leave McGrath out of this deal. I see one cop—state, local or fed, current, ex or on vacation—and your boy's dead."

This time it was Teddy's turn to hang up.

First, money. Then Stick Monroe. Get it all done in one day.

He glanced at the kid. "Probably should have put your shoes on before you ran out. Come on, we've got to take a little hike in the rain."

"Don't hurt my dad. I know he's an asshole, but he—"

"Yeah, yeah. Let's get moving. It's payday."

Thirty-One

◆━━◦⟳◦━━◆

"What a crazy bastard," Bruce said, shaking his head after he discovered his junked rowboat was, indeed, missing. "He could have sunk and drowned. Anyone could have seen him out on the water in a leaky rowboat."

J.B. nodded. The drizzle had let up, but the fog was starting to roll in, adding to his overall sense of foreboding. "Shelton doesn't necessarily think things through."

"Like that guy who stuck a knife in your throat?"

"Yeah, Bruce. Like him."

Bruce shrugged. "Sorry. That was tactless."

J.B. stood on the water's edge, the horizon no longer visible through the encroaching fog. The bright fall leaves—yellow-leafed birches, red-leafed maples—penetrated the grayness, and he could hear gulls but couldn't see them, couldn't place where they were. He'd checked his messages on his way down here. Sally Meintz had called to tell him she'd worked until 2:00 a.m. on his little mission and that Luke Castellane collected expensive weapons. She'd had to dig deep to find that one out.

"Christ, you've got your FBI face on," Bruce said. "Mind if I take a look around my cottage, see if Teddy camped out there last night?"

"Bruce, you don't need my permission." J.B. sighed. "Yeah, go ahead. Let me know if you find anything. I'll try to get hold of Chief Jacobs."

"If I find anything, you'll be the first to know. I'm a simple lobsterman. You're armed."

He headed off, looking as much a part of the landscape as the spruce trees and rocks. J.B. watched the water lap right to the edge of his shoes and felt absolutely no connection between this moment and his life two months ago. How the hell did he get here?

Posey, tell me you don't miss Maine. Tell me a part of you doesn't hate your husband for taking you away from here.

J.B. thought about his father, who could no more imagine life away from Montana than Olivia West could imagine life away from the southern coast of Maine. Zoe wasn't like that, he thought. That was what she'd bring to Jen Periwinkle—he'd seen that in the pages he'd read, however unpolished and awkward. It was what she was meant to do.

An old Taurus sedan rolled into the lobster pound lot.

Betsy O'Keefe climbed out, waving gingerly at J.B. as she walked down to the water, hugging her heavy sweater tightly around her. "Zoe said you'd be out here." She was shaking, her lower lip trembling. "She's talking to the police for me. I didn't want—she said they'd want to talk to me, too, but I can't. Not yet."

"Luke collects guns," he said.

She nodded.

"He thinks one of them was used to kill Patrick West."

"A .357 Colt Python." Her voice was calm but grim, as if she was telling someone they had cancer. "It was stolen last fall. He didn't report it."

"Tell me about Stick Monroe. He's Luke's friend and Zoe's mentor, but he knew about Shelton and did nothing. He's savvy, a retired judge. He had to know Luke's arrangement with Shelton was dangerous."

"He warned Luke—"

"When?"

"The other day, after Zoe got here."

J.B. looked out at the Atlantic. The tide was out, the low-tide smells ripe in the air. "Everyone around here says Olivia West was a great observer of people in her hometown. I think you're a lot like her, Betsy."

"I'm not," she said. "I don't have any instincts about people. I just—" She swallowed, refusing to go on. "I'm worried about Kyle. He hasn't turned up."

J.B. nodded. "I'm worried about him, too."

"Stick—" She turned away, which J.B. read as reluctance to say more than she should, not because she was contemplating outright deception. Betsy O'Keefe was accustomed to keeping confidences, by training, experience and nature. "Stick Monroe's a powerful figure around here. People respect and admire him, but they also like him. He took Zoe under his wing. He was Olivia's friend, Patrick's friend. He's not a wealthy man."

"Luke is," J.B. said.

Betsy licked her lips, still not looking at J.B., but she said, almost inaudibly, "Luke's been making payments to Stick on and off for a year."

"How much?"

"Thirty thousand dollars. Luke's so anal, he's kept a precise record."

Which she'd found. J.B. didn't ask her about that. "Did you talk to Luke about what you know?"

She nodded. "Last night. I didn't tell Zoe. I think she guessed I didn't tell her everything."

"Why tell me?"

"Because you're objective."

In other words, she trusted him to be willing to hear something bad about Stick Monroe. "Stick knew about the missing gun."

"Luke sold a gun to Teddy Shelton, as well," Betsy said. "I told Zoe that part—about the illegal sale, I mean. Stick must have threatened to go to the police and Luke—I know him, Mr. McGrath. I know he'd offer to pay Stick for his silence. That's what Luke does. He pays people." She faltered, her face crumbling in shame. "That's what he did with me. He knew I was drawn to his lifestyle. If he didn't have money, I wouldn't have put up with him. We used each other. Maybe it was that way with Stick."

"Why would Stick take the money?"

"He wouldn't want to tell on Luke. He elicits a kind of sympathy in people—it's hard to explain. The money was a way out. Stick wants to stay in Goose Harbor. It's been his dream to retire here for as long as I can remember."

"He didn't want to know what he knew, so he took money to pretend he didn't know it?" J.B. shook his head. "Maybe, but he also wanted the thirty thousand."

Betsy looked down again and ran her toe over the wet sand. She was wearing sensible walking shoes with white gym socks. J.B. felt sorry for her.

"What else?" he asked. "Get it all out, Betsy. You've waited long enough. If people have done something wrong, the consequences are of their own making, not yours. You're just telling what you know. The police will decide if it's relevant to their investigation."

She looked out at the harbor and squinted at the misting rain, as if she might see something there that would tell her what to do. "I should have said something before, but I didn't. I don't care if I get into trouble—" She took a breath, plunged in. "The evening before Patrick West was killed, he visited Luke on his yacht."

"What time?"

"Late, around ten o'clock."

"Luke told you?"

She shook her head. "He doesn't realize I know. I was interested in him even then, before Olivia died. I was spying on him, to be honest." She smiled lamely, waved off her own embarrassment. "Stupid of me. It was a nice night, and I took a walk on the waterfront. I just wanted to know if he had a woman in his life and I was wasting my time. I saw Patrick—I thought nothing of it."

"Luke never said anything about the visit?"

"No. Never. I decided I wouldn't, either. Patrick West

and Luke were friends. I convinced myself the visit had nothing to do with Patrick's murder."

J.B. waited. She wasn't finished. There was more. Zoe must have sensed the lies and deceptions, the secrets, in her hometown last year. That was why she'd pushed so hard, because the answers were there and she knew it. He'd bet Stick Monroe was one of the people who'd talked her into backing off.

Betsy breathed out, her teeth chattering now, more from nervousness, J.B. thought, than the weather. "Patrick knew Olivia had a soft spot for Luke. We all tried to do right by her. She was so old, such a force in our lives, his perhaps most of all. He never knew his father. Olivia was his only connection to his father—" She caught herself. "I'm being overly dramatic."

This time J.B. spoke. "Do you think Olivia put Patrick up to seeing Luke that night?"

"Not that directly. If Patrick suspected Luke or Kyle of doing something illegal—"

"Selling a gun to Teddy Shelton."

She nodded. "He'd go the extra mile with them, for her sake."

J.B. could feel his physical activity of yesterday and last night—kayaking, chasing bad guys, lovemaking—catching up with him. He needed food, more coffee, a few more hours of sleep. But he wouldn't get them, not yet.

"Betsy, you were with Olivia before she died."

She gasped. "Zoe told you? She said she didn't want to tell anyone!"

Well, well. J.B. hadn't expected this one. "Tell me what, Betsy?"

"Oh—oh, damn. You didn't know. It's not like it matters. Olivia was rambling. She was confused."

"About what?"

Betsy lowered her eyes. "I shouldn't tell you."

"You've gone this far. If you don't tell me, I'll just drag it out of Zoe."

"Olivia was convinced she knew who the killer was," Betsy said, almost mumbling. "She was frustrated because she couldn't tell us the name—she blamed her short-term memory. She wouldn't let go of it."

J.B. grimaced at the thought of an old woman wrestling with such a demon, on her deathbed, no less."She died thinking she knew the identity of her nephew's killer?"

"There was no point in saying anything once she was gone. She was very elderly, and she was dying. I'm sure her shock and grief played into it. She was so convinced. It was sad more than anything else."

Zoe would blame herself for telling her aunt about her nephew's murder—for not letting her die in peace. What a thing to live with. But J.B. stayed focused on Betsy O'Keefe, the nurse and caregiver, the plain woman people underestimated. "I want you to go back to the docks and tell the police everything you just told me. Tell them I think Kyle saw Teddy Shelton throw the grenade and came out to confront him and Shelton snatched him. Tell them I think Stick Monroe's going to kill Shelton and make it look like it was Luke." He paused, but he knew he was right. "They'll know what to do."

"What about you? What are you going to do?"

But J.B. walked her to her car without answering, helped her behind the wheel and made her repeat back to him what he'd told her to do. The police would call in a tactical unit to deal with Shelton, Kyle Castellane and Stick Monroe. They'd all do their jobs.

J.B. stood back from the car. "Tell them to hang on to Zoe." Monroe was her friend, her mentor—this wouldn't be easy. "I'll grab Bruce and get there as soon as I can."

Betsy nodded, and J.B. was surprised to see she looked less shaken and out of control now that she had a mission to accomplish. "I'll do my best."

As she backed out, Bruce called from the brush and birches between the lobster pound and the cottage. "You've got to see this. Jesus."

J.B. joined him in the tangle of wet, flopping undergrowth.

For the first time, Bruce Young actually looked shaken. He pointed to an apple crate half covered in a black tarp. "Check this shit out, J.B. Isn't that a goddamn submachine gun?"

"MP5." J.B. kicked the tarp off and took in the rounds of ammunition, grenades, handguns, most of it illegal to own even if Shelton wasn't a convicted felon. "When you look at what he left behind, it makes you wonder what he took with him, doesn't it?"

Bruce made a face. "Bastard's armed to the fucking

teeth. I'm thinking he took what he could and rowed over to the docks. Leave his truck here, leave the arsenal, misdirect the cops with the stun grenade, keep them on the docks for a while."

J.B. gave him a grim smile. "You're getting good at this."

"I just want to catch lobsters, you know?"

Bruce flipped the tarp back over the apple crate. He had drops of sweat on his upper lip. This wasn't his life, J.B. thought. Illegal weapons, murder. He looked down at the apple crate of Teddy Shelton's prized possessions. "We need to call this in."

"Yeah, sure." Bruce was breathing hard, having trouble taking it all in. He gave the crate a slight kick. "This stuff's small potatoes compared to that last undercover operation of yours, isn't it?"

"Those guys had rocket-propelled grenades. They wanted an Apache helicopter."

Bruce made a stab at a smile. "Teddy'll be jealous, knowing you've seen scarier shit than his stuff."

"It all works," J.B. said, and got out his cell phone. "It all kills."

Thirty-Two

The naked lightbulb at the top of the attic stairs cut through the gloom of the bleak, gray morning. Zoe sat cross-legged on the floor and pulled open the box she'd packed up after her aunt died. Christina sat next to her. They hadn't said a word since they'd opened the attic door and started up the steep steps.

Zoe had no idea if they'd find anything. Maybe she and her sister were grasping at straws. At this point, why not? It was better than grasping at nothing.

After she'd relayed Betsy's story to Donna Jacobs, who would then relay the information to the state detectives and appropriate federal agents, Zoe had gone back to the café, diving into a warm apple-cinnamon muffin, telling herself that was what she needed to do. Sit there and eat muffins. Stay out of the way.

But the café was deserted, and Christina came out from behind her counter with a muffin of her own. Zoe mentioned that Kyle could have asked her anytime about looking in their great-aunt's attic—he could have sneaked in anytime. Why now?

Christina, apparently, had asked that very question when they'd argued last night. He'd been working on the documentary for months. Why the sudden urgency?

"Then I knew," Christina said. "Damn. I knew it was because of me."

At first, Zoe had no idea what Christina was talking about. Then she guessed it—she could see it in her sister's expression, knew it because she *was* her sister. "You know about Aunt Olivia."

"I saw her before she died," Christina said. "She told me she knew who'd killed Dad. She was so convinced, Zoe. It was unbearable. I tried to reassure her. Then she died—and I didn't say anything to you because you didn't say anything to me. If you didn't know, it'd just upset you."

"And what does Kyle think, that Aunt Olivia left a clue behind?"

Christina was positive that was *exactly* what Kyle thought. "He's read all of her Jen Periwinkle novels. He says Aunt Olivia was a master at dropping clues. He couldn't believe she'd die without letting us know somehow who Dad's killer is. He wanted to find it so he could do this big 'ta-da' presentation. You know, like Jen Periwinkle."

Zoe didn't tell her that if Kyle believed there was a clue, he hadn't gone looking for it because of his documentary. He wanted to make sure it didn't finger his father—or him. Not that either was guilty.

She dug into the box she'd put away last year, after the memorial services, after Betsy had moved out, before she'd gone completely off the deep end. She'd collected up the papers on the kitchen table, junk mail, several versions her aunt had done of her own obituary, at least two false starts on a new Jen Periwinkle novel, letters. Nothing looked like anything Zoe needed to save, but she'd left the box for another day, one that hadn't come until now.

Christina pulled out a sheet of typing paper with just *Chapter One* typed at the top. "She didn't get very far, did she? Poor thing. I still can see her hunched over her typewriter, typing with those bony old hands. It's hard to believe when she started writing, she was younger than I am now." She sighed. "God, I miss her."

"I do, too, Chris." Zoe touched her aunt's things, as if they'd somehow bring her closer to them. "I like to think she's still a presence in our lives, don't you?"

"She is in mine. I'd never have the café without her."

Zoe pulled out the obits and laughed and fought tears at the same time. "Leave it to Aunt Olivia to rewrite her own obituary. Dad thought she was nuts—he threatened to get her on Prozac. Maybe I should have brought the new version down to the paper, but I couldn't think."

"What's that?" Christina leaned toward Zoe and pointed to doodles at the bottom of a half-typed page.

"Nothing, I don't know. A tree. A hangman. Betsy probably tried to get her to play hangman—" But Zoe frowned, examining the doodles more closely, noticing the frailty of the pencil lines. They were definitely her aunt's doing, the difficulty she'd had drawing evident. "Chris, Aunt Olivia had a hard time even holding a pencil. Why would she doodle?"

"Maybe it wasn't her."

Zoe shook her head. "No, you can see it was hard for whoever did it—it had to be her. Look, there are places where the pencil went a little wild."

"Jeez, it really is like a Jen Periwinkle clue, isn't it? You know, how she'd find messages in bottles, stuff dropped just in the nick of time."

"But a hangman and a tree?"

"They're line drawings," Christina said. "She didn't fill them in. Maybe that means something."

Zoe held the paper closer to the dim light. "There's a tiny arrow pointing to one of the tree branches. Oh, hell. Chris—a stick, a stick figure."

"Stick Monroe? Zoe!"

"He was here the morning Dad was killed. the other day—" Zoe swallowed, shaking. "Stick mentioned Aunt Olivia was revising her obituary that morning, before I got here."

"You can't possibly think—no." Christina shook her head. "No way."

If there was a name Olivia wouldn't want to remember—a man she would never want to know had killed someone as surely as she knew that day—it was Stick Monroe. Zoe's hands were shaking so badly she had to set the paper down. Not Stick. She had to be wrong.

Christina was equally as horrified. "Why would Aunt Olivia think Stick killed Dad? It can't be!"

"You know what Stick says. Everyone has secrets. Maybe she discovered his secrets."

"Or knew Dad had—but Zoe, Stick wouldn't have the kind of secrets you'd kill your friend to keep from getting out. My God, we *have* to be wrong!"

Zoe stared at the paper and the simple drawings her great-aunt had done in her last hours. "Dad must have been planning to arrest him."

"Stick? For what? It had to be something awful for him to risk killing someone—to kill his own friend." Christina jumped to her feet, and Zoe could feel her sister's agitation, her fear. "You wouldn't kill somebody over unpaid parking tickets."

"Dad stopped by to see Aunt Olivia that morning. If he said something, and then Stick stopped by—Aunt Olivia wouldn't have to say anything. He'd know. But we're getting ahead of ourselves. Just because Aunt Olivia believed she knew Stick killed Dad doesn't mean she was right. A couple of doodles aren't proof of anything." Zoe handed the half-written obituary and its stick drawings to her sister. "Will you take this to the police? J.B. and Bruce must still be at the lobster pound—I'll take my car and go find them."

"Kyle—Zoe, do you think he knows—"

But she broke off, and Zoe didn't answer her sister's half-formed question as they headed back downstairs. They'd taken Christina's car up from the docks, and she drove off alone, with obvious misgivings at leaving Zoe to her own devices. But she didn't plan to waste any time. She had her VW back. She grabbed her keys and charged out the side door.

Stick walked around from the front porch. "Zoe."

He had one hand behind his back. Not a good sign, Zoe thought. You always want to keep their hands in sight. "Hey, Stick, what's up?"

She knew she'd blown it. He'd been her friend since she was a little girl, and he'd killed her father. Murdered him. How could she pretend she didn't know?

His eyes narrowed on her. "Oh, Zoe. Zoe, Zoe. You can't hide it. Not from me."

"Stick—"

"Shh. You don't know what it was like to have Olivia look at me and *know*."

Zoe could barely breathe. "Did you kill her, too?"

"I didn't have to. She was dying. I could see it. Zoe—I have a Zodiac down on the water. I borrowed it from Luke. No one even paid attention. They're all fixated on the idea of Teddy Shelton loose in Goose Harbor with grenades." He swallowed, but didn't look nervous or upset. "I don't have much time. I need you to help me make this work. I've had the plan in place for a year. I've examined all the contingencies. It's my only option left."

He pulled the gun from behind his back. Luke's missing Colt Python. He was Luke's friend. He'd have access to the alarm code—Luke would have given it to him.

He leveled the Colt at Zoe. Had he done it this way with her father?

She refused to panic. "Christina's taking your name to the police."

The shock of seeing Stick—the fury Olivia must have felt at what he'd done—must have been the last straw for her old heart. He'd as good as killed her. Zoe could feel her own rage building, but she knew she had to contain it. If she didn't, she'd die, and so would Teddy Shelton and Kyle Castellane.

"Stay two steps ahead of me," Stick said. "And no cop tricks. I shot your father, Zoe. Don't think I won't shoot you."

Thirty-Three

Christina stumbled out of her car and started to collapse, but Bruce was there, grabbing her around the waist and keeping her on her feet. He and J.B. were at the lobster pound, waiting, as instructed, for the police to get there to take custody of Shelton's arsenal. They'd watched her speed into the lobster pound's dirt lot, so fast J.B. half expected her to drive straight into the water. She'd braked hard and threw open the door, then fell apart.

"Chris," Bruce said gently. "What's wrong?"

She made eye contact with him, her face white. She choked back a sob. "Stick's got Zoe." She couldn't get her breath and thrust a sheet of paper at J.B. "He killed Dad. It's right here."

J.B. took the paper but stayed focused her. "Where are they now?"

"He took her in a Zodiac. Luke's, I think. I was on my way to the police—I saw Stick take her. I didn't know what to do." She was gulping in air. "I don't know who to trust anymore. I didn't want to do anything that would make her situation worse. So I came straight here."

"Stick doesn't know shit about boats," Bruce said. "He's out in this fog? Never mind on purpose, he'll kill Zoe by accident."

Christina, still in Bruce's grasp, seemed steadier. "They headed north."

Bruce dropped his arm. "Come on, McGrath. Let's go. We'll take my boat." He held Christina by the shoulders and gave her an encouraging shake. "You know what to do, right, Chris? Get in your car. Drive back to town. Raise hell."

J.B. thought Bruce did fine with his instructions. "Tell the police Stick took Zoe as a hostage. He's going after Kyle and Shelton.He'll kill them and frame Shelton if he can. He's had time to work out a plan. He'll keep Zoe as his hostage as long as he needs her—"

Bruce coughed, hiding his own shock and fear. "Got it, Chris?"

She nodded. "I—I don't think Stick knows I saw him."

J.B. started to help her back into her car, but she told him she was okay. "Find my sister."

By the time J.B. charged down to the dock, she was backing out quickly and Bruce had his boat untied. J.B. was relieved it wasn't anchored in deep water—they didn't have to waste time with a dinghy. Unlike the heap he'd rented to J.B., it was a new boat with radar, GPS, a proper radio, good traps, fresh paint. The same old orange rain gear hung on a hook in the pilothouse.

Within seconds, they were on their way across the

mouth of the harbor. Clouds, fog and mist had descended on the gray water, reducing visibility, keeping in the pleasure boats and even many of the working boats. Bruce was undeterred by the weather. He got on his radio and learned from a lobster boat heading back toward shore that he'd seen the Zodiac zip out to the islands off the Olivia West Nature Preserve.

He shouted to J.B. over the sounds of the boat's engine. "Marine patrol will send a boat out, but it's a big goddamn ocean. You going to get into trouble for doing this?"

"It'll take an hour for the tac unit to get here. They'll take over once they're in place. Meanwhile, we isolate the incident and wait for help, do what we can to keep Kyle and Zoe alive." And Teddy Shelton, he thought. Stick would kill him, too. Dead, he couldn't argue with Stick's version of events.

"I like my life as a lobsterman," Bruce said.

But his mouth was set in a grim line, and he cranked up the engine and set across the harbor.

Stick had too many balls in the air. Zoe could see it as he tried to steer the Zodiac and keep her from killing him. He had his Colt in one hand. One false move, one falter, and she'd be on him. "Your father almost had Luke convinced to tell him about Teddy Shelton. He really put the pressure on."

"What did you care?"

"Luke had already confessed to me."

The hush money. "You'd kill my father—your *friend*—because you didn't want it to get out that Luke paid you to keep quiet about an illegal gun sale? Come on, Stick. That doesn't make sense."

"Insufficient motive? I tried a murder where a man killed his own brother because he didn't like the way he was chewing his steak."

Zoe didn't let him divert her. "You didn't want your connection to Teddy Shelton to come out. That's why you didn't kill him this past year—you didn't want to draw any attention to him. You must have just prayed for the day he'd leave town."

They were among the small islands off the preserve, but the conditions were difficult—fog, low tide, more drizzle. Stick didn't like boats or the water. His control of the Zodiac was tentative at best. It was a small boat, fast and maneuverable, not as likely as a speedboat or lobster boat to get hung up on rocks or stuck in shallow water at the hands of someone with Stick's lack of experience.

"Teddy Shelton wants me dead," Stick said, almost blandly.

"Then why hasn't he killed you?"

"He had to toy with me first. Get under my skin. Play out his string with Luke and make some money. He had to be careful your father's murder wouldn't get pinned on him."

"If you knew," Zoe said, "why haven't you killed him?"

He grimaced. "Because I'm not a killer."

She could have jumped up and gone for his throat then. "That's not why. Teddy must have something on you. What?"

"I went to see him in prison. I offered to set him up

with a new arsenal after he got out if he would keep something that he knew secret." Stick seemed unable to stop himself, as if it was cathartic to tell her—or he just wanted her to know why he was killing her before he pulled the trigger. "He came up here before his trial— he was out on bail. I should never have set bail for him. He snuck into my house and found a very small stash I had—not much, just a few pictures…." He didn't go on.

Zoe felt her stomach lurch. "Child pornography?"

"I've never touched a minor. *Never*."

"What did you do, tell Teddy it was for research purposes?"

"Yes. Exactly. That *is* what it was for."

"He tried to get you to let him off?"

Stick nodded. "It was too late. I'd only make both our situations worse. He's convinced I favored the prosecution and basically made sure he was convicted."

"Not true?"

"No, of course not. I looked for any legitimate way to get him off. He'd have fared even worse with another judge."

Zoe was sickened, stunned. "So you visited him in prison and offered to set him up with a new arsenal."

"That's why he came to Goose Harbor, but it wasn't enough—not enough guns, not enough to make up for seven years in prison. Teddy wants my hide, too." Stick's voice was matter-of-fact, as if he'd resigned himself to what he had to do.

"How much of this did my father figure out?"

"Most of it. Not all. He wanted Luke to come clean

about selling the gun to Teddy and how I manipulated Luke into paying me."

"You scared Luke into keeping quiet, didn't you? What does he know?"

"Nothing. He's not as worried about selling the gun to Teddy as he is about Kyle. He thinks it's all been about saving his son."

The boat slowed, and they were within only a few yards of Stewart's Cove before its horseshoe-shaped beach came into view.

"Patrick was in uniform that morning because he planned to take me in. I stopped in to see Olivia. She couldn't hide it, Zoe. She knew everything." Stick took in a breath, but Zoe didn't detect even a flicker of regret. "He never saw it coming. That's how I've consoled myself this past year. Knowing he didn't suffer."

"Bastard."

He beached the bow of the boat on the sand and made her get out first. She sank up to her knees in the cold water but slogged to shore as he splashed behind her with the same gun he'd used to murder her father.

He gave her no opportunity to escape or wrestle the Colt from him. She had to be patient. Keep him talking.

He stepped out onto the beach, sand sticking to his bare calves. "Teddy! Come on out. Luke sent me. I've got your bonus money. Let's finish this up and all go home."

Teddy Shelton emerged from the pines with Kyle shielding him, a gun leveled at Kyle's head. Stick seemed unsurprised. "Put the gun down, Teddy. Luke wants his kid back in one piece. Come on. We're all on the same side now. I think a hundred grand will put a lot of things right, don't you?"

"What's Zoe doing here?" Teddy asked, keeping his gun where it was.

"She's my insurance card."

"It was you on the phone earlier, wasn't it? Not Luke. I thought he sounded funny. What about the kid?"

"I'm not here to answer questions," Stick said.

Zoe tried to make eye contact with Kyle, but he was too frightened to focus on anything. He was rigid, just his teeth chattering slightly. She pushed back a wave of sympathy for him and concentrated on the tactical situation. What could she do?

Without warning, Stick stepped to her left and fired the Colt. Zoe immediately dropped to the ground and rolled, saw Teddy fall backward as he yelled out in pain.

Kyle staggered forward, in shock.

"Kyle, run—take cover," Zoe shouted at him.

He obviously didn't know what she meant and dove face first into the sand, as if that'd protect him. But it was better than standing there.

"No one move," Stick ordered. He stood over Zoe, pointing the gun at her. "I'll shoot you, Zoe. Don't think I won't. I can pull this off with you dead right here, right now."

Zoe went still and sat up in the wet sand. Teddy was shouting obscenities and grabbing his left arm. His gun had gone flying, but she couldn't get to it and didn't know if Kyle could see it. She didn't want him trying for it and getting himself killed.

Stick walked over to him and kicked him in the side. "Up."

Kyle obeyed, his front covered in clumps of gray, wet sand, his face ashen. He looked at Zoe, then turned away as if he was embarrassed by his predicament, or maybe just couldn't watch Stick Monroe shoot her.

"You fucking asshole," Teddy spat at Stick. "What the hell are you doing?"

"Delivering a murderer to the police," Stick said.

"*Me?* You're going to pin Patrick West's murder on me?" Teddy snorted in disbelief. "How?"

"I have the murder weapon. You, in your zest to own weapons of all kinds, stole it from Luke and intended to kill Kyle with it, but he instead used it to kill you— after you shot him with your own weapon, mortally wounding him. You'll both be dead, but the evidence will tell the story."

"You'll never pull it off," Teddy said, "not with DNA, blood spattering, all that forensic shit they have nowadays."

"You forget that I'm familiar with all of it."

"What about Zoe?" Kyle asked hoarsely. "What are you going to do with her?"

Zoe was wondering the same thing. But she knew. Stick was going to use her as a hostage to ensure his getaway. Then he'd tie a brick to her feet and dump her in the ocean.

That was what Stick was going to do with her.

He was just smart enough, arrogant enough, to think such a complicated plan, contingent on so much going his way, would work.

"Stick," she said.

"Don't try your negotiating skills on me, Zoe. You never made it to the academy, remember? You quit. You ran away."

Even now, knowing what he'd done, the contempt of this man she'd known and loved for so long stung. She had to steel herself against the affection and respect she'd had for him. Child porn. Extortion. Blackmail. Murder. He'd been living a lie for a long time.

"Screw this," Teddy said, and dove for his gun.

Stick shot him again, hitting him in the thigh but giving Zoe a split second to go for Teddy's gun herself.

But Kyle rolled between her and the .380, and that was that. Stick grabbed her by the hair and jerked her to her feet, sticking the Colt against her ear. "Always so full of yourself."

Kyle surprised her and scooped up Teddy's gun. He was shaking and clearly had no idea what to do now that he had it.

"You can't hold off Teddy and me both," Stick said. "Teddy wants to get the hell out of here, don't you, Teddy?"

Zoe thought Teddy wanted to kill Stick, but she let the judge think he'd succeed in manipulating him again.

"Don't do anything stupid, Kyle," Stick said. "I have a gun to Zoe's head. You know I'll shoot her even if you shoot me. A simple matter of reflexes. And if you take me on, you risk giving Teddy his opening. Don't you think he wants his gun back? If he gets it, you're dead. So if I were you, I'd point that gun at Teddy and let me go."

Kyle was sobbing. "Zoe…"

"Stick's right," she said gently, calmly. "Hold the gun on Shelton. Someone heard those shots. The police must be on their way. Stick won't get far with me."

Kyle nodded, crying openly now. He turned and re-directed the gun at Teddy, who'd sunk back onto the beach, holding his bleeding thigh.

Keeping the gun leveled at her head, Stick marched Zoe back to the Zodiac. He left her no opening this time. Even when he pushed the boat back out into the water and climbed in, he managed to keep the gun on her.

The boat jerked and bucked as he got it up to speed.

The fog was thick now, and Zoe doubted Kyle could even see them ten yards out from shore. He wouldn't be able to tell the tac unit which direction Stick had taken her.

"On your stomach," Stick ordered.

"If you shoot me, J.B. will hunt you to the ends of the earth. He likes that sort of thing."

"Do as I say, Zoe, or I will shoot you."

She turned over onto her stomach on the boat's wet bottom. He used a length of rope to tie her hands behind her back, then his web belt to tie her feet together.

"I should have done this to begin with," he said.

"I would have."

He ignored her gibe. "You don't think I can get out of this, do you? I'd have preferred plan A. It would have made everyone happy. The police, the town and the West family all would have their killer. I could go back to my garden and resume my life there. It's all I ever wanted, you know. A simple life in Goose Harbor."

"With your kiddie porn."

He inhaled sharply, but said nothing.

"You were shocked my father was on to you, weren't you? You *wanted* him dead, for the insult of it." She remembered to control her breathing, tried to keep her muscles relaxed, her hands and feet from swelling against their binds. "You thought you were better and smarter and more worldly, and you assumed you could get away with your games right under his nose. You couldn't. He found out."

"Moral superiority will get you nowhere, Zoe." He sneered at her, and she recognized his arrogance now for what it was—a cover for everything he wasn't. "You're trussed up like the proverbial Christmas goose."

She managed to sit up in the bottom of the boat. She could smell the fog, its dampness seeping into her. Gulls, ubiquitous to the shore, cried in the grayness. Her father hadn't died in the fog. He'd died on a beautiful, cloudless morning.

"I don't owe anyone anything," Stick said, as if he were talking to himself.

"Yes, you do. You owe a debt to society for killing a police officer in the performance of his duty."

Stick lurched suddenly and kicked her in the stomach. She moaned, doubling over in pain. She hadn't taken a kick like that since training for the state police.

"Don't you dare talk to me about debts to society. Do you know how many people I've had go through my courtroom in my life? Criminals. Lowlifes. Scum. Dirtbags. Sociopaths, drug addicts, alcoholics, murderers, terrorists—"

"Pedophiles?"

He kicked her again.

"Go ahead. Keep kicking me. Give yourself a heart attack. You're not young anymore, Stick. How many more years do you think you have?"

This time he ignored her. They were on the northwest shore of Sutherland Island. She saw the rocks where she and J.B. had taken their break. She thought of him among his ancestors' tombstones, touching their names as he must have tried to absorb their connection to him.

She remembered what he'd said about the boathouse with the new lock. She stared up at Stick. "You've got another boat."

He didn't deny it. "Didn't you think I had a contingency plan? I've had a year, Zoe. A quick change of appearance, a new boat—I'll be long gone before anyone even realizes I have you." He eased back on the speed, taking the Zodiac around a rocky point, toward the boathouse. "Zoe, I want a simple life. The bad times are over for me. My trip to the dark side. Now I'm back."

"You just pumped two bullets into a man. You intended to kill him, and Kyle, and you still intend to kill me." She tried to move, but winced in pain. "You just kicked the hell out of me. Your bad times aren't over, Stick. Don't delude yourself."

"When I was on the bench, I sent people away for the rest of their lives who would never kill anyone again if they were set free. They were no longer a danger to society. That's me, Zoe. I don't need to be in prison. After today, I won't be a danger to anyone."

"Today's a pretty big day, Stick."

He reddened at her sarcasm, but didn't kick her again. When he thought he'd escaped and didn't need her as a hostage, he'd pitch her overboard. Zoe had no idea how long she had, but she hoped Special Agent McGrath was good at what he did and at least bought her some time, gave her an opening, to save her own skin.

Thirty-Four

Bruce came in as close to the cove as he could without grounding his boat, and J.B. jumped into the water, gun drawn, never mind that Kyle Castellane had called to him that it was okay, he had things under control.

Nothing was under control.

When he reached him, the kid's fingers were so cold and stiff from shock, he had trouble letting loose of the gun. He was sitting on a rock with Teddy Shelton down in the sand, complaining about bleeding to death. J.B. did a quick check of Shelton's wounds, but he didn't appear to be in imminent danger.

"He's got Zoe," Kyle said. "Stick—the fuck. He put a gun to her head and took her with him in the Zodiac. He wanted to kill me and Shelton, but I had the gun and he couldn't risk it."

J.B. nodded. "Did you see which way he went?"

"I couldn't with the fog, and I was afraid to take my eyes off Shelton."

"It's okay. You just have to hang on for another few

minutes." He gave the kid an encouraging smile. "The cops are on their way by land and by sea."

"Zoe—if Stick killed her father, he'll kill her, too."

"I know."

Teddy moaned. "I hope you kill the fuck. I should have done it a year ago."

Kyle tilted his chin up, and J.B. could see the kid was trying to be brave. "I was wrong about everything. Why don't you go? Give me the gun back. Shelton's in no shape to make a move on me, not with a bullet in his leg and another in his shoulder."

But J.B. wasn't leaving Kyle alone with even a wounded Teddy Shelton. He could hear the police moving closer, and he had his badge out when they arrived and informed them he wasn't sticking around. "Tell marine patrol Sutherland Island. An old boathouse on the north end. Stick Monroe's been planning his escape for a long time."

They'd have to contend with the fog. He was close to Sutherland Island. He had Bruce and knew he'd be game to navigate among the islands. As far as J.B. was concerned, he had no other choice. He had to act or Zoe would be dead.

He splashed back out to the lobster boat, Bruce hauled him in, and they were off.

"Sutherland Island," J.B. said.

"My great-great-grandmother was born on that island."

"Mine, too."

Bruce glanced at him. "The fog's a bitch. I can't make any promises."

"If it's a bitch for us, it's a bitch for Stick."

"A bigger bitch. I know what I'm doing. Stick doesn't."

Stick hadn't counted on the fog. He even told Zoe so after he dumped her into the speedboat he had hidden in the boathouse, paid for with the money he'd gotten off Luke to keep his bumbling gun deal secret. Zoe didn't think Stick had been honest about having reformed.

Apparently he had another boat waiting farther north, thus creating two additional hurdles for the police. They'd expect him to go south. He'd go north—and change boats.

But he didn't know the islands, and even on a good day, the currents and swirls and underwater ledges would be treacherous for an experienced boater. On a bad day, an inexperienced boater like Stick Monroe was way over his head on this one small stretch of Maine's southern coast.

Zoe heard him muttering that one island looked like another. Good. She hoped he was lost. It'd give the tac unit and J.B. more time to find her.

Her hands and feet ached. Her cut from yesterday had opened up again.

The distinctive purr of a lobster boat off in the fog roused her. She didn't know if Stick had heard it, too. They were hugging the shore of what he apparently thought was still Sutherland Island, but it wasn't. It was one of the two smaller islands.

The lobster boat came around the tip, just barely visible in the milky fog.

She knew it was Bruce's. She knew J.B. was on it.

Stick swore and gunned the engine, going too fast for the conditions. He was coming to a narrow passage between the two tiny islands. In low tide conditions, it would be mud, impassable. "I can't see in this goddamn fog. Once I get out of these islands—"

"You want to avoid the narrow passage between the two small islands out here," Zoe said, trying to play on his confusion. "It's right up there. It's treacherous—nothing but mud and tide pools at low tide. There's a deep channel near Sutherland, but I hope you get lost and end up stuck in the mud."

He ignored her and glanced back, the lobster boat gaining distance on them. Zoe knew J.B. wouldn't do anything precipitous. It was a hostage situation. He'd isolate them and get the tac unit in there.

Unless she made it *not* a hostage situation.

Stick turned the boat, and Zoe heaved herself to her feet. Without hesitation, she rolled over and dropped into the water like a hunk of bad bait.

The water was cold and deep, and she sank, in case Stick decided to waste time trying to shoot her. His boat could outrun the lobster boat. All he needed was enough time to disappear into the fog.

No shots.

Zoe concentrated on not drowning. Moving mermaid style, she thrashed her way to the surface, gulped in air and tried to stay afloat.

"Just pretend she's a fish," Bruce was saying somewhere in the fog. "Hook her and pull her in."

"Go after Stick." She spit out saltwater, her hands and feet numb. "Don't let him get away. I can float."

But Bruce maneuvered his boat alongside her as if she were a stray lobster pot, and J.B. had a long metal pole that he managed to shove between her bound hands and the small of her back.

"Don't try to be gentle," Bruce told him. "Just snap her on in like a big, fat fish. Mind her head."

J.B. hauled her to the side of the boat, then he and Bruce grabbed her by her hands and feet and waistband and pulled her in, coughing, spitting. Her stomach ached where Stick had kicked her. Bruce handed J.B. his Leatherman to cut the ropes on her hands and ankles. Zoe tried to get to her feet, but her elbows hurt from having been bent back for so long and the blood was still rushing back into her fingers and her feet.

J.B. managed a smile at her. "You'd have aced drown-proofing, babe."

"Stick—"

"I'm on him," Bruce said, back at the wheel. "The dumb-ass went up West Passage."

Zoe nodded, shivering. "It's mud at low tide."

J.B. winked at her. "Even I knew that."

Bruce pulled his boat as close to the mud flats as he could without running aground himself.

Up ahead, through the swirling fog and mist, Zoe saw that Stick was in his boat, trying to get it to move in the mud, only digging himself in deeper. She could hear him cursing, as if he of all people was entitled to get away.

J.B. had his gun out and called to him. "Freeze, Monroe. FBI. Put your hands up."

Stick complied. He was maybe thirty feet away.

"Don't move," J.B. ordered. "Keep your hands up where I can see them."

Bruce radioed the police. He glanced back at Zoe. "Did you steer him into the mud flats?"

"Misdirected," she said. "I knew he wouldn't believe me."

J.B. didn't take his eyes off Stick, and she was vaguely aware of thinking that if she was J.B., she'd do the same. She wouldn't shoot a man with his hands up. She wouldn't shoot him even if he was the man who'd killed her father.

"How long before the tac unit gets here?" she asked.

"As long as it takes," J.B. said without moving.

"I can spell you."

"I'm good."

But Stick didn't last.

He went for his gun, and J.B. shot him.

Thirty-Five

The rain, the ocean and the wind pounded and swirled and howled outside the house where Olivia West had lived for a century. J.B. sat in the front room while Zoe and Bruce, like the childhood friends they were, argued over the fire they were trying to light. J.B. wasn't following the particulars, but finally Bruce looked around at him. "You're from Montana, McGrath. You must know how to light a fire. You do it."

"I can do it," Zoe said.

"Fine. Do it." Bruce got to his feet. "You remember how?"

She scowled at him, but J.B. knew that Bruce saw what J.B. saw, that Zoe hadn't even begun to come to terms with what had happened today. It was late, long after dinnertime, but none of them had eaten since morning. J.B. had drunk a cup of bad coffee at the Goose Harbor police station, where he'd told the Maine state police, the local police and the Special Agent in

Charge of the Boston field office everything that had transpired since he'd arrived in town.

Donna Jacobs had left him alone to do a little more explaining to the SAC. "Hell of a vacation, McGrath," the SAC, a super-fit guy in his mid-forties, said. "How'd you get mixed up in this mess? A woman?"

A woman.

He watched Zoe pile her kindling in the fireplace the way she liked it and strike a match, the fire catching, spreading. She rolled back onto her knees and waited, as if it were the most important thing in the world that her fire not go out.

After J.B. shot Stick, she rolled herself out of the lobster boat and swam, not gracefully, until she could stand, then raced to Stick. She tried to revive him. J.B. had peeled her off her dead friend and wrapped her in his arms to keep her from going into hypothermia.

She didn't cry. She clung to him and said she should have seen it, she should have known her father was going after Stick. Olivia had seen it. Why hadn't she? But her father had stopped by to see his aunt almost every day of his life—he'd have told her things he didn't tell his cop daughter. And Olivia West had lived in Goose Harbor for a century—she was a keen observer of its residents, her friends, her neighbors, her family. She hadn't known it was Stick in the way Patrick and Zoe, two cops, would know it, but as a woman who'd lived a long life and who had wisdom and instincts.

It hadn't been a stranger, not to her, Patrick or Zoe.

It had been a friend. Zoe's mentor. A man who'd let himself slip to the point of no return.

From the way the state police treated their former colleague, J.B. could tell Zoe had been a damn good cop. They'd been proud of her. But there wasn't one of them, he knew, who thought she should come back.

And he hadn't even told them about the rose tattoo.

"Fire looks good," Bruce said.

When she turned, the flames glowed in her eyes, distant, almost a charcoal gray now, but she smiled. "Told you."

"You law enforcement types." Bruce sank back against the couch and groaned. "I get up this morning thinking I'm going to catch a few lobsters, and next thing my boat's a crime scene and I'm charging across the harbor with an armed and dangerous federal agent."

"You did okay out there today," J.B. said.

"Damn straight. You'd never have found anyone in that fog without me." But J.B. could see how shaken Bruce was over today's events. His teasing tone was for Zoe's benefit, to keep her from sinking too deep. "You two want me to get out of here?"

But it was too late. Christina burst in with food from the café, lobster rolls and fresh apples, an untouched wild blueberry pie. She'd obviously been crying. J.B. guessed it had something to do with Kyle Castellane. He wasn't a bad kid, and he'd been through a lot today, but he had more growing up to do. Christina knew who she was, what she wanted in life. Kyle wasn't ready for her.

"You West girls," Bruce said. "Tough as nails."

He helped set food on the table.

Zoe got stiffly to her feet and sat next to J.B. as she stared at her fire. "I've been over it a thousand times, and I don't know what else I could have done. I keep thinking if I hadn't gotten in the boat with him to begin with, or if I'd stopped him in the nature preserve—"

"You did stop him. You kept him from killing both Kyle and Shelton."

"Kyle helped."

"Good. It's about time the kid stood on his own two feet."

"He was afraid his father had killed Dad. Can you imagine? That was what the documentary was about— a cover so he could find out the truth. Stick must have suspected, and that's why he broke into the house and café. An FBI agent was sniffing around—Stick couldn't hide it anymore. He had to know what Kyle knew."

"He must have been worried Olivia managed to leave behind a clue."

"She wasn't confused. She was shocked and horrified and her mind wouldn't let her produce the name— but she knew who killed Dad. If I'd known it was someone from Goose Harbor, I'd never have left. I'd have kept digging, come hell or high water."

"Zoe, you're going to play this day over another thousand times. You know that, don't you?"

Her eyelids were drooping. She leaned against his shoulder, and by the time Bruce and Christina called them for dinner, she was asleep.

* * *

Betsy had finished packing her things. She carried her suitcases out to the afterdeck and realized she didn't like boats that much. For a day trip, maybe. Not to live in.

Luke was there in his rain gear, like he was a lobsterman or something. The rain dripped off his orange rain hat. He looked so sad. "I blew it with you, Betsy."

She nodded. "You did."

"I'm seeing someone after I get this legal mess sorted out and head south. I need help. I'll come back next summer. If you're still here, maybe—" He shrugged. "Who knows."

"Yeah. Who knows."

"It's a lot to ask you to forgive me."

"At least you can see you need forgiveness. That's a start."

His mouth had a grim set to it, but there was none of the usual defensive arrogance about him, no contempt, none of the mannerisms that he used to keep the world at bay. "Patrick West shouldn't have died. I could have done something."

"Maybe. You'll never know for sure."

"Kyle—I was so afraid he'd done something impulsive, stupid. No matter what I did, there was this nagging doubt. He's a young man with a lot of anger, creativity, drama."

"You wouldn't have been the first father duped."

"It was always at the back of my mind that he could have had a secret life, a problem with the law that he let get out of hand." Luke's voice was steady, as if he'd gone over this so many times in his mind that it was rote now. "He could have taken the Python out for target practice and accidentally shot Patrick. I didn't know. I didn't want to know."

"Stick manipulated all of you. He played you, Kyle, Teddy." Betsy shook her head in amazement. "It's all so insane."

"Kyle's abandoned his documentary. He—he had his questions about me, too." Luke touched her wet hair, a gentle, simple gesture that was so unlike him. "What are you going to do?"

She shrugged. "I don't know yet. Maybe I'll see you next summer, okay?"

"Yeah. Okay."

She carried her suitcases out onto the docks, slick with rain, the wind blowing hard as she walked out to her car. It was an awful night. She was soaked. But she drove up to the library, and nobody said anything when she went into the Olivia West Room and sat for a while.

J.B. went back to Washington to sort out his own life, and during the month he left her alone in Goose Harbor, he sent Zoe a rose-something every day. She had red roses, pink roses, yellow roses. One white rose. Rose notepaper. Rose powder. Rose bath oil. Rose hand lotion. Rose potpourri. Rose wrapping paper. Rosehip jam.

Her favorite was the print of beach roses.

It went on and on and made her laugh every time, made her miss him, but she knew he wouldn't come back until the month was up. He'd decreed it. She needed time.

She ran the three-mile loop in the nature preserve two mornings a week. It wasn't easy at first, but she did it. And she kayaked. She and Christina went at high tide and paddled between the islands where Stick had run aground. They saw a hawk perched atop a spruce tree, as if there just for them.

Zoe also got another tattoo. A tiny orchid on her ankle. She drove down to Connecticut for it and stopped to see Charlie and Bea Jericho. She showed them her scarf, which she'd finished at night by the fire, and out on the porch when the autumn winds weren't howling. Bea said she had potential as a knitter. Zoe took that to mean her scarf still looked like a dead snake.

The leaves had dropped. The tourists had gone home. The summer people had left. Luke Castellane, in town late while he sorted out his legal problems, donated Sutherland Island to the nature preserve in Olivia's memory. Zoe tried not to look at it as a ploy to get probation.

Every day, Zoe wrote. It was still her secret. She bought more pillows and a more comfortable rug—just in case—and tried a fountain pen, gel pens, Flairs. All she asked of herself was to have fun. Whatever came after that—well, so be it. But her Jen Periwinkle was something else. She'd come to life in Zoe's mind, and on paper. The granddaughter of Olivia's agent had been in touch, just to check in—Zoe suspected Special Agent J. B. McGrath had had something to do with it.

Then an antique rose pin Olivia West and Posey Sutherland might have worn as teenagers arrived in the mail, and Zoe couldn't stand it anymore. She decided to pack up her car and find her way to Washington, D.C., and McGrath's door.

She'd been good at tracking down people at one time.

But she didn't get very far. The next morning when she was ready to leave, Bruce's truck turned up her driveway and J.B. got out. "My spies were in touch." He walked toward her in his jeans and leather vest. "I had to fly up here."

"Bruce. That big mouth."

J.B. smiled. "I never reveal my sources."

"*Sources* is too polite. He's a snitch. You two—"

"We're distant cousins."

"I wasn't running. I was going to find you."

"That's what Bruce thought. He was worried you'd get arrested in D.C., or get me in trouble again."

"Uh-huh. Like you need my help getting in trouble."

"No more undercover work for me," he said. "I train undercover agents now. I show them the scar on my throat. If they don't run, they're in. If they don't get scared, they're out."

"Why do I never know when you're serious?"

"Because I like to keep you off balance." But he was in front of her now, close enough that he could slip an arm around the small of her back and kiss her. "Miss me?"

"You have no idea—"

"But I do. I spent this last month alone, too."

"J.B.—"

He touched her mouth with one finger. "Before you go any further, I want to tell you that I'm not done with the bureau yet. I'm not going back undercover, but I'm not standing down. I need you to understand that."

She nodded. "It's what I've been expecting. I've been fantasizing about life in Washington. Hydrangea. Prowling the Smithsonian. It sounds like an adventure." She smiled, kissing him this time, and she whispered her only secret. "I want to write, J.B."

"I know."

"But I'm not ready to sit up here for the next seventy years and do it. This'll make a great second home, don't you think?"

"Zoe—"

"I love you. My God, J.B., I love you so much. Do you want me to stand on the bluff and yell it across the harbor?"

He inhaled sharply, caught her up with both arms and lifted her. "And I thought I was going to have to drag that out of you. Bruce said—"

"Since when are you discussing me with Bruce?"

"He knows I love you. He's known it from day one. Ah, Zoe." He swung her in a circle in the driveway and laughed in a way she hadn't heard before, then set her down. "I flew out to Montana and brought Olivia's letters to my grandmother back with me."

Zoe stared at him. "What?"

"I'm giving them to you. You can burn them if you want. They had a grand sense of adventure, the two of them, each in her own way. Posey married and went off to Montana and died young, Olivia stayed here and never married and lived to a ripe old age. It's what happened."

"J.B.—"

"I thought we could bring the letters up to that attic nook of yours and read them." He smiled. "Or not."

"I put a new rug up there."

"Did you? Like minds and all that, because that's your present for today."

And he went back to Bruce's truck and got the letters and a rug that he flung out right there in the driveway. It wasn't as soft as the one she picked out, but it had a big fat red rose right in the middle of it.

"Spies, ha. You bought that rug and couldn't stand it anymore yourself."

He winked at her. "As I said, like minds."

Zoe scooped up the rug and followed him onto the side porch, pausing to look out at the ocean churning under the gray November sky. She remembered how she and her sister had stood on the rocks and scattered Olivia's and her father's ashes in the water, and she smiled, knowing they both were at peace.

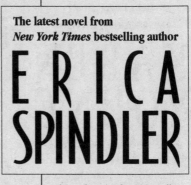

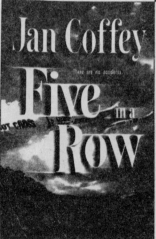